W9-BWK-148

Resounding praise for the incomparable *USA Today* bestselling author

"A REMARKABLE WRITER."
Lisa Kleypas

"SAMANTHA JAMES WRITES EXACTLY THE SORT OF BOOK I LOVE TO READ."
Linda Lael Miller

"JAMES DELIVERS DELICIOUS AND EXCITING ROMANCE . . . WITH EXCELLENTLY DRAWN, COMPLEX CHARACTERS."
Publishers Weekly

"READERS WILL ADORE HER ENDEARING, THREE-DIMENSIONAL CHARACTERS."
Romantic Times

"SAMANTHA JAMES TUGS ON THE HEARTSTRINGS."
Catherine Anderson

By Samantha James

Every Wish Fulfilled
Gabriel's Bride
His Wicked Promise
His Wicked Ways
Just One Kiss
My Lord Conqueror
One Moonlit Night
A Perfect Bride
The Truest Heart

Coming Soon

A Perfect Groom

SAMANTHA JAMES

A Perfect Bride

AVON BOOKS
An Imprint of HarperCollins*Publishers*

This is a work of fiction. Names, characters, places, and incidents are products of the author's imagination or are used fictitiously and are not to be construed as real. Any resemblance to actual events, locales, organizations, or persons, living or dead, is entirely coincidental.

AVON BOOKS
An Imprint of HarperCollins*Publishers*
10 East 53rd Street
New York, New York 10022-5299

ISBN: 0-7394-4472-7

Printed in the U.S.A.

Prologue

England

1794

Sebastian Lloyd William Sterling lay in his bed, his eyes wide open, a cold, hard knot in his belly as he stared at the shadows flickering on the wall. He made no pretense at sleep, though he'd screwed his eyes shut and pretended slumber when Nurse had cracked the door ajar and peeked in on him earlier.

But then, sleep never came easily when Mama and Papa were fighting. Sebastian's window was open, for the day had been warm for late September, and his chamber was directly above Mama's suite of rooms. And in the night, in the dark, their voices carried.

It was hardly the first time he'd heard them fighting, of course. This last year had been particularly bad, not just in London during the Season, but here at Thurston Hall. It happened often, particularly when they had guests. And Mama loved to entertain. They argued about Mama's infidelities. They bickered about Mama's gay, frivolous nature and unseemly behavior.

The observations came from Papa, of course, for William Sterling, marquess of Thurston, was not a man to turn a blind eye to anything that displeased him. He was far more likely to mete out punishment and criticism. Indeed, when Sebastian searched his mind as far back as he could remember, he could not recall a time his father had praised him—or anyone, for that matter.

When Sebastian had crawled into bed tonight, he'd known a quarrel was inevitable. Indeed, he'd tensely awaited the moment it would begin, for his parents had hosted a country house party this weekend and the last guest had departed earlier this evening.

But tonight . . . it was the worst of rows. Sebastian clamped his hands over his ears, but he couldn't drown out the sound. Papa raved and bellowed and cursed. Mama railed and argued and shrilled. He couldn't stop them. No one could. When they quarreled, the servants tiptoed down the corridors and kept their distance.

Finally a door slammed belowstairs.

The house went utterly silent.

Papa, he knew, would remove himself to his study and a bottle of gin. Oh, his mood would be vile in the morn, his eyes red-rimmed and swollen. Already Sebastian could envision his tight-lipped glower, and he did not relish the prospect of the coming day. His riding lesson was scheduled, and Papa always observed when they were in residence at the Hall. He was used to Papa's brittle comments and harsh disapproval, but no doubt tomorrow Papa would be more scathing than usual. The boy sighed. He would have to try to keep his younger brother, Justin, away from Papa as well. Sebastian knew better than to provoke Papa when he was in a mood, but Justin . . .

Quietly the little boy lay in the dark, not moving a muscle. He lay there for a long, long time. Finally he crept from his bed and crossed the floor. Always he checked on his brother and sister on those nights his parents feuded. Why, he knew not. Perhaps because he was the eldest—wasn't it his duty to watch over his siblings?

He crept furtively down the hall. Nurse, he knew, was already asleep—he'd heard snores coming from her room. Once she'd scolded him soundly when she'd discovered him in the library at midnight. But Sebastian didn't fear the dark, as some children did; in fact, the night gave him a welcome opportunity for solitude seldom accorded him. His tutors weren't there to badger him. Nurse wasn't there to keep an ever vigilant eye on him. The servants weren't forever trailing at his heels.

Silently he trod past the schoolroom and into Justin's chamber. Four years his junior, Justin was asleep and frowning sternly, his lower lip thrust out fiercely. Bad dreams? Sebastian wondered. He brushed back the dark hair so like his own. When he touched his brother's protruding lower lip, it went back in—but only for a second.

Farther down the hall, three-year-old Julianna lay curled on her side, her knees huddled to her chest, her favorite doll clutched beneath her chin. Silken, chestnut ringlets fanned out over the pillow. Sebastian tucked the lace coverlet more tightly about her form. His baby sister looked like an angel, he decided fondly.

Outside, the circle of the moon had already begun

its downward arc high in the night sky. The moon seemed impossibly bright, impossibly huge. A hundred stars glittered and winked, so close he fancied he had only to stretch out a hand to touch them.

Before he knew it, he was standing outside. Moving down the drive, he paused beneath the outstretched branches of a stately elm tree. He stood transfixed, still staring up at the awesome sky, when a flutter of leaves across the drive caught his attention.

He blinked. "Mama?"

His mother didn't see him standing in the shadows.

He stepped out from behind the tree. As always, Mama was dressed in the height of style. She wore a plaid pelisse and carried a matching reticule, a feathered cap jauntily poised atop raven-dark curls.

Just as Julianna resembled an angel, he decided, his mama was surely the most divinely beautiful creature on earth.

She stopped dead in her tracks. "Sebastian!" She sounded peeved. "Whatever are you doing here?"

Sebastian crossed to where she had halted. Tilting his head, he regarded her. Though his years on this earth numbered but ten, already he stood slightly taller than his petite mother.

"I couldn't sleep, Mama."

Mama made no answer. Instead she appeared rather vexed.

Beyond her shoulder, he saw a carriage roll to a halt just beyond the bend in the drive. His eyes narrowed. He glanced from the carriage to the portmanteau in her hand.

"Are you going somewhere, Mama?"

She took a deep breath. "Yes. Yes, pet, I am."

"Where are you going, Mama?"

Mama's expression underwent a lightning transformation. "La, but I don't know! To Paris perhaps," she said gaily. "Or Venice. Ah, yes, Venice. The weather will be lovely this time of year. And it's been ages since I've been there. Why, it's been ages since I've been anywhere on the Continent."

There was a strange feeling tightening the middle of his stomach. Young as he was, that Mama should depart in the middle of the night didn't seem quite right.

"Venice is very far away, Mama. Don't you like it here at Thurston Hall?" That someone might not like the stately manor house, the neatly trimmed gardens and rolling hills that surrounded Thurston Hall, was difficult for Sebastian to comprehend. He loved his ancestral home. Why, seven generations of Sterlings had been born here. When he wasn't at his lessons, he loved nothing more than to race his pony up the hills and down the other sides.

Someday, he thought proudly, when he was a man, Thurston Hall and all the other family estates would be his. That was why he must apply himself diligently to his lessons, why he could not shun responsibility. The title of marquess and all that it entailed was not something to be taken lightly. And it was Thurston Hall he cherished most.

Still waiting for his mother's response, he gazed at her. Mama glanced over her shoulder toward the carriage. The door was open now; he had no trouble discerning the outline of a man's form.

Mama turned back. "I just . . . I don't know how to put this. I simply can't stay with your papa anymore. I thought I could be a mother and a wife, but . . . well, it's just not my way. Your papa is too strict and . . .

well, I know you're young, but you're acquainted with his temper. I need more, my pet. I need life and gaiety and parties. And if I stay, he will surely stifle the life from me!"

Sebastian knew his mother loved being adored above all else. She loved being the center of attention. And he knew that Mama had lovers. Not so long ago, guests from London had visited. Sebastian had seen one man in particular gazing boldly at Mama. He knew that men liked to look at Mama. And that Mama gazed back. Before long, Mama and the man had slipped out onto the terrace.

They weren't aware of it, but Sebastian had followed.

It was there he saw them kiss. One . . . two . . . three ardent kisses.

Kisses never shared with Papa.

Mama didn't know he'd seen, of course. He hadn't told her. He hadn't told anyone, certainly not his father, for he was well aware another row would ensue. It was then that Sebastian first began to comprehend the meaning of the word *infidelity* . . .

And Mama's *lovers*.

It was a secret he'd tucked away deep in his soul . . .

He had the awful feeling that tonight was another secret he would keep.

"Daphne!"

It was the man inside the carriage—the same man whom he'd seen kiss Mama so ardently? he wondered. He couldn't tell.

Mama spun around and gave a wave, then turned back to Sebastian, who pressed his lips together.

"I must go," she said briskly. "Now come. Give Mama a hug."

Sebastian remained where he was, the wet grass soaking the hem of his nightshirt and chilling his bare feet. "Papa will be displeased," he said.

"Your papa's always displeased. Now go inside and scurry back to your bed. And look after your brother and sister for me, will you, pet?" She gave a tinkling little laugh. "La, why am I even asking? I know you will. You're such a good little boy."

She smiled and pinched his cheek, then dropped a kiss atop his head, almost as if it were an afterthought. And then she was running toward the carriage.

A moment later the man handed her inside, then followed her up. For an instant, just before the door was swept shut, their silhouettes were clearly visible in the moonlight. The man's head swooped down. Mama eagerly lifted her face for his kiss, and the familiar tinkle of laughter drifted on the air . . .

It was the last he saw of dear Mama.

One

London
Late March 1815

Devon St. James was in a dreadful fix.

Two days hence, the rent was due on the cellar room where she lived. Her landlord, Mr. Phillips, had raised it to an outrageous sum. Devon was both furious and amazed, for the room was scarcely able to accommodate a stool and the narrow bed she had shared with Mama before she died. To make matters worse, he'd informed her but yesterday, the wretch!

"Thieving monster," Devon muttered under her breath. She tugged almost viciously at the ribbons of her bonnet. The same treatment was accorded the ties of the voluminous cloak she flung over her shoulders. A sad, limp affair, its hem ratty and uneven, it was far too large for a frame as small as hers. In places it nearly touched the ale-spotted, pitted plank flooring beneath her feet. But it served its purpose—as did the remainder of her clothing—and for that she was grateful.

Carefully smoothing a hand over the rounded

mound of her belly, she paused at the back entrance to the Crow's Nest, the tavern near the Strand where she worked. Shutting the door firmly behind her, she stepped out into the damp, misty night. Not a night went by that she didn't dread the long walk home through the crisscross of dark alleyways. Tonight it was even later than usual before the last patron had stumbled from the taproom. Seeking to fortify herself, she reminded herself she'd made the journey safely for nearly a year now.

A year. God above, *a year*.

For the space of a heartbeat, a wave of bleakness chilled her soul. God, but it felt as if a lifetime had passed since then! When Mama had died, the loss was like a knife to the heart. Indeed, she thought with a pang, at times it was difficult to refrain from discouragement. But something inside would not allow her to resign herself to working as a barmaid forever. Mama had hated that she worked there—and so did she. No, she would not give up her hopes and dreams. Indeed, she was more determined than ever . . .

Someday she would find a way out of St. Giles. Some *way* . . .

It was a vow made long ago. A vow she was determined not to forsake.

But how was another matter, for Phillips's words of this morning echoed in her brain. Though it had cost her dearly, she had swallowed her pride and pleaded with him. If he would only allow her some time to cover the sharp increase in rent . . .

"I will not!" he had snarled. "Me mind is made up. Ye'll pay, missy, else ye'll find yerself out on the street!"

His angry flare had left her in no doubt. He meant what he said.

He was, she decided blackly, a scoundrel. She had despised him for years now, for the wretch had always been rude and hateful to her mother. But however much she might wish Phillips to the devil and beyond, it would not solve her own dire straits.

Only money could do that.

Continuing on toward St. Martin's Lane, Devon considered the precious stash of coins nestled in the left pocket of her gown; her wages had come due today. Only a week ago, she'd been so certain there would be more than enough to cover the rent! She'd even imagined she might be able to buy another gown, and improve her chances of obtaining employment other than as a barmaid. But now it would take every penny of her wages to cover the rent . . . and more.

A chill seized hold of her, a chill that had nothing to do with the cool night air. Dear God, what if Phillips *did* cast her out?

Rounding the corner, she managed to quell the dread roiling in her belly. Instead she directed her attention back to her surroundings. It was quiet, as quiet as it could be in this part of London. Darkness smothered the rooftops. During the day, horses and carriages jostled for room along narrow streets. Tradesmen's shouts filled the air, struggling to be heard above the bustle of activity.

Her cloak flapped about her ankles as she hurried past the Seven Dials—not easy given the bulk of her middle. She slipped once on the cobbles, slick from an earlier shower. The girth of her belly made her balance tricky, but she managed to right herself without mishap. Her gaze swept around again as she did so. There was no one about.

"Your plight might be easier were you to take some of the patrons in the back room now and then," Bridget had commented earlier that day. "That's what I do when I'm in need of a shilling or two."

The ease with which she advised was telling—Bridget scarcely gave a second thought to such activity. While Devon was aware that Bridget meant well, she could hardly do as Bridget suggested. For she refused to make her living on her back.

Another promise she'd made to herself.

As she tugged her cloak more closely about the bulk of her middle, her gaze encompassed the next corner. God knew, the streets of St. Giles were mean and merciless—no place for a lady.

Especially at night.

Of course, not that she was a real lady, as Mama had been. Though Mama had worked as a seamstress for as long as Devon could remember, she knew that her mother had been employed as a governess before she was born.

But society, she thought with a trace of bitterness, was not forgiving of an unmarried woman with a child at her breast, and it was that which had forced her mother into poverty.

Almost without knowing it, her hand stole to the pocket of her gown. Warm fingertips brushed against cool metal. She fingered the cross. Remembrance flooded through her . . . As Mama had breathed her last, Devon had slipped the necklace from her mother's pocket . . . and into her own. The clasp was broken—the reason Mama had carried it in her pocket.

It was Devon who had broken it.

Twice in her life she'd made her mother cry. That was one of those times, and the memory of it still provoked a stab of guilt in her chest. She had no idea of the value of the necklace, nor did it matter. The necklace was Mama's most treasured possession.

Now it was *her* most treasured possession.

Never would she part with it. Never. No matter what price it would fetch, no matter how hunger gnawed at her belly, no matter if she had to sleep in the rain and the cold—pray God it would not come to that! For as long as she had it, she had a part of her mother.

Pulling up her cloak, Devon skirted a puddle left by an earlier rain shower. On either side of her, the houses huddled together like shivering children in a biting wind. A ragged woman slept in a doorway, bony knees huddled to her scarecrow frame.

Despite her earlier resolve, a dry fear touched Devon's spine. *I don't want to be like her,* she thought with a touch of desperation. *I don't!*

Her steps slowed. All at once, she recalled the boardinghouse on Buckeridge Street where they'd lived for a time when she was younger. It was a vile, smelly place filled with scum and decay, and both she and Mama had hated it there. She reminded herself that they had survived hunger and squalor.

Yet they had never been homeless. There was always a roof above their heads, no matter that it sometimes leaked like water through a sieve.

Taking a breath, she battled a rising despair. She could not give in. Staunchly she told herself she had her wits, her determination . . . and her mother's necklace.

"What 'ave we 'ere? Why, a lady with a fondness for the laddies!"

The voice rang eerily into the night. Devon stopped short. A man blocked her way. Another stepped from the shadows, just to her left.

"Hello, dearie."

The fine hairs on the back of Devon's neck prickled. And somehow she knew she'd remember the sound of that oily voice for the rest of her days . . .

He beckoned. "Come here, dearie. Come to Harry!"

"Leave off," protested the other. "I saw her first!"

"Ah, but she's closer to me, Freddie!"

Harry. Freddie. Her breath caught in her throat. As the names tumbled through her mind, her heart plummeted. She knew this pair—or at least she knew *of* them. They belonged to one of the most frightening gangs that roamed St. Giles!

"Wot say we share, eh, Freddie?"

The suggestion came from Harry, a coarse-faced man dressed in a filthy tweed jacket, a top hat tipped jauntily on his head. Beside him, Freddie grinned, displaying yellow, rotting teeth. Vile-looking creatures they were, both of them men of sinister countenance, ageless in the soul, their behavior ruled by perhaps the oldest of provocations.

Greed.

Oh, yes, she could see it in their eyes. And now Freddie blocked her way. He was smaller than his brother, not much taller than she.

She flung her head up. By God, she would show no fear.

But feel it she did. The cold breath of terror trickled along her spine. Her breath caught in her throat.

She willed herself not to panic. Mama had always told her she possessed a sound constitution. She would not scream. Indeed, what good would it do?

Earlier she had given thanks that not a soul was about. But now . . .

She managed to shield her fear behind a wall of bravado. "What do you want?" she asked sharply.

"Depends on wot ye got to give!" There was a sinister rumble to Freddie's laugh. He stepped near, grabbing her chin. The streets were ill-lit and dark, but as if to aid him, a full moon slid from behind a cloud. He tilted her face to the sky. "Oh, but we've caught ourselves a pretty one, Harry!" he crowed. "Will ye look at those eyes! Pure gold, they are!"

Devon cursed her forgetfulness. She always took great care with her clothing when she left the Crow's Nest each night. The brim of her bonnet was wide enough to help shield her face; the crown was deep enough that she was able to stuff her mane of thick, golden tresses within. As an extra precaution, she usually smudged her face with soot to hide the youthful curve of her cheeks and neck. But she'd been anxious to be on her way tonight, and she'd forgotten.

She jerked her chin from Freddie's grip. "I have nothing," she said levelly. "Now leave me be. Or would you prey on an innocent woman?" Oh, a ridiculous question, that! This pair would prey upon any and all! "Can you not see I'm soon to give birth?" She jutted out her stomach so that her girth protruded from the cloak. And it was on her belly that his gaze lingered.

But not in the way she hoped.

"Oh, I can see," Freddie said with a wink. "And we be glad to see ye like the laddies, eh, Harry?"

Harry bowed to her with a great flourish. "Indeed, Freddie."

Freddie's narrow lips twisted in a smile. He gave a nod. "What's that ye have there in yer pocket?"

Devon paled. Too late she realized she had done the one thing in the world she should never have done. Her hands had plunged protectively into the pockets of her gown. Her mind sprang to the knife tucked away in her boot. Drat, but they were so close! They would be upon her before she could reach it!

She dragged her hands out so they could see. "Nothing," she said quickly. "Now leave me be!"

"Let's just 'ave a look, shall we?"

This was a feat with which they were familiar and quite accomplished. Harry's nimble fingers found the pouch with her precious stash of coins in one pocket. With a hoot Freddie snatched her necklace from the other.

Something exploded inside her.

"No!" she cried. They could steal her coin, beat her senseless, but they would not take her necklace! The only way she would see it gone was if they left her dead on the street. Heedless of the danger, she reacted without thinking, darting after Freddie. Harry had already disappeared into the murky depths of the alley, but Devon paid no mind. Throwing out a hand, she managed to grab a fistful of Freddie's coat.

It was enough to topple him. Together they tumbled heavily to the ground. But all at once he had her by the throat. "Bitch!" He squeezed; she could feel the ragged edge of his nails biting into the soft flesh just below her jaw.

She struggled to breathe. A faint, choking sound

emerged . . . it bore no resemblance to a scream. She raked at his face, but it was no use. Then she remembered . . .

The knife tucked at the side of her boot.

Freddie squeezed. Devon clawed at him desperately, certain her neck would snap with the pressure of his bony fingers. A grating laugh seared the air.

The world blackened. Desperately she fought against it. Her fingertips closed about the knife's handle. Gritting her teeth, she drove upward with all her might, then wrenched it back.

Air rushed back into her lungs. Through the meager light she saw Freddie's eyes bulge, as if they would pop from their sockets. Little did she realize the surprise on his face mirrored hers, for it was then she realized the blade had reached its mark.

"Ye . . . ye've killed me!" he said faintly.

Devon waited no longer. With a cry she shoved at his shoulders. Weak, stunned, Devon rolled away. As she pushed herself to her knees, she saw the knife, still in her hand. Blood dripped from the blade onto the cobblestones. In horror she let it fall from her hand.

It was then she chanced to see her necklace, just beyond her knees. With a frantic cry of relief, she snatched it up and clasped it to her breasts.

Behind her, there was a groan. Her heart gave a great bound. It was Freddie!

Run! chanted a voice in her mind. *You must run!*

Too late. He'd seized hold of her dagger. She twisted, even as a tremendous force hit her from behind. She pitched forward, skidding headlong across damp, slippery stone. Searing fire burned through her, like a red-hot poker, at the place where her shoulder blade curved into her side. A scream shrilled in her ears . . . her own, she realized.

In the swirling mist of her vision, she was aware of Freddie staggering to his feet and shuffling toward the alley where Harry had disappeared.

Freddie's dragging footsteps faded. Devon's mind hazed. The world seemed to dangle. She felt dizzy and sick. And she'd fallen in a puddle, she realized hazily. Beneath her cheek, the cobblestones were rough and wet; she could feel the dampness seeping through her gown. Her teeth began to chatter. She had been cold before, but not like this, for this was like a numbing, icy blast that came from within and spread to every part of her, a cold that made her shiver from the inside out.

Memory flashed inside her, the memory of Mama's last hours. She had whispered of the cold, and she had shivered and shaken . . .

Oh, God. Was she dying then? *No*! her mind cried. *I don't want to die, not like this. Not in the dark and the cold . . .*

Biting deep into her lip, she choked back a sob—she knew there was no use in crying out.

For there was no one to hear. No one to care. For this was St. Giles, home of beggars and thieves, the poor and the unwanted.

Two

Damn his brother's foolhardy nature!

The Sterling family carriage careened around the corner onto St. Martin's Lane, a grand affair of shining black and gleaming silver. To any onlookers (of which there were few, given the ungodly hour), the splendidly sumptuous vehicle was sorely out of place in the filthy streets of St. Giles. Inside the vehicle, Sebastian Sterling held on tightly, both to the strap and to his temper—it was rare he ever truly *lost* his temper—but admittedly, the edges were a bit frayed.

True, he'd spent a very pleasant evening at the Farthingales' dinner party—a lively affair, to be sure, for it had lasted until well after midnight. Justin had been invited as well but had chosen not to attend, it seemed. Indeed, Stokes, the butler, had informed Sebastian as Sebastian left his town house that Justin planned to spend the night gaming.

So it was that Sebastian had stopped at White's after leaving the Farthingales. Though Sebastian and Justin lived beneath the same roof, it seemed they only encountered each other in passing these days. Since Julianna was traveling, there was no one home but the servants, who were certainly all abed by now; perhaps he and Justin might share a brandy together. Besides, it was only right to apprise his brother of his plans before Justin read about them in tomorrow's gossips . . .

But Justin was not at White's. His friend Gideon, however, was. And it was Gideon, deep in his cups—God, was he ever anything *but* deep in his cups?—who disclosed he'd seen Justin but a short time earlier . . .

At a gaming hell in St. Giles.

And it was that which accounted for the carriage's breakneck pace . . .

Outside, Sebastian could hear Jimmy, his driver, urging the horses on. Damn Justin's recklessness! he thought again. By God, but there were times he swore his brother cared about nothing, not any*one* or any*thing*. What the blazes was Justin thinking, to come to such a place? Ah, he reflected furiously, but that was Justin. His life consisted of but three pursuits—gambling, whoring, and drinking. As for Gideon . . . well, they were rakehells, both of them, and he wasn't sure who was worse!

Under other circumstances, Sebastian wouldn't have dared stray into the heart of St. Giles, for it was surely the very scourge of the earth, rife with pickpockets, thieves . . . and worse. It seemed a man could scarcely walk down any street in London these days without risk of being robbed. But in an area such as this, a man risked losing not only his watch, but his very life . . .

His jaw clamped together hard. Little wonder, he decided blackly, that he preferred Thurston Hall to London.

The carriage veered precariously. As Jimmy negotiated the turn, Sebastian shifted to accommodate the movement. Yet in the next instant, the carriage swerved abruptly and lurched to a halt. Sebastian found himself flung across the seat so violently, he narrowly escaped cracking his head.

He righted himself and flung open the door. "Jimmy! Is this it?"

Jimmy hadn't moved from his perch atop the cab. "No, my lord," he said with a shake of his head.

"Then drive on, man!" Sebastian couldn't curb his impatience.

Jimmy pointed a finger. "My lord, there be a body in the street!"

No doubt whoever it was had had too much to drink. Sebastian very nearly advised his man to simply move it and drive on.

But something stopped him. His gaze narrowed. Perhaps it was the way the "body," as Jimmy called it, lay sprawled against the uneven brick, beneath the folds of the cloak that all but enshrouded what looked to be a surprisingly small form. His booted heels rapped sharply on the brick as he leaped down and strode forward with purposeful steps. Jimmy remained where he was in the seat, looking around with wary eyes, as if he feared they would be set upon by thieves and minions at any moment.

Hardly an unlikely possibility, Sebastian conceded silently.

Sebastian crouched down beside her, his mind working. She was filthy and bedraggled. A whore who'd imbibed too heavily? Or perhaps it was a trick, a ruse to bring him in close, so she could snatch his pocketbook.

Guardedly he shook her, drawing his hand back quickly. Damn. He'd left his gloves on the seat in the carriage. Ah, well, too late now.

"Mistress!" he said loudly. "Mistress, wake up!"

She remained motionless.

An odd sensation washed over him. His wariness vanished. His gaze slid sharply to his hand. The tips of his fingers were wet, but it was not the wetness of rain, he realized. This was dark and sticky and thick.

He inhaled sharply. "Christ!" he swore. He moved without conscious volition, swiftly easing her to her side so he could see her. "Mistress," he said urgently, "can you hear me?"

She moved a little, groaning as she raised her head. Sebastian's heart leaped. She was groggy but alive!

Between the darkness and the ridiculously oversized covering he supposed must pass for a bonnet, he couldn't see much of her face. Yet he knew the precise moment awareness set in. When her eyes opened and she spied him bending over her, she cringed and gave a great start. "Don't move," he said quickly. "Don't be frightened."

Her lips parted. Her eyes moved over his features in what seemed a never-ending moment. Then she gave a tiny shake of her head. "You're lost," she whispered, sounding almost mournful, "aren't you?"

Sebastian blinked. He didn't know quite what he'd expected her to say—certainly not *that*.

"Of course I'm not lost."

"Then I must be dreaming." To his utter shock, a small hand came out to touch the center of his lip. "Because no man in the world could possibly be as handsome as you."

An unlikely smile curled his mouth. "You haven't seen my brother," he started to say. He didn't finish, however. All at once the girl's eyes fluttered shut. Sebastian caught her head before it hit the uneven brick. In the next instant he surged to his feet and whirled, the girl in his arms.

"Jimmy!" he bellowed.

But Jimmy had already ascertained his needs. "Here, my lord." The steps were down, the carriage door wide open.

Sebastian clambered inside, laying the girl on the seat. Jimmy peered within. "Where to, my lord?"

Sebastian glanced down at the girl's still figure. Christ, she needed a physician. He thought of Dr. Winslow, the family physician, only to recall that Winslow had retired to the country late last year. And there was hardly time to scour the city in search of another . . .

"Home," he ordered grimly. "And hurry, Jimmy."

It wasn't Stokes but Justin who opened the door to Sebastian's fashionable town house. "Well, well," Justin drawled, "keeping rather late hours, aren't—" He broke off at the sight of his brother. In his arms was a woman, but hardly the sort his brother usually fancied. Hardly the sort *he* fancied, for that matter.

Her wet, billowing cloak dripped puddles on the highly polished floor. Her head lolled over Sebastian's arm. Her face was turned into his greatcoat.

He raised incredulous eyes to his brother. "Sebastian! What the hell—"

"She's hurt, Justin. Bleeding."

"Good God! Shot?"

"I don't know." Sebastian's tone was clipped and abrupt. "Let's get her upstairs. The yellow room."

In unison the brothers gained the stairs, cleared the landing, and proceeded down the hall, their long-legged strides in perfect accord.

"What the hell happened?"

"I found her sprawled in the street in St. Giles. Jimmy nearly hit her."

"St. Giles! You?" Justin thrust open the bedroom door.

Sebastian spared him a hard look as he brushed by him. "Yes."

By then the butler had appeared, scratching his chest and still dressed in his nightclothes. "My lord, may I be of assistance?"

"Hot water and clean strips of linen," Sebastian ordered. "And please hurry, Stokes."

He lowered his burden to the bed and turned his attention to her. She was soaked and shivering and white as snow. It hadn't taken long to reach his town house—a scant quarter hour—but she hadn't roused again, which worried him.

Particularly when he realized she was heavy with child.

"We've got to find out where she's bleeding." He ripped off the silly bonnet she wore. A cascade of golden waves tumbled over the pillow across his fingers.

He flicked the tresses aside and leaned over her. His patrician nose wrinkled in distaste as he fumbled with the sodden, knotted ties of her cloak. Dingy with age, it was the same muddy color as the Thames. "Christ, what is that stench?" He sniffed. "She smells of fish and smoke—"

"Mmm," Justin agreed. "And stale ale and grease. A noxious blend, isn't it?"

Sebastian cursed at the clumsiness of his big fingers. At last the ties came undone, and he eased the cloak from beneath her, thrusting it to the floor.

"Be careful," Justin warned. "She's rather . . . she appears to be in a delicate condition."

"Yes." Sebastian's gaze roamed quickly over her. She must surely be almost ready to deliver, given the enormous size of her belly, especially considering the narrow frame of her shoulders. He frowned. Yet there was something rather peculiar about her shape . . . Now that her cloak was off, it struck him that her belly looked almost . . .

Lumpy.

Suspicion took root. A prod from a finger revealed her belly to be as soft as it looked. His lips compressed. His hands delved beneath her ragged scrap of gown.

Justin stood just behind his shoulder, watching as a slow curl of twine dropped from his fingers to the sodden cloak now pooled on the elegantly patterned Aubusson carpet. A pillow followed in short order.

"Good heavens." Justin sounded utterly shocked. "She's not—"

"Apparently not."

There was a long, drawn-out pause before he heard Justin's voice. "Why the deuce would a woman pretend to be with child?"

Sebastian made a sound of disgust. "It's a ruse. My guess is that the twine and the pillow are used to conceal her stash."

"Her stash," Justin repeated.

"She's a thief, Justin."

"But she has nothing concealed!"

"Doesn't she?" He spied something in one of her hands, clenched beneath her chin.

He tried to loosen her grip.

Her fingers tightened. "Mine," she muttered. "Mine!"

Tugging, he freed a chain clamped tight in her palm. He spared it no glance, but dumped it into his pocket with an oath. "My God," he muttered, "I've brought home a thief!"

"Oh, come," Justin protested. "You could hardly leave her lying in the streets. She might have been trampled. If it's any consolation, I'd have done the same thing myself."

"What, you've sprouted a conscience now?"

"Who knows? Perhaps I'll even follow in your path and lead a life of utter respectability—though I cannot imagine anything more boring!"

Those acquainted with the pair were aware such banter was commonplace. As they spoke, Sebastian was busy peeling away the rest of her gown.

As it joined the growing pile on the carpet, Justin inhaled. "Look there. She hasn't been shot, she's been stabbed!"

Sebastian saw at the same instant. His gaze settled

on a jagged puncture that seared the flesh of her right side. If she was lucky, perhaps the blade had glanced off a rib. If so, the injury would not be mortal, and the bleeding would stop soon.

Stokes had quietly deposited a tray of linens and water at the bedside. Sebastian grabbed a wad of linen and pushed her to her side, one hand on her shoulder. Before long, a telltale crimson began to seep through the pad. He swore and increased the pressure.

Beneath his hands, the girl twisted. Slim shoulders heaved and she cried out, a sound that resounded within his very bones . . . his very hands. Her head turned, and he saw her eyes were open; she stared directly into his face. They were pleading, those eyes. Alight with a glimmer of gold—most unusual, he noted distantly—a glimmer of life. She was young, no more than twenty, he guessed.

His efforts paid off. It wasn't long before the bleeding began to slow. With Justin's assistance, he pressed a thick, clean pad over the wound, then wrapped several strips of linen over the dressing and around her body to secure it in place.

Only then did he allow himself to breathe. With a tail of cloth, he gently wiped the grime from her cheeks.

"She's frightfully pale," observed Justin.

"I know." Sebastian had already taken note of her ashen color—and the rest of her as well. Her frame was delicate, her limbs petite and slender, much like their sister, Julianna. "Christ, I knew I should have taken her to a physician." He spoke almost to himself.

"And where would you have found one this time of night?" Justin dropped a hand on his shoulder and squeezed. "Besides, I'd trust you far more than I would any physician." His tone lightened. "My brother the hero, tending the wounded on the battlefield. I daresay you've far more experience with such things than many physicians."

Sebastian neither agreed nor disagreed. He had been proud to serve his country in the fight against Napoleon, but upon his return to England from the Peninsula, he was only too glad to relegate his war memories to a far distant place where he need not think of them ever again. Certainly he had never dreamed his skills might be needed again—and in his own home yet!

Carefully he eased his patient to her back.

Complete and utter silence ensued. Perhaps both men were a little taken aback. Perhaps they'd been too engrossed in the commotion to truly take notice of her. But now both he and Justin stared as if spellbound. Neither could help it. Neither could ignore it.

Leave it to Justin to speak the unspeakable. "Well, well, well," he whispered. "Do you know that pale coral rose in the garden at Thurston Hall? Julianna adores it, remember? Sunrise, I believe it's called . . ." Another second of silence. "Her nipples," he finished softly, "are just like that rose."

Sebastian yanked the sheet over her breasts. "Justin! For pity's sake, she's ill!"

"And I am not blind. Nor, I daresay, are you."

He leveled an admonishing frown at Justin. "If possible, I should like to tend her without benefit of your lecherous insight."

"Meaning you wish me to leave?"

"I do," Sebastian said sternly. "But send Stokes

back in with more hot water. Soap, too. And have Tansy fetch one of Julianna's night rails."

"As you say, my lord. But since I'm being banished, I should like to offer a word of advice."

Sebastian glanced up inquiringly.

"Perhaps we should have Stokes stow away the valuables," Justin stated mildly. "Indeed, perhaps we should lock our doors. We've a woman of the streets in the house, you know. She may well rob us blind and murder us in our beds by morning."

Sebastian glowered. Justin merely laughed and closed the door.

Sebastian bent over his patient once more. Clearly Justin considered the situation quite humorous. Damn it all! He needed no reminders that he'd brought a thief into his home . . . sweet Lord, his *home*!

He was still having trouble believing it himself.

Three

Four chimes from the walnut clock in the marbled foyer announced the hour as Sebastian made his way to the study; the sound was lost in the vastness of the domed ceiling. Justin's presence was proclaimed by the pungent smell of smoke from a cheroot.

At Sebastian's entrance, Justin turned. Quickly he abandoned his stance before the warmth of the fire. Crossing the room, he fetched a brandy from a delicate-legged side table.

By the time Justin handed it to him, Sebastian had sprawled in the chair behind his desk. The events of the evening had taken their toll.

"How is she?"

Sebastian took a long, burning draught of brandy and swallowed. "The wound is not so deep as I'd first thought." He rubbed his fingers over the scratchiness of his jaw. He needed to shave, he thought absently. "In time," he said slowly, "I think she'll be fine."

"Excellent." Justin had ambled to the chair across from him. "I must confess, I'm mightily curious as to what you were doing in St. Giles. It's certainly the last place on earth I should have expected to find *you.*"

"Spare me the sarcasm, Justin. When I left for the Farthingale ball, Stokes told me you planned to spend the evening gaming. When I left the Farthingales', I stopped by White's thinking to find you there. It was Gideon who disclosed he'd left you at a club in St. Giles." Sebastian made no secret of his disapproval.

Justin's eyes glinted. "And so you decided to come to my rescue?"

"Something like that."

"I'm a grown man, Sebastian. I don't believe I need to apprise you of my every activity."

"St. Giles is a dangerous place," Sebastian said sharply. "Surely you know that."

"I do. But as you can see, I'm none the worse for it, save for some wretchedly bad wine and a good deal more bad luck."

God knew Justin had ever been in defiance of the strictures placed on him by their father, even before their mother's capricious flight of fancy. The three siblings had grown up knowing they could rely only on one another—he, Justin, and Julianna. But if life's lessons had taught him anything, it was that a man could not be molded . . . *should* not be molded.

Sebastian could never forget the scandal that had ripped their world apart when he was a boy. God knew, he'd lived with it every day since. Justin possessed the charm and vivacity of their mother. He also possessed her wild streak, and that worried him. Julianna had been too young to understand what had happened . . . she missed her mama, but only for a time.

But Justin . . . Their father had tried to confine his headstrong ways. He had tried to restrain him. Sebastian wanted to protect him, but like their mother, Justin had always been one to go his own way. Sebastian had recognized—as perhaps their father had not—that to rein him in, to control him, would only incur his rebellion.

Yet at times he was given to wonder if something more had occurred between their father and Justin. On several occasions, when Sebastian tried to press the issue, Justin chose to dismiss it in that careless, nonchalant way he had.

In truth, Sebastian could appreciate there were some things a man must guard closely within himself.

And he would not mold his brother into something he was not.

"Bad luck," he murmured. "What, you?"

"Indeed. And I would remind you, I arrived home before you, dear brother."

"So you did." Sebastian chuckled, and the tension between the two vanished. "Let it suffice to say that I did not expect to encounter a woman on the streets. Or *of* the streets, in all likelihood. Why else would she be out and about at such an hour?"

Justin frowned. "You don't intend to notify the authorities, do you?"

"What, you think I shouldn't?"

Justin regarded him steadily. "No, I don't."

"But the circumstances are suspicious at best. The

girl was stabbed. Why? What brought it about? Who did it? And where is he now?"

"Precisely. But isn't that all the more reason to wait until she's awake and able to speak, and then see how the game plays out?" When Sebastian said nothing, Justin gave a tiny shake of his head. "After all, it's hardly like you to act impulsively."

It was true. Impulsive was the one thing Sebastian would never be. He preferred order in his life. He was methodical, a meticulous planner. In his mind, it was why he usually achieved what he wanted.

"I hardly consider notifying the authorities an impulsive act," he said slowly. "But I suppose you're right. We should speak with her first."

Justin cocked his head to the side. "I must admit, I'm surprised you agree so readily. Perhaps you've taken a fancy to the chit?"

Sebastian gave a short laugh. "I do believe I prefer my women to be more refined than thieves."

"Ah, yes. There is that matter of respectability. Admit it, though. She does have the most glorious breasts."

Sebastian slanted his brother a thoroughly disgusted look.

"What, Sebastian! Are you going to say you didn't notice? Are you going to say you didn't look?"

Once again Sebastian maintained his silence. But this time he cursed the dull, red flush that crept beneath his skin.

Justin chuckled. "I know better, Sebastian. Lord knows I admire your discretion, but I am your brother, after all. And I'm aware you've kept a number of mistresses over the years. Pray tell, who is the latest?" He tapped a finger to his brow, as if engaged in great concentration. "I have it! Lilly, is it not?"

Sebastian sighed but made no reply. Heaven help him, Justin needed no further encouragement!

"Come now, Sebastian. I know you've a fondness for women."

"As do you." God, what an understatement! He emptied his glass, then set it aside. "There's something you should know, however, before you hear it elsewhere." He paused, then said, "I've decided to take a bride."

Justin erupted into laughter, then all at once stopped short. "Dear God," he said incredulously, "you're serious!"

"Quite."

"And you made the announcement tonight?"

Sebastian smiled to himself. "In a manner of speaking."

"Well, either you did or you didn't."

While Justin listened, Sebastian relayed the scene played out earlier in the evening as Sophia Edwina Richfield, the dowager duchess of Carrington, had made her round of farewells. She'd peered at him in the prim, stately way of hers from beneath snowy white curls. It was then she made her declaration, for that was the dowager's way, ever forthright, ever direct.

"My boy," she stated as she came to him, "it's time you had a wife and children."

Naturally a collective gasp was heard. All sound ceased. There had been little need to peruse the room to be aware that every head had turned, every ear strained to the limit to hear his reply.

And so Sebastian had merely kissed the duchess's hand. "Your Grace," he murmured, "I do believe you may be right."

Sebastian knew then and there what would happen next, for he was a man who did nothing without weighing the consequences. His agreement with the duchess would be bandied about at once. Tongues would wag, and his presence at every party and fete he attended for weeks to come would be noted by the *ton*. What he wore, what he ate, to whom he spoke, and, most notably, the women with whom he danced would most assuredly become fodder for the rags. A regrettable necessity, he supposed.

"You should have attended," he finished with a faint smile. "I'm sure you'd have found it most entertaining."

"The Farthingale affairs are always the most boring, tedious parties imaginable!" Justin rolled his eyes. "But to think you did not seek my counsel before coming to such a momentous decision. You've hurt my feelings tremendously, Sebastian."

"Yes," Sebastian remarked dryly, "so I see. And I know what your counsel would have been."

Justin regarded him through a haze of smoke. "What *is* behind this sudden decision?"

"It's hardly sudden. I've been considering it for some time, if you must know. Besides, most men marry. Have children. It's a matter of duty."

"Ah, yes, duty. How predictable," Justin drawled. "Might I inquire as to the candidates you're considering as your future wife?"

"You may inquire, but I've no particular woman in mind, to be honest. I've simply decided to narrow the field."

"I see. Yet I am given to wonder if the woman exists who can please you."

Sebastian leveled an arch look upon him. "Precisely what does that mean?"

"Forgive me," Justin stated blandly, "but I cannot help but wonder if your requirements may not be rather . . . exacting."

"Explain yourself."

"Gladly. I think you would demand no less of a wife than you do of yourself. In short, a woman of perfection."

Sebastian was ready with a rejoinder. "Not so much a woman of perfection, but the perfect woman for me."

"Well," Justin remarked, "you can certainly be discerning. Society's ladies do tend to follow you about."

"Just as they tend to moon after you."

"The ability to charm the opposite sex certainly seems to be in the blood, doesn't it?"

Caustic sarcasm swathed in silk—how very typical of Justin. Sebastian ignored the jibe about their mother's infidelities.

Justin continued. "I've been telling you for ages you're the most sought-after bachelor in London. Now it's official."

"True," Sebastian agreed. "But let us not mince words. In my case, it's the title they want. The fortune. Which reminds me"—he raised a brow, regarding Justin through a haze of smoke—"isn't it time you considered taking a bride as well?"

Justin dissolved into laughter. "Discharge yourself of the notion at once! I'll never hang up the ladle, and well you know it."

With that, Justin crushed out his cigar and ambled to his feet. Sebastian bid him good night, but did not follow. Loosening his cravat, he poured the last splash of brandy into his glass, then sank down into the big leather chair before the fire.

His fingers rubbed the back of his neck. Christ, what a night! For a long time he simply sat, allowing the peace and solitude of the night to slip into his bones. God knew, after a night like tonight, he needed it. Besides, this was an excellent time to plan and ponder the future . . . and his decision to take a bride.

The duchess was right. It was time he married. Contrary to what Justin might think, it was hardly a sudden decision. No, he'd been thinking about it for weeks now.

It was time. He was ready.

But there would be no mistakes.

There would be no scandal. No slight, no blight upon his name. It was a vow Sebastian had made to himself long, long ago, a vow that drove his every endeavor.

Ten years had passed since he'd assumed the title. There was now no taint, no shame in being a Sterling. Much had changed since then.

Yet in some ways, so very little.

He was still seeing after his brother and sister—wasn't tonight proof of it? Justin hadn't been pleased at his incursion into St. Giles tonight. He smiled slightly, for it was hard to quell such instinct after so many years. Countless times he'd had to remind himself that they must live their own lives, that they must be allowed to make their own choices.

Their own mistakes.

But Sebastian could afford none. For there was the not-so-small matter of duty to consider.

Duty.

His brother despised it. His sister shunned it, though in a different way than Justin. But William Sterling had taught his eldest son well.

To marry was his duty. To his name. To his title. His duty was the legacy left behind by his father and the generations before him.

And yet . . . there was more. Things Justin wouldn't understand, might never understand, for he was so like their mother it frightened him sometimes.

Ah, yes, it was more than duty. He loved Justin and Julianna without question—he was glad their closeness had carried into adulthood. But there was a hunger in him, a yearning for something more. He wanted . . . a family of his own. A child of his own. Hell, a dozen children for that matter, for he would give them all the things he and Justin and Julianna had never had. Indeed, he could imagine no greater pleasure than the feel of a small, warm body snuggled against his chest, in complete and utter trust . . . a child of his blood.

A son. A daughter . . . Sweet Christ, he didn't care which, for the thought of either made his heart swell with emotion. God, but it would be good to hear gay, merry laughter echoing through the rooms—both here at his town house and at Thurston Hall.

But there must be a wife before there could be children, either son *or* daughter.

His fingertip swirled around the rim of his glass again and again. His mood was suddenly pensive. Thanks to his mother, the family name had been mired in scandal throughout much of his childhood.

But at least these last few years had been quiet. The storms had all been weathered, the damage repaired. His father's death had been sudden, and Sebastian had been rather startled to learn he'd been careless with finances the last few years of his life.

But the Sterlings were once again one of the richest families in England. Indeed, he thought with a touch of the cynical air usually displayed by his brother, with power, wealth, and rank came privilege. The dowager duchess too had borne her share of scandal throughout the years. It was said her son had seen to that, and she was now the most influential woman in town!

But Sebastian would not allow scandal to touch his wife and children the way it had touched his brother and sister.

And so, as with all things, Sebastian Sterling knew he must choose carefully. He was a man who preferred order in his life, a man who disliked the unexpected.

At least Justin was right—he needn't cast about for a bride. Of course he didn't possess his brother's classically elegant countenance. As one starry-eyed miss once declared upon her first glimpse of Justin, 'twas as if she'd died and gone to heaven! But Sebastian was too dark, too big, too brawny—too much like a Gypsy, as he'd been teased when he was a boy.

No, Sebastian decided, he wasn't so devilishly handsome as his brother. But he would be a loving father. A good husband. He'd learned from his father's coldness, his harsh, rigid nature . . . his mother's abandonment.

But what of the woman who would be his wife?

It must be done right or not at all.

No simpering miss, to be sure. His wife must be a woman of grace and tact, of gentility and stability; cultured, well-bred, and well-educated. A woman of unswerving loyalty and devotion. A woman of scruples, as strong and staunch as his own. And his wife would be a woman of stable nature, a loving, attentive mother.

Something shifted inside him, something that caught at the very center of his heart. Dear God, he prayed fervently, above all, a loving mother!

And beauty? Nay, he decided. Many a man would demand that of a bride. Not he. Oh, he was not opposed to a pleasing countenance. If she was a woman fair to look upon, comely of feature and shapely of form, all the better. But it was her inner beauty that mattered most.

He smiled suddenly. Justin would call him a fool, that outward beauty was not so high on his list. Sebastian was well aware of his brother's tastes; Justin would not deign even to glance at a woman who was not a diamond of the first water.

His smile ebbed. His heart squeezed.

Dear God, she could be a toad. As long as she loved him and would never leave. He was determined he wouldn't make the same mistakes as his father and mother. Dear God, not with his children.

Or his wife.

The brandy decanter was nearly drained to the dregs before he arose and mounted the stairs. At the top he paused. His gaze was drawn to the first door on the right, which stood slightly ajar.

He'd best look in on her, his uninvited houseguest. He was suddenly reminded of what Justin had said.

Perhaps we should have Stokes stow away the valuables. Indeed, perhaps we should lock our doors. We've a woman of the streets in the house, you know. She may well rob us blind and murder us in our beds by morning.

He thought of the necklace the girl had gripped so tightly in her palm. It still warmed his pocket. Amazing that she'd held it throughout the ordeal; she must have been in considerable pain, and who knew how long she'd been injured before he discovered her? But then greed was a powerful incentive. He knew a costly piece when he saw it, and he suspected this was the genuine article.

His mouth thinned. She had a great deal to answer for, that much was certain.

Almost before he was aware of it, he was standing over her. A frail sliver of moonbeam seeped in through the windowpanes, trickling over her form.

What else was it Justin had said? That Sebastian had taken a fancy to her?

Ludicrous.

It was just as he'd told Justin. The chit was a thief. A pickpocket. God only knew what else! That so little was known about the circumstances in which she'd been injured was troubling. As soon as she was able, it would have to be sorted out.

His eyes drifted over her.

One small hand, the hand that had clutched the necklace, lay curled against her chest. He'd carefully washed the mud and stench from her body and clad her in one of his sister's night rails. Odd thing, but once she was clean, he'd had to remind himself she was a thief. A street urchin.

Not that he'd ever encountered one in quite so intimate a fashion as he had this one. His lips quirked at the thought, then slipped away.

Slowly his gaze slid over her. She slept, but restlessly, it seemed. She'd kicked aside the covering he'd drawn over her. Her small mouth trembled slightly. Slender brows rose aslant above those extraordinary eyes that reminded him of topaz.

Respectability be damned! he thought.

For a thieving woman of the streets, she was remarkably fine. There was no denying her wild beauty and . . . God above, but he felt almost lascivious!

Was it the pose? Or the woman herself? Beneath the fine lawn of the night rail, her skin glimmered in the firelight. The night rail lay bunched about her thighs, slender and white. Her legs shifted; a small hand moved to her chest, then dropped to one side. Her breasts rose and fell rhythmically, her nipples round coral disks that thrust out impudently.

There was no hiding her frank sensuality. Sebastian took a deep breath, aware of something totally unexpected tightening in his belly. It was hardly a gentlemanly thing to do . . . But there was no withholding a lingering, intensely masculine admiration of the tawny mane that spilled across the pillow in silken chaos, gleaming like sunlit honey; of tender, well-shaped limbs, the velvet hollow of her belly. And . . . yes . . . oh, yes . . .

Those glorious, glorious breasts.

Four

It was the shiver of a presence that woke Devon. The unfamiliar cadence of a voice . . . a man's voice, deep and cultured and melodious. Searchingly Devon turned her head toward the sound. Her body shifted.

"Easy, now," said the voice. "You've been hurt."

Hurt, her mind echoed vaguely. A strange stillness seemed to drift in her head, abruptly snared by memory. A shudder tore through her. She saw Harry and Freddie, circling like vultures. She remembered falling, hurtling into a black void where there was nothing but cold, seeping through, clear to her very bones . . . she'd been cold before, but not like that. Never like that! And there had been the terrifying fear that no one would hear. That she would lie there and die, like Mama, in the cold and the dark . . .

But she wasn't cold now, she realized. There was a

dull ache in her side, but she was cocooned in softness and warmth as never before.

And someone sat close. *Very* close.

With that awareness, Devon struggled to bring the image into focus. A man sat beside her, so near she could have reached out and touched his sleeve. Even sitting down, he was astonishingly large, his shoulders surely as wide as the Thames. Behind him, standing across the room, was another man, whose rich, dark hair was but a shade lighter.

Devon scarcely gave the other man a second consideration. No, it was the man beside her who captured and commanded her attention and made her breath slip away. She remembered now. She remembered waking and seeing *him* . . . the jolt of fear that passed through her at finding this huge man crouched over her.

It wasn't just his size that radiated power. It was more, far more, for his was a presence that could hardly go unnoticed, not by her, or anyone else, she suspected.

His clothing was sheer elegance. Not a single wrinkle marred the fabric of his coat. Beneath was a royal blue silk waistcoat and fine cambric shirt. His cravat was spotlessly white, almost blindingly so, particularly against the bronze of his skin.

His eyes were sharply, penetratingly gray, set deep beneath craggy black brows and hair of darkest midnight. His jaw was square and cleanly shaven to the skin, totally unlike the bristly, bewhiskered men she was used to encountering. The only hint of softness in his angled, supremely masculine face was a clefted chin.

"Where am I?" The words came out sounding hoarse; she sounded nothing like herself.

"I found you injured in the streets. I brought you here, to my house in Mayfair."

Mayfair. Devon's gaze circled slowly around the chamber. She stared. Somehow she couldn't stop herself. Draperies of yellow silk hung at the window, tied with a silver cord. The walls were papered and patterned in roses. She was lying in a bed the size of which she'd never imagined, a bed so soft she felt as if she were floating on a cloud. In truth, but for the fiery ache in her side, she might have been in a dreamworld.

His speech was clipped and precise, like her mother's. "You are a gentleman." She spoke unthinkingly. "And this house . . . it's so grand! 'Tis what I imagined some fine lord's might be like."

The merest hint of a smile graced his chiseled lips.

Devon blinked. "Are you a lord?"

He gave a half bow. "Sebastian Sterling, marquess of Thurston, at your service. And this is my brother Justin."

Devon was dumbfounded. By Jove, a marquess!

"Miss." The other gentleman gave a slight nod. His gaze didn't possess the piercing sharpness of that of the marquess, but he watched her closely.

"What about you?" asked the marquess. "Have you a name?"

She swallowed. "Devon. Devon St. James."

"Well, Miss St. James, now that you're a guest in my home, perhaps you'd care to tell me of the night's . . . activities."

There was a masked coolness in his regard. Only

then did Devon perceive it. As she did, her memories sharpened. With unremitting clarity, she remembered the feel of Freddie's fingers around her neck, cutting off her breath. That, she realized belatedly, was why it felt as if needles were slashing her throat when she spoke, why she was so hoarse.

Freddie, she thought wildly. She remembered gripping her dagger and thrusting it forward, the odd sensation of cloth tearing and flesh giving way . . . how he'd staggered away. She nearly cried out. Where was he? What had happened to him?

Her gaze lifted. "There was a man," she said unsteadily. "Where is he?"

The marquess shook his head. "When I found you, you were alone."

"But he was there! I tell you he was there!"

"And once again, I must tell you, you were alone. Clearly you did not sustain your injuries yourself. So tell us about this man you were with."

"I wasn't *with* him. I—"

All at once she broke off. The way he was looking at her . . .

"Miss St. James? Pray continue."

It was easy to see what he thought of her. He continued to regard her as if she were a maggot, and she was suddenly furious. Why, she was surprised he had brought himself to sit within arm's length of her.

Devon would not hide from what she was. She could not *change* what she was. She had grown up in the dirty, fetid streets of St. Giles, where she'd learned the hard way that trust was not something to be given lightly.

Marquess or no, she would not allow him to steal her pride from her, for indeed, it was all she had. Besides, she knew his kind. Long before Mama had died, Devon had determined she would not fail, that she would fulfill her promise to find a better life for herself. She'd gone to the great houses of the city, seeking other work. From the time she was very young, Devon had labored. She'd cleaned fish at the docks, swept paths for the gentry as they crossed the street or descended a carriage, and carried slop from the kitchens, for Mama's work as a seamstress was barely enough for food and lodgings.

But there were no positions to be found in the households of the lords and ladies of London, or indeed any reputable establishment, not as maid or cook or kitchen wench. One look at her and the door was promptly slammed in her face. She did her best to stay presentable, but it wasn't always easy—she'd placed a basin outside the door to catch rainwater in order to bathe, but some wretched soul had stolen it. If she was well scrubbed and rosy-cheeked, perhaps it might have made a difference. And it hadn't helped that she'd outgrown her ragged gown some years ago. There was no money to spare for cloth, though Mama had mended and let out the seams as much as she could.

"Miss St. James, why do I have the feeling there's something you're not telling us?"

Her sharp retort died in her throat. Justin's gaze was nearly as sharp as his brother's. She felt herself pale, all at once uneasy. These two were blue bloods, and blue bloods had no use for people like her! If she admitted she had stabbed Freddie, what would they do?

She would be hauled off to the authorities with nary a thought.

"Miss St. James? Is something wrong?"

Her heart thumped wildly. "Nothing's wrong," she said quickly. It was part fear, part defiance that compelled her answer. But suddenly she started.

"My necklace!" Her hand moved frantically on the satin counterpane. "My necklace! Where is it? I cannot lose it. I had it, I know I did—"

"Set your mind at ease. It's in a safe place."

But his expression lent her no ease. "It's mine! I want it back!"

He got to his feet. It skittered through her mind that on his feet he was a giant. She watched as he walked to the ornately carved marble fireplace, then turned to face her, strong hands linked behind his back. Near the door, his brother continued to look on.

"When the rightful owner has been determined," he said with a lift of one brow, "the rightful owner shall have it back."

"The rightful owner . . . What do you mean?"

His eyes had gone the color of stone. "It means I am not a half-wit, Miss St. James. I do have a very good idea how your injury was sustained, and I'll not be tricked. A quarrel among thieves, for instance—"

"I am not a thief!" she cried. "My purse was stolen!"

"Your purse," he repeated. "Stuffed with your coin, I expect."

"Yes. Yes! There were two men, you see—"

"Oh, so now there were two. And hoodlums, no doubt."

There was an awful, twisting feeling in the pit of her stomach.

"I must give you credit, Miss St. James. You speak far better than I expected."

Her chin climbed high. "My mother was well-spoken."

"And who was your mother?"

"Why, the queen of England!"

"That would make you a princess. In that case, I commend most highly your penchant for disguise."

Devon followed his gaze across the room. Draped across a high-backed chair near the door was her ragged cloak, her gown . . . and the pillow she'd stuffed beneath it.

Damn his arrogance! How dare he pass judgment on her!

Like her mother before her, she was different from those who lived and worked in the filthy back alleys of London. Despite those differences—or perhaps because of them—she had learned to survive. It wasn't that she was meaner or stronger—such a notion was laughable—or even that she was smarter. But she was wise enough to avoid circumstances that might place her in situations that were less than desirable.

The very reason for such attire. If one must brave the streets each night, it was better done this way. Upon commencing her employment at the Crow's Nest, Devon had considered dressing like a lad, but alas, there was little chance of being mistaken for a lad, not with her breasts and hair constantly tumbling in a wild curtain about her shoulders. At least like this, she didn't look so different from the beggars and thieves. And thankfully, there were few who were wont to look twice at a woman who, as Bridget was fond of saying, appeared ready to deliver the burden in her belly at any moment.

"One cannot help but wonder what you were doing about at such a late hour. Out taking the air, perhaps?"

She stared at him. There was no mistaking his meaning. "Not only do you think I am a thief, you think I am a trollop."

He made no reply, nor was there a need to. It was there in the way those crystalline eyes measured the entire length of her form.

Devon, her ire blazing, dragged the counterpane up to her chin. The urge to do bodily harm was indeed paramount in her mind.

"What did you say your name was?" she asked coolly. "Lord Shyte?"

He stiffened visibly. "I beg your pardon?"

"Oh, do forgive my lapse in memory. It must have been Lord Arse—"

Three strides brought him back across the room and to the bedside. "Watch your tongue, Miss St. James. I'll not have the language of the gutter spoken in my house. But then, I suppose I should expect no less from a woman of the streets."

He stood above her. Tall. Not threatening, but certainly imposing. But Devon was too angry to recant her recklessness. Throughout her life, there had been times she despaired of her quick, impetuous nature, but this was not one of them.

"Then perhaps I should leave, sir!"

"Not until you are well." A peremptory command, no less!

Their eyes dueled. "I'll have you know my father was from a family finer than yours!" she spouted. "And he lived in a house far grander than this one!"

"Ah, yes, with your mother the queen. Do forgive *my* lapse in memory. Though indeed, I have the feeling there's much more you could tell me about last night."

"I think not."

"Then perhaps I should return when you're more disposed to converse."

"Perhaps you shouldn't return at all."

"Oh, but I shall. And I promise we shall continue our discussion." But he made no effort to depart, remaining at the bedside, regarding her in that assessing manner she already disliked.

She plucked at the soft folds of the gown she wore. "This is not mine," she muttered.

"No. It belongs to my sister, Julianna, who is traveling on the Continent. If she were here, she would be the one to nurse you, and not I. She's always been one to tend poor animals and such."

Devon gritted her teeth. "I am not an animal."

"I apologize. It was a poor choice of words."

He didn't sound very apologetic. Devon glared. "I suppose it was you who put me in this night rail as well."

"I did indeed."

Heat flooded her face. "I thought you said you were a marquess!"

"I am."

"Then have you no servants?" Her shock had turned to outrage. "Why, I'm surprised you deigned to lay a finger on someone so obviously inferior!"

His smile held little mirth. "Oh, it would take a good deal more to put me off. So think of me as your nurse, Miss St. James, and rest assured I shall endeavor to make your recovery a speedy one. And," he added smoothly when he saw her gaping, "if you're going to ask why we didn't summon a physician . . . well, I daresay a physician would have asked more questions than you appear willing to answer."

Devon checked her biting retort. He was right; she should mind her tongue. Mama had often chided her for not guarding it more closely. She resented his arrogance and overbearing manner, but there was little she could do about her fate right now. She reminded herself she was warm and dry—and far away from Harry and Freddie.

He shifted, suddenly so close she could smell the starch of his shirt. She tried to recoil from his nearness, but there was nowhere to go. His fingertips slid over the delicate skin just below her ear, down the side of her neck.

"You've bruises there," he observed grimly.

Devon said nothing. She tried to read the thoughts behind the depths of his eyes, but she could not peer within, any more than she could have peered down the darkest alley on a moonless night.

"Would you care to tell me how you came by them?"

The burning in her side was suddenly intense and throbbing, but it was like nothing compared to the ache in her breast. Black despair slipped over her heart. What was the use? His kind would never believe her.

"No," she muttered.

"Are you in pain?"

Though his expression was intent, the harshness was gone from his voice. Devon refused to be lured. Mutely she shook her head.

He persisted. "Perhaps some laudanum—"

"What, to coax me into talking?"

Silence. "No," he said finally. "It will help you rest."

"I shall be fine." She pressed her lips together, horrified to discover that tears lurked but a heartbeat away. She was determined not to reveal how close she was to breaking down, but if he stayed any longer, she wasn't sure she could stop them.

She averted her gaze. "If you don't mind, I'd like to be alone now."

From the corner of her eye, she saw his brother's shadow shift toward the door, but the marquess had yet to move. She could feel his gaze boring into her.

"You must be hungry. I'll send someone up with food."

"Fine," she muttered. "As long as it isn't you."

"Given your present state, Miss St. James, I shall pretend I didn't hear that." He gave a slight bow. "In the meantime I shall look forward to our next meeting."

Devon, on the other hand, most certainly did *not*.

Five

Outside in the hall, Justin crossed his arms over his chest and regarded Sebastian. "Quite the termagant, isn't she?"

Sebastian snorted. "Termagant? I can think of a word far more fitting and much less proper."

The corner of Justin's mouth twitched. "The girl has gumption, you must admit. I found it vastly amusing when she called you Lord Shyte."

"I'm sure you did, and I agree she has gumption. But she's hiding something, Justin. I'm sure of it."

A gleam entered Justin's eyes. "Shall we entertain a wager?"

"You'd lose," Sebastian predicted bluntly.

Justin merely laughed.

After dinner that evening, Sebastian retired to the library and his favorite chair. The day had been a busy one. Business had occupied much of the afternoon, as well as nagging thoughts of the girl upstairs. He still wasn't sure precisely what they'd gotten into. Although, he reflected wryly, it appeared she was doing her best to forget *him*. He'd looked in on her once, but the instant she saw him, she screwed her eyes shut and pretended to be asleep.

The Wetherby ball was tonight, but he'd sent a note declining. He didn't feel right about leaving an injured woman alone with just the servants to tend her. No doubt the gossips would be all abuzz, wondering at his absence, particularly after his announcement at the Farthingales', but the decision had been an easy one.

His search for a bride would simply have to commence later.

Settling into his chair, he reached for the newspaper. It had arrived earlier in the afternoon, but this was the first chance he'd had to read it.

It wasn't long before he heard Justin come in, then call for the carriage to be brought round in an hour's time. Justin stopped in the doorway.

"I thought you'd be dressing for the Wetherby ball."

Sebastian shook his head. "I think not," he said dryly. With his thumb he gestured toward the ceiling.

"Ah, yes. I forgot. You'll be guarding the silver." Justin stripped off his gloves. "How is she, by the way?"

"Better than I expected, though she still doesn't seem to have taken much of a liking to me."

"Yes. One can only wonder why . . ." Justin paused. "Are you sure you won't attend the Wetherby ball?"

"I'm sure."

"You won't find the perfect bride sitting here at home. I vow all of London's lovelies will be there."

"And they'll all be looking at you. Besides, as I have survived over thirty years without a bride, there's no harm in waiting awhile longer." Sebastian flipped open the paper.

Justin chuckled. "I think you're wrong there. In fact, I know it." Before he could stop him, Justin grabbed the paper in hand. Rattling it with a flourish, he cleared his throat. "Here," he announced, "is the latest in today's society column." He proceeded to quote.

Ladies, set your caps! According to the marquess of Thurston, the city's most celebrated bachelor, Thurston's search for a bride is on . . .

"Oh, Lord," Sebastian muttered, snatching it back into his grasp.

"I vow, Sebastian, after that juicy tidbit all the lovelies will be disappointed you're not present. And I shall simply have to console them somehow."

"Oh, I'm sure you'll find a way." Sebastian was already ensconced in his paper.

"Oh, I shall. Have a pleasant evening."

But Justin had scarcely crossed the room before Sebastian erupted with a curse. Justin glanced back over his shoulder. "What is it?"

Sebastian's expression was grim. "I knew it! I knew she was hiding something!"

Justin looked at him sharply. "What do you mean?"

Sebastian flicked a finger at the newspaper. "Remember the man she spoke of? Well, a man was found dead on the street adjacent to where I found our esteemed houseguest."

"Good Lord."

"He was apparently a member of a gang in St. Giles." Two white lines had formed beside Sebastian's mouth. " There was a dagger discovered near his body."

Justin looked at his brother. "Surely," he said slowly, "you don't think—"

"What I think is that another visit to the lovely Miss St. James is in order. I do believe she can shed some light on the matter." He reached the door and yanked it open. "Christ," he muttered, "I should never have brought her here."

Justin was right beside him as he mounted the stairs. In the yellow room, Devon was sitting back against the pillows. Tansy, one of the maids, had just removed a tray from her lap. In some distant part of him, Sebastian was pleased to note she'd eaten nearly all of her dinner.

Her chin came up when she saw him. "Well, if it isn't my lord Shyte!"

Sebastian smiled thinly. "It's good to see you're feeling better. Perhaps you'll be more obliging with the truth." He stopped at the side of the bed and tossed the newspaper on her lap. "I think you'll find this bit of news most interesting." He rapped a finger on the headline.

Wide golden eyes traveled from his face to the paper. She spoke not a word.

"Well?" he demanded.

She maintained her silence.

"Miss St. James?"

She gave a little shake of her head. "I-I can't read. I mean . . . I know all the letters, but I-I can't put them together into words, except for my name."

Inwardly Sebastian cursed himself for a heel. He should have known!

"Well, then, I shall oblige." He picked up the paper. "A man was found in St. Giles this morning. Just a short distance away from where I found *you*."

Her color was distinctly paler.

"According to the story, a woman was seen wearing a long, mud-colored cloak and a large bonnet."

Her gaze slid to her bedraggled bonnet, hanging on the post of the silk-striped damask chair across the room.

He continued. "'The woman,'" he quoted, "was given to a plump disposition." He cast a pointed look at the pillow on the chair, then back to her face.

She was chewing her lower lip. His gaze pinned hers, then hers slipped away. A guilty look, if ever there was one.

"This man was struck down, Miss St. James. Stabbed in the chest."

"What?" she said faintly. "Are you saying that he's dead?"

"Indeed. There was a dagger by his side. The constable is speculating it's the murder weapon."

"Oh, God," she whispered.

"Thus my question. Was this man struck down by your hand?"

Her lips parted. It was not the answer he sought; yet in truth, her stricken expression was the only answer he needed.

"Who struck first?"

She avoided his gaze. "The dagger is mine," she admitted, her tone very low. "But it wasn't what you think. Truly it wasn't."

"Were you trying to steal from him?"

Her eyes slid back to his. "No!"

"Was it a lovers' tiff then?"

"A lovers' . . . I have no lover," she gasped. "I told you last night he was trying to steal from me! He stole my wages, and he tried to steal my necklace!"

Sebastian ignored the tremulous quiver of those lush lips and pressed on. The time was ripe to pluck at the truth, and he knew it.

"The paper claims he was a member of a gang," Sebastian said. "Did you know him?"

"No. I swear, I did not. I only knew *of* him." She shuddered. "His name was Freddie." Her gaze skipped to Justin, who had moved to the end of the bed.

"All we ask is the truth," Justin said quietly.

"They blocked my way—Freddie and his brother Harry." Her eyes flashed accusingly as she addressed Sebastian. "I told you there were two of them. Harry reached into my pocket and grabbed my purse. He ran down the alley with it. Freddie tried to take my necklace from the other. I didn't care if they stole my wages, but I couldn't let them take my necklace! I tried to stop Freddie, but he put his hands around my throat, and I couldn't breathe! I remember, I reached for the dagger. It was in my boot."

Sebastian's gaze now rested on the side of her neck. *So that was how she'd come by those bruises,* he thought. *When Freddie tried to strangle her.*

Justin spoke his thoughts aloud. "It must have

been Harry who returned and found Freddie's body."

"Not necessarily," said Sebastian. "It could have been someone else. But perhaps he's the one who informed the police—"

Devon shook her head. "No. He wouldn't dare, for fear of being caught himself. But it could have been one of his cronies planted a bug in the constable's ear." She blinked rapidly and looked down. Sebastian frowned.

"Either way," she said, her voice scarcely above a whisper, "it doesn't matter. He's looking for me, and so is the constable."

"They're looking for a woman with a large belly, a cloak, and a ridiculous bonnet," Sebastian pointed out. "For a woman who claims she's not a thief, you were certainly dressed like one."

That brought her head up in a flash. "Do not presume to call me that which I am not. It seems I am a murderer, but I am not a thief!"

"How do you make your living then?"

"I work at the Crow's Nest, I daresay an establishment two fine gentlemen like yourselves are scarcely wont to visit."

Such impertinence! Why, she sounded a veritable hoity-toity miss!

He glanced at Justin. "It's an alehouse not far from the docks," Justin supplied.

No wonder she'd smelled of fish and smoke and ale!

He addressed her once more. "You certainly went to great lengths to conceal your form."

"Not for the reason you believe!"

He raised his brows. "I should like to hear that reason," he said calmly.

Her eyes were smoldering. He strongly suspected that had she possessed the strength, she'd have cheerfully fastened her fingers around *his* neck.

"I rent a room from a man named Phillips, in a house near Shelton Street. It's very late when I make my way home. If you must know, it—it's my way of protecting myself."

Sebastian and Justin looked at each other. Both men were clearly confused.

Their guest looked at them both as if they were dolts. "Men seldom look twice at a woman heavy with child. At least that was my experience until last night." She paused. "I didn't mean to kill Freddie," she said quaveringly. "I only meant to stop him."

A plausible explanation. Perhaps the better question was if it was a truthful one. Carefully Sebastian regarded her, gauging the way those soft pink lips had begun to tremble. Or was it but a trick of the evening light? Perhaps her defiance was nothing but sheer bravado.

She looked at Sebastian. "You should have left me there," she said, her voice very low. "It would have been better—"

"Nonsense!" His tone was sharp.

"It's true," she said bitterly. "The constable will never believe me, nor will the magistrate. I'm poor. I'm from St. Giles. That's all the reason they need to hang me. And Harry . . ." A shiver ran through her. "He's mean. Cruel. I could see it in his eyes. And I-I killed his brother. If he ever finds me, he'll make me wish I *had* died."

This time it was Justin who spoke sharply. "See here now, there's no need for such talk! And there's no need to be afraid. You'll come to no harm here in this house, Sebastian and I will see to it. Indeed, you may stay as long as you wish." He rose and strode to the door. His hand was already on the gleaming brass handle. "But come. You should be resting. Therefore, we bid you good night."

There was little doubt Justin possessed the Sterling arrogance. Sebastian had no choice but to follow him into the corridor. Justin was leaning against the wall when Sebastian closed the door.

"Was it only last night you said something about *me* taking a fancy to the chit?" Sebastian gave him a long, considering look. "I do wonder if it isn't *you* who's been taken in by her . . . how shall I put this . . . considerable charms."

"Rubbish." The word was a bald dismissal. "Despite appearances, I'm not so shallow as all that. She's in trouble. We can't turn her out. And we can't turn her in." Justin arched a brow when Sebastian said nothing. "Oh, come. Surely you don't think she's a murderer?"

Sebastian hesitated, aware of a tug-of-war churning inside him. "No," he admitted. "But can we ignore the fact she's from St. Giles? Home to beggars. Thieves. Prostitutes—"

"Oh, I see. You think she's a woman of easy virtue?"

Sebastian's mouth compressed. "More likely a woman of *no* virtue."

"The streets of St. Giles are a mean, dirty place, Sebastian. One can hardly remain innocent living there."

"Precisely the point. Just because she claims she's not a thief doesn't mean she isn't."

"She's in dire straits, Sebastian. If we go to the police, it's quite likely they won't listen to her. From her own admission, she killed Freddie. She comes from a place where her background alone is a crime. What if the police are more interested in securing a conviction than meting out justice? It won't matter that she was trying to defend herself. Thief or no, she doesn't deserve to hang."

It was a disturbing observation. "I'm aware of that," Sebastian said quietly. "It's entirely possible they'll take the view that there will be one less undesirable on the street." But now that undesirable was in his home, and in all truth, he couldn't say he was particularly pleased that Justin had offered the woman safe harbor indefinitely. "Considering you informed her she could remain as long as she wants, I do hope this woman doesn't take it into her head that she can become a permanent houseguest."

"Well, in that case she would no longer be a guest, would she?"

"In that case, perhaps you can take her with you when you find a town house of your own. You mentioned the possibility not long ago, I believe."

"Oh, I'm in no hurry."

"So I've noticed."

"My dear, elder brother, I should like to point out two things. For one, it was you who brought the dear lady Devon here—"

"Thank you for that reminder," Sebastian put in.

"As for the other, I vow you'd be rather lonely in this monstrous house all alone."

"Julianna may be off traveling, but she still resides here," he reminded Justin. "And I must say, I do wish our dear sister were here to tend this upstart!"

"As you said yourself, she's already on the mend."

"It will be some time before she's completely well. She could use some meat on her bones, in case you hadn't noticed."

"I did. Considering your opinion of her, I'm surprised *you* noticed."

Guilt stabbed inside Sebastian, swiftly set aside. "I am not an insensitive brute, Justin."

Justin's expression proclaimed otherwise.

"I daresay there's a woman in London who might consider *you* an insensitive brute."

"Oh, I daresay more than one." Justin's eyes gleamed. He paused, the laughter fading from his expression. "She was terrified, Sebastian, and trying very hard not to cry."

A vision impaled itself in his mind, a vision of eyes glistening like jeweled amber. He'd told himself they weren't tears. God knew, he didn't deal well with weeping females. They tore at his heart. They burned his very soul. Julianna could attest to that. A downward glance, a tremulous lip, a smothered sob . . . he was lost. Not that Julianna was the weak, whimpering type. Far from it. Yet for all that she was staunch and strong, he knew of no one more tenderhearted than she. And when she or any woman cried, Sebastian simply could not abide it. He could not remain unaffected. He could not turn his back and walk away. He did whatever he could, whatever must be done, to chase away those tears.

Now his brother's rare chastisement only made him feel worse. Good Lord, even Justin, who should have been immune to a woman's tears, who'd broken more hearts than all the rakes in London combined, had been moved.

Oh, hell. *Hell*. Perhaps he *was* an insensitive brute.

And indeed, the chit was in dire straits.

"Perhaps some inquiries should be made into her statements," he said quietly, "in particular, this wretch named Harry."

Justin nodded. "I'll see to it." He turned toward the stairs.

"Oh, and Justin?"

His brother glanced over his shoulder.

"We must take care it isn't known the inquiries came from us."

Justin cocked his head. "What?" he drawled. "Am I not a man of the utmost discretion?"

"Never." Nary a breath was wasted on the observation.

"Ah." His brother's smile was purely wicked, purely rakish, purely Justin. "You mean rarely, do you not?"

"I think you're quite aware what I mean."

Justin's smile ebbed. His countenance became unusually somber. "I am," he said. "And rest assured, brother, that you may count on me."

Their eyes met. A faint smile curled Sebastian's lips. "I know," he said softly.

Six

Behind the door, Devon sank back against the pillows with a sob. She was furious. Devastated as never before, sick to the dregs of her soul.

A cold ache settled around her heart. Her mother would have been appalled that she had even possessed a dagger, let alone used it. She had promised Mama once that she would never steal or whore or beg.

Instead she'd killed a man.

Guilt raged inside her. She had wanted out of St. Giles, wanted it above all else! Ah, but at what cost?

Her heart twisted. Sebastian Sterling was convinced she was a thief. *A thief*.

Never would Devon have dreamed of stealing. *Never*.

At least, never again.

For she *had* stolen once, a sweetened pastry from a confectionary. It had been so tempting, sitting on a pretty white plate painted with blue and yellow flowers, drizzled with honey. The shopkeeper's back was turned, and she knew he would never see. With no more thought she snatched it from the plate and ran for all she was worth, all the way home.

There, in the attic, she sank down upon the floor. She still remembered the way she'd crammed it in her mouth. The taste was incredible. Lusciously sweet.

But Devon knew better. She hadn't even been particularly hungry . . .

Mama had caught her. "You stole it, didn't you!"

The pastry in her mouth turned to sand. It was all she could do to swallow it.

There had been no need to answer.

Mama was furious. "You will not steal, Devon St. James. We may live among the wicked, but *we* are not wicked."

To this day, Devon remembered the way she had felt. So guilty. So greedy.

They had both cried afterward . . . the first time she'd made her mother cry.

And now tears threatened again, but she blinked them back. She couldn't cry. *She wouldn't.* She couldn't change things. Freddie was dead.

Nor could she stay here, in this house. His house. Not when he didn't want her here. But she *would* have her necklace back.

And then she would leave.

Her gaze swung to the door. Determinedly she pushed aside the coverlet, easing to the side of the bed. The room spun giddily. The world seemed to dangle on end. She sat for a moment, pressing a shaky hand to her forehead. More than anything, she longed to crawl back within the inviting warmth of this soft, wonderfully wide bed. It was such a lovely room . . . What, she wondered yearningly, would it be like to live in such grandeur, to wear such soft garments as the night rail that even now cocooned her body? The rich wood floor was so highly polished she was certain she could see her reflection in it, had she tried. With the sunny yellow bed hangings and gaily patterned coverlet, it was like being in the midst of a sunbeam.

But *he* didn't want her here.

Just then she spied her bonnet, atop the chair. What was it he'd said?

They're looking for a woman with a large belly, a cloak, and a ridiculous bonnet.

Her bonnet was most certainly *not* ridiculous, she thought furiously. Why, she prized it above all else! Mama had always bemoaned the fact that she'd never been able to buy her a bonnet. Devon vividly remembered the day she'd found it on the streets, shortly before she'd begun working at the Crow's Nest. She'd been ecstatic, for it was her first. It mattered not that it was blemished and stained, or that the profusion of yellow silk feathers and matching trim no longer stood straight and proud. She had imagined some pretty young miss twirling her umbrella and strolling in Hyde Park on a sunlit day; indeed, she'd fancied that *she* was the young woman. And now it *was* hers, and for Devon, a find beyond price.

Pressing her lips together, she slid from the bed to the floor. The effort sent pain streaking through her side. She stood cautiously for a moment, feeling her strength wane and fighting it desperately. Her knees went weak. She was stiff and sore and couldn't even straighten her spine. She felt like an ancient hag and probably looked it.

All of a sudden the door opened.

"Bloody hell," said a voice. "What the devil do you think you're doing?"

She fixed an eye on him.

"I should think it would be obvious. I'm leaving. And I thought you said the language of the gutter wouldn't be spoken in your house. No doubt it's different for the master, eh, my lord Shyte?"

Sebastian ignored the jibe. She looked ridiculous, standing there in that seedy, silly bonnet. He crossed his arms over his chest and regarded her. "How the devil do you propose to do that?"

"As you can see, I shall be walking." Almost defiantly she tugged at the ribbons on her bonnet. "And you shan't stop me."

"You shall no more walk out than you walked in." Hunched over, she was swaying as if she were tipsy—she looked ready to tumble over at any moment.

But her eyes blazed rebelliously. Justin was right. She was a termagant, a stubborn one at that.

"What do you propose to wear?" he asked.

"I'm afraid this night rail will have to do. But you needn't worry. I'll return it to your sister. Why, perhaps she'd even like the use of my clothing since I was given the use of hers."

The hoity-toity miss again! Oh, but it was a role she'd played well, for the chit was surely high in the instep!

"Oh, I doubt that." His eyes slid over her. "As practical as my sister Julianna is, she's a bit more discriminating when it comes to choice of gown. But perhaps it's a good thing Tansy mended your cloak and gown and cleaned your boots. I confess, I didn't understand why she bothered."

"Please thank her for me then. Now, where are they?"

Sebastian gestured to the highboy. He crossed to stand beside it and opened the door. "Come get them, if you like."

The look she cast him was distinctly withering. She took one step, then managed another. With a grimace, she tried to straighten upright and failed. The nightgown gaped, offering a considerable and unconstrained view of swelling generous curves. He availed himself of the opportunity.

She saw.

"Why, you pompous, blue-blooded ass!" Her curse spoke glaringly of her roots in St. Giles. She clenched her fist and aimed at his jaw.

It was a pitiable effort. She pitched straight into his arms and he didn't even have to move.

"You missed," he said calmly.

"Let me go! You don't want me here."

She was leaning against him heavily, glowering through the bright golden screen of her hair. It spilled over her shoulder . . . and across his sleeve. A most unusual color, he mused distantly, thick and curling and lustrous, as if it had been poured through by burnished rays of the day's last sunlight.

He sighed. "My dear young woman, you are injured. Need I remind you that you are in my care?"

"Your care! Why you bothered, I've no idea, for you've made your feelings about me quite clear. Besides, I don't like the way you look at me!"

Sebastian blinked. "I beg your pardon?"

"You look at me in quite the same manner as the men at the Crow's Nest. But I am not a strumpet!"

A claim of righteous indignation, if ever he'd heard one.

"So if you're going to look at me, sir, look me in the eye!"

Sir. A distinct improvement over "blue-blooded ass." A *vast* improvement from Lord Shyte. It appeared he was gaining status in her eyes.

This time he was careful to gaze into those eyes, as strikingly unusual as her hair. Surrounded by thick, dark lashes, they were almost golden, quite unlike anything he'd ever seen before.

"You're right. It wasn't a very gentlemanly thing to do."

"I'm glad you realize it." She tipped her head back to look at him, and as she did, her bonnet tumbled to the floor.

"My bonnet!" she cried. "Oh, please, I must have it!"

"It's quite wretched," he said before thinking better of it.

She gave a cry. "It's not wretched! It's beautiful and it's mine. And so is my necklace, and as soon as I have it back, I'll be on my way."

Her lips were tremulous, her eyes suspiciously bright. *Please,* he prayed, *not tears.*

A strangled sob . . . and something inside him constricted. Damn, but he should have known. A torrent was imminent if he didn't act quickly. Even as the thought spun through his mind, she tried to push her way through him to retrieve her bonnet. His hold tightened, a confining restraint that was gentle but uncompromisingly firm.

"You can't leave," he reminded her. "What about the constable?"

"To the devil with the constable!"

If she stayed, something would have to be done about her language.

"What about Harry?"

The question brought her gaze to his in a heartbeat. "Harry?" she whispered.

He could almost feel her terror. God knew, he decided grimly, he could certainly see it.

"Yes."

"You think he'll come after me?" Her tone wasn't entirely steady.

"I don't know." It was the truth. "He won't find you here. He'd never think to look here. Mayfair might as well be a world away from St. Giles."

Her eyes clung to his. "You won't let him find me?"

"Absolutely not."

Her strength gave way. Unable to remain on her feet any longer, she sank into his arms. This time there was no outburst as he scooped her up. He was nearly to the bed when she said urgently, "Wait! My bonnet . . . please, will you fetch it?"

Sebastian obligingly retraced his steps. She clung to his neck as he bent to retrieve it. Carefully he lowered her to the bed, then handed the bonnet to her.

She wasted no time dragging it over her head.

He watched as she wiped the tears from her eyes. In all truth, Sebastian couldn't say what came over him. The next thing he knew, he found himself sitting on the side of the bed.

"You need to rest and lie quietly, Devon."

Her eyes had been half closed. At the sound of his

voice, she opened one. "I don't believe I gave you leave to call me by my given name," she said with a frown.

A statement of remarkable hauteur, considering she'd just been in his arms and was now in his bed. Well, not his bed precisely, but it *was* his house.

The makings of a smile tugged at the corners of his mouth, swiftly suppressed, lest she see it. "May I?" he asked gravely.

"May you what?"

She was exhausted; he knew it by the shadows that ringed her eyes.

"May I call you Devon?"

"I suppose you may." She eyed him. "But what am I to call you then?"

"Most definitely *not* Lord Shyte."

A glimmer of a smile crossed her lips. "You prefer Lord Arse?"

"Devon!" He raised his brows. "I do believe we've just begun to engage a truce, you and I. Please, let's not jeopardize it. And Sebastian will do quite nicely, I believe."

Their eyes caught. All at once her smile wavered. She averted her head. "I really didn't want to leave," she confided in a small voice.

"You didn't?"

"No. It was only because you looked so dreadfully stern."

How flattering, he thought. Did she regard him as such an ogre then? "Yes, I know," he murmured. "Justin is the pretty one, not I."

Her gaze slid back. "What do you mean?"

"My dear, you just said I looked dreadful."

She frowned. "Dreadfully stern, not dreadful."

She was decidedly emphatic, so much so that Sebastian was a little taken aback. But then he remembered the night he'd found her. *Handsome,* she'd called him. *Him.* He said nothing, merely sat there for a moment, a strange sensation in his chest. Before long, her eyelids began to droop. Then all at once she shuddered.

Sebastian leaned forward, fighting a startlingly compelling urge to brush a wayward curl from her cheek. "What's wrong?" he asked softly.

"I remember lying in the street, in the cold." Her voice plunged to a whisper. "I don't want to wake up like that again."

Suddenly her hands were in his. Not soft and delicate and gloved, like a lady's, but chapped and red and dry. Yet so very small within his.

His fingers curled around hers. "You won't," he said quietly. "Now lie back and sleep, Devon."

"I don't think I can. I"—she hesitated—"I'm afraid."

"Of what?"

"That when I wake, it'll all be gone. That you'll be gone."

He felt inexplicably pleased.

"And your brother, too. Justin."

Justin, he echoed dryly. Of course.

His grip on her fingers tightened. "I promise it'll all be here when you awake."

Her eyelids trembled; she hovered on the verge of sleep. A wispy sigh emerged. "This room . . . it's so lovely. Truly it is. Oh, Sebastian, I . . . I wish I could stay here forever."

Sebastian's heart caught. She hadn't cried about Harry, but she'd cried about that silly bonnet. He'd have laughed at the picture she presented, that damnable bonnet lopsided and drooping crookedly on her forehead, if it weren't so sad; there was something very poignant about her just now. Even weak as a kitten, she'd fought him—not just a battle of words, but quite literally! He suppressed a smile as he thought of the punch she'd tried to throw at him. He'd never known a woman quite so filled with spirit, unless it was Julianna. Yet somehow at this moment, the fractious Miss Devon St. James was so fragile, he was half afraid to touch her.

But somehow he couldn't stop himself either.

Her eyes drifted shut. She murmured something inaudible.

Very slowly, with the tip of a finger, he traced the small curve of her nose, the piquant fullness of her lips, the fine-boned delicacy of her jaw. "Hush," he whispered. An odd sensation knotted in his belly, making him catch his breath. Sweet Jesus, she was exquisite, her complexion pale and unblemished. And soft, he marveled. So soft, the texture of her lips and skin like mother-of-pearl.

His hand fell away.

Blackmail, he decided blackly. Emotional blackmail by a waif and his rogue of a brother. He didn't know how it had happened, or even why, but somehow he'd been charmed. At the very least, disarmed.

Sweet Jesus, he couldn't turn her out. Even if he wanted to.

Even if she did steal the silver.

Seven

Late the next day Justin came to him in his study. "I sent Avery to check on Devon's story."

Avery had been in the service of the family for nearly twenty years; his loyalty was unquestionable, and Sebastian knew that the footman could be trusted to keep the task given him to himself.

Sebastian tapped his fingers together. "And?"

"To all accounts, it's all true. Where she lived, where she worked."

Sebastian's face was grim by the time he finished. "And the pair she encountered? Harry and Freddie?"

"I'd say she was lucky to escape with her life. A dangerous pair, those two. If she killed Freddie, I've no doubt it was to defend her own life. I only wish Harry would join his brother in the netherworld. The world would be well rid of him."

Sebastian nodded. "Tell Avery to keep his eyes open and his ears peeled."

"Already done," Justin said lightly.

When Justin was gone, Sebastian settled back to work. Work. It was impossible! He tried to put Avery's information about Devon from his mind. He tried to put *her* from his mind. But the fear he'd glimpsed in those beautiful golden eyes continued to haunt him.

And he could still feel those small, icy fingers trapped within his.

It festered in his chest until he could stand it no longer.

It wasn't wise. In fact, it was downright foolish. And damnably impetuous! But he could put it off no longer.

He wouldn't be satisfied until he'd seen for himself where Devon had come from.

An hour later, Sebastian sat among the dockhands that guzzled and swilled at the Crow's Nest. He was dressed much as the other patrons, in rough woolen clothing. His foresight had seen to it that he attracted but a few idle glances as he ducked beneath the sign hanging outside and stepped into the dark, dimly lit establishment.

The interior was small and cramped, the mood rowdy and raucous, the language bawdy. Men crowded next to each other at long, rough-hewn tables. Sebastian took a place at one of the tables.

A plump, straw-haired waitress promptly presented herself. "Ye're new 'ere, aren't ye?" She gave him no chance to answer, but ran a finger down his sleeve. "Wot's yer name?"

"Patrick," he replied without blinking an eye.

"Well, Patrick, I'm Bridget. What's yer pleasure?"

"Ale."

A burly, bearded man across from him banged his tankard on the table. "Blimey, wot about me?" he barked. "Can't a man get another pint round 'ere?"

"Calm yerself, Davey. Yer pint's a-comin'."

"Fine," he boomed. "But where the devil is Devon?"

Every fiber of Sebastian's body came to full alert.

The fellow next to him shrugged. "Haven't seen 'er for a couple o' nights. Timmie thinks she's decided she's too lofty for the likes o' us." He gestured to the barkeep, a hulking man whose meek name belied both his countenance and his girth. "'E's got a new girl startin' in the morn, 'e says. Let's 'ope she's half as fetchin' as our fair Devon, eh?" He offered the fellow a wink.

Sebastian was steaming. When Bridget set a foaming tankard of ale before him, he wasted no time lifting it to his lips. By the time he lowered it, she was on her way back to the bar. The customer sitting at the end of the table grabbed a handful of her skirt and tugged her onto his lap. The suddenness of the move caused the barmaid's heavy breasts to nearly spill out of her gown.

The man crowed. "Ah, now there's a juicy tidbit, eh, lads!"

The girl let out a peal of laughter and they both tumbled onto the floor. He whispered in her ear and pressed something into her hand. She nodded.

Sebastian slapped a coin on the table and rose. There was no need to stay any longer. He'd seen all he needed to.

But once he was outside, he didn't return to the spot where he'd left Jimmy, the coachman. Instead he turned and strode deeper into the heart of St. Giles.

His business here was not yet done.

The hour was indecently late when he returned to Mayfair. As he stepped across the threshold, it crossed his mind that, for that very reason, he should expect Justin to follow soon.

Naturally Justin did.

They came face-to-face in the entrance hall.

"Sebastian?" came the sound of his brother's shocked voice. Justin looked him up and down. "Ye gods, man, what the devil are you wearing?"

Sebastian gave a tight smile and pulled the rough woolen cap from his head. "My name is Patrick," he said with his best Scots burr, "and I'm a sailor from the north."

"Had I chanced to pass you on the street, I should never have guessed it was you!"

"That was the case when I wore this to the Pemberton masquerade a few years back," Sebastian said. "Our houseguest isn't the only one who's a master of disguise."

"Ah, and is she the reason—" He broke off. The very next instant, his elegant nose twitched. He retreated a step, his mouth curling in distaste. "Christ," he said faintly. Suddenly his jaw came together with a snap. "You smell like ale. And smoke. Don't tell me you went to St. Giles!"

Already on his way into the study, Sebastian ignored his accusatory tone. "Very well then. I won't."

Justin was right on his heels. "Damn it," he said tightly, "I told you I sent Avery to check on Devon's story. Didn't you believe me?"

One of Sebastian's hands was on the brandy decanter, the other on the glass beside it. "It wasn't that," he said curtly.

"What then? Was she the one you doubted? Avery? Or me? Or all of us?"

"It wasn't that," Sebastian said heavily. He walked behind his desk and sat. It was a moment before he spoke. "I had to see for myself," he said quietly. "I *had* to." The air was still and silent as he raised the glass to his lips.

Justin took the chair across from him.

Leaning back, he ran a hand through tousled black strands.

"My God," he said in an odd, strained voice. "I feel like I've been to hell and back."

Once he began, it was almost as if he couldn't stop. "I had Jimmy let me off on the outskirts of St. Giles. I'd no more than rounded the corner and I saw a man with no arms. A woman with no legs huddled in the doorway next to the Crow's Nest."

"It's a trick. A ruse. I hope you didn't give them any money."

"Hardly," he said with the haughty air that would have cowed anyone but his brother. "I gave it to the three little urchins with no shoes."

Justin nodded. "Good thinking."

"When I left the Crow's Nest, I walked to Devon's lodgings."

"You what!"

"You heard me. I walked."

Justin leaned forward on an elbow. "Good God, man! Were you approached?"

Sebastian gave a harsh laugh. "Oh, yes! A beggar. I gave him a few coins. He thanked me, then proceeded to try and raid my pockets." The veriest pause, and Sebastian smiled ever so slightly. "He didn't succeed. The next ones"—there was an almost imperceptible widening of his smile—"well, they were a trifle more persistent and would have *very* much liked to continue where the first man left off."

"*They*?"

"Yes. There were two."

"My God," came Justin's mutter, "I do hope you called for help."

Blithely Sebastian raised a hand and curled his fingers toward his palm, pretending to inspect his nails.

"There was no need," he said lightly.

"Balderdash! There was every need!"

Sebastian blew delicately across his knuckles—and met his brother's gaze. "No," he countered mildly, "there was not."

Justin stared.

Sebastian smiled.

"What, you never heard about my days as a prize boxer during my years at Oxford? No, I suppose not, having gone to Cambridge. Ah, but I filled many a purse many a night, dear brother. And I still have the touch, it would seem, for I've come away with nary a scratch."

Justin reached for the decanter. "Well, well, we all have our secrets, don't we? Yet I can't believe you went to St. Giles alone again, and you dare to call me reckless! My God, I need a drink." He tossed the brandy down in two gulps. He was reaching for another when he caught sight of Sebastian's expression.

Slowly he lowered the glass. "There's more?"

"Yes."

"I'm all ears," Justin muttered.

Sebastian rubbed his fingers. "I met Phillips," he said.

"Devon's landlord?"

"Yes. It's my opinion he belongs to a species no higher than a worm."

"So I understand."

"He wasn't particularly happy when this drunken Scots sailor knocked on the wrong door and woke him from a sound sleep."

Justin had finally recovered his usual aplomb. "He actually *believed* you had the wrong house?"

"He did."

"But he changed his tune and was quite accommodating when I chanced to mention I had nowhere to stay for the night. As a matter of fact, he informed me, he had lodgings available."

"So you saw where Devon lived?"

"I did. Shall I tell you about it? The pitch of the roof was so steeply angled I couldn't stand upright. There was but one window. The only furniture was a pallet in the corner. There wasn't even a stool. There was barely enough room to turn around."

Sebastian began to steam all over again. "He called Devon a cheeky little bitch who had run out on him without paying her rent. I wanted to blacken his eyes then and there. Alas, I had my chance. When I informed him I expected more in lodgings than a hovel, he took exception." He flexed his fingers. "Consequently, I took exception to *him*."

His jaw clenched hard. "My God, Justin, you should have seen it. I have never seen a place so vile. And Devon lived there. She *lived* there." He stared into the shadows. "She's not going back there. *Ever*. I won't allow it."

Justin gave Sebastian a long, slow look. "That's quite a statement coming from the man who didn't want her here in the first place." He raised a brow, for Sebastian's expression remained utterly hard. "Why do you look like that? You've bloodied the faces of three men tonight—"

"Four. You forgot Phillips."

"In any case, I don't care to be the next." He paused. "What are your plans for her?"

An arch look.

"I see. No plans yet. Knowing what a stickler you are, I know how that must grate."

"Leave off, Justin."

"Oh, come now. This entire night is very unlike you, Sebastian. I could almost believe that sailor Patrick has done away with my brother." He shook his head in mock reproof. "Drinking. Brawling in the streets," he drawled. "Were Father still alive, I doubt he would have approved."

Sebastian stiffened. Anger was something that came to him neither readily nor without cause. But this was the side of Justin—the caustic side—that he hated. Justin knew it full well, yet there were still occasions when Justin sought to prick his control.

Someday, Sebastian reflected, his brother's acid tongue would land him in trouble, and he would sorely regret it.

Nonetheless, his tone was terse as he advised, "Let us not go there, brother. I try not to look back, and I strongly suggest you do the same."

"Yes, you're right. As usual. But that reminds me of something else, however."

"Which is?"

"Well, far be it from me to point out the propriety of the situation, but we've an unmarried female beneath our roof. And I know how you feel about scandal. So should anything ever be said, I shall take the blame—"

The tension in Sebastian's shoulders vanished. Justin's mercurial nature was sometimes baffling. "Don't be absurd." In that arrogant way that could only belong to a marquess, he went on, "We've given shelter to a poor, unfortunate girl from the streets. The servants are too loyal to question it, or ever betray me."

"True enough. Your reputation is above reproach."

Sebastian quirked a brow. "And yours is beyond reproach."

"Well, I can't argue with that." Justin plucked a cigar from his pocket. "Which reminds me . . . how goes the hunt?"

Sebastian gazed at him blankly. "The hunt? Good Lord, man, I've no plans for hunting."

Justin erupted into laughter. "What, have you given up already?"

Only then did he take Justin's meaning. "My God, finding a bride is the last thing on my mind just now!"

He scowled when Justin merely laughed the harder.

Eight

Devon was healing. She was healing nicely. Within several days she was able to leave the bed. The pain in her side gradually subsided to a dull ache. Soon she was able to sit and walk about the room. Tansy, the cheery little maid who attended her, entered one morning with an armful of Julianna's clothing—at Sebastian's direction, she was told. All were a fine fit in the hips, length, and shoulders, but in the bodice . . . It was hopeless. Her rounded curves swelled above the neckline and there was nothing she could do to hide it. Julianna was clearly less endowed in the bosom than she.

Until she was sixteen, she'd been scrawny and thin, often taken for a child much younger. She'd been so proud when the little buds of her breasts had finally begun to blossom—was there a girl who didn't long to be a woman? But when she'd begun working at the Crow's Nest, she'd grown to hate the hungry, wolfish look that inevitably entered a man's eyes as they traversed up and down her figure, invariably lingering on her chest. They stared at her breasts. They stared at Bridget's. They grabbed and pinched and twisted.

What *was* the fascination men harbored for women's breasts? she had pondered irritably one day. Bridget had shrugged and responded blithely that was simply the way men were. During the time Devon had worked there, she'd never grown accustomed to their leers.

And somehow, she'd always known she never would.

The prospect of returning to work there made her shudder. Indeed, it was the one thing she was determined to avoid at all costs. There had to be a way, she told herself. She had only to find it. Indeed, she told herself stoutly, miracles could happen. Why, the very fact that she was here in Mayfair was proof.

Every morning when she woke in this lovely room so like a burst of sunshine, she reminded herself where she was—a great house in Mayfair, not just a dream conjured up from some deep-seated longing tucked away inside, a longing she hadn't even known she had until now. Ah, but it would be easy to grow used to a life like this! Breakfast in bed. Tea sitting by the window, a blanket tucked over her legs. Dinner before the warmth and glow of a blazing fire. A warming pan to keep her feet toasty at night—heaven itself! No hunger. No worries about pinching her pennies to make her rent.

But she warned herself she mustn't grow too accustomed to it. She prayed that when she was well, Sebastian would allow her to stay long enough that she might find a position in a house such as this. She would work long and hard, if only she didn't have to go back to St. Giles.

Yet for all that her days were filled with hope and comfort, the nights were difficult. When the room was still and she was all alone, a wrenching despair dragged at her insides.

She couldn't forget.

By your hand, Sebastian had said.

And it was.

Freddie was dead because of her. She'd killed a man. *Killed* him.

The knowledge rent her apart.

She lay in bed one night, trying hard to forget. Trying hard not to think. She tossed and turned for what seemed like hours, battling the burning rush of tears against the back of her throat and not always succeeding. It was inevitable, perhaps, that her mind turned to Sebastian, who, according to Tansy, was out for the evening.

If only she knew what to make of him! He looked in on her every day, inquiring how she felt. He was always impeccably dressed, faultlessly polite. And somehow the sight of him always made her tongue feel heavy and clumsy. Perhaps it was because she already knew he possessed a formidable presence.

Only the other morning, she lay in bed as Tansy tidied the room. It seemed wrong to watch as the bright-eyed little maid worked. Finally she'd pushed aside the coverlet, determined to help. Tansy chanced that moment to turn.

"Oh, no, Miss Devon!" she cried. Naturally Sebastian chose that moment to be passing. Her heart gave an odd little leap at the sight of him. His dark gaze traversed from the top of her head to one bare peeping toe, pointed toward the floor. One jet brow climbed high, a silent reproof. Either way, there was no need to utter a word. She wasted no time withdrawing her foot and dragging the covers up to her chin.

To all outward appearances, it seemed his manner toward her had thawed. Yet somehow, she couldn't help but think that he was convinced she was a strumpet. She knew not how to convince him otherwise.

An odd little pain nipped at her insides. Indeed, what did it matter? It wasn't as if she could remain in this house forever.

Some ten days after her arrival, she lit a candle, drew on a robe, and ventured into the hall. It was rather bold, she knew, and she felt quite like the thief Sebastian had branded her. But from the beginning, she'd been intensely curious about this house. Judging by the furnishings of her room, which were so very grand, the marquess must be very rich, she mused to Tansy one day. He was indeed, Tansy assured her with a laugh.

Now it was the wee hours of the morning, and surely there was no one about. It felt good to stretch her legs. Lovely as her room was, it was growing quite tiresome lying about so much.

Making nary a sound, she crept down the stairs and tiptoed through the house, glancing inside the rooms. There was the dining room, with its massive, polished table and silver candelabra. The parlor, where delicate, porcelain vases mingled with dainty figurines, looking ghostly in the moonlight. Everything was elegant, costly, and aristocratic-looking—just like the marquess.

A little in awe, but still determined to indulge her curiosity, she slipped through the nearest door. In the middle of a large, high-ceilinged room, she paused. Tall, paned windows flanked a marble fireplace. Row upon row of books filled the bookcases that lined the walls.

The library.

A painful tightness crowded her heart, her very chest. Her mother would have loved this room, she thought achingly. How she wished Mama was still alive that she might see it! Three months had passed since Mama's death, and there wasn't a day—not a single hour—that Devon didn't miss her dreadfully. Tears welled in her eyes, and she wiped them away.

Trailing her fingers over the arms of the chair drawn up before the fire, she paused. Beneath her fingertips, the leather was smooth, almost buttery soft. In the fireplace, embers still glowed faintly. She could imagine nothing cozier than sitting in this very chair before the blazing warmth of the fire.

Outside, a blustery wind sent an angry pelting of rain against the windows. The storm raged on, making her shiver in remembrance. She hadn't forgotten the feel of the cold and rain seeping through her cloak, into her skin.

It struck her, not for the first time, that she was lucky Sebastian had found her. That he had allowed her to stay.

The corner of her mouth twitched upward. Of course, if he knew she was snooping about his house, he'd likely throw her out on her ear!

The wind howled again. At the door, there was a strange scratching sound.

She ducked behind the chair, her first instinct to hide.

The scratching came again. Louder this time. More insistent. Oh, yes, much more insistent. And this time, accompanied by something that sounded almost like a whine.

Drawn by curiosity, she crept from the library, onward toward the scratching, clutching her candle for all it was worth. Slowly she straightened, then cautiously opened the door.

A gust of wind pummeled her and nearly knocked her from her feet. Something cold and wet darted past her legs into the entrance hall. She choked back a scream, looking down frantically. At her feet, two dark, soulful eyes peered up at her. Devon blinked. A dog! Wet and bedraggled, he shivered from his head to his sopping tail, little wonder since he had been out in this horrid weather. He was quite ugly. His little snout seemed mashed into his face. But somehow it made him all the more endearing. His coat was long and yellow and dragged on the glossy tiled floor. Oh, yes, he was quite stout indeed, for he looked as if he had no legs!

She set the candlestick on a small oval table behind her. Before she knew it, she was on her knees beside him. "Oh, my! You've had quite a drenching, haven't you?" She crouched down before him.

Without hesitation the dog crammed his cold little nose beneath her hand and whined, a pitiful sound that caught at her heart. "Are you hungry?" she crooned.

She could have sworn his eyes brightened.

"Let's just see if we can find you something to eat, shall we?" She mused aloud, "There's a wedge of cheese left over from my dinner." Did dogs like cheese? Well, she would find out. "Now, my little mite. Stay where you are." She pointed a finger at him, then laughed at herself. "My little mite. You need a better name than that, don't you?" She pressed a finger to her lips. "What shall we call you, hmmm? I know. Webster. I shall call you Webster!"

Obviously he approved of the name, for his tail circled madly.

"Excellent," she said, pleased with her choice. "Stay, Webster."

It took her but a few minutes to dart to her room and find the wedge of cheese she'd stowed away in her napkin for later. When she returned, she found he hadn't moved.

"Good boy, Webster." Sinking to her knees again, she pinched off a bit of the soft cheese and held it out.

He needed no coaxing. Eagerly he gobbled it up.

Devon laughed delightedly. He looked up at her expectantly. "Patience, Webster." A virtue she herself had never quite mastered, but no matter.

The rattle of the doorknob snared her attention. Confound it, there was someone there. Sebastian? Justin? Would one of the servants come up to answer the door? Either way, she'd been well and truly caught. There wasn't time to gather Webster and flee up the stairs; she would be seen.

In desperation she seized the dog and pushed him under her night rail. "Don't say a word!" she hissed. *As if he could*, she thought with a half giggle.

A gust of wind swirled about her bare feet. The door clicked. By the time she straightened, Sebastian stood directly before her.

"I wasn't stealing," she said quickly. Only then

did she realize she'd thrust the hand with the cheese behind her back.

Sebastian made no response, merely tipped his head slightly to the side, as if in inquiry.

Devon swallowed. Her eyes trickled upward, taking in broad shoulders covered in wool, the intricate knot of his cravat, the corded column of his neck. There was a sharp stab deep in the pit of her belly, something she couldn't identify. Standing so close to him again, all she could think was that he was so handsome, so intensely masculine, so unlike any man she'd ever met before . . .

It seemed strange to face him on her feet; it was not a posture she cared to maintain for very long, she decided vaguely. He was so tall that to do so would surely put a crick in her neck.

Meanwhile, his eyes were occupied with traveling the length of her. She wished she'd taken the time to tidy her hair . . . But what foolishness was this? She was abruptly irritated with herself. Why did she care how she looked before him? He'd made his opinion of her quite clear, and she knew there would be no changing his mind.

Damn! Now he was regarding her in that probing way that always made her feel distinctly ill-at-ease.

Her hand fluttered nervously to her throat. "What is it?"

"Nothing. I'm simply pleased that you're looking so well. The color is back in your cheeks." He stepped closer.

Devon battled the urge to step back, then remembered the dog beneath her skirts. "Oh, yes," she intoned brightly. "I'm doing so much better." Confound it, she couldn't stand here forever with Webster planted between her legs. Heavens, but he was cold!

"Indeed you are," Sebastian said softly. "You're no longer tottering into my arms."

Devon flushed, aware of a hot tide of color rising clear to the roots of her hair. At the mention of his arms, her pulse skittered. They had been strong, those arms, secure and warm and . . . and all at once the heat in her cheeks was shooting through every part of her, clear to the tips of her toes. Ah, yes, his arms . . .

In truth, a most safe and comfortable place to be.

Between her legs, she felt Webster circle and plop down.

The hem of her dressing gown fluttered as he moved. The heat inside her was forgotten. She froze, but her heart jolted forward. *No*, she thought in horror. *Oh, no*. Her gaze darted to Sebastian's face. Had he noticed?

His gaze slid down and halted. One bushy black brow climbed aloft in that imperious way he had.

For indeed, Sebastian *had* noticed. What the deuce? he wondered.

He lifted a dark brow. "Miss St. James," he began.

"Devon. We agreed that you should call me Devon, remember? And that I should call you Sebastian."

"Very well then. Tell me, Devon, what do you have under your gown?"

"'Tis not my gown. 'Tis your sister's."

The chit was stalling. Shifting her feet from one to the other. *And* looking decidedly guilty.

"But you, Devon, are wearing it. Therefore, it is yours."

The flutter came again. Her feet shifted, as if to cover the movement.

Sebastian narrowed his eyes. He could see . . . No. It couldn't possibly be. By Jove, it was a tail!

"Are you hiding something beneath your skirts, Devon?" He might have been asking the time of day.

The tip of her tongue came out to dampen her lips. "Of course not," she denied.

Sebastian scarcely heard. He was too busy gazing at her small and dainty mouth, the unintentional sensual slide of her tongue over her lips.

He wrenched his gaze away. Christ, what the devil was wrong with him? He forced himself back to the matter at hand. "You're quite sure?" he queried.

"Of course. If there were something hiding under my skirts, wouldn't I know it?"

He frowned. She didn't sound terribly certain. "I should hope so," he said, thinking that she was an intolerably bad liar. In all his days, he'd never seen eyes so huge.

Another movement from under her skirts. Now a snout had replaced the tail! A dog's snout, if he wasn't mistaken.

"Perhaps we should see then." Before she could disagree, he bent low and stretched out a hand toward the hem of the dressing gown.

The mutt snarled and lunged from under the robe. Sebastian snatched his hand back just in time. Biting back a curse, he lurched to his feet. "Blasted creature!"

"Oh! Oh, I'm so sorry. It's just that he's hungry."

"Hungry! He looks as if he's never missed a meal in his life!"

She bent and fed the dog the last bit of cheese. "He's cold too," she added, straightening once more. "See the way he's shivering?"

The wretched creature wasn't shivering now. In fact, he looked almost smug!

Sebastian glowered. "This mongrel," he said succinctly, "looks like a fat, long-haired gutter rat."

Her eyes flashed. "And you said *I* looked like a woman of the streets!"

Not any longer, he thought. "He does look as plump in the belly as you did." He cast a pointed look at her middle. "Unlike you, I daresay 'tis not because of any artifice, but rather that he simply likes to eat!"

"He still doesn't look like a gutter rat!"

Sebastian reserved his opinion, for she was looking highly offended. "How the devil did he get inside?" he asked irritably.

Small white teeth dug into the soft pink flesh of her lower lip. "Well," she ventured finally, "I let him in."

Sebastian's gaze narrowed. "He didn't follow you here, did he?"

"Of course not. I heard scratching at the door, and when I opened it, he dashed inside."

"Perhaps he's lost his way." Sebastian seriously doubted anyone would want such a ratty little thing. Briskly he went on, "In that case, we'd best put him back out in case someone comes looking for him—"

"But that's precisely why we shouldn't!"

Devon had gathered up the mutt high in her arms. "He might lose his way again," she fretted. "Please. Can he stay? At least until he's warm and fed and dry?" She went on in a rush. "I'll keep him in my room tonight. He won't be a nuisance, I promise. I-I've named him Webster. And he'll look much better after a bath, I'm sure."

And so had she, said a voice somewhere in the back of his mind. He sighed. "Devon—"

"Please. I can't bear the thought he'll be out in this horrid weather again."

Sebastian planned to refuse. He had every intention of refusing. But all his good intentions melted away as he read the pleading in those wide, golden eyes. And he saw something else there too.

The unmistakable signs of recent tears. God, she'd been crying. *Crying* . . .

In all his life, he didn't know when he'd been so confused. He wanted to demand she tell him why. But something inside stopped him. She looked so . . . so hopeful. And he didn't think he could bear to dash those hopes.

Damn, he thought, vexed. *Damn!* How could a man say no? How could *he*?

"I suppose it wouldn't hurt."

The smile she flashed was blindingly sweet. It reached clear inside and grabbed hold of his heart.

"Thank you, my lor—"

"Sebastian," he reminded her.

"Thank you, Sebastian. Oh, thank you!"

Hugging the dog tightly to her breast, she turned and started toward the stairs. But on the first step, she paused and looked back, biting her lip.

Now, he thought. Now she was going to tell him what was amiss.

"I have a confession." She paused hesitantly. "I . . . um, I . . ." Her gaze sidled away, to the side, then the floor, then the ceiling before returning to his. Even then she didn't meet his eyes directly. "I lied," she said finally.

As if that were great news to him. Sebastian wasn't perturbed though. Indeed, he had to wipe the wry amusement from his face as he crossed his arms over his chest. "You lied?"

She gulped. "It wasn't just that I heard Webster at the door. I-I wanted to see your house."

"You wanted to see my house," he repeated.

She now regarded him as if she expected lightning to strike her down at any instant. "Yes. I couldn't sleep, and I was tired of my room—"

"I thought you said it was a lovely room."

"Oh, it is! But this house is just so beautiful, I wanted to see it all."

"I see."

She peered at him. "You do?"

"Yes."

"And you're not angry?"

"No," he said smoothly. "But now that you're feeling better, there's no need to skulk about in the dark." He paused. "I could have Tansy show you about tomorrow, if you'd like. I'd do it myself, but I'm afraid Justin and I have business in the country tomorrow. Then I've an engagement in the evening . . ." He watched her closely. "Would you like that?"

Her mouth opened. She was gawking, he realized, all at once struggling against the impulse to laugh. He had the most insane urge to stride up to her, place his fingers on her chin, and close her lips with the seal of his own . . .

He shook off the thought and answered for her. "Yes? Excellent, then. Oh, and Devon? Feel free to use any room you wish. I assure you, they're all better seen in the light of day. Then I won't have to worry about you tumbling down the stairs in the dead of night."

"Oh," she said weakly. "That's quite thoughtful of you."

"It's my pleasure," he said softly.

And heaven help him, it was. She was smiling again, that same beaming smile that nearly stole his breath. He'd have done anything to make her face glow with pleasure the way it was right now.

Long after the door to her room had clicked shut, Sebastian was still standing in the entrance hall. Only then did he ask himself if he'd gone quite mad.

Because somehow, he'd managed to acquire not just one urchin . . . but two.

Nine

When Devon awoke, Webster sat up, eyes bright, tail wagging madly. He didn't look quite so ugly this morning, but as she'd noted last night, a bath was sorely needed.

She and Tansy tackled the task. During the process she made a rather revealing discovery about the little creature. Two of them, in fact. The first made her chuckle, and was of little consequence one way or the other. As for the second . . . well, she wasn't quite sure how to break it to Sebastian, or even if she should.

Afterward Tansy took her through the house. As she stepped into each room, all she could think was that Sebastian was right. The house was better seen in the light of day. Elegantly carved moldings framed the ceilings, windows, and doors; the furnishings combined both luxury and comfort. Brightly hued bouquets graced many of the side tables, freshening the air. It was too early in the year for such blooms, and Devon wondered where on earth they came from, but she was too embarrassed to ask. Even with Tansy, she didn't want to sound as ignorant as she was.

The blustery weather of the night before had given way to sunshine, a reminder that the warmth of spring was nearly upon them. Tansy had pointed out a small garden to the rear of the house. When Tansy went back to work, Devon tugged a shawl over her shoulders—another item borrowed from the absent Julianna—and slipped outside.

The garden, enclosed by red brick on all sides, was filled with manicured bushes and trees. Devon caught her breath in admiration. In summer it would be lovely, filled with the perfume of flowers and vibrant with greenery. Passing beneath a wooden archway, she followed a grassy walkway to a stone bench angled in the far corner. Tilting her head back, she let the sun wash over her face, feeling the breeze swirl around her, watching sunbeams skitter through the treetops. When dusk began to fall, she reluctantly returned inside.

She took dinner in her room, then ventured down to the library. She had just seated herself in the leather chair that had beckoned so invitingly last night when she heard a low male voice.

"Hello there."

It was Justin. Something akin to disappointment shot through her, and she almost found herself wishing it were Sebastian. Dear God, what the deuce had come over her, to find herself yearning to see Sebastian again? It made no sense, no sense at all, especially considering his opinion of her. For some reason she'd yet to figure out, when she was in his presence, her state of mind was a maelstrom of emotion. She felt uncertain of herself, of her feelings, for they swirled in every direction. She wasn't afraid of him, indeed she had no qualms about standing up to him.

If the truth be told, she was in awe of him. It wasn't just his height, though she'd never encountered a man of such size. Nor was it his dark, dashingly handsome good looks. He was different from all the men she'd known in her life. At the Crow's Nest, the men swaggered and crowed and bragged about themselves and their achievements. She'd always found it vastly annoying.

But clearly Sebastian had no need of it. He exuded an air of almost careless confidence and poise. Why, he need not say a word. One need only *look* at him and know he was a cut above—a man of supreme ability in whatever endeavor he might choose.

He fascinated her, even as she fiercely resented his air of commanding superiority.

But last night he'd been so nice. Even . . . sweet. He hadn't wanted to, but he'd let the dog stay. He hadn't been angry that she'd been nosing around his house in the dead of night, like the thief he was convinced she was.

She couldn't help but recall the night she'd staggered from bed and announced her intention to leave his house. She'd ended up toppling into his arms instead . . . Her memory of what followed was hazy, but she could have sworn he caressed her face, her lips, a touch so infinitely gentle it made her want to cry out just thinking of it . . .

Pushing the disturbing image from her mind, she focused on the man before her. She liked Justin, she told herself stoutly. His manner conveyed an almost careless self-confidence, but he wasn't pretentious—at least not with her—and Devon liked that. She'd known him but a short time, but unlike Sebastian, with whom she was forever tongue-tied, Justin was remarkably easy to talk to. Only the day before he'd blithely stated his days were spent gambling and riding and racing, his nights in pursuits that, as he put it, weren't quite fit for feminine ears.

Devon, of course, was *all* ears.

"So you are a rake," she'd pronounced. She couldn't say that she approved.

He clicked his heels and gave her a wink. "The handsomest man in all England, or so it's said."

Devon didn't even have to consider. Handsome, yes. But handsom*est*? Not so, for in her mind Sebastian was surely the handsomest man in all England.

She eyed him. "Are you quite full of yourself, sir?"

He chuckled. "That's the most flattering thing that's been said about me. Truth be told, I'm also known as a reprobate. A rascal, as well as some names I fear I cannot repeat in your company."

"Oh, I doubt you're as bad as all that."

"Oh, I am, I assure you. Sebastian is the gentleman of the family. He was quite the war hero, you know, tending the wounded under fire in the Peninsula. I daresay he'd have made a fine physician. He has the patience of a saint."

Devon wasn't surprised to learn he was a hero. A man of intensity, that was what she sensed about him. As for patience, if Devon was doubtful, she couldn't help it. She was convinced *she* didn't bring on that particular tendency.

Justin took a seat on the wing chair opposite her.

As he did, a black, wet nose sniffed about his ankles. "Well, hello, there! Who's this?"

Devon told him about the events of the prior evening. "I don't think your brother was terribly pleased," she finished.

"Oh, he won't mind. When we were children, Julianna was always bringing home some poor creature. I remember once she brought in a squirrel that had fallen from a tree. Mother, of course, screamed and had the vapors."

"Does your mother live in London too?"

A shadow seemed to pass across his face. Was it sadness? she wondered. A moment passed before Justin answered. "No. Our parents are both dead. At any rate, I'm on my way out. But Sebastian told me you were up and about, so I decided I must stop and see you."

"Is he here?" She did her best to sound offhand, but her insides were suddenly twisted in knots. "He mentioned last night he had an engagement this evening."

"Yes. The dowager duchess of Carrington is giving a ball tonight. He's upstairs dressing. I wasn't invited, I'm afraid. Acceptance in society, you see, hinges on the duchess's approval. I do believe the duchess tolerates me only because she's fond of Sebastian. Not that I plan to while away the evening in regret. These things tend to be incredibly tedious affairs."

To Devon, a ball sounded terribly exciting. "You're being sarcastic, aren't you?"

"Always," he retorted. He extended a hand toward the dog, giving a slight laugh as a rough, wet tongue came out to lap his fingers. "Quite an affectionate little creature, eh?"

Neither of them was aware that Sebastian hovered near the door, watching the two of them. Certainly they seemed to get on well together, he decided. It ran through his mind that the two of them would have made a striking couple, Justin's hair so dark and gleaming, Devon's all shining and gold . . . Good God, what was wrong with him? He felt almost jealous.

Feeling quite the intruder, he advanced into the library . . . and was promptly greeted by a low growl.

Justin looked up. "Dumpling doesn't seem to like you, old chap."

"*Dumpling*!" Sebastian's brows shot high as he glanced at Devon. "I thought you said his name was Webster."

Devon smiled weakly. "It was. I've had to change it, I'm afraid."

"Change it? Why?" he asked baldly.

"Because he is a she."

The mongrel was female! No wonder the creature liked Justin and not him!

"My God," he said. "You can't name her Dumpling!"

"Why not? You made mention of the fact she obviously likes to eat. And she does look a bit like a dumpling. It's a fitting name, don't you think?"

Sebastian glanced at the mutt. *Dumpling*, he thought. Why, it almost made him gag!

The object of his scrutiny bared her teeth.

"I do believe Beast would be a fitting name," he muttered.

Devon scolded her sternly. "Stop it, Dumpling."

With a whine the animal sank down onto the floor,

dropping her head onto her paws. But those round black eyes surveyed him warily as he stepped closer.

Justin laughed, earning a reproving glance from Sebastian. He got to his feet. "I believe," he said, "this is my cue to leave. Good night, Sebastian. Devon, pleasant dreams." A courtly bow directed at them both, and he was gone.

Sebastian and Devon were left alone. He watched as Devon moved to warm herself before the fire.

"I trust you had a good day."

"Thank you, I did."

Thank you. She was such a puzzle, he thought, watching as she stretched out her hands. If he hadn't known better, she could almost be mistaken for a prim, proper miss. He'd chanced to pass by her room this morning as she was eating, licking the tips of her fingers. She'd looked up then, and saw where his eyes resided. A most becoming ribbon of scarlet had rushed to her cheeks.

Her fingers dove beneath her napkin.

The remembrance renewed itself as his gaze slid over her slim form, hazily etched by the glow of the fire. She looked very fetching, dressed in a high-waisted gown gathered tight below her breasts, clinging to those generous curves. A simple ribbon tied at the nape restrained the glory of her hair; it hung over one shoulder, a silken, wavy mass of pure gold.

Desire cut through him, a sharp, primitive hunger that wound its way to every part of him. His fingers tingled. He wanted to touch her, trail his fingertips lightly over the vulnerable place where her neck flowed into the slender slope of her back, to toy with the wisp of fine, downy hairs that curled at her nape and feel her shiver.

Precisely what it was that alerted him, Sebastian wasn't certain. But all at once he felt himself pulled up short. Her head was bowed low, her fingers clamped together before her.

"Devon?" Her name was a sound of uncharacteristic uncertainty.

There was no reply.

Sebastian stared incredulously. "Devon," he said again, "are you crying?"

She presented him with the slender lines of her back.

Without thought, without word, he scooped her up in his arms.

The mongrel pushed up on its haunches.

"Bite me, Beast," he hissed, "and I'll bite you back."

The beast sat.

In but an instant, Devon was tucked in his embrace—and they were both tucked in the roomy depths of his favorite chair. He turned his attention to the woman in his arms. "You were crying last night too, weren't you?"

"I wasn't!" she wailed.

Sebastian sighed. "Devon, I cannot abide weeping females."

"I'm . . . not . . . weeping."

But she was. Her narrow shoulders heaved up and down. She was positively blubbering.

Seeking desperately to console her, he said, "You'll be pleased to know I've called in a modiste for you. She'll arrive promptly at ten tomorrow morning."

Her lips parted. "A modiste?"

"Yes. A dressmaker."

Tears welled in her eyes anew, shimmering tears that speared his very heart.

Now what the devil had he done? Sebastian was wholly bewildered. He'd never before met a woman who did not wax poetic over a new gown!

In truth, he'd never met a woman the likes of Devon.

His long legs sprawled before him, he sighed. "Devon, will you please tell me what's wrong?"

Her cold little nose was buried in the ruffles at his throat. She was shaking, gulping, trying to hold back sobs.

He tipped her chin to his, the gesture immeasurably gentle. "Devon, you must tell me what is wrong." For all its softness, it was a command.

Still nothing. Was she being stubborn? Defiant? Or was it simply that she didn't hear?

"Devon," he intoned more forcefully.

He felt the ragged breath she drew. "My God," she said through a watery sob, "you are a nag!"

"I prefer to think of it as persistence. Either way, I'm sure you find it quite vexing."

"I do! But . . . you won't leave me alone until I tell you, will you?"

"No," he answered frankly. "Now tell me what it is that distresses you so."

Hot tears seeped through the starched white of his shirt; they reached his very soul.

"I'm . . . not . . . sure I can explain."

"Try," he said gently.

"It just . . . it all seems so wrong . . . I mean, look at me. I'm living in a grand house in Mayfair, of all places. Mayfair! There's a-a dressmaker coming to visit . . . a dressmaker! And what have I done to deserve it? I"—her voice wobbled traitorously—"I killed a man. I killed Freddie."

He gathered her closer, so close his breath stirred the fine hairs on her temple. "Listen to me, Devon. You did what you had to do, in order to stay alive. If you hadn't, Freddie would have killed you."

"I know. *I know.*" Tears streamed down her face. "But there's a part of me that says I don't deserve such treatment. And then there's you—"

"Me!" Sebastian was utterly taken aback.

"Yes!" she wailed. "Why are you doing this? Why are you being so generous? I don't belong here. You don't even know me. You don't even *like* me."

"That's not true." Staunchly he defended himself.

"It is. I know what you think of me. So if you want me to leave—"

"I don't want you to leave. I want to help you. And"—she might as well be aware of it now—"you are *not* going back to St. Giles. I forbid it."

"I won't be a burden!"

"Devon, please do not argue with me."

"Then please don't treat me in such a manner. You can't forbid me anything! And you can't tell me what to do!"

Sebastian pressed his lips together, trying not to glower. This was definitely stubbornness, he decided.

"Sebastian, did you hear me? I won't be a burden!"

"And do you hear me? You are *not* a burden, Devon. *You are not.*" He spoke the last three words with emphatic emphasis.

"Then let me earn my keep." Her tears had begun to dry. Lifting her head, she stared up at him earnestly. "I've been thinking about it, Sebastian. Let me help Tansy or one of the other maids. Or perhaps I could help in the kitchen."

He made a sound low in his throat. "You will not!"

"Why not? I've done it before."

"Well, you'll not be doing it again. Devon, for pity's sake, I don't intend for you to be a servant."

"I won't be a charity case."

"I'm not giving you charity. I'm simply lending assistance where assistance is needed." He detected more than a hint of obstinacy in her regard. "Besides, I can well afford to feed you . . . yes, definitely you"—he tipped his head to the side as though to consider—"though I'm not so sure about Be . . . Dumpling."

With this last, he endeavored to lighten her spirits. He succeeded.

He ran a fingertip over her lips. "Is that a smile I see?" he murmured. A voice inside warned he was treading dangerously. Treading where he should not. The feel of her . . . and the way she looked at him, all golden eyes and golden hair, her lips tilting up in the slightest of smiles . . .

He felt that smile as well, beneath the tips of his fingers. His own joined in, and with that, a wispy little sigh emerged from her lips.

"This is a lovely room."

"I agree." His mouth brushed her cheek as he spoke. He fought the urge to linger. "We're sitting in my favorite chair, in my favorite room."

Her eyes widened.

"How odd. I'd decided that too, when I came downstairs." She seemed in no hurry to remove her head from his shoulder. She lay against him, no longer sobbing, her body fluid, one small hand curled against his chest.

"Sebastian," she whispered, "have you read all these books?"

Sweet Jesus. She was speaking of reading, while he was thinking of what it would be like to carry her up the stairs to his bed, strip away her layers of clothing, and make love to her the whole night through.

He felt himself tempted. Seduced by the beguiling charm of a lovely little urchin from St. Giles. But he didn't want to frighten her. Or argue.

"Hardly," he murmured.

"Why not?" She sounded amazed that he hadn't.

"Well, to begin with, there are a great many."

"If I lived here, I should make it a point to read every book in this room." Her gaze flitted away. "If I could read, that is," she said, her voice very low.

Sebastian frowned. "Tell me, Devon." He voiced the question that had been preying on his mind. "How is it you speak as you do yet cannot read?"

He sensed her reluctance to answer. "You mentioned your mother was well-spoken," he prompted.

She nodded. "Mama made her living as a governess before I was born," she said at last. "And, well, I shall be honest. She wanted to teach me to read, but I was stubborn."

His lips quirked. A startling revelation, that. At least she was honest enough to admit it—and not too stubborn.

"Since there was no money for books," she continued, "I saw little point in learning to read. I disappointed her, I think," she said in a small voice. "But now I wish I hadn't been so willful or defiant, because perhaps then I might be a governess, like she was. Or a companion to a widow in need of company."

"What about your father, Devon?"

Her eyes grew shadowed. "He died before I was born."

"And that's what sent your mother into a life of poverty? She had no family to whom she could turn?"

"Only a sister who died when they were young. The only employment she could find was work as a seamstress. Unfortunately she could never find anything that paid well."

"The two of you were very close, weren't you?"

She nodded. "Her name was Amelia," she said softly, "Amelia St. James."

A governess, he thought, mulling it over in his mind. She wanted to be a governess like her mother. Could it be done? *Should* it? She was halfway there. He sensed it instinctively.

"If you like," he said slowly, "I could teach you to read."

She stared. "You would?"

"I would." He paused. "The modiste will be here tomorrow, but we could begin the following morning."

"Oh, Sebastian," she breathed, "I would like that. I would like that very much." But her joy was all too fleeting. All at once, her lips trembled. "Sebastian, I"—her voice caught—"I don't know what to say—"

"No tears," he advised sternly.

"No tears," she whispered, but she was smiling, smiling in a way that made him want to spin circles on his head in every square in the city just to see her face light up the way it was now.

His arms tightened, just a little. She twisted slightly against him.

His blood began to pound once more. She lay with her hip nestled against the pillar of his maleness, which began to swell and throb, straining high against his trousers. Did she feel it? No. She gave no sign of it. Her face was turned at just such an angle that the delicate column of her throat lay open to him—like an invitation to a man on the brink of starvation.

A veritable feast.

A temptation that must be vanquished.

Yet even as the realization tumbled through his mind, he ached with the need to brush his mouth over that delicious arch and ever so slowly work his way up to the lush sweetness of her lips . . .

She sat up slowly, shifting in his lap.

Against him. Against the part of him he dared not think about.

Never before had he endured such agony.

Gritting his teeth, he helped her to her feet. He turned his body slightly aside, to hide the evidence of his arousal. Once she was up, she gave a shake of her head.

"Oh, dear. I must look a fright."

"You look beautiful, Devon."

She made a face. "Thank you for saying so, but I know I look dreadful when I cry. My eyes get puffy and red."

Sebastian pulled a handkerchief from his pocket and mopped her cheeks. "Better now?"

She nodded obediently.

She blew her nose, a distinctly unladylike sound.

He wanted to laugh. He wanted to hold this contradictory creature—one moment sharp as a blade, the next soft as a kitten—in his arms and never let go.

Oh, God, this was crazy.

A hand brushed at the front of his shirt and jacket. He sucked in a breath. Oh, Christ, if she touched him *there*, even brushed him accidentally, it would start all over again . . .

"Oh, my, I've wrinkled you. And you look so dashing and splendid."

Before he could respond, she said the oddest thing. "My mother would have liked you, I think."

"And what about you, Devon St. James?"

"I didn't like you at all that first night. Or the next day, either. *Especially* the next."

The day she'd tried to punch him. Such candor startled him, but he was beginning to realize that was simply Devon.

"But now . . . Well, I do believe you're a nice man, Sebastian Sterling."

Nice. God knew he wasn't thinking nice thoughts. The warm, scented hollow at the base of her throat beckoned him, reminding him of other soft, velvet hollows he already knew lay hidden beneath the fabric of her gown.

Ah, yes, his thoughts were decidedly impure. "Thank you," he said almost gruffly.

"Justin too is a very nice man."

Nice. Certainly he'd never heard a woman refer to Justin as nice. A hoarse laugh erupted. "Ye gods, don't ever say that to his face. He fancies himself quite dangerous."

A faint line appeared between her delicate brows. "Dangerous?"

"Yes. It's bandied about that no lady is safe when he is near." He smiled slightly. "If the truth be known, I do believe it."

Devon blinked. "And what about you, sir? Are you a dangerous man?"

"I highly doubt it. Justin says I'm the most honorable and proper man he knows."

"You're the finest man he knows too."

"What, did he say that?"

"Not in those words," she admitted. "But that was what he meant. I sensed it. And he said you have the patience of a saint."

"Did he?" Sebastian was oddly pleased.

A loud knock sounded on the door. "My lord," called a voice, "your carriage is ready."

Devon stepped back. "I won't keep you any longer then."

Sebastian didn't move. Questioning eyes scoured her face.

She read his thoughts. "See? I'm not weeping. Not anymore." She took his hand and pressed it to her cheek.

Every muscle in his body clenched. They stood but a breath apart. Her skirts brushed the folds of his coat.

His chest rose in an uneven breath. Dangerous, she'd said. Dear God, *she* was the one who was dangerous. Strange feelings coursed through him. Feelings of desire. Of need. Feelings that had no place in this moment . . . in this situation. She was in his house. Under his care. My God, he was supposed to be searching for a bride . . . He had to forcibly remind himself who she was, where they were . . . and why.

Justin was wrong. He had no patience, no patience at all. He wanted to drag her close, kiss her mouth, and never stop.

He settled for raising her hand to his lips.

"Are you sure you'll be all right?"

She nodded.

He almost wished she would say no.

He wanted to say to hell with his plans, to hell with reason, to hell with the duchess's ball. He wanted to say to hell with the world and stay right here.

But in the end he obeyed the sway of his mind. He did what he'd been trained to do from the time he was a boy.

For Sebastian was a man ever to do his duty. And so he went to the duchess's ball and danced with every twittering young lady who had taken her place in society.

But every moment he was thinking of Devon.

And he carried with him the disturbing image of shimmering golden eyes all through the night.

Ten

Promptly at nine two days later Devon presented herself in the library. Sebastian was already there, seated behind a leather-topped desk. A spear of sunlight shone through the windowpanes, bringing into sharp relief the heavy arch of his brows, the blade of his long, elegant nose, the turn of cleanly sculpted lips.

A strange sensation seized hold of her. She stood rooted to the floor, unable to move. All at once the simple act of breathing was a chore she could scarcely muster. And what was this odd tightness in her breast? She knew instinctively that it had little to do with an actual shortage of air. And everything to do with him, his sheer, masculine presence.

He was busily writing on a sheet of parchment. If he was aware that she stood on the threshold, he gave no sign of it. Devon's gaze slipped to his hands; they were large and strong, his fingers lean and dark.

Her breath still dangling, she watched as he folded the parchment neatly into thirds, sealed it with a drop of hot wax, and imprinted it with his crest. The sight of his hands made her want to hide her own, and she smothered them in her skirts. Though Tansy gave her a salve to massage into them each night, still they were chapped and dry.

He must have heard her then. Pushing back his chair, he got to his feet, an easy smile on his lips.

"Well," he murmured, "I see you're ready and eager."

Hastily Devon recovered herself. Lifting her chin, she stepped forward. "That I am," she announced briskly. Advancing into the room, she trailed a fingertip along the heavy volumes that lined the bookshelves.

Taking a deep breath, she pulled one out. "This one," she said emphatically, running a finger along the gilt-edged binding. "I want to be able to read this one."

He glanced at the cover, then back to her face. "You will," he said firmly. "Your resolve will serve you well, Devon."

Belatedly she peered at it curiously. "What *is* this book?"

He glanced at the cover. "It's a book of English folklore. Fairy stories. One of Julianna's favorites, as I recall." He paused. "If you like this one, there are a pair of brothers who write wondrous tales, tales that enchant, I'm told. I believe their second book was published just this year."

"Then I shall read both of those, too," Devon vowed.

Something flitted across his features.

"What is it? I thought you were convinced I could do this."

"I am, Devon. *I am.* But I fear I spoke too soon. The books I'm thinking of are written in German."

"By two brothers, you say?"

"Yes. By the name of Grimm."

"You and Justin live in this grand house. Perhaps someday the two of you will take up writing fairy stories."

"Fairy stories?" His smile was fleeting. Devon could have sworn that something almost sad lurked in the back of his eyes. "Trust me, Devon, that's a task better left to the brothers Grimm."

Devon replaced the book on the shelf, then turned back to him. "Do you read German?"

"Yes. Not a pretty language, I fear. I'm told I have a horrid accent."

To Devon, that he could speak—and read!—another language besides their own was astounding.

"Do you know other languages too?" She posed the question half in jest.

"Just Greek and Latin, of course."

Of course. The matter of her education all at once seemed an obstacle she wasn't quite sure she was ready to take on.

Her expression must have given her away. "But there's no need for you to learn Greek or Latin. Or German," he amended hastily. "A smattering of French, no more."

"French! Whatever for?" Devon was aghast. "We were just at war with them. We don't even like them!"

He laughed softly. "I know. Far be it for me to say I understand it, but it's a strange world we live in. All things French are much coveted—their fashions, why, even their chefs! A dressmaker is no longer a dressmaker, but a modiste. And French is something children are expected to learn, and so, I fear, must their governess."

Devon considered this. "Do you have a French chef?"

"Lord, no! I'm quite content with my very English *cook,*" he emphasized.

Still, Devon was caught squarely between hope and fear. "What else must I learn?" she asked carefully.

"I shall endeavor to teach you history and geography, how to keep accounts. And when my sister Julianna returns from the Continent, she can instruct you in the finer points of being a lady. Music, dancing, embroidery and drawing, things like that. Julianna is quite accomplished at watercolors."

Embroidery? Heaven help her, she lacked Mama's skill with the needle. As for watercolors, what if she proved even *less* proficient? Her heart sank like a stone.

Almost before she was aware of it, lean fingers slipped beneath her chin. With but the touch of thumb and forefinger, he summoned her eyes to his.

"Don't look like that, Devon. You can do this," he encouraged. "I have every faith in you."

Devon's mind was racing. Could she? How long would it take? Perhaps the better question was how much time she had. She had no idea how long Sebastian would allow her to remain in his house.

She wanted desperately to believe him. Somehow his quiet sincerity made *her* believe.

She *could* do this, she told herself fiercely. She could learn to read and all the other things as well.

The incentive was a powerful one; she had no intention of returning to work at the Crow's Nest. She refused to go back to St. Giles. She would not be weak. She would not be meek. This was her one chance to better her life, and she was a fool if she didn't make the most of this opportunity.

The beginnings of a smile appeared. "Then, sir, I suggest we dally no longer."

Keen gray eyes glimmered their approval. "Capital idea," he praised. His tone turned brisk. "Now, I believe you mentioned you know your letters?"

She nodded. "My mother used to sketch them out in the dirt. I think I remember them." Linking her fingers together before her, she closed her eyes and began to recite, "A—B—C—"

"Excellent." Sebastian gave an approving nod. "That will make it easier, I think. For you'll find that the ability to read and write is the key to everything. . . ."

Thus her lessons commenced.

For the next four days, faithfully between the hours of nine and four, Sebastian and Devon were closeted together, either in the library or his study. They stopped only for luncheon, and ended with tea. He was a man of his word, of punctuality, for he was never even a minute late.

He was also a creature of habit.

Little wonder then that guilt surged high in Devon's chest when she stopped at the door to his chamber one morning.

The lure was irresistible. The maid had just exited his chamber, her arms full of linen. Devon was already familiar with the ways of the household. She knew the woman wouldn't be back. Nor would Sebastian; she'd heard the rumble of his baritone downstairs a moment earlier.

Holding her breath, she stepped inside.

The room was much like its occupant—massive and dark, the furnishings intensely masculine. She crept past an immense four-poster bed and bypassed the shaving stand. A scant heartbeat later, she opened the door of a massive armoire. The scent of crisp, starched linen immediately surrounded her—Sebastian's scent. Trying not to disturb anything, her fingers darted behind a stack of neatly folded neck cloths. It made her feel quite odd, touching Sebastian's clothing. Why, it was almost as if she were touching *him*. Pushing aside the troubling sensation, she renewed her search, concentrating her efforts.

Drat! There was nothing.

She swung around, her gaze lighting on the chest of drawers. Her heart clamoring madly, she wrenched open the top drawer. Atop the dresser, a delicate urn tipped wildly; she rescued it just in time. Chiding herself, she opened the next drawer. Biting back her impatience, she reached for the third. It was then the light from the window reflected on something bright. Was it her necklace? Her pulse singing in excitement, she started to reach for it.

Something brushed her skirts. Panicked, she looked down. With a shaky laugh, she reached to pat Dumpling on the head, then reached inside the drawer once more.

A growl of warning vibrated in Dumpling's chest.

Devon froze. Her hand snapped back. She knew,

even before she glanced over her shoulder that she'd been caught red-handed. How the devil could such a big man be so quiet?

Her cheeks burning, she turned. Sebastian was but three paces away. It was a pose of indolent ease, his arms crossed over his chest, one shoulder propped against the wall. Snug fawn breeches outlined every hard muscle in his legs. His black jacket stretched taut against the span of his chest. His feet were shod in sleek black boots.

He appeared relaxed. Even comfortable. Faith, was there anything that rattled this man's composure? He was utterly calm. Her insides lurched, for she realized then it was an ominous calm. His dark features were etched in brittle reproof, his jaw set squarely, the cleft in his chin even more pronounced.

Her cheeks burned, yet she would not be cowed.

"Well, Devon," he said, his tone one of frigid politeness, "have you anything to say for yourself?"

"Yes," she muttered. "Must you always sneak up on me?"

His features blackened further. "I suppose you're going to tell me you're not stealing this time either."

"I am not. I'm looking for my necklace!"

"Why not ask me for it?"

"Would you have given it to me?" she shot back.

Something flickered across his features, something that sent a surge of anger through her blood.

"Would you?" she demanded.

"I don't know."

Her eyes flashed accusingly. "Then you see why I did not. If anything, you are the thief! You took it from me, Sebastian."

"Your possession of that necklace hardly ensures that it's yours. And I would remind you, it's broken."

"*I* broke it!"

"Well, at least you admit it. I suppose there's no need to ask how it happened, is there?" This last was accompanied by a knowing arch of brow.

Even if he'd asked, she wouldn't have told him. She was too incensed with his high-handedness and with his jab, for with it a vivid rush of memory surfaced in her mind.

Devon would never forget that long-ago day she'd broken the clasp. It was rare that she asked after her father. It caused her mother such distress that she'd quickly learned not to broach the subject; Mama had always said little save that he was a man of upstanding bloodlines. The scant information Devon had gleaned was little comfort, though, when the other children jeered and called her bastard.

"You said my papa was a gentleman!" she cried one day.

A pained expression flitted across her mother's gentle features. "He was," said Mama.

"Then why do the other children call me bastard?" Devon screamed. "Why?"

Never would she forget the stricken look on Mama's face. With a hand she reached out and brushed a burnished curl from Devon's cheek.

"Devon," she murmured, "oh, my sweet, sweet child . . ."

It was then Mama told her the truth. "One summer when I was young, I attended the nieces of a-a very wealthy family. I fell in love that summer, Devon. I fell in love with the son of the master and mistress of the house. It was he who gave me this." She touched the cross at her throat. "I was foolish, for he was far beyond my reach, far above me in station. When I confessed my love, he said he couldn't marry me—*wouldn't* marry me. He . . . he rejected me."

So it was true. Her father *was* a man of fine family. But hardly a fine man.

Her voice bleached with pain, Mama went on. "I ran away to London, for I had no family of my own. Scant weeks later I discovered he'd been killed in a riding accident. By then, I knew I carried his child in my womb." Her words grew choked. "Work was scarce, but I couldn't give you up . . . I couldn't! Nor could I appeal to his family. Perhaps it was pride. Perhaps it was stubbornness—much like you possess, I think. Most of all, I was afraid, so very afraid! His family had the power and wealth to take you away, and it was something I knew I could never allow, especially once I saw you." Wistfulness flitted across her features. She toyed with the necklace around her neck.

"You have his passion," she whispered. "His impulsiveness. And your eyes are so like his. So like his . . ."

But at her mother's confession, Devon was angry as Amelia had never been. She was angry at the haunting sadness that lived inside her mother, that even now filled her eyes.

Despite his rejection, her mother had never stopped loving her father. But Devon hated him, hated him for causing her mother pain and using her body. Incensed, she tore the necklace from her mother's neck.

"Why do you wear this?" she screamed. "*Why*?"

Mama began to weep.

It was the last time they spoke of her father—the last time she'd made her mother cry. Devon never forgave herself for making her mother weep that day, for in that moment came the awareness that for her mother, the necklace was both a torment and a comfort. It was much the same for Devon. Besides its sentimental value, it reminded her of all her mother endured, of all that Devon should strive for.

Slowly she raised her eyes to Sebastian's. "That necklace is mine," she said fiercely. "It was given to my mother by a-a well-to-do fellow."

"Your protests grow tiring, Devon. I confess, you give an admirable performance. I'd truly begun to believe you weren't a thief. But now it seems I must warn you. I refuse to be taken advantage of. I won't be fleeced."

Fleeced! Through her teeth, she said, "I promised my mother I would never steal or whore or beg, and I will not."

His silence proclaimed his disbelief only too well. Outraged, she called him a name so foul she could scarce believe she'd said it.

"Did your mother teach you to swear too?"

"My mother never *heard* me swear. She was the kindest, most gentle soul on this earth, and I would never have dishonored her so. You, however, are another matter."

"So I gather. A pity you've never learned to control your tongue." The clench of his jaw bespoke his disapproval.

Devon relished it. "What, sir," she said with caustic sweetness. "Is my language more than you expected?"

"On the contrary. It's everything I expected."

They stood toe-to-toe now. As he spoke, he leaned close. Devon's smile evaporated. Her mouth went dry. Her heart thumped almost painfully. The possibility that he was about to kiss her skittered through her mind. Oh, an absurd thought, that! Yet all at once the turf had changed. Confronted by bold, brazen masculinity, she felt her pulse begin to hammer. But she wouldn't retreat. She wouldn't give him the satisfaction.

Tilting her head back, she discovered his leisurely assessing gaze wandering down her neck, across the exposed skin of her chest.

It settled on her generous swell of cleavage.

"Stop looking at my bosoms!"

"My dear," he drawled, "you have but one bosom."

Anger rocketed. "Well, *stop looking!*"

Their eyes tangled. "Let us be frank with each other, Devon. I paid a visit to the Crow's Nest. I saw the other barmaid—Bridget, I believe. Yes, her name was Bridget."

Devon felt as if her face was on fire. A scalding shame spilled through her, clear to the farthest reaches of her soul. But far surpassing it was an anger that spiraled higher with each second. Sebastian had gone there to check on her story. To check on *her*.

"She appeared to have no distaste for the man whose hands were in her bodice and beneath her skirts."

"Bridget," she said levelly, "is not a harlot."

His lip curled in distaste. "If that is what you think, then your morals are most assuredly displaced."

Devon opened her mouth, prepared to deliver a cutting retort. Before she could say a word, he spoke.

"There's no question she's a harlot. What then, I wonder, does that make you?"

Devon slapped him, as hard as she could.

His shock was gratifying.

" 'Tis a logical assumption," he defended himself stiffly.

"You bloody prig!"

"What, are we back to that again?"

"You are," she charged, her voice shaking. "You are a hypocrite, and yes, I do know what *that* word means. You dare to deride me, yet you can't stop gawking at my breasts. I've seen you looking when you thought *I* wasn't looking!"

"Were you covered decently, I might be able to."

She gasped. "Kindly remember, sir, it was you who put me in this dress!" The modiste had yet to deliver any of her new gowns.

"Because I thought you were of a size with Julianna."

"Obviously I am not," she said tightly.

A dull, red flush had begun to creep up his neck. "The truth is," he muttered, "you fill Julianna's gowns in a way Julianna does not."

"And of course I'm to blame."

"What about the gown you were wearing the night I found you? By God, if you're not a doxy, you certainly looked like one."

"You're determined to think the worst of me, aren't you?" she lashed out furiously. "How dare you," she said, her eyes blazing. "How dare you stand in judgment of Bridget—of me—you in your fine house with your fancy ways!" She jabbed a finger squarely in the middle of his broad chest. "I daresay you've not spent your entire life chastely. Indeed, I daresay there's been more than one woman in your bed!"

At first he was startled, then clearly affronted. "I am a man," he stated.

As if that explained everything. As if that explained *anything*. And spoken, she decided coolly, like a man who thought he was entitled to every woman in sight.

Granted, there was no arguing the fact, for his was a vital, intensely masculine presence. From the very first time she'd laid eyes on him, a sizzle of awareness had sparked in her body. It stood to reason that probably many other women would find his wide shoulders, narrow hips, and raven hair as devastatingly attractive as she.

Furthermore, the evidence was irrefutable. Her gaze drifted lower. His gentleman's clothing did little to hide his long-boned strength. He was built like a stallion.

His jaw jutted out. "Stop looking at my . . . my—"

"Crotch?" she supplied.

"Don't be vulgar," he warned tightly.

She responded quite pleasantly. "If I wanted to be vulgar, I'd have said—"

"That's quite enough, Devon!"

Calmly she returned her eyes to his thunderous features. "You said you were a man. I thought I should verify."

Later Devon would be mortified that she dared to speak so audaciously. But not now. She wanted to gloat. He'd just been given a sample of how he'd treated her, and she was certain he didn't like it!

She squared her shoulders. Back to the matter at hand. Coolly she stated, "Now that we've established that you haven't spent your life chastely, tell me this. Have you ever lain with a woman and *paid* her?"

He gazed down his long, supposedly superior nose at her.

"Have you, my lord?"

"I had no need to pay a woman to lie with me," he said abruptly. "But even if I had—"

Devon interrupted him. "Let me guess, my lord. I daresay it's different for you blue bloods, isn't it?" She gave him no chance to respond. "I admit, I'm curious. Do you keep a mistress? Do you supply her house and clothing and—"

"That is none of your affair," he said sternly. "And you are impertinent, Devon."

Devon snorted. There was no need for an answer. She had it right there.

She looked him straight in the eye. "You've never had to wonder where and when your next meal will come from, Sebastian. You've never spent a night shivering in cold. So do not dare to judge me. Do not dare to judge Bridget. Yes, she takes men in the back room. Yes, she does it for the money it will bring—how else is she to feed her brothers and sisters?" Her eyes simmered.

Gathering her skirts in her hands, she prepared to exit.

Before she left, she turned and looked him directly in the eyes. "And just so you know, I *will* have my necklace back before I leave."

Eleven

When Sebastian strode into his chamber and caught Devon with her hands in his drawers—well, perhaps not literally!—he'd been furious, both at her and himself. He'd been gullible, for he'd begun to entertain the notion that he was wrong about her. But her presence in his room proved otherwise.

He'd called himself every kind of fool, that he had succumbed in such a way; that he'd been blinded by her lush sensuality . . . and, yes, her charm.

She was impetuous. Impulsive. She provoked him. She aggravated him. She was neither coy nor shy. She was half lady, half wildcat, and totally unpredictable.

Ah, yes. Her charm . . .

He wanted to shake her even as he longed to drag her into his arms and kiss her until she could speak no more. When he caught her in his room going through his things all he could think about was pulling her close, trapping those temptingly mutinous lips to his, and kissing her until they were both wild with desire. He wanted to plunge his hands into her bodice and fill his hands with bountiful, creamy flesh, bare her breasts and curl his tongue around those delectably colored nipples.

Her breasts.

There was no question she was extremely sensitive about that particular part of her anatomy, and not in the way a man would hope. He hadn't realized his scrutiny was so transparent. Or maybe it was simply that he'd never dreamed she would take him to task as she had.

How lame he'd sounded! *Look me in the eye*, she'd insisted the night she had determined to flee. And she was right. He *did* look when he thought she didn't see. But even Justin managed to keep his eyes above her neck! In the far recesses of his mind, he wondered what she would be like in bed. Ah, but there was one way to find out, he decided with black humor.

Not bloody likely, though. He'd gained no favor with her this day.

"Hell and damnation," he said aloud.

Absently he fingered the plane of his cheek. Christ, it was still throbbing! He was still having difficulty believing she'd slapped him. Never before had Sebastian been slapped. Never had there been occasion for him to be slapped. Of course, never had he *said* what he just had either.

Shame bit deep. In all honesty, he must acknowledge the truth. He'd branded as whores those women who spread their legs for any and every man willing to pay their price—women like Bridget. He'd held them in the utmost disdain, without once ever really considering the reasons a woman might take up such a life. Perhaps it had been in his mind that it was a conscious choice; certainly he'd never considered there might be a need behind it—a need like brothers and sisters!

And he wondered . . . had Devon been hungry? Cold? He had the awful feeling she had.

It came to him then . . . Until he'd met Devon, he'd really given precious little thought to those less fortunate than he. But not all paupers were thieves and robbers, the dregs of the earth—like Harry and Freddie. No doubt there were many like Devon's mother, Amelia St. James, a woman left on her own with a child to care for . . . a woman left to the mercy of the fates.

But he must give credit where credit was due. Devon had done a fine job of turning the tables.

Adorable. That's what she'd been. Absolutely adorable. Why, it almost made him want to laugh, the idea that he'd been lectured by a waif!

Not that he'd been inclined to laugh when she'd slapped him. Indeed, she'd given him quite a lot to think about.

He didn't wait long before hurrying into the hall. He didn't entirely trust her not to plunge headlong into the streets once again. She was in a fine enough temper to do exactly that.

His step quickened. In his haste, he nearly ran down Tansy, who had just rounded the corner. Her arms were wrapped around a large box.

"My lord," she cried, her eyes sparkling. "My lord, look! This just arrived from the modiste. Miss Devon will be so pleased, don't you think?"

Would she? After the scene in his room, Sebastian wished he could be sure. "If you don't mind, Tansy, I'll see that it's delivered to Miss Devon."

Tansy curtsied. "As you wish, my lord."

The maid was gone from sight when Sebastian knocked at Devon's door.

"Who is it?"

Sebastian frowned. Her voice was faintly muffled. Was she weeping?

Sebastian didn't answer. He didn't dare. Instead he stepped boldly within.

Devon was just rising from the bed. She sat up, her eyes blazing when she saw him. From her post at the end of the bed, Beast snarled. Sebastian set the parcel down near the door. Plucking the mongrel from her perch, Sebastian retraced his steps, set her on her bum in the hall, shut the door against her whiskered little snout, and turned back to Devon.

"Must you forever plague me?" she cried.

"It would seem so."

She watched his progress across the chamber, then at the last instant swung her head away.

Sebastian wouldn't be dissuaded. He pulled her to her feet. She tried to snatch her hands back; Sebastian wouldn't let her.

"Devon," he implored, his voice very low. "Look at me."

Her gaze was flush with the center of his chest. "No," she denied almost frantically. "*No.*"

Cursing, he slipped his fingers beneath her chin. "Devon, please. *Please.*"

Long, spiky lashes fluttered closed, then lifted. She stared at him with huge, liquid eyes. Sebastian's breath caught. She wasn't weeping, but she was dangerously close. He felt her wounded pride in the quavering breath she drew, and her pain hurt him to the bottom of his soul.

He addressed her, his regard steady. He'd never been so solemnly intent. "Devon," he said, "my conduct today was appalling. I apologize most heartily for saying what I did. It was wrong of me to judge Bridget so harshly." He paused. "And you, Devon. It was wrong of me to judge *you*, especially when I've come to know you."

A strangled sound emerged from her lips. She flung herself against him, holding tight and clinging. His arms closed about her.

"Oh, Sebastian, I'm sorry too. I shouldn't have sneaked into your room. And it was horrid of me to slap you. Did it hurt?"

A faint smile curled his lips. "It would take more than a slap from a little thing like you to hurt me," he lied.

She'd tipped her head back to peer up at him, her expression rife with utter concern. The golden splendor of her hair, loosely coiled on her crown an hour earlier, had tumbled down to spill about her shoulders in artless disarray. At his denial, she smiled in relief.

Something twisted deep in Sebastian's gut, something wholly beyond the boundaries of his control. He knew, as surely as the sun had risen and would set this very day, that he was going to do something incredibly stupid. Something insane. Something he hadn't planned, though, God knew, he'd thought about almost day and night since the moment she'd arrived in his house. He knew he had to taste those soft pink lips poised beneath his own . . .

Or die.

And so, for the length of a heartbeat, his mouth closed over hers. She started in surprise, but she didn't draw back. In some distant part of him, he'd been convinced she would; that she didn't made his heart soar and his chest swell.

Christ, she was but a wisp against the breadth of his large-boned form. The scent of her hair was dizzying, the feel of her intoxicating. He held her tightly, half afraid he might crush her. But she swayed against him, and the tremulous rush of warm, moist breath against his mouth seared him to the bone.

It was but a whisper of a kiss, a fraction of all he desired, tempered by the certainty that if he gave in to the rising clamor in his veins, he'd have backed her up against the bed, thrown up her skirts, and plunged himself to her womb and beyond.

Sanity returned abruptly. He dragged his mouth away and stepped back.

Clear, wide-set eyes opened. She blinked, as if in confusion.

He cleared his throat. "Forgive me," he said quietly.

She gave a little shake of her head, averting her eyes. "It's all right—"

"No," he said very deliberately, "it is not. A gentleman wouldn't have done that. *I* shouldn't have done that."

"Then why did you?"

This time he was the one who looked away. "I don't know."

Now he could practically feel the weight of her regard. Wondering. Mutely questioning. If she pressed him, how the hell was he to answer? He couldn't tell her the truth—that when he looked at her, he ached to bare her breasts and body to his lips and tongue, and to hell with everything else.

Sebastian never would have considered himself a coward, but in that instant he did. He couldn't have met her gaze if his life depended on it!

After what was surely the most uncomfortable moment in his life, she nodded toward the large, beribboned box. "What have you there?" she murmured.

Quickly he retrieved the box and placed it on the bed. "Tansy said this just arrived." He beckoned her forward. "Go ahead, open it."

Almost gingerly, she tugged at the white satin ribbon, then removed the lid. Frowning, she leaned forward and parted filmy layers of tissue.

"The first of your gowns from the modiste," he said by way of explanation. "I daresay, a timely arrival."

She flushed and bit her lip, but her eyes were dancing as she pulled a day gown of blue and white sprigged muslin from the box. "Oh, Sebastian," she cried, "how lovely!" A sheer, white shift and petticoat came next. Devon exclaimed delightedly over each.

Some of the tension left his shoulders. "Try it on," he suggested.

"Oh, yes. *Yes.*" Her face lit up. "You'll have to help me with the buttons, though."

Before he could respond, she grabbed up the gown and undergarments and darted behind the screen.

There was a rustle of clothing, and the dress she'd been wearing dropped over the screen.

Sebastian's head traveled from the screen to the door. He really should fetch Tansy, he thought.

You just called yourself a gentleman, came a mocking voice in his head. *Why don't you act like one?*

Because this is Devon, and none of the usual rules apply here.

There was little debate. His feet remained rooted to the floor.

He wasn't about to inform her he was far more adept at helping a woman *out* of her clothes than *into* them.

Idly he picked up a dainty white bonnet, running his fingers over the ribbons. "There's a bonnet too," he called to Devon. "Now you can get rid of that ratty old thing you came here with." Distastefully he eyed the object in question, looped around a bedpost.

"I shall not!" came Devon's immediate and vehement protest. "I cherish that bonnet! It was my very first, you know."

Sebastian shrugged. There was no accounting for a female's tastes when it came to fashion. When Julianna was young, she'd been stubbornly attached to a ghastly green fluff of a frock that she insisted on wearing every day. Nurse complained that it had to be peeled away amid wails and screams every morning that she was not allowed to wear it. When she finally outgrew it, she insisted on having several frocks made in black, declaring herself in mourning for the loss of her most beloved gown.

"Stockings and garters," he said when Devon reappeared.

They were snatched from his hand. "Turn aside," she commanded.

Sebastian obliged, but he could still see from the

corner of his eye. Perched on a chair, she tugged her skirts to her knees and drew on the fine white silk, securing each while Sebastian admired the turn of slim, shapely ankles and calves. With amusement he realized he might have been the lamppost outside for all the notice she took of him.

"Slippers?" he queried, passing them her way. He stooped obligingly. A hand against his shoulder, she slipped on first one and then the other. A pair of delicate lace gloves came next.

With a swirl of skirts, she presented him with her back. The gown was loose about her shoulders. He wanted to rip it off, not do the damn thing up! A row of tiny pearl buttons awaited his attention. His mouth dry, he stared at the supple length of her back, divided by the delicate groove of her spine, covered by a shift so sheer he had no trouble discerning the creamy flesh beneath. Almost reluctantly, his fingers complied. Doggedly he willed aside the impulse to press his mouth against the silken expanse of her nape, bared to allow him access to the buttons.

Unconsciously he measured the width of one hand against the nip of her waist. His hands were big and dark in contrast to her fairness and dainty, fine-boned form. He felt almost ungainly and uncouth—he, Sebastian Sterling, Marquess of Thurston, and she, a waif!

All at once he frowned. "Devon, where are your stays?"

"I don't like them. I won't wear them. They're torture devices."

"A lady always wears stays."

Her chin firmed. "Well, *I* won't. I never have and I never will."

She wasn't wearing stays. She never wore stays. She would *never* wear stays. She spoke of torture. By Jove, she was a mistress of torture, for his was never-ending!

But in truth she didn't need them. Had he not seen for himself, *felt* for himself, he'd never have guessed.

The task completed, he steered her toward the gilt-edged cheval mirror in the corner. Where before she'd been almost dancing in excitement, now, oddly enough, she almost had to be prodded into position. She stood for an instant, her chin bowed low, before finally lifting her head to gaze at her reflection.

She stared. "Oh," she whispered, and then again, "*Oh*." She ran a hand over the bodice. "It fits," she breathed. "Sebastian, it fits!"

She was positively glowing.

Their eyes met in the mirror. "What do you think?" she said breathlessly.

"Well," he said thoughtfully. "I think something is missing."

"What?" She voiced her concern. "What?"

"I'm not sure." He pretended to study her, first one way, then the other.

Her hand fluttered to her throat, a gesture of uncertainty.

"Yes. My thoughts exactly."

He withdrew something from his pocket. Her eyes never wavered from his as he slipped a finely etched chain of silver around her neck. The cross came to rest in the shallow hollow of her throat.

"My necklace." She ran her fingertips over the shiny surface, almost reverently. "You had it repaired," she whispered, then bit her lip.

"Yes," he admitted with a rueful smile. In truth

he'd sent it to a jeweler the day after he'd gone to St. Giles.

Slowly she turned. Her eyes, dark and questioning, sought his. "Why?" she asked, a ragged tremor to the word. "Sebastian, why? I thought—"

"You were right," he explained softly. "It wasn't mine to keep."

She bit her lip, her eyes misty. "Sebastian, I-I don't know what to say."

Naked emotion flashed across her features. It seemed such a simple thing—so effortless—yet it brought her so much pleasure. For perhaps the first time in his life, Sebastian felt humble.

"Say thank you," he said lightly.

She did, but not in the way he expected.

With both hands she reached up, tangled her fingers in the dark hair on his nape, and tugged his head down to hers.

Without a word, she kissed him full on the lips.

A dozen warning bells clanged inside Sebastian, telling him that he'd been right. For if the other kiss had been sweet . . .

This one was sweeter still.

Twelve

Devon had been kissed before—if the mashing of wet, slobbering lips against her own could be construed as kissing. Always before at the Crow's Nest, her skin crawled and she ducked and squirmed away, seeking to evade the lustful advances pressed upon her person. It was something she endured, for the sake of preserving her job.

But this was neither lust nor lechery.

Nor was she unwilling.

For with Sebastian, she wanted to be caught and captured. Imprisoned forever. And if she wanted to squirm, it was to squirm closer still.

It lasted but a moment, yet it was seared in her heart forever.

Never had Devon experienced anything like the touch of Sebastian's mouth against her own. She'd longed desperately to clamp her hands around his back and burrow her fingers beneath his shirt, to discover the sleek tautness of muscle and skin. And if the kiss had only lasted longer, perhaps she would have done precisely that.

And in the days that followed, she couldn't forget. Sebastian had kissed her. He'd *kissed* her.

Perhaps it was silly. Perhaps it was stupid, but she could have sworn something more than comfort had resided in his kiss. Something smoky and heady and heated that hinted of smoldering sensuality. She'd suffered a stab of hurt when he apologized. But she reminded herself he was a man of impeccable manners.

For something had happened that day in her chamber. Devon couldn't identify precisely what it was, but every time she thought of that kiss—which was nearly every waking moment!—her toes curled in her slippers all over again.

It made her glance at him when he sat at his desk working. That overpowering awareness of him made her pulse clamor and goose bumps rise upon her skin whenever he came near. The very sight of him made her insides quiver. Sometimes she even begged his assistance when it wasn't really needed, for her reading skills were improving vastly. One afternoon she cast a subtle glance at the cleft in his chin, the squareness of his jaw, already dark with the shadow of his beard.

Her regard must have lingered longer than she realized. Very soon she heard his voice. "Devon," he said patiently, "are you paying attention?"

"No," she almost blurted. "I'm too busy looking at you."

The next afternoon prompted a dreamily earnest contemplation, for he sat next to her for the longest time. The figures he'd set before her were a blur. She could hear his quill scratching and pausing—his explanations fell on deaf ears.

Even when he was sitting, the top of her head barely reached his shoulders. He was so tall and powerful and handsome . . . His scent was clean and fresh. Every so often, his sleeve brushed hers. She fancied he did it on purpose, that her mere presence set him on fire inside. Wiggling her bottom, she scooted closer to the edge of her chair . . . and him.

There. That was better. For now, if she turned her head just so, and he chanced to do the same, their lips would have been but a breath apart . . .

Would he feel compelled to kiss her again? The prospect of his mouth on hers, warm and smooth, made her shiver inside.

At that precise moment a most horrifying awareness set in. For it appeared that while she had been preoccupied with her most riveting, fascinating catalog of Sebastian's assets, her examination had not gone unnoticed.

Only he hardly looked enamored.

He replaced the quill in the inkpot and turned to her. "Devon," he queried, "is there something you need to attend to?"

She regarded him blankly.

"Let me be blunt then. Do you need to use the water closet?"

"No!" she gasped.

"You're wiggling," he pointed out.

A hot tide of color rushed to her cheeks. "Not because of that!"

He propped an elbow on the leather-topped table. "What then?"

By now Devon was sure her face was flaming.

How could she tell him she admired him? That she thought he was the most divinely handsome man ever put on this earth?

"Does your side pain you?" he asked suddenly.

"No. I feel a slight twinge only when I take a deep breath." To be sure, she could hardly breathe when he was near.

He nodded, those clear gray eyes unerringly direct. "What is on your mind then?"

"Nothing," she said. "Why do you say that?"

Very gently he said, "Because you were staring at me. You are *still* staring at me."

"Oh," she said, her voice very small. "I'm sorry. It's just that . . . you smell," she blurted.

Now he was the one who was taken aback. "I beg your pardon?"

"Oh, I don't mean that you smell *bad*," she hastened to assure him. "It's just that I've never been around a man who smells the way you do. So crisp and clean, like starch and—and something else—"

"It's just a . . . a blend of bay rum." He appeared at a loss for words.

"And it smells heavenly, truly it does, Sebastian! And I . . . I . . . oh, my," she finished weakly. "I suppose no other woman has ever told you that, has she?"

"That I smell? In a word, no."

"And I suppose it's the kind of thing a lady should *never* say to a gentleman."

"Quite so," he agreed.

She plucked at the folds of her skirt. "I suppose you think I'm silly."

"No." A twinkle appeared in his eyes. A smile lurked at the corners of his mouth.

"Oh!" she cried. "You're making light of me!"

"Not at all! Though I'll admit our conversations do tend to verge on the"—his lips quirked—"unusual."

"Are you laughing at me?" she demanded.

"A little."

At least he didn't lie.

"It's just that I feel like I can be myself with you," she confided. "I don't have to pretend to things I don't know." She bit her lip. "But I'm sorry. I won't say such things again—"

"Don't," he interrupted with a shake of his head. "Don't be sorry. Don't be afraid to tell me anything. Don't be afraid to *ask* me anything." Devon was shocked to see his tiny smile had vanished. "And don't betray yourself, Devon. Don't betray who you are for anyone." His regard was oddly penetrating, his tone quietly intent.

His hands caught hers where they lay on her lap. "Do you understand?"

Her eyes roved searchingly over his features. She was shocked to discover a lump in her throat. "You don't mind if I say what I please?"

"Not at all."

"And I can ask you anything?"

"Anything you please," he vowed.

"Then tell me, my lord, how on earth you manage to shave"—she leaned forward, her eyes dancing—"*there!*" Her fingertip dropped squarely in the cleft of his chin.

He laughed, the sound low and melodious. "Very carefully," he told her, rubbing a hand over the bristly hardness of his chin.

In that moment her heart surely melted.

* * *

That was the way it was whenever they were together. Devon's senses hummed. Her heart sang. She loved the way the corners of his mouth quirked upward when he was trying to appear severe and struggling not to laugh at her, the way he'd done that day in the library.

She liked making him laugh, for at times she sensed he was altogether too serious.

Six weeks of living in the Sterling household had given Devon a glimpse of life in the *ton*. Each morning, while Sebastian perused his *Public Ledger*, she sat beside him, making small talk with Charles, the footman. For the most part absorbed in his paper, Sebastian interjected a word now and then, idly sipping his tea.

Walking in one morning, Justin pronounced them the stodgiest pair he'd ever seen. It was during breakfast where Devon learned about the frivolous amusements of the *ton*, for Justin often regaled them with accounts of his previous evening's activities—a censored version, she strongly suspected. Still, she enjoyed hearing who among the *ton* vied for the prized vouchers to Almack's, which would gain them admittance to that most exclusive of clubs, as well as who was seen with whom riding in Hyde Park.

"Good morning," Sebastian greeted several mornings later.

"Good morning," she returned softly, busy buttering a roll.

Against her bare leg came a nudge. When Charles stepped between them to pour Sebastian's tea, she took a sip of chocolate. With the other hand she reached down.

When the footman stepped aside, Sebastian's gaze was fixed on her. "Devon, I saw that."

"Saw what?"

"Please do not feed Beast under the table."

"*Dumpling* needs her nourishment too." It was horrid of her to tease him so, for he and Beast were still feuding; they continued to regard each other in mutual disdain.

"Devon, *Beast* does not walk, she waddles. Her belly drags upon the ground. She has the appetite of a horse. The last thing she needs is more nourishment, including the choice tidbits of meat I know you give her every night."

Devon nearly choked. She pressed a napkin to her lips. Why, it was the very thing Dumpling needed!

"Besides which," he grumbled, "'tis a waste of perfectly good food."

Oh, Lord, never say he didn't *know*! But apparently he didn't. Nor did she know quite how to tell him. He would not be pleased . . .

Now, she decided, might be a good time to change the subject.

She glanced at the parade of footmen streaming back and forth through the entryway. "What's all the commotion?"

"They're getting ready for tonight."

"Tonight?"

"Yes. I'm hosting a dinner party." He peered at her over the top of the *Ledger*. "Didn't I tell you?"

Devon shook her head.

She wasn't surprised, of course. Invitations poured into the house with predictable regularity. Sebastian sifted through them every morning. To fetes, to balls, to soirees. Why, if he attended all of them, he'd never have slept! Naturally, he would have to take his turn hosting such affairs.

Devon was well aware she would never be a part of this elegant, privileged life. But she was living on the fringes, and the lure was irresistible . . .

"Sebastian?" she murmured.

"Hmmm?"

She hesitated. "Do you mind if I watch?"

The newspaper lowered. He was silent, looking at her for the longest time. Devon began to wonder if she'd said something wrong.

"I'll stay out of sight," she said in a rush. "Your guests won't even know I'm here. I'll be quiet as a mouse, neither seen nor heard. Please say yes, Sebastian. I promise, I won't embarrass you."

She held her breath and waited, waited forever it seemed. Something flickered in his eyes, and then he spoke.

"I'm not worried about any such thing." He smiled slightly. "Of course you may watch."

Devon leaped up and threw her arms around him, her eyes shining. "Thank you," she sang out. "Oh, thank you!"

Sebastian watched her go, filled with an odd jumble of emotions. The little things that gave Devon such pleasure—my God, to watch a party she couldn't even attend! He'd been remiss in not telling her earlier about the festivities. If he could have canceled it, he would have, but the gossipmongers of the *ton* would have asked too many questions. His mouth twisted. Christ, but he wished he could recant his foolish announcement about taking a bride. In truth, it had been nothing but a bother. He had little patience for the addle-brained twits who constantly threw themselves in his path. So much had happened since he'd made the declaration. *Too* much. Why, it was that very night that he had brought Devon into his house . . . and into his life.

A heavy weight sat in the middle of his chest, an oppressive weight. He heartily disliked the feeling that she must be banished, hidden away from all eyes; it didn't set well at all. She was sweet and lovely and enchanting, and he'd never felt so low and dirty and mean. Devon thought nothing of it, but he did. Yet it couldn't be helped.

As much as he wished otherwise, he couldn't invite her, for it was just as Justin had once reminded him. The *ton*, he feared, would surely look askance at the fact that she was an unmarried woman living beneath the same roof as two unmarried men, would not be forgiving of such a fact, no matter the circumstances. If Julianna were here, it would be a different situation entirely. But alas, he'd received a note just yesterday that she was now in Italy and might stay longer. And God knew, he couldn't blame her, not after her wretched experience of the last year. For she too had been the unwitting victim of an unavoidable scandal . . . little wonder she had vowed she would never marry!

Scandal. The word felt vile to his very soul. God, but he despised it with every pore of his being!

Which, he thought grimly, made him all the more determined that Devon avoid all hint of scandal. If she were to attend tonight, there would be questions he was not yet prepared to answer—she might never gain the post of governess she sought. When the time was right, he decided, they would come up with a story to explain her presence, a story that would leave her reputation intact.

Too, the situation with Harry made him uneasy. He'd said nothing to Devon, but Justin's sources had advised that Harry was still searching for the pregnant woman who had killed his brother, a realization that sent a chill through his bones. He wouldn't risk exposing her—not to the police or to Harry.

Damn, he thought tiredly, but it couldn't be helped.

Later that evening Devon installed herself on the balcony behind a potted fern. It was a perfect spot, for she could observe the festivities firsthand without being seen. If she was lucky, she told herself stoutly, she might learn a thing or two about proper behavior.

It was like something out of the fairy stories she'd just finished. Urns of fresh flowers sweetened the air with their light, delicate scent. The ladies wore swirling concoctions of silks and satins that shimmered in the candlelight, pearls and jewels at their throats and ears, their curls beribboned and plumed. The gentlemen were bedecked in pantaloons and tight-fitting jackets, the points of their collars stiff and high. It was an enthralling sight—and this but a dinner party.

But her eyes returned to Sebastian, again and again. He strolled among his guests with that careless, natural grace only he possessed. He stopped once, turning his head so that she was allowed a glimpse of his strong, sensuous lips and rugged jaw. Had she been standing, the very sight of him would have turned her knees to water.

She didn't notice that Justin was missing until she saw him strolling lightly up the stairs.

Devon pressed her back against the wall. "Rats!" she whispered as he stood beside her. "Have I been seen?"

"No," he assured her. "I didn't even realize you were here until I reached the landing."

"I wasn't eavesdropping," she said quickly.

A devilish glint appeared in his eye. "Oh, but Devon"—he gave a shake of his head—"the things you might learn if you did. Why, you could end up a wealthy woman far into your old age." Devon was still trying to figure out precisely what that meant when he gestured with a finger. "Scoot to the left and look between the rails. You'll be able to see everything. As a child, one learns these things."

Devon obliged, and indeed, he was right. She could now see into the dining room as well as the drawing room.

"And later, if you should chance to see three beautiful *demoiselles* flee into the garden with me"—his smile was recklessly bold—"don't tell anyone it was me."

"Three!" Devon was shocked.

"For a dare I'll make it four."

"You are incorrigible!" She scolded him without heat, for she knew he was teasing. She peered down again. "Sebastian told me this was a small gathering. My word, but there must be a hundred people down there."

"You see that man, standing at the far end of the fireplace?"

Devon nodded.

"That is Viscount Temberly. He stuffs his pantaloons to enhance his—how may I put this delicately?—his masculine endowments. Or perhaps I should say his lack thereof."

Devon cuffed him in the shoulder. "I am not so gullible. No man would do such a thing!"

"Wouldn't he? Ask the widow Blakewell standing next to him. She knows. No doubt far better than his wife."

Her mouth opened, then closed.

An odd look passed over his features, but then he was laughing. "What, are you shocked? Ah, Devon, don't delude yourself. Temberly's wife too has had her"—a meaningful pause—"diversions."

"What about Sebastian?" Her heart was suddenly beating very hard. "Is his mistress here?"

Justin regarded her for a full minute in what looked to be sheer astonishment. Then he said, "He told you about her? He hasn't even told *me* about her!"

"Well, not in so many words . . . I guessed," she admitted.

He nodded. "Sebastian is very closemouthed when it comes to such things. But to answer your question, no, she's not here. To be honest, I've never seen any of his paramours. But I've heard she's an actress named Lilly."

Devon let out the breath she'd been holding.

"Sebastian would never be so crass as to consort with his mistress openly, not with this crowd. Believe it or not, you see before you the crème de la crème of the *ton*."

Devon leaned forward intently as he pointed out a duke, and an earl and his countess.

"And there is the grande dame of them all, the dowager duchess of Carrington."

The duchess was quite diminutive in size, her white hair covered by a seed-pearl cap. Though assisted by a cane, she carried herself in a way that left Devon in no doubt that she was a woman of distinguished importance. Devon found herself rather in awe of her.

"Sebastian went to her ball the night after I found Dumpling."

"Yes, I recall. I do believe she has the most sumptuous house in London—and that but one of a dozen."

Devon found it difficult to imagine a house grander than this one, and so she said.

"I daresay the devil himself could be received in society if he was received by the duchess. The duke died about ten years ago, as I recall. Her son, Marcus, is gone too, for many a year now. Her husband's nephew inherited the dukedom, but they're not close. Sebastian is convinced she's made society her playground because she has no one else."

"How lonely, and how sad," Devon murmured, still looking at her. "Did Marcus die in infancy?"

"God, no! To all accounts, Marcus was a rake who would put even me to shame. Affairs with married women, affairs with *un*married women, duels . . . The duchess weathered each scandal, for she adored him and tried to rein him in. She was devastated when she lost him."

"How did it happen?"

"He fell from his horse and broke his neck."

Devon stared at the duchess for a long moment. Her son was exactly the sort of man Devon despised. Yet what good had the dowager's wealth and riches done for her? Her houses were empty, and perhaps so was her heart.

"What, Devon, are you feeling sorry for her?" Justin sounded astonished.

"Well," she began.

"Don't," he said baldly. "She can take a man down with a look. A word and he's cut to a ninny. She says what she thinks and she thinks what she likes."

The trace of a smile crossed Devon's lips. Mama had often said that about *her*.

"And when she begins to brandish that damn cane of hers . . . God help anyone who chances to be in the line of fire."

Devon couldn't help it. She chuckled aloud. "A fearsome woman then."

"A *most* fearsome woman," he agreed.

"Sebastian doesn't appear to fear her." She made the observation almost proudly.

"There's no question Sebastian can hold his own. Look there. The duchess has slipped her arm through his. And I do believe where Sebastian is concerned, she'd love to play matchmaker."

Matchmaker?

"You see? She's piloting him towards Miss Darby. A good, biddable lass, but without enough starch for Sebastian. He'd be bored silly with her." From his perch above, Justin laughed softly. Cheering, she wondered, or jeering? With Justin, she could never be quite sure.

"That's the way, old man. Steer the old gal to a chair, exhibit your most courtly bow while driving home your point . . . oh, ever the gallant to young and old alike, that's my brother."

Devon couldn't take her eyes off Sebastian. He'd barely turned aside from the duchess when a bevy of beauties surrounded him.

Her smile was no more. "For pity's sake," she said peevishly, "do they wish to smother him?"

"An apt observation, Devon." Justin's laughter had grown mocking. "Sebastian made the announcement not long ago that he would begin his search for a bride."

Devon's heart caught. Her breath grew painfully shallow. "A bride?" she echoed faintly.

"Yes. He's the marquess of Thurston, and he's not getting any younger. He'll need his heir and spare. And those women smothering my brother down there, well, they're all hoping to snare a husband. The gossips are full of speculation about who will be the bride-to-be."

In her lap Devon's fingers pulled at each other. She had gone very still inside.

"But no woman will ever *snare* him. I know my brother, and when he weds, it will be a woman of his own choosing, not one who chooses him. I daresay that's why none of those clucking young chicks gathered about him now will be his bride—they're too damn eager. God knows, no hint of scandal dare taint his future bride's past. When Sebastian marries it will be a most proper young woman, a woman of unquestionable lineage and impeccable behavior."

"A blue blood," Devon said slowly.

"A blue blood," he confirmed. "Nothing less will do for Sebastian." He hitched his chin toward the corner, where a woman had paused before the harp. "If I were to wager, I'd lay odds on Penelope Harding. She's quiet. Intelligent. Genteel."

Devon didn't want to look. She didn't want to see the woman who might well end up Sebastian's bride. Yet no power on earth could have stopped her.

The lump in her throat was almost painful. "She's quite lovely," she said wistfully.

Petite, with sleek black hair, Penelope Harding was arranging her skirts over a stool before the harp. Even as Devon watched, Sebastian joined her. He said something. Penelope nodded, her exquisite features lighting up. Lace-tipped fingers reached out to strum the strings of the harp.

She began to sing.

The room was filled with the sweetest, purest sound that Devon had ever heard.

Long after Justin's return to the party, long after the last note had died, long after the applause had ended and the guests moved into the dining room, Devon sat alone in the dark. Unmoving.

Desperately trying to wish away the rending ache in her breast.

Perhaps it was Justin's words. Perhaps it was the way everyone in the room had paused to listen in wonderment to the sweet-voiced Penelope. Perhaps it was the way Sebastian had immediately lent his hand to help the stunning Penelope to her feet. She sang like an angel. And dressed in gleaming white silk, she looked like one too.

Devon gazed down at her lap. She suddenly felt cheap and tawdry, sitting there in her pretty new gown.

When the evening began, she had almost fancied herself in love with Sebastian.

But now, with the night almost ended, she swallowed a pang. To fall in love with a man like Sebastian . . . that would be unwise, she told herself. Very, very unwise. For Sebastian was as far above her as a star glittering high in a moonlit sky.

And she was just a pebble in the mire.

As for the kiss they'd shared, no wonder he'd apologized. She was a fool to think it had been anything beyond a whim.

She would do well to remember that.

Thirteen

A few days later Sebastian entered the library to find Devon sitting in a chair, her legs dangling over the side.

"My dear, a lady always has her feet on the ground."

"And a gentleman is never without his coat." She glanced pointedly at his forearms, bare where he'd rolled up his sleeves.

"Touché." He cocked a brow but made no effort to slip on his coat, which lay draped over the chair behind his desk. He seated himself, then looked her over. "A bit testy today, are we?"

Her eyes flashed.

"Perhaps luncheon didn't agree with you then?"

There was no reply. She was supposed to be studying her geography. She'd spent much of the morning at the writing table, staring into space, an expression of consternation on her lovely features.

Rising from his desk, he moved to the globe alongside it. "Devon?" He gestured her forward.

With a sigh she rose.

"Where is the Cape of Good Hope?"

She gestured vaguely in the vicinity of the North Pole.

"Interesting," he commented dryly. "That was not where it was yesterday."

Her mouth turned down. "What does it matter? I'm never going there anyway."

This was serious, he decided.

"Very well, then. Show me where London is. I know you've been there."

Grudgingly she made a tiny circle with a fingertip.

"Very good," he approved.

Devon didn't look at him. The set of her shoulders was stiff. She seemed very unlike herself; she'd been subdued of late, without her usual brimming vibrance.

"Are you ill, Devon?"

"No. And you are growing quite tiresome, sir."

"And you are being quite inattentive."

At least he'd managed to gain her attention.

Her gaze finally swung to his. "Why are you bothering with this, Sebastian? With me? After you come home from your parties in the evening, you're up until the wee hours of the morning. I know. I've seen the light burning under the door."

He subjected her to a cautiously guarded scrutiny. The faint shadows beneath her eyes bore out the fact that she wasn't sleeping. So she hadn't ceased her nocturnal wandering. He wasn't about to challenge her now, not in the mood she was in.

"I like the night," he said lightly. "I always have."

True as the statement was, it was clear he hadn't convinced her.

Yet there was no question it was difficult to attend to work during their lessons. Sometimes when she stood bent over the long, mahogany table at the center of the room, he eyed that delectable little bottom swaying first one way, then the other, her brow furrowed in concentration. She didn't want him looking at her breasts, so he contented himself with the view at hand.

But it was more than that.

The duties that had always been so important to him were almost an afterthought. He'd far rather spend time with Devon than at the social affairs that demanded his presence so he could search for a bride. With Devon, there was no need to stand on social graces or formality. He didn't have to stand behind his title. As for Devon, well, she was certainly never boring. No matter her lack of knowledge; she was keenly intelligent and had only to gain it. She didn't mince words and she didn't hide behind incessant chatter, simpering laughter, and empty, mindless conversation. She was entertaining as no other woman had ever been.

He didn't want to give that up—thus his late hours. And he wasn't about to set her aside. Until now she had reveled in her studies.

"This isn't about me," he said. "I thought you enjoyed learning."

"I do."

A grudging, less than enthusiastic response—and one she wouldn't have made two weeks ago. He frowned. "You've been acting strangely these last few days. What's wrong?"

Her gaze slid away. "Nothing," she said in a small voice.

"I know you better than that," he said firmly. "Have you changed your mind? I thought you wanted to be a governess."

"I do. But . . ."

The hesitation declared her misery, which in turn played on his heartstrings. Bracing his hip against his desk, he reached for her, catching his fingers around hers and tugging her close.

"But what?" His gaze roved over her features.

Soft, pink lips compressed tightly.

"Devon—" he began in soft warning.

"Oh, all right! If you must know, I—I can't sing."

Sebastian blinked.

"I beg your pardon?"

"You heard me. If I ever did, there would be a stampede through the doors and into the streets."

For a heartbeat Sebastian simply stared at her dumbly. Then understanding dawned.

"You heard Penelope."

She nodded miserably.

He wanted very much to laugh, but for the sake of his own preservation, suspected he didn't dare. "Devon," he said carefully, "few can sing like Penelope."

His tack didn't appear to be working. Perhaps encouragement was what was needed.

He tried again. "It may be that you just think you can't sing."

"No," she said almost frantically. "I can't. Listen."

She commenced a quavering, cracking melody. Sebastian hastily extinguished what he feared she might construe—and rightly so!—as a look of pain.

In the corner Beast sat up and howled.

Sebastian shot the mongrel a quelling look.

Devon had finished and now gazed at him expectantly. Sebastian took in the discouraged slump of her shoulders. By Jove, he needed to tread more carefully than ever right now. Her ego seemed particularly fragile.

"Devon, there's more to being a lady than the ability to sing."

"Yes," she said bitterly, "I know."

"Perhaps your talent lies in the pianoforte—"

"Perhaps I have no talent at all."

He studied her. "Odd. I didn't think you were the type to give in so easily."

"Give in, give up, I daresay I'm doing neither. I'm being honest. You value honesty, don't you?"

"Most highly."

"Then stop trying to goad me."

"I am hardly trying to—"

"Please, Sebastian, let me finish. It's not just Penelope. I saw the ladies at your dinner party. And I can never be a lady like that. Ever," she said fiercely. "I'm not sulking. I'm not envious—or perhaps I am! Oh, I know as a governess I wouldn't be privy to such affairs. I'm aware a governess or companion can never aspire to climb to the same scale as society's upper crust. But if I am to teach their children, or sit as companion to some rich old woman, I must have the proper deportment—"

"You'll *have* the proper deportment if you sit up straight."

"It's not just that." She waved a finger at the globe, the volumes spread out on the tabletop. Her features grew pained. "It's everything. I can't sew; how the devil can I learn to embroider? I helped my mother with a gown once, and ended up sewing the sleeves up tight as a drum! I'll never be able to sketch, there's no sense in even trying—I'll likely vex your poor sister into a premature grave! I'll never learn French. I'm still trying to read our own language." Her voice broke ever so slightly. She steadied it before going on bravely. "I don't think I have a prayer, Sebastian. I thought I could do this. But there's so very much to learn—"

"Devon, hush."

"Sebastian, I—"

"*Hush.*"

Her lovely lips were quivering. Sebastian's heart contracted.

"Listen to me, Devon," he said softly, "and listen well. I am ever so pleased at the inroads you've made in your education. It's truly quite amazing."

She gave a tiny shake of her head. "You're just saying that."

"No." He was adamant. "I am not. I believe you're simply feeling overwhelmed. It's not surprising, really. You've taken in an incredible amount of knowledge in a very short time. What has it been? A little over a month since we began? No more than that, surely."

With a fingertip, he traced the two faint lines etched between the delicate bridge of her nose. "Now," he said gravely. "Have I made you feel better?"

Her eyes clung to his, as if to seek whether he spoke sincerely. She must have been satisfied, for at last she nodded. "Yes, you have." Her tone was solemn, but her lips had curled up in a wispy smile. "You always do."

Sebastian caught his breath. He wanted to kiss her.

He wanted to kiss her quite badly. But she might think his only intention was to have his way with her, and he didn't want that.

His eyes slid from her, to the globe, and back again. He'd traveled the world over. He'd ridden camels in Egypt. Sweated and steamed in India. Yesterday he'd shown her all the places in the world he'd traveled to.

St. Giles was the only world Devon had ever known.

My God, he thought, *she's been to hell and back.*

"Straighten your spine and take a deep, invigorating breath, my dear. Because I think I know something that will make you feel even better."

He led her into the entrance hall, where he called for the carriage and her cloak.

"Sebastian!" She blinked. "What are you doing?"

"We're going out," he announced.

Her eyes widened. "Out! Where?"

Placing a dainty hand in the crook of his elbow, he smothered it with his own. "To see the world you've never seen."

The coach rolled into the countryside where the air was warm and sweet and the skies blue and brilliant. Devon sat with her nose pressed to the window, utterly entranced by the scenery rushing by outside. Sebastian sat next to her, utterly entranced by *her*.

In a small, picturesque little village outside London, they took supper at a charming roadside inn. She ate with gusto, her spirit regained. She was animated and lively, and Sebastian was heartily glad he'd taken her away for the day. The change in scenery was just what she needed after being stifled in such close quarters for so long.

It was dark when they arrived back in the city. Passing through Grosvenor Square, she twisted her head to look at the sprawling house at the end of the square. He laughed to himself, for she was frankly gawking.

"My word, it looks like a temple in one of your books!"

"It does," he agreed. "The dowager duchess of Carrington lives there."

"Oh, yes, she was at your dinner party the other night. Justin pointed her out."

Several minutes later they passed by a brick-fronted Georgian town house. "Oh, I adore that one! Who lives there?"

"Viscount Temberly."

Her mouth promptly turned down at the corners.

"On second thought, it's quite hideous."

Sebastian raised his brows. "Now that's an about-face," he mused. "Dare I ask why?"

"I don't like him," she said shortly.

"Devon, you don't even know him."

He paused. His regard sharpened, his amusement fled, his mouth thinned. He was suddenly steaming. Temberly wasn't known for keeping his hands to himself when it came to a fetching woman, but Temberly's brother was a good friend, thus he had felt obliged to include the viscount.

But now he wondered if Devon had encountered Temberly the night of his dinner party. Had something happened he didn't know about? Something she hadn't told him? Was that what was responsible for her sleepless nights? By God, if Temberly had so much as looked at her, he would strangle him!

He shifted so he faced her more fully. He'd know if

she was hiding anything. "What," he asked in steely tones, "has Temberly done to earn such disfavor?"

"He has a wife *and* a mistress."

The bunching in his shoulders eased. "How do you know about that? No"—he held up a hand—"let me guess. Justin again." If Sebastian was just a little annoyed, he couldn't help it. Justin not only set tongues to wagging; he was quite adept at wagging his own.

"And you?" she asked calmly. "What about you, Sebastian? Will you keep a mistress when you're wed?"

She referred to his quest for a bride. There was no need to ask how she knew, not that it was a secret, of course. But he'd never spoken of it with her—what need was there? But lately it had been a subject of much speculation in every scandal sheet in the city—and he'd seen her reading the gossips in the paper of late. It had given him a moment's pause when he realized it was the gossips she devoured with such fervor, but he'd thought it would be good for her reading skills.

She'd chided him about honesty. He could be no less than honest. "I don't know."

"You don't know," she repeated.

"No. Certainly I can't exclude the possibility. And the fact is, most gentlemen do."

"I see," she said in honeyed tones. "Tell me. Do you expect your wife to be faithful?"

"She *will* be faithful," he answered grimly, "or she damn well won't be my wife."

"So you will demand her loyalty?"

"Fidelity and loyalty go hand in hand," came his prompt affirmation.

"Correct me then if I misunderstand," she said with an acid bite, "but you expect your wife's unquestioning honor and devotion and faithfulness, while you refuse to give your own?"

"I wouldn't quite put it that way. She will do her duty as a wife and I will do mine as a husband."

"And what if she takes a lover?"

His eyes glinted. "She will not! A man needs to know his heirs are his!"

"Yet you may choose to have a mistress. It's the same, is it not?"

"It most certainly is not!"

She regarded him, the line of her mouth compressed, her golden eyes stormy.

He sighed. "Devon, the ways of the *ton* are different. You don't understand—"

"Oh, I understand," she said coldly. "I understand that it's wrong for a man to have a mistress as well as a wife. A husband should be faithful to his wife, as she should be faithful to him. A man should cherish his wife, as she should cherish him! And for a man supposedly concerned about propriety, I would think you would know that!"

Well, he thought, she was certainly adamant about right and wrong. He snuffed out a laugh before she caught it. Still, he was impressed. Her sermon conveyed an unswerving loyalty. It resounded with faith and commitment between loved ones.

The very values he himself held so dear.

He tried to touch her sleeve; she wrenched her arm away.

"Devon," he said softly, "you might be interested in knowing I no longer have a mistress." Why he was confiding such a thing, he wasn't quite certain.

Yet something inside, something he didn't fully comprehend, compelled it.

"Why should I be interested?" she flared.

Why indeed, he decided, settling back on the cushions. The carriage hit a bump in the road. It swerved a bit, and he reached out to steady her. This time she didn't draw away. The very next instant that upturned little nose was pointed his way again.

"What happened to her?" she inquired stiffly. "The lovely Lilly, isn't it? Did the two of you have a falling out?"

How the devil did she know about Lilly? Ah. Justin again, no doubt, he realized in annoyance.

But he'd started this. Now he wasn't quite sure how to finish it. He could hardly admit he'd gone to Lilly one evening a few nights after Devon's arrival. He'd taken one look at her and felt . . . nothing. Her ardent kiss of greeting left him cold. There was no answering spark, no sizzle of desire.

He'd known then and there that it was over, and so he'd said. Lilly's outrage was natural, he supposed. She'd made quite a scene, until he'd offered a more than generous settlement. Then she had practically purred . . .

Those particular details, however, were not something he intended to reveal to Devon.

"It was time we parted."

"And you let her go, just like that?"

Her tone was rather accusing. Such logic defeated him. He thought she'd be pleased!

"The lovely Lilly, as you call her, will find someone else. Word is she already has."

"But what if she doesn't?"

"She will. That's the way it is with"—there was an awkward pause—"with women like her," he finished.

"I will assume from that declaration that you've had many mistresses then."

Sebastian shifted uncomfortably. It was a statement, not a question. Yet he was aware from her expression that an answer was expected. But how the hell was he supposed to answer *that*? Their conversation had veered off in a direction he hadn't foreseen. Which was precisely why he *should* have expected it, for when was he going to learn to expect the unexpected from Devon?

He found himself in a rare struggle for words. "I am one-and-thirty," he said carefully, "so yes, I've had several mistresses."

"Perhaps you have many children then." Her features were etched with disapproval.

"I don't. I made certain of it." His answer resounded with absolute finality.

"How?" she demanded.

"You know. There are ways." He gestured vaguely. "Men have ways. Women have ways . . ." His voice trailed off. The oddest notion came over him as he stared across at her.

They were almost home. The carriage was slowing as they approached the carriage house.

"Devon," he said cautiously, "surely you're aware of the ways men and women can avoid having children?"

"I am not!" She appeared to be gritting her teeth. "I have no need of such knowledge!"

It took a moment to digest the full import of that vehement assertion. The grasp of his mind faltered. Was she suggesting that . . .

A searing, heartfelt curse blackened the air. "Are you telling me you're a virgin?"

The door opened. A crimson liveried footman bowed, then offered a hand in assistance.

"My lord," she stated primly, "your language is abominable."

"My language will get much worse if you don't answer me!"

She gathered up her skirts and glanced back over her shoulder, her round little chin tipped high. "I do believe," she stated pleasantly, "you may draw your own conclusion."

Fourteen

Devon was a virgin. Sweet Christ, a virgin.

Hours later Sebastian's mind still churned, along with his insides.

Every pore in his being warned it was true. Yet how could that be, living as she had in that wretched hovel in St. Giles? Working at that hellhole, the Crow's Nest? Walking the dangerous streets at night as she had, a woman alone and defenseless, pitted against the very scum of the earth?

But then again, there were the circumstances that had brought her to his house. He found himself revising his conclusion slightly—perhaps she wasn't totally defenseless. She had armed herself with a dagger, and she possessed the strength and fortitude to use it. And she'd employed the very best weapon of all—her wits. The fact that she'd garbed herself as a woman heavy with child was really quite resourceful. Ingenious, even. Still . . .

Just when he thought he knew her . . . he didn't.

She wasn't the harlot he'd first thought. After her tirade the day he'd caught her rifling through his belongings, he'd told himself he couldn't blame her for doing what was necessary to survive. Though he'd given her necklace back, occasionally he found himself speculating about its origins; she wore it always. Once clean, it had looked to be a costly piece. Was it true it was a gift to her mother from a well-to-do fellow?

A virgin. Lord God, a virgin!

A corner of Sebastian's mouth turned up derisively. There was, he decided with black humor, one sure way to find out.

Not likely, he told himself with a self-deprecating laugh. There was little chance he'd be well-received. She was still sizzling when she'd sailed to her room.

It was not in Sebastian's nature to be reckless. It was *not*.

It didn't stop him from wanting to mount the stairs and mount *her*. It didn't stop him from wanting to strip away every last stitch of clothing until she was naked and writhing in his arms. It didn't stop his scalding need to lick and taste and suckle those glorious, glorious breasts until he had his fill. It didn't stop him from yearning to hear her scream and moan with pleasure as he plunged his rod inside her, again and again.

That was the uncivilized part of him.

The civilized part of him wasn't so very different, he admitted. Knowing she was asleep at the top of the stairs tempted him, tempted him mightily.

But not beyond reason. Not beyond his limits, he told himself.

He'd not succumbed thus far, and he *would* not.

He was not a man to indulge his every whim, to obey every base urge that arose, for he was not a man of fancy. Said urges and whims must be considered and weighed. The consequences, whatever those consequences might be, must be calculated and measured before the choice was made to discard or execute.

Besides, she was an innocent—sweet God above, he couldn't lie to himself!—and that only made him burn for her all the more. But she was living under his roof, under his care, his protection. No matter how the flames of desire seared his senses and heated his blood, he would not dishonor her by venting his passion.

Particularly after their exchange in the carriage this evening.

A disconcerting thought struck him then. Had her mother been some man's mistress? Was Devon the result? Was that why she was so staunchly opposed to men with mistresses?

A pang cut through him. God, but this house would be lonely without her. For she filled it with spirit and life and laughter.

As she was filling him.

An odd tightness wedged in his chest, until he could scarcely breathe. He felt almost raw inside. "Devon," he whispered with a touch of raggedness, "ah, Devon, what am I going to do with you?"

Dear God, what would he do *without* her?

His mood verged on brooding. A brandy was what he needed. A good, strong brandy. With purposeful steps, he strode toward the library and his chair. Christ, he needed to think.

But his chair was already occupied.

* * *

Devon was dreaming. Of a day filled with quiet serenity. Of lush summer gardens abrim with greenery, the silvery tinkle of water through a fountain and sunlight streaming through the gauzy white clouds. But, alas, a storm approached. The air was suddenly crackling. Lightning flashed and thunder raged. In her dream, she shifted, wanting to return to that splendid world of sunshine.

"Devon. *Devon*."

She jumped. The thunder was upon her now. In fact, it boomed directly at her ear.

Her eyes drifted open. Sebastian towered over her, his features as blackly fierce as the storm in her dream.

"Go away," she muttered.

He did not.

"Devon, Beast . . . *Dumpling* . . . has taken over my chair."

"For pity's sake," she grumbled sleepily, "you're bigger than she is. Move her." She rolled to her side and prepared to go back to sleep.

"Considering her circumstances, I doubt that's wise."

Full consciousness kicked in. Devon bounded out of bed toward the door. "It's time," she said urgently.

Sebastian was at her heels as she flew down the stairs. "You knew," he bit out furiously. "You knew, didn't you?"

"What!" she retorted. "You mean you didn't?"

He took her elbow, hurrying her along. To reply would have been to incriminate himself further. He was still grumbling when he threw open the library doors. "My God," he muttered under his breath, "that creature is whelping in my chair!"

Devon was just close enough that she could hear. She preceded him inside. "I really thought you would have figured it out by now." She couldn't resist teasing him just a little more. "I mean, really, Sebastian. You must have dogs at your estates. Horses—"

"So that's why she has the appetite of one!"

Devon was hardly well versed in the subject of whelping, but in this, at least, she appeared to have a more extensive knowledge than he.

"I expect so." Devon eased down before Sebastian's chair, taking in Dumpling's situation. Dumpling stopped pawing and circling and lay down, pleading mutely with her mistress. Devon frowned, running a soothing hand along Dumpling's back.

They didn't have long to wait. Not more than a few minutes passed before Dumpling began to whine and yip and cry. Sebastian ceased his pacing before the fireplace.

"Devon," he ground out frantically, "we must do something."

Devon eyed him. He was down to his shirtsleeves, white as his cravat, now but a rumpled pile of silk ground beneath his heels. The ties of his shirt hung open, halfway down his chest. Devon's stomach dropped at the sight of the hair-matted expanse of his chest. Her palms grew damp. His forearms were like that too, large and muscled and covered with silky black hair. She stared in riveted fascination, wondering if the rest of his body was covered likewise.

Hastily she averted her eyes. What the deuce had he asked? Ah, yes.

"She's giving birth, Sebastian. She has to do all the work."

And she did. She yelped and heaved and panted and strained until Sebastian could stand it no longer. He sank to one knee beside Devon. He swallowed hard, then stretched out a hand toward Dumpling.

"That's the way," he said tentatively. "You can do it, girl. I know you can."

Something amazing happened then. A wet, tiny little body slithered into view. Sebastian was still staring when something even more amazing happened.

Dumpling licked his hand.

Three more bodies eventually joined the first. When it appeared no more were forthcoming, Sebastian glanced at her hopefully. "Is she finished, do you think?"

Devon ventured a cautious opinion. "I believe so."

Sebastian released a great, wracking breath. With the back of his hand he wiped the sweat from his brow.

"That was exhausting."

Probably more so for Sebastian, she decided with a grin, than it had been for Dumpling.

She leaned forward. Prudently gauging the new mother's reaction, she picked up the newborns, peering beneath each. Her eyes widened. "Oh, my," she exclaimed. "Sebastian, they're all boys!"

Returned to Dumpling's side, they were making tiny, mewling sounds, instinctively seeking the warmth of their mother. With her nose, Dumpling nudged them close to her belly.

"We should make sure the library stays warm tonight," she said.

"I'll tend the fire myself," he promised.

"And names. They should have names, don't you think?"

"Excellent idea," he approved. "What shall they be?"

"I don't know. Perhaps," she said tentatively, "we should leave it up to you."

"Me! Why?"

"I got to name Dumpling, and I know you've never taken a particular liking to the name *I* chose." The comment was accompanied by a telling, sidelong glance. "So I think it's only right that you should name her babies, especially since they're boys."

Sebastian was looking very pleased. He traced a smooth, hairless tummy. "This one's the biggest," he stated with authority. "And he was born first. Therefore, he shall be the General. This one"—he circled a tiny ear—"the Colonel, I think. Followed by the Major and the Captain, of course."

Devon clapped her hands delightedly. "That's quite clever!"

"Thank you," he returned. "It was my pleasure." He turned his head, his gaze roving warmly over her features. "You look very happy," he told her softly.

"I am," she said simply.

They sat shoulder to shoulder, her nightgown frilled about her bare feet. It was a moment steeped in contentment and satisfaction.

Neither one heard Justin push the door open. "Well, well," he drawled, "if it isn't Mummy and Daddy admiring the brood. How many are there?"

"Four. And all males," Sebastian informed him proudly.

Justin advanced. "I confess, I began to think the blessed event would never occur."

Devon stole a glance at Sebastian, whose expression had gone pained. At the same instant Sebastian leveled a warning glance at Devon. Her shoulders quivered with mirth as she struggled not to laugh.

Justin ambled close to Dumpling. He stretched out an idle hand toward the tiniest puppy.

Dumpling lunged.

Justin leaped back. "She nipped me! By God, I should have known not to trust a female!"

Sebastian laughed outright. "Well, what do you know? You, my good man, have just been disdained," he said mildly. "A first, is it not? Perhaps it's a sign of things to come." He scratched the tummy of the same pup. Dumpling rubbed her head against his hand.

Justin was still scowling. "I'll have you know I've not lost one iota of my charm."

"Oh, come now," Sebastian said, laughing again. "Bite your tongue, lest those words come back to haunt you."

"You'd enjoy that, wouldn't you?"

Sebastian grinned. "I do believe I would."

"Since it's obvious you delight in tormenting me," Justin announced, "I shall take my leave. Good night, Devon. Good night, brother."

Neither of them moved when Justin left. Devon felt herself growing tired again. Her eyelids were heavy, but she didn't want to move. Being so close to Sebastian like this . . . it felt so good. He was all solid, heavy warmth. This . . . this feeling inside her, surrounding her, she longed to never let it go, to savor it forever. For never had she felt so safe. So secure. If she snuggled closer, would he notice . . . ?

The next thing she knew, a muscled arm was sliding about her shoulders and under her knees. She felt herself being borne high in the air.

Her lips brushed the side of his throat. A sleepy protest emerged. "I'm watching Dumpling and her babies."

A laugh rumbled in his chest, beneath the very place where her hand resided. "My sweet, you've been sleeping against my shoulder for the last hour."

My sweet.

All at once her heart squeezed. It was foolish to read more into the words than there really was, she thought with a pang. It was just a careless endearment, something he probably didn't even realize he'd uttered.

"Put your arms around me," he whispered.

But her arms had already stolen around his neck. She pressed her face into his neck, reveling in his latent power.

Her gaze trickled up, past the corded tendons of his neck, to the sculpted beauty of his lips. It never wavered as he carried her with effortless ease up the stairs and into her chamber.

Moonlight seeped in through the curtains, spilling over the stark planes of his features. Her heart aflutter, she took in the raw masculinity of his face. So close she couldn't stop herself, she placed a fingertip on the cleft in his chin that held such fascination for her.

"You're very handsome," she said gravely.

Slowly he lowered her to the rumpled bedcovers. Something flashed in his eyes, and suddenly she felt she could see into his soul. She sensed an uncharacteristic uncertainty.

"I'm not," he said with a shake of his head. "Justin's the handsome one."

Devon sat up. "So are you," she said quietly.

He sighed. "Thank you for saying that, Devon, but I see myself for what I am. And I'm too big. Too dark. When I was young, other children used to call me a Gypsy." Taking her hand, he splayed her fingers wide against his. Next to hers, his were massive. His palm was warm and rough, making her quiver in warm, forbidden places. Even in the dark, the contrast between their skin was marked.

"You see? Your hands . . . they're half the size of mine." A ghost of a smile crossed his lips. "*You're* half the size of me." His hand fell away.

Her regard sharpened. What was this? She sensed an elusive hurt. "You're the talk of the town, Sebastian. Why, every available miss in London vies to be your bride. I saw it myself, in this very house. All those ladies, practically swooning at your feet. Why, you could have your pick of any woman in London."

"Well, that's probably true, but let me enhance your education further, Devon. It's because they yearn to be a marchioness. Not necessarily *my* marchioness. It's a powerful lure. Marriages founded in love are rare. They're usually founded in mutual advantage. And I don't mean to sound petty or small, because I love my brother dearly, but if Justin were the marquess, no one would look twice at me."

Devon was shocked. Dumbfounded. That this supremely confident man could even harbor such a ridiculous notion was totally unbelievable. But even as she felt the shock settle through her, she was also touched beyond measure that he had confided such a thing to her. Not many men, she suspected, would have dared to risk exposing themselves so.

"Indeed, he's known as the handsomest man in all England—"

"Yes, yes, I know about that." She rolled her eyes. "But what you just said . . . that if Justin were the marquess, no one would even look at you . . . Why, that is absolutely not true," she informed him stoutly.

"I'm afraid it is, Devon. I do not delude myself."

"It is not true," she insisted, "and you shouldn't think that. Do you want to know why?"

His lips quirked ever so slightly. "I suspect you're going to tell me."

She clasped his hands between hers—tightly, letting him know she wouldn't countenance any withdrawal—the way he'd once done with her.

"I am. You say you see yourself for what you are. Well, let me tell you what *I* see. I see a man with a splendid chest and marvelous shoulders—why, I noticed it right off! That night when I woke—here in this very bed—I could hardly take my eyes off you. Granted, I speak only for myself, but I can't imagine it would be so very different for other women. I daresay most would admire a man who stands head and shoulders above all others, a man with great hands like yours, a man who makes a woman feel dainty and small and protected. Every morning I see you sitting at your desk, the sunlight making your hair gleam like a raven's, and I think I've never seen a man so dashing as you."

With each breath, with each word, her voice gained

fervor, and so did the emotions welling in her breast.

"You, Sebastian Sterling, are strikingly handsome in a way that . . . well, quite simply . . . you steal my breath away . . . you make me shiver inside. And your brother has certainly never done *that*."

It didn't come out quite the way she intended. Had she said too much? No matter, for it was done. And now she could only pray that she'd managed to convince him.

She braved a tentative glance upward.

The air was suddenly alive with a vibrating tension. Sebastian was staring at her intently. As their eyes collided, something flashed in his, something she'd never seen before. He looked as if he wanted to devour her. Consume her.

She fought an irrational fluttering of her pulse, but it was no use. Everything seemed to stand still, the very world, her very heart. Ah, yes, especially her heart! For one blinding, heart-stopping moment, she was convinced he would kiss her.

She had been cozily warm as he carried her up the stairs, but suddenly she felt hot. They sat so close, a steely hard thigh rode gently against her own. Her breath grew meager. His nearness made her tremble inside. She wanted his touch. She wanted it like nothing she'd ever felt before. Wanted it like misty rain upon sun-parched earth.

His voice came through the charged silence. "Devon," he said, "don't ever . . . *ever* . . . tell a man what you just told me." He leaned forward, his jaw locked tight. "Because the next man will surely ravish you on the spot."

She wanted *him* to ravish her on the spot.

But his smile had vanished, and confusion churned in her belly. His expression was utterly fierce, his features tense and strained.

Her smile ebbed. Her heart quavered, along with her fledgling courage. She stared at him through clouded eyes. Perhaps she'd been blinded. Blinded by the moonlight. Blinded by him. Blinded by all the pent-up emotion held deep in her breast.

She felt herself flailing. She had made blunders before, but Sebastian had never looked like this . . . never like this.

"Promise me, Devon." His fingers now gripped her own, his hold like steel.

The hurt was immense, a giant fist crashing down upon her heart. Her throat ached so badly she could hardly speak. "Sebastian . . ."

"Promise me."

She gave a tiny shake of her head. "I promise," she whispered raggedly. "I promise . . ."

He released her.

Pierced to the quick, she turned her face aside. She couldn't watch him leave. When the door clicked shut, she raised a fist to her lips, smothering a dry sob. She didn't understand! Was it so awful, what she'd said? Had she overstepped her bounds? Been too familiar? When she was with him, she never thought twice about the differences between them. It didn't matter that he was a marquess, and she was a nobody. He was simply Sebastian . . .

But there was no denying the thunderous whirlwind swirling inside him. She had sensed it with all that she possessed. What was it? Anger? Disapproval? She thought of all she'd confided. God knew, it was true, every word. He *was* handsome. Devastatingly so. And she'd thought he would be pleased . . .

Clearly she was wrong.

Sebastian was a man who prided himself on his control. Not only by nature, but by necessity. To repair the shambles his parents had made of the family name, to restore the respect earned by previous generations of his ancestors, there had been no other choice.

In that moment, in that room, his control almost shattered.

It was only by clenching his fists, squeezing his eyes shut, fighting the powerful roil of emotions flying inside him, and lifting his face to the heavens that he was able to empower himself to walk away.

Where he found the strength of will, he didn't know.

He couldn't do it again.

For a man like Sebastian, it was not an easy thing to face. From the beginning, his every instinct had warned that Devon would turn his household upside down. He simply hadn't known how much.

He'd never suspected she'd turn *him* upside down.

He was thoroughly disgusted with himself for feeling the way he did about Devon. He was a man of vigilant deliberation. He hadn't planned this, and he didn't like being caught in this haze of conflicting emotion.

Affection was one thing. He didn't mind that. But this twisting in his vitals, this burning in his soul . . .

I don't need this, he thought. *I don't.* She had his heart, mind, and body ensnared in . . . what? Infatuation? Surely not. He was far too old. Far too smart.

Yet what other explanation was there?

When she was near, he felt wholly out of control, his entire being in upheaval. When he woke in the morning, he thought of her. Only of her . . .

She was the last thing on his mind when sleep drifted in, each and every night.

Christ, she even consumed his dreams! Many a night his traitorous mind swam with searing, blatantly erotic visions of Devon. How many times had he awakened, he wondered, panting and sweating, his rod stiff and swollen like an iron pike?

Always she was naked. *Always* in his arms. He saw her molded against him, his tongue buried in the moist cave of her mouth, a silken leg caught between the hardness of his, their limbs questing restlessly, her breasts burning like a brand against his chest. He saw his hands fill with the luscious globes of those soft, ivory mounds, his fingertips playing a maddeningly elusive rhythm around delectable, sunrise-colored nipples until she cried out and begged for the taste of his mouth. Sometimes she lay beneath him, her legs parted and wide, the clasp of her body hot and wet and tight around his rigid shaft as he drove inside her again and again.

Once the night sky cast a hazy glow about her form, her hair a tangle of gilded moonlight; it spilled over his belly as she pushed herself upright . . . atop him. He couldn't tear his eyes away as she braced herself on his chest and slowly came down on his hardness . . . this, the most startlingly vivid image of all.

He woke with the sheets wet from his seed—Christ, he hadn't spilled himself in his dreams since he was a stripling green lad dreaming of bedding his first woman. Even now he could feel his blood rush hot and thick, a twisting, fisted heat unfurling in his gut.

God, what a joke! *He* was supposed to be teaching her to be a lady, a proper, refined lady of quality.

But there was nothing proper about his thoughts when he was with her. And Sebastian did not like this unreasoning desire. He wasn't sure how to stop it—or even if he could.

Fifteen

Walking into Sebastian's study the next morning was difficult. Facing him, she suspected, would not be easy, for she was still smarting from his rebuke. In fact, she did an about-face at least three times before she was even halfway across the floor of her room. Regardless of what had occurred the night before, she was going to have to face him again sometime. She dreaded it with every fiber of her being, but what would be served by prolonging her agony? Thus reasoning, she threw open her bedroom door and marched down the stairs.

She paused at the door to his study. He was seated behind his desk, busily writing. The morning light cast his profile in stark relief, arresting and noble and proud. Her heart went out to him, for he appeared tired; there were faint grooves beside his mouth.

Her eyes slipped to his hands, so lean and strong. Her pulse gave an odd little flutter. For an instant, she remembered the way he'd fitted their hands together last night. It made her ache inside—and nearly sent her fleeing before he saw her.

But something held her there, some force beyond her control. And when he glanced up and saw her, she didn't look away. She couldn't.

For the span of a heartbeat, their eyes tangled. Sebastian didn't shrink from her regard, but she could detect nothing of his thoughts. She held her breath and braced herself inside, waiting tensely for what would come next.

A heavy brow slanted. His mouth carried the faintest hint of amusement as it curved into a faint smile. "There's no need to stand there," he said almost lightly. "You hardly need an invitation."

Swallowing hard, Devon stepped forward. His demeanor was . . . well, quite normal. It was reassuring . . . and yet *not* so reassuring. He acted as if nothing had happened the previous night.

She didn't know what to make of it. She didn't know what to make of *him*.

So it was that beneath the roof of the Sterling residence, matters continued much as before. The days turned into a week, a week turned into several.

More than ever, Devon was determined not to fail in her studies. She *would* find a post as governess or companion. No matter that she had entered late in the game, she *would* succeed.

And learning to read had opened up the world, in a way she had never dreamed it would. History was a favorite. To her it was never dry or boring. She loved stepping into a world of faraway places and distant times. She had a definite dislike for mathematics, but she applied herself prodigiously, and Sebastian was pleased.

Given her newfound interest, she had taken to reading every night. As long she was here, she was determined to avail herself of Sebastian's library.

On this particular night, just after midnight she closed a small, leather-bound book. Sebastian had found another book of folklore, and she had enjoyed it immensely. She wasn't tired, and she knew she wouldn't sleep if she tried, so why bother?

A visit to the library was in order, she decided. She glanced at Dumpling, sitting in a box next to the fireplace. Her ears pricked up when Devon pushed aside the coverlet and started across the rug, but she remained where she was.

Not so with the General, aptly named and ever the leader. On seeing her rise, he scrambled over the side of the box and bounded forward. The Colonel toddled but a tail behind, and now the Major and the Captain peered sleepily over the side of the fortress, their little heads cocked to the side. Chuckling, Devon scooped up the adventuresome pair, one beneath each arm. Briskly she tucked them back beside their brothers.

"You two stay where you are." Carefully she closed the door behind her. Playful and curious, every day the puppies ventured further from the box and their mother.

It was a ghastly night. Outside the wind howled and rain ran in rivers down the windowpanes.

The library door was open. Light flickered from within. Devon hesitated. Was Sebastian home early from the opera? She didn't want to disturb him if he was working.

"Come in, Devon. Don't be shy."

It was Justin, sprawled in the wing chair beside the secretaire, a glass of finely cut crystal in one hand. From the look of him and the pungent fumes in the air, he'd been imbibing quite heavily.

He saw the way her gaze encompassed the bottle of brandy on the rosewood side table. "An excellent year. Nothing but the best for my brother, you know." In one swallow he drained the contents of the glass.

Devon eyed him. If he relished the spirits so, then why did he grimace?

His voice rang out heartily. "Will you join me, Devon? No? Well, then, stay as you like. Or leave as you like." He reached for the bottle.

"Justin," she said levelly, "I think you've had enough."

"No, I have not. I have not had *nearly* enough."

Devon frowned. "You're rather disagreeable tonight."

"I'm always disagreeable when I'm drunk."

"Then why do you drink?"

"Why does any man drink? To escape life as he knows it."

"Why would you want to escape?" Devon was totally baffled. "You have everything. You're rich and—"

A black laugh erupted. "Devon, you are remarkably naive! Don't you know the life of the privileged is not always so privileged after all?"

"I don't know what you mean, Justin. This isn't like you—"

"Oh, yes, but it is, Devon. It is. Do you mean to tell me you don't see me for what I am? I'm not a do-gooder like Julianna—poor girl, look where it's got her! She's off hiding in Europe!"

Devon stared. She knew Julianna was traveling on the Continent, but . . . hiding?

Only a few days ago Sebastian has received a missive from his sister, stating she'd decided to extend her stay awhile longer. Sebastian hadn't looked pleased. Indeed, there had been a faint worry in his eyes.

"And I'm not like Sebastian. I never was. I never will be."

Taken aback by his abrasiveness, Devon stared.

"I can't live up to my brother's standards of perfection, Devon. My God, how could anyone, so why should I even try? I'm a wastrel. A rogue. Nothing I do pleases my brother, just as nothing I did ever pleased my father. Even Sebastian couldn't please our father."

Devon was too stunned to move.

"I remember hearing Father tell Sebastian that he must never forsake his duty. That he would someday be the marquess. Therefore he must always do what is right and proper. And if Sebastian didn't, Father took out the cane and whipped him. He must be schooled, Father said. He must be groomed. I remember once I tried to stop him. I thought he would kill me. I thought he would kill us both. And then Sebastian whipped me for daring to interfere. He said he could bear it, for it was his duty."

Devon scarcely heard this last. Her mind was still reeling. Their father had beaten Sebastian. *Beaten* him. She wanted to heave.

Justin was right. The life of the privileged wasn't so privileged after all.

"It's a good thing my brother isn't here," Justin finished with a dark smile. "He might disapprove of my drinking."

"Your brother *does* disapprove of your drinking."

Sebastian advanced into the library, fastidiously dressed in a crimson-lined opera cloak and evening clothes. His skin was tightly drawn over his cheekbones, his lips thin.

He looked absolutely ominous.

Justin was oblivious. Or perhaps he simply didn't care. Devon strongly suspected the latter.

With a clink the bottle connected with the rim of the glass.

"Let the tale continue then . . ."

Sebastian turned to Devon. "Please excuse us," he said curtly. "I should like a word with my brother."

"Oh, let her stay," Justin drawled. "It's only right she should be privy to the Sterling family secrets—why, she's practically family." He cocked a brow. "Does she know about Mama running off with her lover and turning her back on her children? No? I thought not."

Justin continued to address Devon.

"The scandal was atrocious, as you can imagine. What kind of woman would desert her children? It was hardly Mama's first infidelity, of course. Though to her credit, she waited until after we children were born. She and her companion, shall we say, were killed crossing the Channel."

"Justin—"

Justin paid no heed. "When Father died, Sebastian gathered up the reins of authority and took up where Father left off. He patched things up so we're received by society in the best drawing rooms in England. No more scandal, except for Julianna's. No one breathes a word of it, though. Why, it's almost as if that scandal too has been forgotten . . . except by poor Julianna, of course."

"That's quite enough," Sebastian warned icily.

An unpleasant smile rimmed Justin's mouth. "Is it? I don't need you to tell me how to run my life, Sebastian."

"Nor do you need me to tell you how to ruin it."

Devon had the feeling she'd been forgotten.

"Spare me the lecture. I'm a man, not a boy."

"Then perhaps it's time you acted like one. You have no sense of duty whatsoever. No sense of responsibility—"

"That's because you have enough for both of us." Justin's mouth twisted. "You're just like Father, you know. The title must come first. Duty must come first. Oh, yes, you fill his shoes quite tidily. Everything in order, always in its proper place . . . every*one* in order."

Sebastian took a step forward. His spine was inflexible, his posture rigid.

"By God," he said tautly, "I should like to—"

"What? Beat me?" Soft, mocking laughter filled the air. "Ah, yes. Oh, but that would make you Father's son indeed . . ."

There was a ringing silence. Justin's eyes locked unflinchingly with Sebastian's. Devon held her breath. For a timeless moment, the Sterling brothers engaged in furious, silent battle.

It was Sebastian who ended it. Turning on his heel, he strode from the library, his face an inscrutable mask.

His shout brought the footmen scrambling from their beds.

"Bring the carriage around," he ordered.

He continued toward the back entrance and the carriage house.

Devon flew after him. "Sebastian, wait!"

He gave no sign he'd even heard.

Damp, moist air rushed in as he flung open the door.

Somehow Devon managed to wedge herself between the frame of the door before he could step through.

"Step aside, if you please."

He was faultlessly polite, his façade one of utmost control. He didn't even look at her.

"Sebastian, where are you going?"

"Away," he snapped.

From the sound of him, he longed to tear someone apart.

She hoped it wouldn't be she.

"Are you all right?"

He made no answer. Strong hands closed about her waist. He set her aside bodily. It flashed through her mind that he looked right through her.

Undeterred, she raced after him, grabbing a fold of his cloak.

He spun around. "Are you trying to choke me?"

She let go. "You haven't answered me, Sebastian. Are you all right?" She peered up at him.

He looked at her then, and she saw it all. Through the rain, through the dark, she caught a glimpse of the ravaged tumult in his soul.

A rush of emotion squeezed her chest . . . She hurt inside, just as she knew that he hurt.

Yet not half as much as he hurt.

For there was something stark and vulnerable and lonely about him just now.

The heavens opened up, and so did her heart. Rain gushed from the skies, a drenching torrent. She stood her ground, uncaring that the rain pelted her face and soaked her nightgown, freezing her to the bone.

She braved a step forward. "You don't look all right."

Cursing beneath his breath, he whipped off his cloak and swung it over her shoulders. "Go inside," he ordered roughly. "You'll catch your death out here."

Engulfed in his warmth, engulfed in *him,* she shook her head, her throat so achingly tight she could not speak.

"Devon."

A world of pain bled through in the sound.

"I can't stay, Devon. I *can't.* Not now. Not tonight."

Devon sensed his frustration, felt it in every fiber of his body, heard his despair in his ragged expulsion of breath. He didn't know whether to push her away or drag her close.

She allowed him no choice, but hurtled herself against him.

"Then take me with you," she pleaded. "Wherever you're going, take me with you."

Sixteen

She caught at his vest . . . She caught at his heart.

Trapped in a maelstrom of emotion, he felt every muscle in his body constrict. He couldn't breathe, for his lungs were on fire. He couldn't find the strength to break away. He couldn't summon the will to leave her behind.

Her heavy hair had fallen down. Already sodden, it lay plastered to her scalp. Her gown clung to her skin—he'd shielded her too late. Dusky rose nipples poked tight little buttons against the silken confinement. Her lashes were spiky and wet . . . Tears or rain? he wondered achingly.

But it was the way she gazed at him . . . her lovely features so fervently expressive, those delicate, small-boned fingers so tightly gripping his vest. She could hide nothing, her golden eyes half pleading, half hopeful.

He felt as if he'd been punched squarely in the gut. "Devon," he said helplessly. "Ah, Devon . . ."

She shifted, moving her right hand, the movement ever so slight. A fingertip poised at the very center of his heart. The others twined even more tightly in his vest.

"Take me with you," she said quaveringly. "Sebastian, please, *take me with you.*"

She wouldn't let go.

Nor could he.

When the carriage sped forward, they were both in it.

Sebastian questioned no further. She pressed him no longer.

It was enough that she was here.

Enough that they were together.

London was left behind, along with the rain. An hour later, they hurtled down the narrow roads, lurching up the hills and chasing down the other side. A half moon slid out from behind a silvery frill of clouds. Sebastian found himself wishing for daylight, that Devon might see the glittering sapphire lakes and lazy placid valleys.

They rounded a curve. A wheel struck a pothole. Devon pitched forward into his lap. His arms closed around her instinctively, but it was a far different instinct indeed that kept her there. When she would have righted herself, there came a wordless sound of protest.

His.

Their eyes caught. Within hers lay a silent question. His embrace tightened, all the answer she appeared to need. When Sebastian tugged her small, slight form against the solid breadth of his chest, she nestled against him, turning her nose against the side of his neck, seeking his warmth. As he arranged the cloak around them both, he fancied he felt her smiling . . .

Dawn bathed the eastern hills in gilded splendor when at last the carriage turned up a long, winding lane, through massive, ivy-twined gates, past clipped, manicured lawns and gardens.

He roused Devon, who had fallen asleep just a short time earlier. She stirred, all sleepy-warm and drowsy. He kissed the small hand curled atop his chest and gently pushed her upright. "We've arrived," he said lightly.

A half smile curled his lips as they approached the house. It was, he decided as always, an impressive sight. Tall, Grecian columns dominated the center of the house. High mullioned windows framed in white marched down each wing. Devon's mouth dropped open as he swung her to the ground.

He smiled crookedly. "Welcome to Thurston Hall," he murmured.

Though Sebastian's appearance at the family estate was unexpected, a crimson-and-gold liveried footman was there to usher them within. Sebastian put Devon into the hands of a capable maid named Jane.

"Why don't you have a bath and a nap?" he suggested. "I'll meet you here at"—he glanced at the grandfather clock ticking near the stairs—"noon-ish."

Her eyes roved searchingly over his features. "And what about you?"

He fingered the stubble on his jaw. "Well," he said thoughtfully, "I suppose I do need a bath and a shave—"

Her mouth curved. "You *always* need a shave."

He was aware her question ran much deeper.

Tenderly he ran the backs of his knuckles over the curve of her cheek, marveling at its texture, uncaring what the servants might think of the caress.

"I'm fine." And he was. The heaviness in his chest had lifted. There was no need to ask himself why. He loved Thurston Hall. Loved it above all else, but this time it had nothing to do with the fact that he was home . . .

And everything to do with the woman at his side.

But at noon Devon wasn't waiting at the bottom of the stairs. Thinking she'd overslept, he rapped lightly on the door of her room. Jane looked up from straightening the bed and informed him she'd departed promptly at a quarter before the hour.

He found her in the portrait gallery. She looked refreshed, her hair combed and drawn back from her face with a ribbon. Her necklace gleamed silver and bright about her throat. Jane had seen fit to clothe her in one of Julianna's gowns. He nearly groaned.

He approached, careful to keep his eyes from dwelling on the expanse of creamy bosom exposed.

"Hello," she greeted. "I was wandering."

Sebastian chuckled. "I should have known. You do have that habit, don't you? Just don't wander too far. You could get lost in this house and no one would find you for weeks."

"Ah, but the real question is this, sir . . . if I were ever lost, would you look for me?"

His gaze roved over her profile, the place where a tiny, silky curl waved into the shell of her ear, the delectable corner of her mouth. "Every minute," he said quietly.

"While searching for missing treasures, no doubt," she teased.

"No, Devon. Only you. I wouldn't rest until I found you." He meant every word.

Her gaze flashed up to his, her eyes mutely questioning. There was a sharp stab in his belly. Oh, Christ, what was he doing? He shouldn't have allowed her to come. But he had, and now it was too late . . . And, God help him, it felt so right, her being here . . .

He smiled slightly. "I must thank you for coming with me. I didn't mean to drag you away in the middle of the night, you know."

"That's not quite how I remember it, but it's generous of you to put it like that."

His smile ebbed. "I'm not sure I can explain it. Justin . . . well, as you saw last night, I couldn't stay. And I just . . . I needed to be here. I needed to see"—for a moment his throat closed off and he struggled to speak—"all this again. I needed to be home."

A small hand crept into his.

He squeezed her fingers, then gestured toward a heavy, gilt-framed painting.

"I see you admire the family portrait. It was painted only a few months before my mother left. My father wouldn't allow it to be hung while he was alive. But I take the view that it belongs here, with the rest of the Sterlings."

"You look very young," she ventured, then bit her lip. "How old were you?"

"I was ten, Justin was six, Julianna was three."

"My, but you were tall even then—not so very far behind your father." Her gaze moved on to the tiny, chestnut-haired little cherub who stood alongside her eldest brother. "Julianna looks very sweet."

Sebastian's eyes softened. "She is. She hasn't

changed a bit since she was a child. She has the most generous, giving nature in the world, with a voice like pure sunshine."

Devon's gaze had moved on to the fine-boned, dark-haired beauty draped in royal blue velvet. Though her expression was properly demure, the vivid sparkle of her eyes betrayed her true nature; it was almost as if she defied the somber-visaged man at her side.

An unseen hand seemed to close around Sebastian's heart. Little wonder, he thought . . .

For that was the way it had always been.

"Your mother is stunning," Devon murmured.

"Yes, she was, wasn't she? Justin greatly resembles her. Julianna has her delicacy, while I have my father's stature."

But not his nature.

Dear God, never that.

As if she knew the precise direction of his thoughts, Devon's scrutiny moved on to the head of the family. The painter had captured William Sterling's essence remarkably—his stern austerity, the disapproval with which he viewed his family . . . why, the world! Even in the portrait, though all of them stood before the fireplace mantel in the library, William Sterling maintained his distance from his wife and children, a distance both physical and emotional.

Sebastian frowned. He looked upon the portrait daily when he was in residence. Odd, but this was something that had escaped his notice until now, the way his father held himself apart.

It was as if he saw the portrait through new eyes . . . through Devon's eyes.

And he wondered, with a touch of his brother's cynicism, if perhaps the Sterling family was cursed when it came to love and marriage. He couldn't imagine Justin taking a wife—what woman would have such a rogue? And Julianna's experience with love had proved disastrous. For she too had borne a scandal of her own . . .

Little wonder she had decided no man would turn her head again.

His marriage would be far different from his parents'. It had to be. It *had* to.

"It must have been awful for you," Devon murmured, "when your mother . . . left."

Beneath the flowing white cambric of his shirt, Sebastian's shoulders went taut.

"I saw her, you know. I saw her leave. I-I've never told that to anyone," he admitted, his voice sounding oddly strained, even to his own ears. "And it was awful, for a long, long time. Julianna was too young to really comprehend. All she knew was that dear Mama was gone. But Justin"—Sebastian shook his head—"it was hardest on him, I think. He has the charm and vivacity of our mother—her wildness. In fact, he's so like her, it frightens me sometimes."

"Why?" she said softly.

A shadow passed over his features. "Justin has a dark side, Devon. You caught a glimpse of it last night. He can be so reckless, as if he doesn't care about anything or anyone."

He paused. "I love him," he said suddenly. "You know that, don't you? I don't want you to think we're constantly at each other's throats."

"I would never think that," Devon stated immediately. "I've seen the two of you together, remember?"

"We both behaved abominably. I shouldn't have allowed myself to lose my temper, especially in front of you."

"You don't have to explain, Sebastian."

"I want to," he said quietly. "Justin can be outrageous, and no one will care. No one will think twice about it. Justin doesn't care a fig about scandal. But I do. Dear God, I still remember how people whispered and stared. At my father. At *us*. It lasted for years . . ."

Perhaps it was the way she looked at him. So earnest. The way she cocked her head to the side and listened. As if she understood the angry hurt that rent his childhood in two.

The ache of remembrance battered him. He tried to steel himself against it and failed. Suddenly it was all pouring out and he had no hope of stopping it. Maybe he didn't *want* to stop it.

"Justin chides me about duty and obligation. He chides me for being so proper. He chides me for being so perfect." He gave a self-deprecating laugh. "As if I had a prayer. As if I *ever* had a prayer. I think you've already guessed the truth, Devon. I envied my brother when I was a child. I envied his looks. I envied his charm. I longed to be out riding and playing as he did, but my tutors wouldn't let me. My father wouldn't let me. I'll never be perfect. But I have to try. It's what I was taught. It's what I am.

"Perhaps Justin is right. Perhaps I *am* like my father. But it's because of him that I have my pride, my pride in my home and my name and my heritage. I hate what happened here, but the Hall is nearer and dearer to my heart than anything else. Perhaps it's selfish. But I can't put it aside. I can't put duty aside.

For it's here in this house I want my children born. It's here I want them raised, as we were—Justin and Julianna and I. It's here I want to make them laugh. To *hear* them laugh. But never to cry. Never to hurt. Not the way Justin did. Not the way *we* did—"

He broke off. Devon's shoulders were heaving. Shocked, he stared at her.

"Devon, what's wrong?"

She didn't answer. She couldn't.

Alarmed, shaken to the marrow of his bones, he pulled her around to face him. "My God, Devon, what's wrong?"

Slowly she lifted her face. "You should hate him, but you don't, do you?"

Sebastian went very still inside. "Who? My father?"

"Yes. *Yes.*"

He shook his head. "I can't. He taught me to respect what I am, who I am. He taught me to *be* who I am."

Warm, wet tears drizzled down her cheeks. She wiped them away with the back of her hand. "Sebastian, *he beat you*. Oh, don't you see? He taught you nothing that wasn't already inside. Nothing that wasn't already there."

He shook his head. "Devon," he refuted gently, "it's kind of you to say so, but you can't know—"

"Oh, but I do," she burst out. She swept a hand toward the portrait. "It's there, Sebastian. It's all there. Your protectiveness. Your loyalty. It's there in the clasp of your hand on Justin's shoulder, the way Julianna's little fist is curled within the other, the adoration in her eyes as she gazes up at you! You took care of them, didn't you? You sheltered them. You held them. You loved them when your parents would not! You were just a boy, but so very much a man already!"

"No, Devon." He felt raw inside. As helpless as he'd felt those stormy years beneath his father's iron rule. "You're wrong. I couldn't help them. I couldn't shield them—"

"You did far more. How can you say you are selfish? Sebastian, you are staunch and strong and—and I think you are, quite possibly, the most wonderful man in the world."

Her pronouncement stunned him. Humbled him. Nearly swept him to his knees.

"Devon," he said hoarsely. "Ah, Devon . . ." There was an awful constriction in his chest. For one perilous moment he was afraid that *he* might cry . . .

He wrapped her close and clung, his mouth against the soft, feathery wisps of hair at her temple.

It was some time before the ability to speak was reclaimed.

When he was able, he pressed a kiss on the fragrant cloud of her hair. Drawing back, he wiped away the glaze of tears from her cheeks with the pad of his thumb, then gazed into the misty depths of her eyes.

"Walk with me," he murmured, a crooked little smile at his lips as he offered his arm. "For if you don't mind, I would very much like to show you my home . . ."

Seventeen

There was never a day more glorious.

Not a cloud marred the sky, a striking shade of pure indigo. The sun's rays spilled down, showering the land with warmth and light. A lazy breeze stirred the air, carrying with it the scent of flowers, the trill of a feminine voice, the rumble of low male laughter.

Hand in hand, they wandered through the grounds, past neatly trimmed hedges and manicured flowerbeds. Eventually their steps took them through a woodland and down a hill where a clear, shallow brook dashed over the rocks. Mid-afternoon, they paused to rest on a bench threaded through with hollyhock.

Devon lowered her bottom, only to bounce upright. "Look," she cried delightedly, "a hare!"

Sebastian pointed toward a copse of trees. "There's another one." Through the grass, several more heads popped up.

Sebastian laughed as she darted first left, then right, spinning and twisting.

"Stop!" he protested. "You're making me dizzy."

"Oh, but they're so darling," she panted. "I wish I could catch just one."

"And what would you do with him? I daresay Dumpling would be jealous."

"I hadn't thought of that," she said worriedly.

"On the other hand, I know what I would do if you caught one." He rubbed his hands together. "We'd have a very tasty meal of roast hare tonight."

She looked stricken. "Oh, you are too cruel! I swear I shall never eat hare again."

But in the next moment, she slanted him a sidelong glance. "I take it we're staying the night then?" She made no effort to disguise her hopefulness.

"Would you like to?"

"Yes," she said promptly.

"Well, I suppose I could give it some thought."

"Not too much thought."

"Devon, you know I give everything a great deal of thought."

"Then let me do it for you. There's little point in leaving now. Even if you did, we wouldn't get back to London until the middle of the night." She sounded quite happy at the prospect. "Therefore we may as well wait."

Subtlety was not her strong suit.

"True. But we'd make it back in time for breakfast. And I know you're fond of Theodore's croissants. On the other hand, I daresay Mr. Jenkins, who has been cook here at Thurston Hall since before I was born, makes the finest roast hare in all England."

Limb by limb, as if he had all the time in the

world, he arranged one booted foot across the other, then leaned back, resting on his elbows.

She was still puffing, her cheeks flushed pink from exertion. In consternation she regarded his pose of indolent grace. In turn, she jammed first one fist against her hips, then the other.

Her fingers wiggled. "Sebastian?" she queried.

"Hmmm?" Closing his eyes, he turned his face up into the sun.

"What is your decision? Are we departing for London?"

"We're still here, aren't we?"

"That we are."

"Then I'm wondering what's keeping you."

"Keeping me?"

"Yes." Opening an eye, he gave a flick of his wrist. "Catch my dinner."

Devon blinked. "You want me to catch your dinner?"

"I believe that's what I just said."

"While you sit there and watch?"

"Yes. That's the price for staying, my dear."

A mischievous smile played across her lips. "In that case, perhaps we should bargain."

That sounded interesting. He sat up. "What do you propose?"

He missed the irrepressible mirth alight in her eyes. He was too busy watching as she slowly tugged off one of her slippers. Sebastian's heart began to hammer. Good Lord. This was too much to hope for. Too much to comprehend. And interesting wasn't the word for it at all—

The slipper sailed high above his head.

The second hit him squarely in the chest.

"I'll catch your dinner, my lord, but first you have to catch me!"

Sebastian was too stunned to move. "Devon—"

"Do you concede victory, my high-and-mighty marquess?"

No man could resist a challenge such as that.

The chase was on.

He was convinced he had the advantage. Devon made sure he didn't. He'd thought she was exhausted. But she danced and weaved, and oh, but she was quick! His lungs burning, his legs aching so that he was certain he'd never walk again, he collapsed at the base of an oak tree.

"My God, I haven't done that since I was a boy."

She would have dashed by yet again, but he snared her by the waist and brought her down beside him. Still laughing, Devon sank down in a froth of skirts. "I'll tell you a secret. I've *never* done that. And I've never done this either."

Her toes wiggled in the thick, lush grass. They were slim and round and pink, as delectable as the rest of her. God, but that didn't bear thinking about! Her slippers were halfway across the meadow, not that she seemed to care.

They shared the very same thought.

She intercepted his look and giggled. "I know, it's quite unladylike."

Sebastian felt his heart turn over. Being with her like this . . . Oh, God. He had no words to describe it. More than anything, he longed to lean over and part her lips, cover her mouth with his, hold her with their hearts pressed together as one. But something stopped him. He didn't want anything to ruin this moment. It was too precious. Too sweet. Too . . . perfect.

There was a bond between them. A link. Something far beyond friendship. Far beyond desire.

Far beyond his power to master.

He didn't fight it. He couldn't. For somehow he was beginning to recognize this was a battle he could not win.

Was he the only one who felt it?

He leaned back in the grass, watching as the sun played hide-and-seek through the branches. Throwing up an arm, he shielded his eyes against the glare, adjusting his head slightly so he could see her. She sat with her back against the tree trunk, bare feet stretched out before her.

A fingertip traced the squareness of his jaw, the wispiest caress. That same fingertip traced the channeled grooves beside his mouth.

"You didn't sleep a wink last night, did you?"

"No," he admitted.

"Then sleep now."

"I'd much rather look at you." The admission slipped out before he could stop it, and then he didn't care.

Above him, moist, red lips burgeoned into a smile. A thick curl slipped over her shoulder, spilling onto his chest. Absently she pushed it behind her ear. It was all he could do not to wind that silken lock about his fist and drag her mouth down to his. She was such a rare beauty, he acknowledged with a surge of pride, and she didn't even know it. Both innocent and alluring. Spirited and demure.

Reaching over, she pulled his head onto her lap.

Small, delicate fingers stroked the furrows in his brow, sifting through his hair. Somehow he stilled the questing in his gut. Amazingly, her ministrations were making him drowsy. Peace settled into his bones, his very being. The world was spinning away but he didn't care.

"Sebastian?" she whispered.

Sebastian didn't hear. He was sleeping, a sleep more peaceful than any he'd ever known.

Mr. Jenkins himself served supper that night. He saw to every detail himself, placing an elaborate silver tray before his master and his companion with zeal.

"Roast hare," he announced. "My specialty."

With a flourish, he placed a succulent slice on her plate. Hands behind his back, he stood and awaited her verdict.

Devon's eyes were huge. Her gaze swung to Sebastian's.

"Taste it," Sebastian advised lightly. "I promise, it will melt in your mouth."

Behind his napkin, Sebastian nearly choked with laughter as she swallowed it whole.

Miraculously, Devon did not choke. She managed a beaming smile and glowing praise. "Oh, it's simply delightful!" she gushed. "Quite the most wonderful thing I've ever tasted in my life!"

Mr. Jenkins left the dining room a happy man.

Sebastian promptly found himself the recipient of an arch glare. "I do believe you planned that."

"Not so," he assured her with absolute gravity, his palms raised high.

Sebastian devoured both his portion of hare and

hers with relish. After dinner, he invited her to play chess, a game he'd taught her during their lessons. While Devon accorded her attention to the chessboard between them, he devoted his attention to her, watching as she swirled her wine, raised it to her lips, and filled her mouth.

A droplet lingered at the corner. A dainty finger wiped it away while she contemplated her move.

He tried to avert his gaze and failed.

She frowned at him. "What are you looking at?"

"I was just admiring."

"Admiring what?"

"The craftsmanship of this rook."

The artlessness of her beauty.

"That is not a rook. That is a pawn!"

And he was but a pawn in her grasp. Molten need rose hot in his loins. So acutely attuned to her was he that had she given the slightest sign she would welcome him, he'd have leaped across the table, thrown up her gown, and dragged her atop him.

Sweet Christ, he'd never bedded a woman on the floor before in his life.

"Sebastian, are you paying attention?"

"Yes," he lied.

In three moves the game was done.

She trounced him soundly.

"You're pouting," she said when they arose from the table.

"I am not."

"Well, you must be moping then."

Sebastian was amused. "Why would I be moping?"

"Because you're stuck here in the country with me. Because I've taken you away from your diversions."

He laughed. "Hardly."

"Well, if you were in London, where would you be?"

"Probably having a brandy in the library with you."

"That will hardly gain you the bride you seek, now will it?"

"I suppose not."

"Well," she said breathlessly, "I have a theory as to why you've yet to find your bride."

Sebastian did, too, and it had everything to do with this bewitching little urchin who had somehow slipped her way into his life and his heart.

A jet brow rose expectantly.

"I think . . . perhaps you need some advice in dealing with a lady."

The glimmer of a smile crossed his lips. "You think so, do you?"

"I do. For instance, if you were at one of your grand affairs in London, there would surely be a great many ladies about."

None so lovely as you.

"So, let us pretend then. You must choose a lady. And since I am here, well"—she gave an exaggerated sigh—"I fear I must stand in for your lady."

She hardly sounded distressed at the prospect.

"Perhaps I should whisk the lady away from the drawing room for a turn in the garden," he said.

He did precisely that, setting off down the path that wound through the garden. Surrounded by flowers, immersed in moonlight, he guided her past trees and hedges.

They stopped near a high stone wall. A profusion of tiny white roses climbed the adjacent side, lending the night its fragrant perfume. Nearby was a wide stone bench. The windows behind them cast a hazy glow of candlelight.

She glanced around. "Very good," she praised. "Now, since you have your lady alone in the garden, I wonder . . . would you kiss her?"

His mouth quirked. "A gentleman never kisses a lady before they are wed."

For an instant she was speechless. Then she asked, "Do you mean to say you would wed a woman without kissing her? I would certainly never wed a man without kissing him!"

Her emphatic declaration nearly set him off. It occurred to him somewhat belatedly that the chit was flirting with him!

And doing quite a smashingly good job.

"Well," he amended cautiously, "I might, if I particularly liked the lady. If I were feeling particularly"—he stole a sidelong glance at her—"amorous."

"You might? But you're not sure?"

"No."

"Oh, dear. Perhaps you need lessons then."

"Ah," he said softly. "Now there's a thought."

She had turned so that she faced him. The wall was to her back.

Their eyes locked. Their legs brushed. Their fingertips touched.

"Perhaps," she said breathlessly, "you should kiss *me*."

"Perhaps I should." He lifted his hands, feigning helplessness. "What shall I do?"

"To begin with, I think you should be closer."

He moved so that her slippered feet were aligned squarely between his booted feet. The lapels of his jacket brushed the ruffled bodice at her breast. Very deliberately he placed his hands alongside the wall behind her.

For Sebastian had joined the game with relish.

God, but her expression was priceless. Her gaze skidded to the left, then the right, then climbed to his face. Her mouth rounded, along with her eyes.

He knew the precise moment she realized she was trapped against the wall and trapped against *him*.

His mouth curved, a slow-growing smile more befitting a rake than a gentleman.

"Now what?" he asked silkily.

"Well," she whispered, the sound half strangled, "you must kiss me." He saw the way she swallowed. "It's the man who does the kissing, is it not?"

Not always. His mind filled with images of her lush, sweet mouth pressing warm, wanton kisses down his chest. Her unbound hair swirling around and over his skin, down his belly, clear to his loins. He envisioned that hot, sweet mouth closing on his . . .

He nearly groaned. What the blazes was it she'd said? Ah, yes.

Some devil seized hold of him. He smiled wickedly. It was she who had begun this game, but by God, he would continue it.

"Tell me how," was all he said.

He watched as the tip of her tongue darted over her lips, driving him half mad.

"Press your lips to mine," she directed earnestly.

He gave her a quick, maidenly peck. They touched nowhere . . . but on the lips.

"How was that?"

"Sadly lacking," she grumbled. "You must try again. But . . . harder this time."

"Harder as in . . . more?" he asked silkily. "Or harder as in . . . *this*?"

Bending his head, Sebastian took her mouth in a long, unbroken kiss that was fierce and ravenous and tender all at once.

They were both breathing raggedly by the time he raised his head. Her eyes flicked open to stare directly into his. She was clawing at the wall behind her.

"I must commend you, sir," she gasped. "You are as good a pupil as you are a teacher."

Sebastian's hands closed around her waist. With an odd little laugh he caught her into his hungry embrace, giving in to the need clamoring inside him. Oh, Christ, he thought. This was insanity. Madness. Yet from the start, there had always been a spark between them. Sebastian knew it. And he knew that Devon knew it too; just as he was aware that, in her innocence, she was experimenting. Testing these feelings of desire coming alive inside her. It was up to him to stop it, for he was the one with the experience. If unchecked, he knew where play such as this might easily lead . . .

But all the reasons he should release her flew right out of his mind. For in some strange way he didn't fully understand, all this was new to him too. He'd been with women before. After all, he was a man with needs and desires, and he had indulged those desires.

But this was different. Devon was different. A voice within warned he should let her go, but there wasn't a chance. It felt too good. *She* felt so good. And above all, being with her like this . . . It felt so right. It had never been quite so right with any other woman . . . And when her arms stole around his neck, that spark between them exploded into a blaze.

A surge of pure possessiveness shot through him. That too was like nothing he'd ever felt before.

She pressed herself against him, making them both tautly aware of the rigid swell of his rod. Her hands found his back. Her nails dug into his shoulders. Heat quickened beneath his skin, sending a shudder of awareness all through him.

There was a breath. A sigh. A whisper. All of them his.

"Devon," he whispered.

She lifted her face to his, her eyes shining like jeweled amber. "Remember the first time, Sebastian? When I asked why you kissed me?"

He trailed a finger over the tilt of her brows, down the pertness of her nose, the beguiling shape of her mouth. Dear God, he'd never forget.

"I was so afraid you'd never kiss me again, with me being who I am and all—" The words were a tremulous cry against his cheek.

"Devon, don't." His arms engulfed her once more. He clung to her as desperately as she clung to him.

"It's just that . . . I thought you were going to . . . oh, several times . . ."

"I wanted to. A hundred times. A thousand."

"You did? Truly?" She drew back to look at him, her eyes swimming.

"Yes. God, yes." His eyes darkened. "I did. Every day. By God, I will—"

And well he might have . . .

But nearby, he heard the sound of a door opening—the terrace.

They both froze.

Eighteen

Perhaps it had begun as a game, her light-hearted enticement of this man, for this had been a night like no other. A night of thrills and enchantment and magic. A night filled with promise. . . . It was much later that Devon asked herself where she had ever found the reckless daring to say what she did. To do what she did. Perhaps it was because she wanted this day to last forever.

And this night to never end.

For the temptation was irresistible . . . and *he* was irresistible.

Once he had kissed her. *Once.*

And for the chance to experience the searing warmth of his mouth on hers yet again, Devon would have done . . . anything.

Indeed, she had.

But he wanted it too.

For though it was she who had begun this game, it

was Sebastian who seized control. His passionate mastery of her mouth left no doubt.

Her heart pounding, she stood raptly as his fingers traced over her brows, her nose, the outline of her mouth. And when she gazed into glowing silver eyes, what she saw there made her pulse pound and her heart sing and her nipples grow all tight and tingly. The sweep of hard arms around her back acquainted her with every muscle, every sinew. The breeches he wore were skintight and thin, allowing her to feel every taut, masculine part of him . . .

Everything.

"Devon," he whispered.

It came to her then.

It came in the midst of a moment, the midst of a breath, the midst of a heartbeat . . .

She loved Sebastian. She loved his pride. The arrogance that drove her to distraction. His fierce protectiveness of those held near and dear to his heart.

She clung to him, offering up tremulous lips to his, uncaring if he saw clear to her soul and beyond.

But the kiss she so craved was not to be.

"Sebastian?" called a voice. "Devon?"

The footsteps were coming closer.

Sebastian raised his head. Beneath his breath, a curse seared the air—rather long, quite vivid, and startlingly eye-opening to the woman clasped tight in his arms. "It's Justin. What the *hell* is he doing here?"

The minute she and Sebastian stepped into the drawing room, Dumpling hurtled toward her. Devon sank down to her heels and was immediately surrounded by five little balls of fur. The pups yipped and licked at her until she was breathless and laughing.

An indulgent smile lighting his features, Sebastian helped her to her feet.

"My little darlings!" she crooned. "Oh, I missed you!"

"Well, there's no question they missed you," said Justin. "I thought you'd be pleased to see them."

"How thoughtful of you. Thank you."

She felt Sebastian's regard as she levered herself on tiptoe to graze Justin's cheek with lips still moist from the wash of his tongue. She glimpsed a strange expression flit across his features. Was he jealous? Her pulse skittered at the thought.

He lifted a brow. "And where, my dear girl, is mine?" He wasted no time in the query.

The heat in his eyes made her heart race. She wrinkled her nose. "You forgot Dumpling," she informed him pertly.

Justin turned to Sebastian, who stood slightly aside, arms folded across his chest.

"Good evening, Sebastian."

Sebastian gave a curt nod.

Devon's sharp eyes surveyed the pair, noting the stilted, awkward strain between the two. She accurately read the tension in Sebastian's posture. His shoulders went up, then down, and she knew he fought it. And Justin was having a difficult time meeting his brother's gaze.

Smoothing her palms down the front of her gown, she raised a hand and pretended to smother a yawn. "Well, Justin," she said lightly, "I hate to be rude since you've only just arrived, but I think I'll retire." An urge to be mischievous bubbled up. "The journey here last night was quite tiring."

Justin had the grace to look sheepish.

Sebastian escorted her to the foot of the stairs and bid her good night.

"Good night, Devon," he said softly.

She stood on the second step, so that their eyes were almost level. More than anything, she wanted to reach out, tangle her fingers in the thick hair that grew low on his nape, and bring his mouth to hers.

She knew from the way his gaze fastened on her lips that he wanted it too.

"Good night," she whispered. She had to force herself to walk away.

At the landing she paused and looked down.

Sebastian hadn't moved. The burning in his eyes made her heart skip a beat.

When Devon was gone from sight, Sebastian rejoined his brother in the drawing room. Justin sprawled in the pink-and-cream Queen Anne chair near the French doors. His gaze encompassed the marble staircase.

"Why," Justin remarked, "do I have the feeling I've just been duly chastised?"

"Not so. If you had been, you'd know it."

"Well then, perhaps *you'd* like to have at me."

"I wouldn't dream of it."

Sebastian stopped at the rosewood parquet table near the Chippendale settee. He dipped the neck of a crystal decanter into a glass, then paused.

"Perhaps you'd care for a brandy too," he drawled.

Justin groaned. "Never again."

"Promises, promises." At last Sebastian smiled. He took the chair across from Justin, whose hands were kneading his temples.

"Nursing a headache, are we?"

"My God, you don't know what a headache is! Between Dumpling yowling the minute Devon left, the pups joining in, and the anvil in my brain . . . my God, it was the longest night of my life."

Sebastian's smile ebbed. He set aside his glass. "I know the feeling," he said quietly.

For the longest time Justin just looked at him. "I knew you'd be here," he said finally. "I had to come."

"I know." Sebastian reached for a cigar box from India. Flipping it open, he nodded to Justin—a peace offering, of sorts.

Justin declined with a shake of his head. "Sebastian," he began, "I—" He cleared his throat, then glanced away. "Ah, hell," he muttered. "*Hell.*"

The ghost of a smile crept across Sebastian's lips. "That just about says it all, doesn't it?"

"Damn straight," Justin muttered.

The ice was broken, the tension thawed.

"If it makes you feel any better, I bought you a case of that Scotch whisky you like."

Sebastian cocked a brow. "For me or for you?"

"I can't abide the stuff! Talk about poison!" Justin pulled a face. After a moment he glanced toward the stairs. "I take it I have Devon to thank for calming your temper."

"You might say that."

"Quite a change from the woman you dragged in from the gutter that night, eh?"

"Amen."

"I take it the lessons are going well?"

"Extremely." But it was a lesson of a far different sort that filled Sebastian's mind . . . Aloud he said, "She beat me at chess tonight."

"You probably let her win. You always let *me* win."

"You were a poor loser. You still are."

Justin arched a sardonic brow. "Well, I won't argue with that." He stretched out his legs. "She's come so far. But tell me the truth, Sebastian. What do you think her chances are for securing a post as governess or companion?"

Justin had just voiced the question that had been nagging at Sebastian for some time now. "It's not so much her chances, as the fact that I don't think I like the idea of her becoming a governess," he stated abruptly. "My God, what if she *does* land employment? She's young. She's beautiful. What if the master of the house decides she's fair game? I don't want her to become the target of some man's lust! And it's entirely within the realm of possibility. Hell, even probability."

There. It was out. The very thing that nagged at his insides. The very thing he'd dared not allow himself to ponder these many weeks with Devon as his pupil. He'd lost sight of the true purpose of their lessons. He'd lost sight of everything but the sheer pleasure of simply being with her! Was it a conscious choice, the way he'd neatly sidestepped the end result? Perhaps he'd kept it at bay on purpose, deliberately keeping it dammed inside. Somehow, along the way, the time spent together had become something far more precious—far more meaningful.

And Devon felt the same.

Goddamn it, why the hell did Justin have to bring it up?

"Yes," Justin concurred. "It's occurred to me as well."

A brooding darkness had slipped over Sebastian. Once started, he couldn't seem to stop. "You don't know Devon like I do. If that were to happen, she wouldn't like it. She wouldn't stand for it." An awful fear gripped his mind.

Nor, it seemed, was he the only one to feel it. "If that were the case," Justin observed, "she might easily end up on the streets again."

"That can't be allowed to happen." Sebastian's mouth thinned. "She deserves a better life than what she's had."

"My thoughts exactly." Justin hesitated. "But there might be another solution."

Sebastian frowned. "What?"

"Well, I was thinking . . . perhaps we could find her a husband."

"A husband!"

Justin leaned an arm on his chair. He looked amused. "Why do you sound like that?"

"Like what?"

"Vastly irritated, if you must know. And the way you're scowling—"

"I'm not."

"But you are." The laughter faded from Justin's features. He was abruptly sober.

"Sebastian," he murmured, "may I be frank?"

"What, you're asking this time?"

Something about the way Justin was eyeing him alerted Sebastian. He felt himself tense.

"Sebastian," Justin said carefully, "God knows I am the last man to consider myself an astute observer of human nature. But when the two of you walked in from the terrace, the strangest notion passed through my mind. When I saw Devon on your arm tonight, I could have sworn the two of you were—"

"A stroll about the garden," Sebastian interrupted coolly.

"A splendid night for it too."

"Quite," Sebastian agreed curtly. "And I know what you're getting at, so let us put the matter to rest. Yes, I have a certain affection for Devon. So do you. But my conduct toward her has always been that of a gentleman." Why he made it a point of saying so, he didn't know.

Or perhaps he did.

"I'm not suggesting otherwise," Justin said. "Besides, you're a marquess. And Devon is—"

He didn't want to hear him say it. "I'm quite aware of who she is," he cut in sharply.

Justin's eyes flickered. "There's no need to bite my head off."

If Sebastian was short with Justin, it couldn't be helped. He was aware he was being difficult, but there was a world of turmoil churning in his gut. He didn't like uncertainty. He didn't like it when plans went awry. And when it came to the subject of Devon taking a husband, he passed the boundaries of civility.

Justin gave a short little laugh. "You're right, of course. You would never disregard your upbringing so. And I completely forgot your search for a bride—after all, it's high time you married. Christ, what was

I thinking? You would never be so wild, to act on your feelings with no regard for the future or what might come of it."

Sebastian was still simmering. Maybe he was a fool, but Justin's suggestion had taken him wholly by surprise. He was totally unprepared to deal with it.

But no. It wasn't just that. He didn't *want* to deal with this.

He neither confirmed nor denied Justin's statement. Was Justin's the voice of reason? Or the voice of suspicion?

And he wondered . . . Did he fool Justin? He couldn't be sure, for Justin was an expert at hiding his thoughts. Justin might suspect, he decided slowly. But he didn't know for certain.

Nothing happened tonight, reminded a niggling little voice from within. *Not tonight in the garden, or any other night.*

Not yet anyway.

But he wanted it. He wanted it past bearing. Beyond caution.

"Even if those feelings were there," Justin added.

Sebastian narrowed his eyes. He gave his brother a keenly assessing stare.

Justin spread his hands wide. "What? Why do you look at me like that?"

"This is certainly a change for you."

"Well, you want me to act responsibly, don't you?"

"Indeed," Sebastian said coolly. "But I'm wondering where all this wisdom comes from."

Justin gave a little smile. "One too many brandies, I expect. At any rate, where was this discussion leading? Ah, yes. In lieu of finding a post for Devon as governess, perhaps we should find her a husband instead."

A husband. A *husband*.

Sebastian could barely digest the word. He clamped his jaws together. The idea of Devon with another man made him feel livid inside. Even that little kiss bestowed on Justin's cheek was like a burr under his skin. Innocuous though it was, he didn't want Devon's lips touching anyone's but his, even his brother's.

But wasn't it the perfect solution? The voice of reason now resounded in *his* head. With a husband to look after Devon, he wouldn't have to worry about her ending up on the streets again.

So why did he want to strangle Justin for even daring to suggest it?

Damn. *Damn!* Why the devil couldn't Justin have stayed in London?

Justin continued. "As you said, we've both become quite fond of her. And I think it's fair to say we only want the best for her."

Sebastian made no reply.

"With a husband she'll be safe from Harry."

She was safe from Harry with *him*.

But she wasn't safe *from* him.

He wanted to tell Justin to shut the hell up.

Instead he inquired curtly, "Whom do you have in mind?"

Before Justin had a chance to answer, his mouth turned down. "Not one of your disreputable cronies, I hope!"

"I really haven't given it much consideration," Justin admitted. "But since you and Devon are here in the country . . . well, the Hall is a good place, don't you think? Far from the prying eyes of London. We could introduce her to some of the local gentry, perhaps. We could say she's a friend of Julianna's. We'll think of something."

As long as she's near, came a taunt from somewhere deep in his mind, *she'll tempt you.*

But with the temptation removed, so would the urges.

Sebastian didn't want to think of it at all. The idea of Devon in another man's arms—another man's bed—made him want to swear and rage and tear someone apart.

He'd never before felt savage.

He did now.

"A small, informal supper the day after tomorrow," he said. "Invite Evans and Mason and Westfield."

Justin raised a quizzical brow. "Evans and Mason will suit, I suppose. But Westfield? He's old enough to be her father!"

"He's one of the wealthiest merchants in the county. Perhaps he'll die and leave her his holdings." Sebastian was only half jesting. "She can take care of herself then."

Justin nodded his assent. "I'll see to it in the morning."

God, what a hypocrite he was!

Yet Justin was right. He couldn't think of himself. It was Devon who was important. Her safety was paramount. Nothing else mattered.

There was a vile, bitter taste in his mouth. A black, gaping hole where his heart should have been.

Less than an hour had passed since Justin's arrival. Less than an hour since he'd held Devon in his arms. Less than an hour since shy, tremulous lips clung sweetly beneath his. Less than an hour since he imagined what it would be like to make slow, burning love to her until dawn's first light burnished the sky; to make her introduction to passion as exquisitely delightful for her as he knew it would be for him. Of dragging out every last, lingering caress so it lasted until the sun and the stars and the night exploded, and the world was no more.

Sweet Christ, in those blissful seconds with her mouth warm and trembling beneath his, he'd even planned it.

But it would never happen. Not tonight. Not with him.

Not ever.

His head began to pound. An acrid bitterness seared his veins. He didn't even hear as Justin bid him good night.

The night aged, the moon journeyed across the sky, and his mood grew blacker. Sebastian was not a man who drank to excess. He indulged his taste for spirits in moderation. The last time he'd been thoroughly, rousingly foxed was during his early days at Oxford.

But that night, he followed his brother's lead of the night before.

By dawn the brandy decanter was empty.

Nineteen

"Justin and I have invited a few friends over tomorrow evening. I thought you might like to join us."

The announcement came at luncheon the next day, in such an offhand, careless manner that it took a moment for Devon to grasp his meaning.

But when she did, her heart surely stopped. Slowly she lowered her spoon to her saucer, the fingers of her other hand curling toward her palm.

Mutely questioning, she lifted her gaze to Sebastian's face. The dazzling white of his cravat brought out the bronze in his skin.

Their eyes caught. She stared at him, with thudding heart and wavering breath. Was he saying what she thought he was?

"A very informal gathering. A bite to eat. A little conversation." His smile was easy, his manner calm. Lightly he stroked her fingers.

Reassured, Devon felt her heart flutter, then soar.

He wanted her to meet some of his friends! The realization washed over her that this wasn't like the dinner party he'd held in London. Granted, he hadn't made it a point of saying so then, but Devon had known that her presence was to remain secret from his guests. But this was different—there was no need to hide away on the balcony.

Wavering a thin line somewhere between elation and apprehension, she bit her lip. "They won't think it's odd I'm here?"

"We'll say you dropped by for a few days, an unexpected visit to surprise Julianna. This isn't London. The usual formalities needn't be observed so strictly here."

Devon nodded, her heart so full she could scarcely speak. Sebastian wanted to introduce her to his friends! He wasn't ashamed of her.

When the next evening came, she rummaged through the armoire. Shortly after their arrival, Sebastian had sent a man back to London for her clothing; a trunk had arrived earlier that day. Now she impatiently discarded first one gown, then another. The process was repeated half a dozen times before she finally settled on a dinner gown of jade watered silk, the most elegant of those Sebastian had had made.

Jane helped her bathe and dress that night. The girl was quiet and sweet, but Devon found herself wishing for Tansy. Tansy's vivacious chatter would have calmed her jittery nerves.

At last Jane stepped back. Devon rose from the dressing table, her steps carrying her to the mirror in the corner. A swell of nervous anxiety lodged in her breast. She didn't want to look. She was *afraid* to look.

But she couldn't stand here forever either.

Jade green silk draped her form, floating in soft folds to the tops of her slippers. As was the fashion, the neckline dipped low; it clung to her breasts almost lovingly. The cut was simple but elegant. The same gold satin ribbon cinched beneath her breasts also edged the hem and delicate, puffed sleeves. But Jane, it appeared, had quite a knack with dressing hair. She'd managed to tame Devon's unruly mane, catching it at the back of her head and allowing a soft fluff of curls to spill over one shoulder.

But beyond her own image swirled another—her mind recalled the night of Sebastian's dinner party in London. She saw anew the cluster of ladies surrounding him, clad in shimmering satin and lace, their hair adorned with feathers and fripperies, jewels shining at their throats and ears, rings encircling their fingers.

Panic flooded her. A hand strayed to her mother's necklace, catching the cross between her fingertips. She had no jewels, no trinkets, only this. Would Sebastian think her a dowdy simpleton? She felt suddenly ill-equipped and gauche.

"Miss," came Jane's voice from behind her, "oh, miss, I must say, the color of that gown was surely made for you! It reflects the bright little sparkles in your eyes—why, they're jewel-bright! If you don't mind my saying so, you look enchanting." Jane clamped her hands together before her. "Miss, you're a vision!"

Devon turned, impulsively catching the maid's hands. "Oh, Jane, do you really think so?"

"I do," came the enthusiastic affirmation. "I truly do!"

Devon reached out and gave her a heartfelt hug, her earlier misgivings banished. "Thanks to your efforts, Jane."

With Jane's praise ringing in her ears, she left the room.

Sebastian stood at the bottom of the stairs when she began her descent. He looked dark and striking, his big hands tucked idly in the pockets of his trousers. Justin was several paces behind him. She clung to the cool, carved wood of the handrail, her heart knocking wildly. Inside she was shaking, but determined not to show it. She wanted desperately to please him. She wanted to please him so much it hurt inside. She wanted him to see the same enchanting vision that Jane had. To hear him say she was beautiful . . .

Both men chanced to glance up at the same time.

Justin's cigar dropped from his mouth. Devon bit back a laugh as he swore and scrambled to retrieve it.

Her gaze was riveted on Sebastian, and God help her, his on her! Everything else faded to oblivion. Every ounce of her being was focused on him, and she had the oddest sensation it was the same for him, for there lurked in the depths of his eyes a banked, simmering heat that made her knees weak and her pulse clamor wildly. A strange feeling settled in her middle.

Slowly she closed the distance between them. Three more steps. Two . . .

All the while, his searing gaze never left her, nor did he speak.

At last she halted before him. He said nothing. The corners of Devon's lips curved upward.

"Well, sir, have you nothing to say?"

His gaze roved tenderly over her upturned features—and settled on her mouth.

His eyes were for her alone . . . and so were his next words.

"I can think of nothing except . . . you steal my breath away."

Softly he spoke, so softly she had to strain to hear . . . but Devon would never forget . . .

A tremendous rush of emotion swept through her, for those were the very words she'd spoken to him the night he'd carried her to her room after the pups' birth. Something passed between them, something almost painfully sweet and darkly intimate. Joy spilled through her, lighting her very soul. Her throat clogged. She felt near to bursting with emotion, and for an instant, speech was wholly beyond her capabilities. All she could do was smile tremulously.

An answering smile grazed his lips. Capturing her hand, he pressed a kiss to lace-covered fingertips.

Together they approached the drawing room. Justin was busy greeting the three gentleman who sat near the fire. A light supper had been set out on a table nearby.

The gravity of what she was about to do set in. She was about to play the part of a lady when she was anything *but* a lady.

"Stop," she said.

Sebastian glanced inquiringly at her.

A tremor shook her. Cold, clammy fingers clutched at his elbow.

"Sebastian," she said frantically, "what if they know who I am? What I am? That I'm a fraud? What if I do something I shouldn't? What if I spill wine in my lap or trip over my feet or use the wrong fork? I don't want to shame you or embarrass you."

Sebastian stopped short, glancing down into wide, amber eyes. He felt her insecurity with every fiber in his soul. But suddenly filling his mind's eye was the way she'd looked just moments ago as she floated down the stairs.

He hadn't moved. He couldn't.

Nor could he drag his eyes from her as she came near. Young and enchanting, she was a far cry from the bedraggled, half-dead urchin he had carried in from the streets. Though she had been a beauty even then.

And now, that beauty shone brighter still.

But one thought filled Sebastian's mind.

She could rival any of society's beauties. She could *surpass* any of society's beauties. It hit him with a staggering compulsion then. Why, it was almost as if she were born for this moment. Born *to* it.

But her wide, frightened eyes squeezed his very heart. And as her expression clearly gave testament to, all this was new to her. If she was unsure and uneasy, who could blame her?

A vile taste burned his throat, his very being. For one shattering instant Sebastian didn't know whom he hated more—Justin for suggesting they marry her off, or himself for agreeing.

They should have told her, whispered a fleeting voice in the back of his mind. It wasn't right that she didn't know . . . But she would surely rebel. It was better this way, for there would be time enough later . . .

He was suddenly filled with a scathing self-derision. Christ! he thought disgustedly. Who the hell did he and Justin think they were? Pretending to save her indeed . . .

Her first appearance to test her newfound skills and he was throwing her to the wolves.

No wonder he felt like a beast.

His feelings were swiftly masked. "You won't," he vowed, and smothered her fingers with his. He gave her no chance to argue or falter, but steered her into the drawing room toward his guests.

And she didn't. She walked into the room, her spine straight, her head held high.

"Gentleman, I should like you to meet Miss Devon St. James, an old friend of my sister's. Miss St. James dropped by to visit dear Julianna, but alas, Julianna is still traveling on the Continent. Nonetheless, I hope you'll join me in welcoming her this evening to Thurston Hall."

At the sight of her, the three gentleman aligned on the sofa popped up like well-oiled springs. Just as he'd known they would, Sebastian decided grimly, the pack swarmed . . .

Mason, a decent-looking chap Sebastian had never disliked until this moment, had already seized her hand and was carrying it to his lips—on the very spot he'd already claimed as his.

"Miss St. James, our local banker, Mr. Mason."

"Mr. Mason, I'm delighted."

He moved on to Evans, who executed a smart bow. "Should you ever find yourself in need of a solicitor, I daresay Mr. Evans will do a fine job."

"Charmed, I'm sure, Mr. Evans." Devon smiled up at him.

Westfield jumped into the act. "James Westfield, Miss St. James." He smoothed the gray hairs back from his temple. "How are you liking our countryside?"

Devon laughed. "It's quite delightful after the stifling air of London."

Their eyes caught. Sebastian had but one thought: He'd never been so proud of her.

He'd never despised himself more.

For with every second, with every word, her confidence bloomed. She was like a fragile blossom come newly into the world and reveling in warmth and sunshine. She laughed. She chatted.

It went off perfectly.

For Sebastian, the evening lasted an eternity. Evans, Mason, and Westfield stayed far longer than he would have liked. Devon retired not long after they departed. Before her cheery good night, she glowingly pronounced it a thoroughly enjoyable evening.

Left alone in the drawing room, the two brothers were steaming. Justin crossed his arms over his chest and turned to Sebastian, his lips tight.

"Well," he stated coolly, "that went well."

Sebastian fixed him with a glare of pure ice. "She did splendidly, and you know it."

"Yes, I do know it, and I don't mean Devon," Justin pointed out stiffly. "I'm referring to your choice of prospective husbands. Why, those three buffoons could hardly keep their hands off her."

While *he*, Sebastian reflected furiously, could hardly keep his hands off them. All the more reason to see her wed, he told himself, and quickly.

"And did you see Westfield? He used his quizzing glass to look at her br—"

"Yes," Sebastian growled, "I saw."

"Well, they won't do. Any of them."

Sebastian said nothing.

Justin eyed him. "Don't tell me you favor one of those three!"

"I do not," Sebastian affirmed, his tone dangerously low. "Devon will not be marrying Mason, or Evans, and certainly not Westfield."

"I see. Well, then, in that case, I'm heading back to London."

"Tonight?"

"Yes. Devon may find the London air stifling, but I can't wait to get back."

Sebastian was well aware Justin was chafing. He'd been prowling restlessly all day, so he wasn't surprised that Justin wouldn't wait until morning to return to London. Why, that Justin had even chosen to follow him here was amazing. Justin usually avoided Thurston Hall like the plague. Besides that, two days in the country tended to have that effect on a man of Justin's nature.

He accompanied Justin to the front door and onto the steps, where a footman had already deposited his bags.

Justin turned to him. "It seems we accomplished little tonight. My God, can you imagine Devon being married to any of those three idiots! A suitable candidate for her hand isn't just going to stumble into our paths. Where do you suggest we look next?"

Justin's practicality was beginning to set his nerves on edge, for at the moment, it wasn't something Sebastian really wanted to consider. But wasn't that the whole point of tonight's exercise?

"We've already established that my friends are out," Justin continued, "but perhaps one of yours—"

"Out of the question." Sebastian cut him off abruptly. He could not bear to see Devon wed to one of his friends! "We'll just have to try again," he told Justin curtly. "We need to marry her off, and quickly. Should it come to it, I'm sure the right husband can be found with a little added jingle in his pocket."

"I suppose that's a possibility," Justin agreed. He paused. "How long will you remain here at the Hall?"

Sebastian shook his head. "I'm not sure."

"Well," Justin said, "if I should come up with any brilliant solutions, I shall return." A brief salute, and he was gone.

Sebastian stepped back into the entrance hall, slowly closing the doors. A shadowy darkness spilled through him. God, but his head ached abominably, and he damn well knew a night's rest wouldn't cure it.

A rustle behind him snared his attention. He turned sharply, for he'd thought he was alone.

He was not.

A small figure stood in the shadows, there near the foot of the grand staircase.

Devon.

Their eyes locked endlessly. Hers were wide and unblinking, impossibly gold, the only hint of color in her white face.

She did not speak. She simply stared at him.

A vast, empty silence stretched between them.

And in the stillness of that never-ending moment, Sebastian damned himself to the very pits of hell and beyond—as he knew she damned him. Chilling certainty swept over him, and he knew, beyond thought, beyond reason . . .

Sweet Christ, she'd heard every word.

Twenty

There was a heavy, suffocating pressure on Devon's chest. It reminded her how once, when she was young, she'd been running through the streets and a pock-marked youth had stuck out his foot. She'd tripped on her skirts, falling flat on her face, the air driven from her lungs so that she couldn't breathe. Her ears had been roaring. She'd been terrified beyond measure, for there was fire in her lungs, and all she could do was lie there, unable to move, trying desperately to breathe.

But that was not the worst of it. Hot shame flooded her, to the core of her being. When at last she was able to gather the presence of mind to drag in a harsh breath, she stumbled to her feet and ran the other way.

She felt the same way now.

The muscles in her face seemed frozen. Her limbs were like ice. She was certain if she moved, her very skin would crack.

Everything inside her rebelled. She refused to believe what she'd just heard. Sebastian could never be so cruel, so devious! But there was no denying it, no denying the truth. For she could still hear him, his voice playing over and over, echoing in her mind until she wanted to retch.

I'm sure the right husband can be found with a little added jingle in his pocket.

Her insides twisted into a sick, ugly knot. Her face felt horribly hot. She battled a stinging rush of tears. Through some miracle, her throat locked tight against them.

Numbly she looked at him. For an instant she sensed that he was as stunned as she. She didn't want to believe it, for this was Sebastian, whom she trusted. Sebastian, whom she loved.

"You would . . . *pay* a man to marry me?"

Delivered into that awful quiet, her voice was but a rusty sliver of sound. Lord, it actually *hurt* to say the words aloud.

The tension was nearly unbearable. In silence she confronted him, staring at him with eyes so dry they burned. And all the while Sebastian remained unmoving. The set of his shoulders reflected a quiet resignation.

"Tell me, Sebastian. You would pay a man to take me into his home and into his bed?"

The silence ripened. Sebastian remained still as a statue, his gray eyes fixed on her face. He didn't even blink. And somehow that smothering quiet was far more devastating than anything he might have said.

Her eyes squeezed shut, then opened. Something flickered across his dark features then, something that might have been guilt.

An immense wave of pain swept over her. She pressed icy-cold fingertips to trembling lips. "Oh, God," she said brokenly, and then again, "*Oh, God.*"

With a swirl of skirts, she flung herself headlong up the stairs. Behind her, there was a muttered curse. Footsteps pounded behind her, but she ran harder.

Why couldn't he leave her be? Hadn't he done enough? All she wanted was to be left alone. But just as she crossed the threshold of her room, the toe of one slipper caught on the hem of her gown. She sprawled across the floor, and it was just as before. The breath driven from her chest, she struggled to regain her footing and her breath.

Sebastian was already there. His hands on her waist, he tried to help her up.

"Leave me be!" she shouted. Wildly she swung an elbow.

He ducked just in time to save his nose. Abruptly he released her.

On her feet now, Devon faced him squarely. "Get out!"

He did not. Instead, with the calm, decisive manner that only he possessed, he closed the door very neatly with the heel of his hand. With the same economy of movement he locked the door and deposited the key in the pocket of his waistcoat.

Devon's gaze traveled from his pocket to his face. "What the bloody hell do you think you're doing?"

"You're distraught," he stated quietly.

"And you're a bastard," she charged feelingly. She'd progressed from shock to sheer, simmering rage. Her hand floated to her breast, a mocking parody. "Oh, la, how could I have forgotten! Despite your diligently tireless efforts to make me into a lady, I am the one who is a bastard, am I not?"

Their eyes tangled. "Do not belittle yourself, Devon. You are ever a lady and you know it. You proved it tonight. Besides, your origins have nothing to do with this—"

"Oh, but I beg to differ! My origins, as you like to put it, have everything to do with this. I told you once that I promised my mother I would never whore or steal or beg. You didn't believe me then, and it's clear your opinion of me has not changed!" She lashed out furiously. "I wouldn't make my living on my back then, and I won't do it now. I won't let you make a whore of me."

"A whore! For pity's sake, Devon—"

"You would pay a man to take me into his home and into his bed! You would *pay* him!" she cried. "Isn't that the same as whoring? Well, I won't let you. Do you hear? I won't let you!"

He stepped close. "Devon," he said, his voice low and taut. "Devon, please."

She gave a tiny shake of her head. Even now, when she was so angry and despairing, his nearness made her ache inside. All at once she felt as if she stood on the very precipice of the earth. And she didn't know whether to leap away, into the darkness . . .

Or hurl herself straight into Sebastian's arms.

But she was too hurt. Too angry.

Bitterness scored her soul. She raised her face to his. "Tonight was no casual evening of entertainment, was it? It was something else. Something calculated. Oh, but I should have known. Naturally you would have *planned* it, as you plan everything. Perhaps I should be flattered you didn't decide to auction me off to the highest bidder tonight after dinner."

Her scorn pricked him. A dull red flush crept beneath the bronze of his skin.

"Devon, you have to listen—"

"I don't! You tricked me, Sebastian. You tricked me! I wanted to be a governess, a companion, and you knew it. Was I such a miserable failure then? Is that what you foresee?"

"No. *No!*"

"Then if you wanted to be rid of me, all you had to do was say it!"

"Rid of you . . . My God," he said, stunned. "That's not it at all!"

When he reached for her, she wrenched away.

He was undaunted. He caught her shoulders in his grasp and gave her a little shake.

"Devon, you have to listen to me. It's not what you think. You're so sweet and lovely, and once I found out you were a virgin . . . we were afraid, Justin and I . . . that you would end up at the whim and whimsy of some unscrupulous wretch who would try to take advantage of your innocence! And I knew you would never stand for it, I knew it! I couldn't stand the thought that you might end up on the streets again . . . I wanted to shield you, to keep you from harm's way. I needed to know that you would be cared for always. Never cold . . . never hungry . . ."

She knew that he was saying he wanted to protect her. Perhaps in some far distant part of her, she *did* understand. But her hurt and feelings of betrayal were still too fresh.

Suddenly it was all spilling out. "I was so excited tonight . . . I thought . . . you wanted to introduce me to your friends! I didn't want to fail, Sebastian. I wanted to make you proud. I wanted to be all you taught me to be."

"You are," he said fiercely. "You were. And I *was* proud. You looked beautiful tonight. You *are* beautiful. Don't you know any man would be glad to have you at his side?"

Her heart cried out, *Any man but you*.

"Do you remember that night in my room, when you carried me to bed?"

A smile appeared from nowhere. "You told me I was handsome. That I stole your breath away."

"I'd have given myself to you that night." The confession tripped off her tongue, torn from deep inside. "Then you told me not to *ever* tell another man what I'd just told you. I-I was so ashamed, I thought I'd die. I didn't know what I'd done that was so wrong."

That fleeting smile vanished. "You did nothing wrong," he said, his voice oddly strained. "It was me. And I wanted it too, I swear. It was just . . . if things were different . . . if *I* were different." His voice trailed off.

Her eyes filled with tears.

"Oh, Christ," he said raggedly, "don't cry." He sounded as raw and tortured as she felt. Catching her around the waist, he dragged her close. He rocked her back and forth. "Don't cry, love. It tears me apart when you do."

Her fingers twisted into the fabric of his shirt. This was all she'd ever wanted—to be locked fast within the binding protection of his strong embrace. But not like this. Not when he was filled with regret, and she with pain. Not when she ached to the bottom of her soul. Try though she might, she couldn't withhold the dry, heartbreaking little sob that broke from her throat.

His arms tightened, his hold fiercely urgent. Lean fingers slipped beneath her hair, urging her face into the notch where his neck met his shoulder. A single tear leaked from beneath her lashes.

"I never meant to hurt you. It's the last thing I want. Do you forgive me?" Fingers beneath her chin, he smoothed a tangled curl from her cheek. Wordlessly he captured her chin, bringing her gaze to his. As he lowered his head, their lips hovered but a breath apart.

"Devon, please tell me you forgive me."

Their eyes clung. "I want to. But—" Trapped in a maelstrom of conflicting turmoil, she took a deep, tremulous breath. "I don't know what I think," she burst out, her voice choked with tears. "I don't know what to believe."

A warm, blunted fingertip trailed over the lilting arch of her brows, the rounded pertness of her nose, the slant of her cheek, the tender cord at the side of her neck. Her heart pounding, Devon stood paralyzed beneath his touch, so gentle, so unbearably gentle.

His mouth grazed hers. Their breath mingled. "Believe this," he whispered. "Believe me," he said against her mouth, into it.

And then he kissed her.

Her heart constricted, for his kiss was far more than she expected, yet no more than she desired. With the feel of his mouth warm and hard upon hers, the tight knot of fear inside her slipped away. And she wondered how on earth a mere kiss could be both tender and fierce, fiery and restrained all at once.

Yet it was, and she dreaded the moment it would end. The impossible sweetness of his mouth upon hers was balm to her wounded soul. The tumult within her slipped away, and in its stead was a fiery yearning, like hot, gilded sunlight streaming through her. There was only Sebastian. Hungry for more of this sweet sensation, hungry for *him*, her lips parted beneath the wordless demand of his.

The expert tutelage of his tongue brought her own out of hiding. When her tongue touched his, there was a low, vibrating growl deep in his chest. She could feel his arms hard around her back, drawing her closer and closer until there was no part of him she could not feel. Her hands were splayed against the broad plane of his chest. She was searingly aware of the aroused thickness of his maleness hard against the softness of her belly.

A fingertip traced the delicate sweep of her collarbone, then strayed lower, an almost maddening caress across the bare skin above the neckline of her bodice.

Devon's heart leaped. Her breathing hastened. Sebastian's breath echoed almost harshly in the back of her throat. His knuckles skimmed the rounded tops of her breasts. They were burning and aching, peculiarly heavy. Pinpricks of sensation stabbed there at the peaks. She held her breath, suspended in an agony of longing. Sweet Lord, would he never . . .

Suddenly, almost impatiently, that lean, dark hand dipped beneath the neckline of her gown. Strong fingers cupped her fullness, taking its weight in the palm of his hand. A lone fingertip swirled a maddening rhythm around and around her nipple, coming close but never quite touching the dark, straining center. And when at last his thumb raked across one turgid peak, sheer pleasure jolted her, a bolt of lightning.

Everything inside went weak. She melted against him, feeling her nipples tighten and pucker beneath that tauntingly elusive caress.

When at last he released her mouth, she clutched at him lest she fall in a heap at his feet.

He rested his forehead against hers. Within his eyes glimmered a scalding heat. "I want you," he whispered.

The words were low, his tone almost gritty. His intensity sent an odd little shiver all through her.

Her gaze enchained to his, she couldn't look away.

"Devon," he whispered, "do you know what I'm saying?"

Her heart was throbbing so that she could scarcely hear. She swallowed, mutely questioning.

His gaze pierced even deeper.

"I want you," he said again. "I want to make love to you."

His stark honesty made her quiver inside. In that moment he surely possessed her inside and out. Sheer emotion filled her until she thought she would burst. She struggled to speak, but all that emerged was a choked, strangled sound. Mutely placing her fingertips on the hollow of his cheek, she let the gesture say what she could not.

The next thing she knew, her feet were no longer beneath her. She felt herself borne high in the air. He started toward the bed in the corner, then abruptly stopped. His gaze swiveled from the pretty flowered coverlet to the door.

Devon faltered. "Sebastian, what's wrong? I-I thought—"

"Not here," he said with a shake of his head. His eyes snared hers. "I want you in my room"—his eyes darkened—"and in my bed."

He was already striding forward.

Devon wanted to weep all over again . . . but this time from happiness.

Twenty-one

Holding her, listening to her pour out her anguish, feeling the tremor that shook her limbs, the icy clasp of her fingers, that single, scalding tear hot against his flesh . . . Sebastian felt something tug at the very center of his being. He knew he was lost the instant he touched her.

No, that wasn't right. He'd been lost far longer. He'd been lost since that rainy night he'd carried her into his town house . . . straight into his heart.

He was tired of battling against himself. He could fight this burning longing inside him no more. It was too strong. Too intense. Too overwhelming. It was something he could never conquer—never even *hope* to conquer.

Nor did he want to. Not now. He had no conscience. He had no scruples. There was no time for guilt, for rationalization. Society's rules were cast aside. His world narrowed until nothing else existed.

There was only Devon.

Devon in his arms . . . in his bed.

His, he thought fiercely. *His.*

Slowly he lowered her to the floor, so that she stood before him.

A blazing fire in the hearth offered light and warmth. The heavy crimson draperies at the window were parted, revealing a full moon that rendered the room nearly light as day. Her slender form was cast in muted shades of silver and gold. The feelings crowding his chest were half pleasure, half pain. She looked ethereal. Like an angel. His gaze roved over her fine-boned features, exquisitely aristocratic. In some faraway part of him, he couldn't help but wonder . . . Who was she? Who was she really?

Small, slippered feet were planted squarely between his. Her hair had come loose, spilling over her shoulder. He slipped his fingers beneath the profusion of silken tendrils, curling his hand around the side of her neck. His thumb rested on the vulnerable hollow of her throat, slipping beneath her necklace. He could feel the wild thrumming of her pulse, as rampant as his own.

Very gently he tilted her face to his. His gaze roved over her features.

On her lips was the wispiest of smiles, the most beautiful sight he'd ever seen. Never able to hide her feelings, her expression betrayed her every thought. It was almost as if he saw clear to her heart . . . and what he saw was a shining sweetness, a purity of feeling that struck him like a blow to the belly. Her eyes were brilliant and unwavering, pure topaz. He had tasted for himself the sweetly unguarded yielding of her lips. And he knew, with a certainty that resounded in every part of him, that she'd have let him do anything, anything he wanted.

A thunder of emotion roared through him, for it was a heady, giddy sensation, almost akin to power. Yet it was also a moment fraught with contrariness. He stood rooted to the floor. Oddly enough, he was half afraid to move, for fear that she would disappear, that all his dreams were for naught. That this night would never be . . .

With slow deliberation he removed his jacket, his waistcoat, then finally his shirt.

When his naked chest came into view, the tip of her tongue emerged to wet her lips, leaving them damp and dewy, sending an explosion of desire all through him.

"Devon. Oh, God, Devon . . ." His head came down. His mouth sought hers. He went a little mad then, crushing her against him. He kissed her like a man half starved, long and lingering, drugged by the intoxicating knowledge that there was no need to hold back.

His head was spinning. "Devon," he whispered, kissing the tender spot just before her ear. "My sweet, sweet Devon." His mouth was on the arch of her throat, his hands warm on on her shoulders. A flick of his fingers, and her bodice slipped down to bunch at her hips.

She inhaled sharply. Sebastian reluctantly raised his head. Her eyelids lifted. She gazed up at him, her eyes smoky and dazed.

Sebastian's breath dammed in his throat. She stood before him, half naked, half shy, half temptress.

Her breasts were even more glorious than he remembered—round, gleaming mounds of flesh that stood out from her chest, lush and delectably full, tipped by perfect, voluptuous peaks of pale coral. Her lungs expanded in a deep, tremulous breath—quite inadvertently, he guessed—setting those lush, jutting mounds all aquiver.

He clenched his teeth, for in that instant, surely every ounce of blood in his body rushed to the head of his member. He could feel it pulsing, throbbing like a heartbeat there, a wanton need he had no hope of controlling.

Vaguely he marveled that he didn't spill himself in that instant, embarrassing them both.

But Devon, he suspected, was feeling enough of that for both of them.

"Sebastian?"

His name was but a thread of sound, underscored by more than a hint of uncertainty. He sensed a fleeting panic. His gaze came back up to hers, and the tightly strung tension within him eased. A laugh snagged halfway up his throat. Quickly he stifled it. Her eyes were huge. She had noted his avid attention, and her cheeks were stained the same enchanting color as her nipples. She was not, he reminded himself, a woman of savoir faire. She swallowed, and her hands started to come up as she instinctively sought to shield herself.

He thwarted her with gentle insistence. Catching her hands, he threaded her fingers through his and tucked them against her sides.

"Don't go all shy on me, sweet," he said softly. He pressed a reassuring kiss to the corner of her lips. "Don't be afraid."

"I'm not afraid," she countered breathlessly. "I was just thinking that—that I'm glad it's not daylight."

Of all that she could have said, that was the last thing he expected. But that was his Devon, ever forthright, ever direct.

It was nerves that prompted the admission, he decided. He took her mouth, the contact slow and unhurried until her nervous tension began to subside. One last kiss on softly parted lips . . . and then his mouth slid with slow heat, pursuing a relentless path down, across the very top of gently rising flesh.

He knelt before her, his head poised between the scented harbor of her breasts. She jerked when she felt the moist heat of his breath, but she didn't retreat. He released her hands, aware of them fluttering, touching the sleek binding of his shoulders, then flitting away. Back and away. Back and away . . .

His own hands displayed no such hesitation. They were otherwise engaged, filled with her tender bounty. His fingertips grazed the tips of her breasts. Though it was but a fleeting, wispy caress, the budding crests swelled hard and taut against his palm.

"Sebastian," she said weakly.

He squeezed gently. Her nipples stood up, thrusting stiffly erect, offered up before him in tempting sacrifice, but he deferred the invitation. She was exquisitely sensitive there, he noted appreciatively.

"Let me touch you," he implored, his voice muffled by soft, succulent flesh. "Let me love you."

As he spoke, he traced a lazily erotic pattern around and around dusky pink crowns, deliberately avoiding the darkly rouged center.

"Sebastian," she groaned.

He stole a glance upward. Her teeth dug into her

lower lip, as if she were trying hard to keep from crying out.

"What, love? What do you want?"

Her breath came in shallow little pants. "I want . . ."

"Tell me, love. I'll give it to you, I swear."

"I want your mouth on my . . . on my breasts. Is that terribly . . . unladylike?"

He gave a half laugh. "No, sweet, that's desire. But tell me where on your breasts," he teased. "Where . . . precisely?"

Coming to this point had been a long, arduous journey. But now he felt as if he were coming home—as if a great weight had been lifted from his shoulders—and he couldn't resist teasing her just a little.

With the tip of his tongue he delicately touched one swollen, straining peak. "Here?" he queried

Her breath tumbled out with a rush. Her nails dug into the hard flesh of his shoulders.

Enflamed, he sucked the whole of her nipple into his mouth. Pulling strongly, his mouth hot and torrid, sucking hard on first one, then the other, until she whimpered and swayed and his hold was all that held her upright.

A shivering cry pierced the air. A fierce possessiveness shot through him, and he surged upright with her in his arms. Three steps and his precious burden was deposited on his bed, minus her gown, now puddled in the spot so recently vacated.

His own clothing was dealt with just as deftly, the buttons of his trousers torn from their berth. His palms on either side of her head, he eased down atop her, mindful of his weight.

Bare, silken arms slipped up to encircle his neck.

Her fingers at his nape, she caught his head. Tangling her fingers in his hair, she pulled his mouth down to hers. He inhaled sharply, for now his burning shaft rode between the notch at the top of her thighs. Beneath him, she shifted restlessly, searchingly, and he wondered if she knew what havoc she wrought with her questing, untutored movements.

Desire churned in his belly. His entire body was on fire. Her nipples burned into his chest, still moist with the damp wash of his tongue. The urge to thrust wildly, to plunge himself hard and deep was overwhelming.

Easy, he warned himself. He felt raw and greedy and carnal. His shaft was so painfully rigid he thought he would surely split his skin. But he knew he must have a care. This was her first time. He must be gentle.

For he wanted to cause her no more pain.

Slowing the wanton fever of their kiss, he eased to his side. With the heel of his hand, he skimmed the smoothness of her belly, tangled his fingers in the golden fleece atop her thighs. With bold intent, he skimmed her secret cleft, tracing damp, furrowed heat before one long, strong finger burrowed within warm, pliant flesh.

He felt her gasp and she stiffened. He soothed her with lips and tongue, their breath swirling together as he gauged the limits of her passage. At last she relaxed. Her hips lifted, and he burrowed deeper within her.

Her body yielded. With his thumb he circled her secret pleasure button. His finger sank deeper, gliding, stroking, gently stretching. Sweat beaded his upper lip. He ached with the need to exchange his finger with his rod. Not yet, he cautioned himself. Could she take more? he wondered wildly.

She could . . . and did.

She was so warm, so sleek and hot. With his thumb he pressed the nub of her desire, rubbing and circling, pleasuring her until her head rose from the pillow and she moaned, a shimmering cry that echoed in the back of his throat.

He tore his mouth from hers and stared down at her. Her eyes opened, dazed and smoky. She clutched at him. "Please," she gasped, "Oh, Sebastian, please." Her thighs parted, opening wide.

Some nameless emotion swept him in its tide. With one hand he guided himself inside her, his control obliterated. He gasped, his crown probing through hot, sleek curls. Oh, God. His lungs were scalding. He could barely breathe. He nudged her cleft, feeling her sleek, wet passage stretch to accept him . . .

And then cursed the very heavens themselves.

For despite his most stringent preparations, her frail barrier of innocence barred him entrance. And though he wanted his possession to be slow and unhurried and careful, the feel of her silken channel clasped tight around his surging helm tempted him past bearing. Knowing he was the first, that no other man had touched her like this, sent a raw, primitive rush shooting through his veins.

His eyes squeezed shut. Blindly he thrust . . .

Her tiny little cry was like a knife to the heart. He knew she tried to smother it, but it was too late. Sebastian despised himself in that moment. Christ, if he'd hurt her . . .

Fool! A voice inside him chastised fiercely. How could he not? She was so tiny. And he was not.

His gaze slid to where their bodies met, where dark, wiry curls mingled with silken fleece. It was a sight of blatant intimacy—a sight so rawly erotic his mouth went dry. Christ, and she'd taken but half his length . . .

Torture. Ecstasy. Which was it? Oh, God. How could he stop? How could he *not*?

Though every instinct urged him to seat himself to the hilt, he couldn't. He froze, just as terrified to withdraw, afraid of causing her still more pain.

"Sebastian?" Her breath rushed by his ear. Her fingers strayed to his nape, touched his hair, a soft cry of confusion on her lips. "Sebastian . . . What's wrong?"

He hated himself for the sudden doubt that clouded her beautiful golden eyes.

"I hurt you," was all he could say. "I hurt you."

Her fingers stilled. "You didn't," she said faintly.

He could feel himself pulsing. Against her. Inside her. "I did," he said hoarsely. "I heard you. Oh, God, Devon, I want you so much! Can't you feel how I want you?" His eyes darkened. "But I'm afraid. Afraid I'll hurt you again." He floundered. "You're so tiny," he whispered. "And I'm so—"

Understanding dawned. Suddenly her fingertips were on the hardness of his mouth, quelling the flow of words. "I'm fine!" she cried softly. "Truly!" Even as she spoke, silken thighs clamped tight around his, as if she sought to imprison him fast within her. Slender arms locked around his shoulders.

Her lips formed a tremulous smile, lips that hovered but a breath beneath his. In her eyes shone a depth of emotion so pure and unguarded he felt humbled.

"Take me now," she whispered. "Make me yours."

"Devon," he ground out.

Her smile wavered. "You'll hurt me if you don't." Her voice caught on a half sob. "You'll hurt me if you *won't*." Her voice finally broke, and so did he.

He plunged forward, a powerful lunge that took him to the gate of her womb. Her tender chasm more than gave way. Hot, clinging flesh melted around his heat and hardness; it was impossible to tell where his body ended and hers began.

"I belong to you now," she cried against his throat. "I do."

He buried his head in the hollow of her shoulder. "Devon." He whispered her name, a half-strangled sound, for he had no breath for more. "*Devon*."

His mouth took hers, a fiery exchange of sweetness. Passion soared. Again and again he slammed inside her, yielding to the blind, white-hot need that consumed them both.

Her back arched. Her hips sought his, their bodies in perfect union. Her nails scraped his back. Her head tossed from side to side on the pillow, then all at once she screamed and went rigid, convulsing tight around his searing heat.

Her spasms fueled his own. Hurtling toward the edge, he drove inside her one last time. A shudder wracked his form. He groaned hoarsely, for nothing could have prepared him for this. His seed erupted, spurting again and again, hot and scalding.

It was the most powerful, intense orgasm he'd ever experienced.

Moved to the depths of his being, he had to wait a very long time before he was able to gather the strength to roll to his side. Cradling her against him, he bent his head and kissed her mouth, with long, lingering sweetness.

And all the while she was smiling.

He trailed a finger over her nose. "Go to sleep, minx," he whispered.

"Yes, my lord," she surprised him by saying promptly.

And the deed was done nearly as promptly.

Sebastian was amazed. He wasn't sure if he should be pleased or offended. As for him, he knew that sleep would not come so easily with this enchanting creature in his bed.

Alas, he was wrong.

Twenty-two

It was the click of the door that woke her.

Prying open an eye, she saw Sebastian striding across the chamber, clad in a crimson brocade robe. She must have been sleeping quite heavily, for she hadn't been aware of his leaving the bed. The last thing she remembered was being held fast against his length, his arms a haven that shielded her from all harm. She recalled stirring once. His arms came harder around her, as if he couldn't bear to let her go.

A wondrous thought, that. She wanted to savor not just the heated passion that sizzled between them but the breathless feeling of closeness, of belonging. She needed to stow it away deep inside for the days when . . . But no. *No.* She wouldn't think about that. She wanted to allow nothing to taint this, the most precious memory of her life.

He came to sit beside her on the bed, one hand behind his back. The other drifted over the slope of one bare shoulder. Hers lay curled on the counterpane, just beneath her chin. He plucked it from its resting place. With his lips he nuzzled each knuckle. He turned her palm so that it lay cradled within his, then kissed each fingertip in turn.

In all her days Devon had never felt anything so exquisitely erotic.

"Good morning," he said at last.

That much belated greeting made her sorely want to laugh. The tenderness that lurked in his gray eyes made her throat ache. It struck her then that she was happy. Deliriously happy. She couldn't remember ever feeling quite so comfortably content.

"Did you sleep well?" he said gently.

"I did," she returned softly, then frowned. "But obviously you did not, if you're up prowling about at this hour." She took in the lingering shadows of night that had only now begun to recede through the window. She scolded him gently. "You work entirely too hard, Sebastian—"

"I wasn't working. I was in the garden."

"The garden! At this hour?"

"It's sunrise." He pointed toward the window, where the eastern sky was awash with a dozen shades of pearly coral.

Devon peered at him closely. His mouth quirked, as if he found something vastly amusing. Why, he appeared almost mischievous!

Sebastian . . . mischievous?

The polished refinement that so defined the essence of this man—the aristocratic marquess of Thurston—was gone. His robe was loosely knotted at his waist. It revealed a dark slice of bronzed chest, a sight of such stark virility that her stomach clenched oddly. With his jaw dark and shadowed with his beard, he was as unabashedly masculine as ever. But there was a difference now.

A lock of dark hair spilled onto his forehead. She'd never seen him so relaxed, even carefree. His air of boyish playfulness made her heart turn over.

Cautiously she decided it might also be cause for alarm. "Sebastian?" she queried sweetly.

"Yes, love?"

"What do you have behind your back?"

Dark brows climbed high. "Why, not a thing!" His expression and tone were in complete accord—both vehemently declared his innocence.

And both were negated when he scooted back just a smidgen.

Determinedly Devon surged forward. Too late she remembered she wasn't wearing a single stitch of clothing. With a gasp she lunged for the coverlet.

It was rescued just in the nick of time. Not that he hadn't seen her before—glory be, he'd kissed and caressed every square inch of her! But it was no longer night, and, well, if she was feeling rather shy, she couldn't help it. This business of appearing naked before him was something that would take a little time to become accustomed to.

It didn't help that Sebastian was laughing outright, the rogue! Devon glared, trying to summon an indignant outrage. While she wasn't precisely apprehensive, she was definitely suspicious of the unholy gleam that lit his eyes to pure silver. For the first time she glimpsed a hint of the rake.

Soft lips pursed. "Show me what you're hiding."

"I'll do more than show you." That devilish smile widened. "What say I let you guess?"

"Agreed," she stated promptly.

"Then lay back against the pillow, and bring your hands alongside your head."

She did as he requested. "Like this?" she said breathlessly.

"Exactly like that. Now, hush, my little love, and close your eyes."

My little love. The endearment made her blood sing. If she'd been deliriously happy before, she was positively ecstatic now.

Velvety softness traced the tip of her nose, tickled her cheeks and came to rest against the center of her lips. Scent that was incredibly sweet assailed her.

She inhaled deeply. Her fingers curled into her palms. "A rose," she said breathlessly. "That's why you were in the garden."

"Just so," he murmured. "Now, you may open your eyes. But be very still. I'm conducting an experiment."

The next thing she knew, the coverlet lay bunched around her hips. On the fringes of her vision, she could see her naked breasts, creamy ivory flesh tipped with coral. So much for modesty, she decided hazily, feeling the heat of a blush proclaim her embarrassment.

But she didn't move.

Sebastian's gaze was locked on her breasts. His eyes had gone dark. A long, hushed silence followed. The play of emotion on his features took her by storm. She felt herself touched beyond measure as both awe and wonder sped across his features.

"Glorious. Absolutely . . . glorious." With almost agonizing slowness, that tender rosebud traced the boundaries of one breast, dipped into the valley between, only to scale the other. There it trailed a tormenting path around the dusky summit.

"Sunrise," he whispered, "is what this rose is called. And my God, but he was right . . . your nipples . . . are the exact same color as this rose."

Devon, almost mesmerized by the reverence she sensed in him, was on the verge of reaching for him. She stopped in mid-movement.

"He?" she echoed. "*He*?" She swallowed hard. "Sebastian, who do you mean? *Who* was right?"

He blinked, finally dragging his eyes from her breasts. "Why, Justin. He said that your nip—"

"Yes, *that* I heard! But do you mean to say that Justin . . . that your brother *saw* my"—faith, but she could hardly bring herself to say it—"my breasts?"

"I'm afraid so," he said cheerfully.

Devon was mortified. "No," she moaned. "It's not true."

"Well," he said lightly, "if you don't believe me, then you'll simply have to ask him yourself."

Devon dove for the coverlet. "Oh, God," she moaned. "I shall never be able to face him again."

Sebastian chuckled richly. "Oh, come, it's not as bad as all that."

"It didn't happen to you!" She glared at him over the satin binding. "Precisely when did this occur?"

"The night of your injury."

She gasped. "So while I lay helplessly, the two of you ogled me!"

"It wasn't like that." He laughed. "He helped me bandage your side. When it was done, I eased you to your back and that's when—"

"Sebastian! You needn't say any more!"

"But we weren't ogling," he protested. "I was very gallant. I immediately covered you up. I was feeling rather possessive of you even then, you know."

"Is that supposed to make me feel better?"

He made no response. Instead his smile deepened.

"What?" she said weakly. "There's more?"

His eyes were dancing with mirth. "Well, I didn't allow Justin to ogle. But perhaps I did, just a bit. Because I fear I must confess . . ." He paused dramatically.

"What now?" she groaned.

"I admired your glorious breasts again," he confided softly, "later that night."

"You are the most wicked man to ever walk this earth!"

"Thank you," he said gravely, "I don't believe anyone has ever called me wicked before. I must say, I rather think I like it."

She clubbed him with the pillow. "You, sir, are no gentleman!"

"Would you feel better if I allowed you to ogle me?" Jet brows slashed up and down.

Devon couldn't help it. He looked silly. Ridiculous, really. Oh, she tried to contain it, but a smile emerged, and then a giggle. And one became two . . . Sebastian tugged her into his powerful embrace. Together they collapsed onto the bed in a fit of laughter.

And when it was over . . . he simply held her. Held her in a blessedly simple moment, where the outside world ceased to exist.

At length, they stirred. Sebastian curled his fingers around an ear, smoothing a tangle of gold away from her cheek. Devon's smile was tremulous and suddenly tenuous as well. Her lips parted. She tried to summon some light, breezy phrase, but the rise of a dark brow revealed she'd given herself away.

Unable to stop herself, she buried her face against

the breadth of his shoulder. With his knuckles, Sebastian brushed the downy curve of her cheek.

"What is it?" he murmured. "You can tell me anything, Devon. You can *say* anything. Don't you know that?" Threading his fingers in her hair, he pulled her head back so he could see her.

Her breath caught painfully, for suddenly she couldn't erase the fear seated deep in her breast. She loved him. She loved him so much, but where would it lead? *Oh, Sebastian,* she longed to cry, *what will happen next*? Did he still intend to marry her off? No. He couldn't. She wouldn't.

But what about him? What about his quest for a bride? Who would he choose . . . ?

"Devon," he said softly. Insistently.

She swallowed. "Very well then," she said, her voice very small. "When you walked in this morning, I was afraid."

"Afraid! Of what?"

Her gaze skipped away. "I thought you might be sorry about last night"—she took a breath—"sorry that we—"

"Hush. *Hush*. Now then, look at me. No, not the window behind me. No, not at my ears! Ah, yes, that's the way."

Reluctantly she complied. There was no mistaking the gravity of his features. Yet there was something brewing in the depths of his eyes—a trace of unlikely amusement.

She dragged in an unsteady breath. "Are you trying to make me laugh?"

"I don't know," he responded. "Am I succeeding?"

Devon didn't laugh, but she *did* smile—oh, but she couldn't stop the veriest hint from crossing her lips.

Sebastian returned that smile, his own just as fleeting. With the pad of his thumb he caressed the side of her neck. "I am not sorry. I am *not*," he emphasized. "I have no regrets. Absolutely none."

The tenderness that lurked in his eyes nearly made her come undone. "Truly?" She started to raise her hand to touch the bristly stubble on his cheek. He snared it and pressed a kiss to her palm, then twined their fingers and brought their clasped hands down to rest on one steely thigh.

His gaze pinioned hers.

"Devon," he said, his voice very low, "last night was very precious to me. And I should like to savor it." He paused, and she sensed he was at an uncharacteristic loss for words. "Accept that what we shared was something very rare. Something very unique. Because it is, you know."

"I know," she whispered.

"I want nothing to ruin it. Are we agreed?"

Devon nodded mutely, incapable of doing more. Imprisoned deep in the web of his gaze, in that moment she could deny him nothing. His husky declaration made her insides turn to mush.

Lean fingers slipped beneath the tumbled cloud of her hair. His kiss was long and thorough. She sighed, feeling as if she'd been turned inside out.

It was a long, long time before Sebastian lifted his head. They gazed at each other, each with a silly little smile.

"Well," Devon murmured after a moment, "I suppose I should rise."

"Stay right where you are!" came his swift, vehement order. "I'm coming back to bed. I'm feeling distinctly lazy."

"Lazy! You?" It was a comment made not entirely in jest. "You are a very busy man. I'm sure you've correspondence to attend to, the business of your estates and such."

"All that can wait. *You* cannot. And I give you fair warning. We may very well not leave this room for an entire week."

"A week! What about your work? Your duties?"

"To hell with the future. To hell with duty. I have you alone. All to myself. And I intend to take every advantage of it."

He started to slip off his robe, but she stopped him with a protest. "No," she said. "Let me." Her fingertips stole beneath the shoulders of his robe, tracing over the knotted hardness of his shoulders, sliding along warm, hard flesh.

"Are you making advances toward me, my good woman?"

He'd teased her unmercifully just a short time ago, but perhaps it was time he discovered turnabout was fair play. "I am, good sir," she replied.

"Remember last night?" he murmured silkily. "You said you were glad it wasn't daylight. You were shy about being seen in the light, I believe."

"So I was. But I do believe I've changed my mind. In fact," she stated, "I'm wondering what you would look like in the daylight." She paused, a little amazed at her own daring. "*Naked*," she emphasized.

He played along. "But I'm not," he said. "Naked, that is."

"Not yet you're not. But you soon will be. And then, sir, why, I may even do a bit of ogling myself."

He laughed huskily. "I do believe I hear a sultry promise in your voice."

"I do believe you're right." Boldly she pushed the robe off his shoulders.

His eyes had gone dark. "Devon," he whispered, "you're so beautiful."

"And so are you."

"I'm not. I am a—"

"You *are*," she insisted. As if to convince him, nimble fingers made quick work of the knot at his waist.

"Next to you, I feel like a great oaf."

"Ah," she said, her eyes gleaming, "but I like that. I like that you're so large and strong. You make me feel safe and warm. And I especially like this." She tangled her fingers in the springy dark hair on his chest and smiled directly into fiercely glowing gray eyes.

He wanted her, she thought, glorying in the revelation. *Sebastian wanted her*.

"Why," she went on, "this very morning I was thinking about the first time I saw you, looking so stiff and starched, your jacket fitting you so tightly there was nary a pucker or a wrinkle. I never guessed that your chest was covered with this dark, wonderful hair . . . But I liked it when you took off your jacket. And it sent a little thrill through me whenever you would roll up your sleeves. I used to look at your arms. Your hands. And I imagined what the rest of you might look like."

"Devon," he said hoarsely.

The sheet had slithered down her body long ago. Leaning forward, she pressed her nipples against the dark fur on his chest. She shifted, carefully straddling his thighs. She pressed her mouth against the cleft of his chin, allowing her tongue to trace the tiny indentation.

"Do you know," she said with a tinkling little laugh, "I've always wanted to do that?"

"My God, Devon"—strong hands settled possessively on the nip of her waist—"do you have any idea what you're doing to me?"

"What, good sir? What am I doing to you?"

"Look down, my dear."

She obeyed without thought . . . Her eyes opened wide. "Oh, my," she gasped.

"Oh, yes," Sebastian groaned thickly. "Oh, *yes*."

Twenty-three

The next three mornings were spent in similar fashion, in lazy contentment marked by long, languorous hours wrapped in each other's arms. London was a world away. Throughout each day, scarcely a moment went by that Devon was not at his side. They walked in the garden, her hand engulfed snugly in his. They wandered along the river and basked in the sun, sometimes in amiable silence, sometimes in laughing playfulness.

It wasn't difficult to understand why Sebastian loved Thurston Hall the way he did. That day in the portrait gallery, he'd stated the Hall was nearer and dearer to his heart than anything else. There was a simplicity of life here in the country, a blessed peacefulness that pervaded all, a calming serenity that could never exist in the frenzied pace of London. Here the rest of the world was shut out, eons away.

He'd told her that what they shared was something rare. Something unique. And how right he was! He touched her often—the fleeting sweep of a finger along the line of her jaw, the merest caress of his fingertips against hers. It was as if he couldn't get enough of her!

He cared for her. Cared for her deeply. It was there in the sizzle of his gaze when he made love to her, in every intimate glance that passed between them, every kiss bestowed upon her lips.

When she was with him, she felt like bursting with all that she felt. She loved him with every beat of her heart, every pore of her body, every fiber of her soul. And being with him like this . . . there could be no greater pleasure. She wanted it to go on and on, to never end. For when she was with him, there was no tomorrow. Only now. Only today. Only the wonder of belonging to him, of *being* with him.

And knowing Sebastian felt the same was sheer bliss.

One week after their arrival, they retired to the library after dinner, where they spent the next hour. Their game of chess concluded, Devon rose and moved to stand before the terrace doors. She stood there a moment, idly locking her hands behind her back and gazing out where a crescent moon shimmered in the sky. Turning back to Sebastian, she saw that he'd ambled to his feet.

"I have the feeling I'm boring you to distraction, Devon. I can't have that, now can I?" His brow raised in a show of rakishness. "We've played cards. Enjoyed a game of chess. Pray tell," he drawled, "is there some other sort of entertainment in which I might interest you?"

"There may well be," she countered daringly, even

as she blushed. "Perhaps you have some suggestions?"

His eyes turned to smoke. "I have several, in fact." Heat simmered in his eyes, so intense she felt scorched by it. "Come here and I'll see if I can tempt you."

Devon's pulse began to race. Her steps carried her forward without conscious thought. The instant she was within reach, he trapped her against him.

His hands rested on the swell of her hips. His lips hovered just above hers, so near the breath they shared was the very same. "I may shock you," he advised silkily.

A thrill went through her. "Shock me," she invited recklessly.

She caught a glimpse of his eyes, fiery and aglow, in the instant before his mouth swooped down to capture hers. A hand at the small of her back, he fitted her against him, allowing her to feel the rigid pulse beat of desire throbbing in his loins. Devon shivered, drowning in the hot, melting splendor of his kiss.

Neither of them was aware that the library door had opened and closed.

Justin took one look at the pair and swore, a blistering oath.

Devon started. Her hands caught at his jacket. "It's Justin," she gasped.

Sebastian paid no need. His grip on her waist tightened. He went right on kissing moist, passion-drenched lips. "Go away, Justin." He spoke without looking at his brother, without even raising his head.

"Sebastian," came a blunt, arch demand, "please

do me the courtesy of looking at me when I speak to you!"

Sebastian finally lifted his head. His arms tightened protectively. He gazed at Justin over the top of Devon's head. "What do you want?" he asked curtly.

Devon's initial shock at Justin's presence had been replaced by an acute embarrassment. She longed to bury her head against Sebastian's chest and burrow inside his jacket, but . . . well, it wasn't as if either of them could hide! She was going to have to face Justin sometime, so it might as well be now. Hauling in a deep breath, she turned and stepped to Sebastian's side. Sebastian allowed the movement, but kept a possessive hand at her waist, anchoring her close.

Justin, she saw, had taken up a stance near the card table. His expression was a stone-cold reflection of his voice. "I think you'd better let go of her."

Sebastian stiffened. He gave his brother a frosty stare. "I think not," he said in clipped tones. "And the next time, please do *me* the courtesy of knocking before you enter."

Justin's eyes narrowed. "Do you think I don't see what's happening here? You have no business touching her, Sebastian, and you know it. You certainly have no business *kissing* her. So I suggest you leave her alone," he said, his tone hard, "before she's ruined—"

All at once he stopped short. He glanced from Sebastian's taut features to Devon. "Dear God," he said numbly. "It's too late, isn't it?"

Devon's face had turned scarlet. Heat scalded her to the very tips of her toes.

"Justin," she said faintly, "it's all right."

"No, Devon, it's not all right."

Devon's fingers coiled in her skirts. Her lips parted, but no sound emerged. Justin was angry with Sebastian, not her. Something surfaced in his eyes, something she couldn't decipher. Pity?

He gazed at her directly. "This can't happen, Devon. It can't."

There was a horrible constriction in her throat. She wanted to clamp her hands over her ears so she didn't have to listen. She gave a shake of her head. "Justin—"

"It's not my intention to hurt you. I'm only trying to spare you! Damn it, do you have to make me say it? He won't marry you."

The words burned clear to her heart, gouging her to the core.

"He won't marry you," Justin repeated, as if once weren't enough. "He'd never risk the scandal." A shattering pause. "He'll marry someone like Penelope Harding."

Her breath left her lungs in a rush. Sebastian's arm had slipped away. She stood rooted to the floor, alone as never before. She raised a hand to her lips, still swollen from his kiss.

"Devon!" Justin implored softly. "Do you hear me? He'll break your heart."

No power on earth could have stopped her then. Trembling both inside and out, she transferred her gaze to Sebastian, to his frozen expression, to the tight lines etched around his mouth and eyes. Beside her, his body had gone taut and rigid.

He looked away.

And Devon knew. *She knew.*

Something inside her withered and died. It wasn't that he couldn't. He *wouldn't*. And there was a world of difference.

It wasn't Justin's frankness that wounded her. That she could accept. But Justin was wrong, she thought distantly. Sebastian couldn't break her heart. It was already broken. She could feel it shattering into a million shards . . . If he had wrenched it from her breast, the pain would have been no less.

With a stricken cry, she bolted for the stairs.

Sebastian grabbed at her hand. "Devon!" He would have been right behind her, if Justin hadn't stopped him.

He grabbed Sebastian's elbow. "Leave her alone."

Sebastian spun around. "Take your hands off me!" he hissed. "Haven't you done enough?"

Justin released him, but he didn't back down. Toe-to-toe, they faced each other. "I was honest, Sebastian. That's more than you can say."

"Stay out of this!" Sebastian warned sharply. "This is none of your affair."

"I'm *making* it my affair! My God, don't you realize what you've done? You. Ever proper. My sainted brother—"

"I've never pretended to be a saint, Justin! You know that!"

"Oh, now there's an excuse." Justin's tone was scathing. "God, and they call me a scoundrel!"

Sebastian's eyes were burning. "Who the hell are you to lecture me?"

"Exactly. *Exactly*. Christ, you even convinced me I was wrong about the two of you. You told me I was! I thought you could be trusted with her. I thought you were too noble to do anything *ig*noble. I thought that you, above all people, would do the right thing and leave her alone."

"Shut up!" Sebastian snarled.

"I will not! Do you think I didn't see the stars in her eyes? She was an innocent, wasn't she?"

"That's none of your business!"

Justin made a sound of disgust. "I came here with a list of suitable candidates for her hand, yet what do I find? The very thing we were supposed to prevent—Devon in the master's arms. Ah, but I wonder"—his tone was cutting—"what man will want your leavings? She deserves someone who'll love her, Sebastian. Someone who'll take care of her. Who'll give her everything she's never had. Or do you think to keep her here at your convenience, to make her your whore?"

Sebastian's hands balled into fists. "She's not a whore!"

"Oh, pardon me. Your mistress then. Your wife, when you deign to choose one, will surely love that." Justin gave a harsh laugh. "Oh, but I'm sure you'll figure out something. Planning was always your strong suit, wasn't it?"

Sebastian's breath whistled in. His big hands clenched at his sides. He wanted to pummel his brother's pretty face.

"By God," he said through clenched teeth, "if you weren't my brother, I'd—" He took a step forward, only to abruptly check himself.

Justin's eyes glittered. "Go ahead," he challenged. "I do believe we're both spoiling for a little rough-and-tumble."

Tension sizzled between them. Their eyes locked. They matched each other, blistering stare for blistering stare, a moment of sheer, utter tautness.

It was the closest they'd come to blows since they were children, and they both knew it.

It was Sebastian who ended the brittle stalemate.

His lips ominously thin, he walked stiffly to the door. "Get out, Justin." His expression was icy, his tone glacial. "Get out before I throw you out."

Devon lay curled on the bed, huddled in a tight little ball. She couldn't cry. In all her days she'd never experienced such depth of despair. When Mama had died, she'd felt as if a part of her heart had been chipped away. It was only now that the pain had began to ease.

But this was a hurt that went far beyond tears, a pain she feared she would carry inside forever.

This last week with Sebastian . . . She'd wanted so desperately to believe it could go on forever. That what they shared was more than moments of rapturous ecstasy, of churning, twisting limbs and clinging lips. She wanted to believe that their hearts were entwined as surely as their bodies.

But they could not shut away the outside world forever.

They could not shut away the truth.

She couldn't be angry with Justin, she just couldn't.

She was far too angry with herself. In the depths of her soul, she'd always known he would never marry her. Bitterly she acknowledged he'd told her as much, the night she'd discovered he intended to marry her off. What was it he'd said?

If things were different . . . if I *were different.*

No, she could not change who she was. She could not change *what* she was.

And neither could he.

Ah, yes, she thought, it was better to know the truth now than to live a fool's dream.

In sheer, utter desolation, she dropped her cheek on her hand.

It was then she heard it . . . the click of the door. Pushing her heavy mane from her face, she saw the outline of a tall, powerful form in the doorway.

Slowly she pushed herself upright. In that instant her heart surely ceased to beat. It resumed with thick, dull strokes. Her mind teetered. Time swung away.

In but a heartbeat, Sebastian was standing at the bedside. Strong hands slid beneath her. She felt the sweep of powerful arms about her, lifting high in the air.

Dumbly she stared at his profile, etched in moonlight. His features were drawn and taut. She felt in him a purposeful determination that was somehow almost fierce.

Deep in her throat, she made a low, choked sound.

His hold tightened. His pace quickened. Without a word, without a sound, he carried her down the hall to his chamber. The coverings raked aside, he deposited her on the mattress. Before she could draw breath, she was caught once more in the cage of his arms.

His embrace was almost crushing, so tight she could feel the throb of his heart beneath the place where her hand coiled on his chest. It echoed the drumbeat of her own, hard and fast.

A crippling wave of pain washed over her. She lay in his bed, she thought wildly, the bed where he would lie with his wife. In the house where his children would be born, the very bed where his children would be born—and this, from his lips!

She could not bear it. She could not.

"Why are you doing this?" she cried, uncaring that her voice was laden thick with tears.

With stark, wrenching clarity, she recalled the night of Sebastian's dinner party. Justin had predicted then that Sebastian would marry only a proper young woman of impeccable breeding and lineage.

A blue blood.

Devon knew why—because of the scandal his mother had caused. He would make no choices that would embroil him in similar scandal, she acknowledged bitterly. He would never marry *her*, a woman of tainted bloodlines.

Foolish though it was, she longed for him to whisper that he loved her as she loved him. She yearned to hear him vow she would be his wife, that her roots in St. Giles did not matter, nor his sense of duty or propriety.

But hers was a fleeting, blighted hope. He shook his head, his expression so ravaged she nearly cried out; his eyes mirrored her suffering and bleakness.

She gave a dry, jagged sob. "Let me go!" she cried.

A tortured groan ripped from his throat. "I can't! Don't you see, I can't give you up! I can't let you go!"

His fingers caught at her chin. He whispered her name, a sound of agony, and then his mouth came down on hers. She tasted a desperation born of pain and passion and hot, fiery need—her own was just as fierce. She surrendered her lips with a low, helpless moan. She could withhold nothing from this man. By the time he raised his head, she was gasping.

Her clothes were impatiently stripped away, along with his. Naked, he came down beside her. With lips and hands and tongue, he greedily charted sleek, feminine flesh. But Devon was just as greedy.

Her knuckles grazed the hair-roughened grid of his belly. Her fingers tangled in the nest at his groin. Her fingers closed tight around his shaft, taut and rigid. He was hot. Burning hot. But she reveled in the way he swelled and surged, the way he throbbed against her palm . . . into it.

His hips bucked forward. "Yes," he said thickly. "That's the way. Oh, God, Devon . . ."

She didn't release him, but explored him boldly, allowing her fingers to trip down the length of his shaft, then dance back up, a heated, shattering rhythm that made him gasp.

"Enough! I can stand no more!" His breath scraping and harsh, her hand engulfed in his, he turned her onto her back.

One fiery stroke embedded him deep inside her. Her sheath abrim with him, his heat and strength and power, she moaned aloud.

He pulled back, leaving the head of his shaft buried inside her. It wasn't enough, not nearly enough. Feeling empty and bereft, she clutched at his hips, seeking to bring him back inside.

His eyes rained down on her like molten fire. "You're mine," he said raggedly. "Mine."

He plunged once more. His thrusts quickened until he was driving almost wildly, so deep he touched her very soul. Their lovemaking tinged with a dark desperation, her hands slipped to ride the frantic plunge of his hips. Her nails dug into the clench of his buttocks, loving the feel of him.

Each pounding thrust hurtled her closer to the edge. Her thighs tightened around his, as if to imprison him, bind him to her forever. She tried to stave off her climax, but it was too intense. Her inner muscles convulsed around his rod. There was the sound of whimpering—her own, she realized dimly—and then there was no more conscious thought. Sebastian erupted inside her, and the world exploded, her release as searing and blistering as his.

In the aftermath, Sebastian lay with an arm flung across his eyes. Spent and trembling, Devon turned her face into the pillow.

A single, scalding tear leaked from the corner of her eye.

She had wondered what would happen next . . . and now she knew.

I can't let you go.

His raw, stark whisper echoed in the chambers of her mind until she wanted to scream aloud with the pain it wrought.

Justin was right. Sebastian wouldn't marry her. He would make her his mistress . . .

But Devon would be no man's mistress.

If she stayed with him, she would be a whore, the very thing she had vowed she would never be. She would never betray her mother in such a way. She would never betray *herself* in such a way.

It struck her then . . . From the moment she'd learned she was a bastard, Devon had despised the man who had fathered her. She had never truly understood her mother's plight—rejected by a man she would always love, no matter that he'd hurt her beyond measure . . . She'd never truly understood the endless sadness that lurked in her mother's eyes.

Now she did.

In a way, she admitted achingly, she had taken the very same path as her mother. And there was a bitter truth that must be faced.

She loved Sebastian, would *always* love him. But Sebastian belonged to a world far different and far above her own.

But unlike her mother, she wouldn't give in to her despair or live her life in regret, wishing for something that could never be.

She was stronger than that.

As difficult a choice as it was, she knew what she had to do.

When they returned to London, the two of them must part.

Twenty-four

Once Devon had drifted off to sleep, Sebastian rose and slipped on his robe. Lifting her carefully in his arms, he carried her back to her own bed. He needed to think, and he couldn't think with her beside him.

She stirred when he pulled the counterpane over her shoulders. Holding his breath, he watched and waited until she had quieted. Bending low, he kissed her softly on the mouth, trailing a finger down the fragile curve of her jaw.

A tiny whimper broke from her lips.

An oppressive tightness filled his chest, crushing the very air from his lungs. He had done this. He alone was responsible for the shadows in her eyes, the anguish in her soul.

Christ, he wanted to shove his hand through the wall! Instead he hauled in an unsteady breath and straightened. Walking away from her was the hardest thing he'd ever done.

Almost before he was aware of it, he found himself standing beneath the tree where he'd last seen his mother so many years ago.

Oddly, it wasn't his mother's image that haunted him. His eyes squeezed shut, but all he could see was Devon . . . her hair a silken halo spilling down her back. Devon, small and delicate, grinning impishly at him, her eyes alight in sheer gold.

His eyes opened. All at once it was as if he'd been caught in the rampage of a wind that battered him across the earth and back.

Nothing could ever erase her memory. Time would never blunt the sharpness of his craving for her.

She was unforgettable.

And what he'd done was unforgivable.

He'd just stabbed himself in the back.

Worse, he'd stabbed *her* in the back.

A scathing self-derision blackened his soul. He had reminded himself over and over that she could never be his. He should never have touched her, but he had, and now they both paid the price.

All along he'd told himself he had a stake in her future. But he couldn't share it.

The situation was . . . impossible.

It all came down to a matter of responsibility. A matter of duty.

Duty.

The word left a vile taste in his mouth, choking him until he could not breathe.

All his life he'd done what was expected of a man in his position. He'd expected to marry a woman of the *ton*, a woman of culture and worldliness. His mouth twisted. Oh, but he'd been so smug! He'd thought he had everything all planned out. He would produce an heir, thus preserving the family name and heritage. He'd told himself his life would be full, that he would be content.

Indeed, his duty compelled it.

But now those well-laid plans went against everything he wanted . . . or been *told* he wanted. He was torn between what was right . . . and what was proper. What he wanted to do . . . and what he *should* do.

Nothing had turned out as he'd planned. He stabbed his fingers against his forehead, his heart in a stranglehold.

If it were up to him, he'd marry Devon in a heartbeat. It didn't matter that she was poor. Take away his wealth, his power, and his title, and what was he? Just a man like any other. No *better* than any other.

But Devon . . . Devon was a woman like no other.

Justin's words battered his mind. *She deserves someone who'll love her. Someone who'll take care of her. Someone who'll give her everything she's never had.*

He had been taking care of her. *He* was giving her everything she'd never had.

And he loved her. God help him, he *did*.

But it wasn't so simple . . . or was it? Would society accept her as his wife? He flinched at the names she would be called. No doubt it wouldn't bother Justin if they were shunned. Justin, cynic that he was, would probably bask in what he would surely perceive as his elder brother's rebellion against society.

From the time his mother had deserted them, Sebastian had vowed there would be no scandal in his life, no taint upon his name. But suddenly it didn't seem to matter. He and Justin could weather another disgrace.

But what of Julianna?

Sweet, sweet, Julianna. Could she bear another scandal? He thought of the horrid incident that had sent her into hiding for months. He hated the thought she might suffer still more disgrace, for his lovely sister did not deserve the wretched fate that Providence had cast upon her.

And neither did Devon.

He suddenly remembered the way she'd looked that day gliding down the stairs, so full of hope and youth and eagerness. She had placed such trust in him. Such faith.

And he had betrayed her. He had betrayed them both.

Suddenly he knew . . . He would not betray her again. He would *not*.

Conviction thundered in his heart, roared through his blood.

Duty, he thought again. Duty be damned! Christ, what did he care about duty? He'd give it all up—his fortune, his home—if only she would be his wife.

He wanted her. He wanted her at his side. Tomorrow. Forever. And he didn't give a *damn* what the world might say. He owed it to Devon to make it right . . .

And he owed it to himself to be happy.

It was near dawn when he finally tumbled into bed. The burden that had driven him outside was no more. Tomorrow, he decided, closing his eyes. Tomorrow everything would be different.

It was later than usual when Sebastian arose. He bathed and dressed quickly with the help of his valet, anxious to see Devon. After he traversed the length of the corridor, a hasty glance revealed that her chamber was empty, the bed linens already changed. At the bottom of the stairs, he chanced to see one of the maids.

"Alice, do you know where I might find Miss Devon?"

The girl's eyes were huge. "I believe she's outside having a stroll." She nodded in the direction of the wide double doors.

Sebastian nodded and walked away. Judging from the girl's reaction, he guessed the servants had exchanged a good bit of gossip this morning. Well, it couldn't be helped.

His boot heels echoed as he crossed the entrance hall. A footman hurriedly opened the door, and he stepped outside. A blistering curse leaped to his lips when he saw a carriage had halted before the manse. By George, if it was Justin again, he would—

It was not.

A sumptuous affair of black lacquer trimmed with red and gold, it belonged to the dowager duchess of Carrington. She had an estate nearby and sometimes called on him when she was in residence.

Sebastian was not particularly pleased. God, could no one leave them alone?

One of the duchess's footmen had already alighted. He stood at the ready when the carriage door swung open. The dowager descended. Smothering his displeasure, Sebastian prepared to greet her.

It was then he spied Devon at the bottom of the stairs. She stood frozen, her pose a reflection of her uncertainty.

The duchess had noticed her as well, and summoned her forward with a slashing movement of her cane.

Sebastian held his breath. The diminutive figure in white spoke, but he couldn't hear what was said. And now she was looking Devon up and down—and offering an elbow for Devon to escort her inside!

Sebastian maintained his stance. Once the duchess was inside, he closed the door and bowed low over her hand. "Your Grace," he murmured. "How nice to see you again."

"I'm on my way back to London," she announced crisply. "I'd heard you were at Thurston Hall, and it's been ages since I've seen you." She eyed Devon with undisguised candor. "Who is this lovely young lady?"

Sebastian inclined his head. "Your Grace, may I present Miss Devon St. James. Devon, the dowager duchess of Carrington."

Devon sank into a curtsy. "Your Grace, I'm very pleased to meet you."

Sebastian couldn't have been prouder. But the duchess continued her perusal of Devon.

"St. James," she repeated. "I know that name." She fumbled for her quizzing glass. "My word, but your eyes are most unusual. 'Tis almost uncanny, for they are remarkably like—" All at once she stopped short. She raised her quizzing glass and peered at Devon, who was obviously discomfited. "Turn this way, girl," she commanded. "Yes, that's it. Now the other way—"

The duchess's gaze had settled on Devon's throat. "That necklace," she said in an odd voice. "How came you by it?"

Devon's pulse was suddenly thudding. The

duchess's regard was so strange. She raised her fingertips to the cross. Her chin climbed high.

"This necklace," she stated with quiet dignity, "was my mother's—she wore it always. It was given to her by my father before I was born." She glanced at Sebastian. Did he expect her to change her story? She couldn't alter the truth!

But he merely regarded her calmly. It was the duchess who broke the silence.

Aging fingers grasped at Devon's sleeve. "Who was your mother, child? Who was she?"

Devon took a breath. "She's dead now. But her name was Ame—"

But even as she spoke the name Amelia, it was echoed by the duchess.

"Amelia," the old woman finished. "Amelia St. James."

Devon was dumbfounded. How could she possibly know—

The duchess was swaying. Her face was pasty white. Alarmed, Devon latched on to her elbow, steadying her. Sebastian had grabbed the other arm. Together they guided her to a chair in the drawing room.

"Your Grace!" Sebastian said. "Are you unwell?"

The duchess shook her head. "I'm fine. Truly I am. Just give me a moment to catch my breath." She paused, then beckoned to Devon.

"Come here, child. Come here and let me look at you."

Devon sank down before her. The duchess stretched out a hand. Devon grasped it instinctively, seeking to infuse some of her warmth into the duchess's cold fingers. No sound passed between them, but the duchess's eyes scoured Devon's features. She was relieved to note some of the color had begun to seep back into the old woman's lined cheeks.

Devon took a deep, steadying breath, gathering her composure. Her mind was racing. No doubt she was about to overstep her bounds, but she didn't care.

"Your Grace," she burst out, "I don't understand. You knew my mother's name. How is it possible . . . how?"

The merest hint of a smile passed over her face. "Because the necklace you wear"—her fingertips brushed the delicate silver chain—"was once mine."

Behind Devon, Sebastian inhaled sharply.

Neither woman heard.

"No," Devon said faintly, "that cannot be—"

"It's true, child." The old woman's eyes filled with tears. "It was I who gave it to my son, Marcus. He died many years ago."

Marcus. The duchess's son. The rake that Justin had spoken of, the night of Sebastian's dinner party.

"Shortly before his death," the duchess continued, "he told me he'd given it to a woman he'd been involved with. Oh, but I was so angry! But now I know . . . that woman was Amelia"—she paused—"your mother."

A half-formed suspicion began to bloom in Devon's mind. She grappled with it, for it was almost too outrageous to believe . . .

"You knew my mother," she stated faintly.

"Yes, child, I knew her. She attended my nieces one summer—oh, so very long ago! I was very fond of Amelia, you know. And Marcus, well . . . He had a way about him, a way that charmed the ladies, but—there is no delicate way to put this, I fear—he was a rascal. A womanizer. I suspected that perhaps Amelia had developed a *tendre* for Marcus. But I didn't know for certain, until now. Amelia departed very abruptly, you see. One morning she was simply gone. She left behind only a note saying that she must leave. I remember I was so shocked! We never heard from her again. I never really understood why she left . . . until now."

The duchess stripped off her gloves. Gnarled fingers smoothed Devon's hair, traced the arch of a slender brow, the gesture not entirely steady. Her fingers beneath her chin, she brought Devon's gaze to hers.

"You resemble your mother greatly, child. But your eyes—oh, those beautiful, golden eyes"—the duchess's voice began to shake as surely as her hand—"are purely my son's."

Devon felt numb, almost dizzy. She could barely speak for the emotion that crowded her chest. "Your Grace," she said around the lump in her throat, "surely you do not mean—"

"I do. *I do.* You are Amelia's child, her child by my son. Her child by my Marcus." The duchess reached out and gripped Devon's hands. "You are my granddaughter," she whispered. "My God, I am your grandmama!"

The duchess broke down.

So did Devon. With a sob she wrapped her arms around the old woman and clung. Together they wept.

Twenty-five

They were both crying—sobbing actually—and Sebastian had the feeling he could have been a fly on the wall for all that either took note of his presence. Heart-wrenching sobs, happy sobs. For a man with his aversion to tears, it was difficult to tolerate either. Yet watching the pair, he felt a twist of his own heart. It was impossible to remain unmoved.

It was incredible, really. He remembered that day in London when Devon had spouted that her father was from a family finer than his—sweet Lord, it was true! Devon was related to the duchess!

Definitely feeling the odd man out, he stood awkwardly for a moment. Finally he excused himself—not that either woman noticed—and went to find a servant to ask that tea be brought to the drawing room.

He waited until the tray was ready before entering the drawing room again. Mercifully the sobs had dried out. The duchess sat with Devon's hand clasped tight within her own. At his entrance, both glanced over at him.

He smiled slightly. "I took the liberty of ordering tea." He nodded to the maid to deposit the silver tea service on a small rosewood table. "Devon," he said lightly, "will you pour?"

She reached to comply. Their fingertips brushed as she passed him a finely etched cup of Wedgwood china. She drew back as if she'd been burned, then quickly turned her head aside. Sebastian's mouth turned down. Dammit, why wouldn't she look at him?

"My granddaughter was just telling me she spent most of her life in St. Giles," the duchess stated in her forthright manner. "As you can imagine, this day has been one of profound revelations. But I confess, I am confounded to find her in *your* household."

She glanced between Sebastian and Devon. Devon made a jerky movement. Her mouth opened, but before she could say a word, Sebastian raised a hand to stave off any response she might have made.

"I found her injured in the streets of St. Giles. I took her to my home in London." Quietly he relayed what had happened.

When he finished, the duchess sat very still. "So you rescued my granddaughter from hooligans," she said at last. "And you've been caring for her all this time."

Beneath the statement was a disturbing undertone. Sebastian did not shirk from the old woman's critical scrutiny, but matched her regard head-on. "No one in London knew of her presence in my home, Your Grace."

"I trust we may keep it as such?"

Sebastian inclined his head. "You have my word."

"Excellent," she pronounced. She rose to her feet. "Devon, my cane, please."

Devon pressed it in her hand. The duchess wasted no time swinging it toward Alice, who had returned to take the tea tray. "You, there, young woman! Please see to it that Miss St. James's belongings are packed and taken to my carriage."

Devon's lips parted. "Your Grace?" she murmured questioningly.

The duchess must have sensed her dilemma. "Yes, dear, you're coming with me." She smiled at Devon's stunned expression. "What! Did you expect me to learn of your existence and then fly off as if it were no consequence?"

"In all honesty, I didn't know what to expect," she admitted. "I-I still don't." She went on, her voice very low. "I do not mean to question your judgment, Your Grace—"

"Grandmama," the duchess corrected gently.

"Grandmama," Devon allowed haltingly. She bit her lip, then suddenly blurted, "May I be blunt?"

The duchess's eyes were twinkling. "My dear, you'll soon discover I know no other way."

"No matter who my father was, the fact remains, I am, and will always be, a bastard. And considering your position in society—"

The duchess was shaking her head. "Say no more, my dear, say no more, for it's my turn to be blunt. Of course there will be talk. Do I care? No. I've no intention of hiding who you are. I fully intend to embrace you as my granddaughter, and if society chooses to turn their back on me, then that is simply their loss. I'm far too old to care what anyone thinks!"

Devon bit her lip. "There's something else you should know."

"Out with it then."

Devon swallowed hard. "My mother loved your son till the day she died," she confided. The agony in her heart bled through to her voice. "But I . . . I always hated him for making her love him, and not caring. I-I just thought you should know."

To her surprise, the duchess's expression grew pained. "I can accept that, child, for no one knows better than I what a rogue Marcus was. I truly regret what happened to your mother, for I was very fond of her. There is much of her compassion in you, I think. And perhaps there is something you should know as well. For all of his faults, I loved Marcus, loved him as only a mother could. He was my only child and"—her voice grew unsteady—"and you are a part of him . . . *you*. My granddaughter. My child, I-I am blessed! There is nothing else to say, only that—I should like very much if we should get to know one another." There were tears in the duchess's eyes as she stretched out an imploring hand.

Her throat aching, Devon gripped her fingers tightly, touched to the depths of her soul. "I should like that too," she whispered.

"Then let us be off." Once again brisk, the duchess hobbled to her feet. She glanced at Sebastian. "Sebastian, will you see us out?"

Sebastian rose and straightened to his full height. More than ever he felt like an outcast. "Your Grace," he began.

Her voice cut across his. "I owe you a great debt, Sebastian. But now that I've learned of my granddaughter's existence, I consider myself charged with her responsibility. Rest assured, I am fully capable of seeing to her care and protection."

"Of that I have no doubt, Your Grace." His tone was pleasant but his eyes were snapping. "However, if you please—"

"It's a long journey to London for an old woman such as I. I should like to reach home before midnight." The duchess bid him farewell. "Good-bye, Sebastian." Ever the commanding lady, she set off toward the entrance hall.

The butler was in place, ready to usher her out. He bowed low as the duchess swept by.

Sebastian bit back a curse. His jaw clamped together hard. He had to forcibly remind himself this was the dowager duchess of Carrington he was dealing with. Devon followed her grandmother's lead toward the door.

"Devon," he said, his voice very low.

Her shoulders stiffened. He knew she heard him then. Yet still she continued in her grandmother's wake.

Two long strides brought him apace. His fingers curled into her elbow.

Her pace quickened. "Let me go."

His grip tightened. He swung her around.

"Devon, please look at me."

She refused. She focused on the intricate tie of his cravat, the mirrored frame behind him, everywhere but his face.

"My dear?"

The duchess again. Sebastian cursed beneath his breath. His head swung around sharply. The old woman had seen and was glaring at him.

His fingers uncurled. Once released, Devon practically sprang away like a hare released from a trap!

It didn't set well with Sebastian. It didn't set well at all. There had been no chance to talk about last night about his feelings—his decision—no chance to talk about anything!

His hands were tied, goddamn it. The duchess was whisking Devon away to London, away from *him* . . .

And there wasn't a bloody thing he could do about it.

It didn't take long for Sebastian to decide upon his course of action. Within the hour, his carriage was hurtling down the road behind the duchess's. When he departed Thurston Hall, it was in his mind to plant himself on the duchess's doorstep, no matter the hour. During the long ride back to London, however, his good sense prevailed. The memory of their emotional meeting had struck a chord in him; he reminded himself they were entitled to some time alone together. Thus his impulsiveness was curtailed, but most certainly not his intention.

At precisely three o'clock the next afternoon, Sebastian crossed Grosvenor Square to the duchess's residence. Two sharp raps with the brass knocker, and the front door swung wide.

The duchess's butler, Reginald, a tall, thin-lipped man of spare demeanor, peered at him. Sebastian passed his card into white-gloved fingertips.

"I wish to see Miss St. James."

That the butler didn't bat an eye was testament to his training. "This way, my lord."

He was shown to the vast expanse of the drawing room. He did not sit in the chair where he was directed, but paced the room. Indeed, he could have negotiated the length of the room and back with his eyes closed, so well had he memorized the layout. Still no one came. Finally he flipped out his pocket watch and glanced at it.

A quarter past the hour.

What the devil? Had he been forgotten? Tolerance was in short supply today. Impatient, he spun around, fully intending to give the butler a piece of his mind—

The thump of the cane alerted him.

"Good afternoon," greeted the duchess.

He executed a smart bow. "Your Grace," he murmured. In truth, he wanted to shout his irritation. "How nice to see you again. I fear, however, that Reginald misunderstood. I asked to see your granddaughter."

"There was no misunderstanding," the duchess replied evenly. "Devon is resting."

"Then please have a maid awaken her and tell her I wish to see her. In the meantime, I shall wait." He ambled to the nearest chair and sat, arranging one booted foot atop the other in negligent ease.

When he glanced up, she stood before him, a fire-breathing dragon if ever he'd seen one.

"This is my house, Sebastian. And I don't believe I care for your attitude."

"Then perhaps you should leave the room. Indeed, I prefer it."

"Young man, I could—" She stopped short and fixed him with a glare.

A black brow arched high. "Yes?" he inquired. Polite though he sounded, his guard was already up. The battle lines had been drawn. Having not slept a wink last night, chafing inside at the wait he'd just been forced to endure, he was in a disagreeable mood and didn't give a fig if she knew it. In fact, perhaps it was *best* if she knew it.

"I am sorely tempted to have Reginald throw you out!"

His brow remained cocked high. "You wouldn't," was all he said. "He couldn't."

"I should," she snapped, "and will! If it were not for the fact I've always been fond of you—"

"And I of you," he interjected pleasantly. "But it occurs to me perhaps we should both speak our minds."

"By all means." The words were gracious; her tone was not. In fact, the old gal thwacked the cane between her elegantly shod feet.

Sebastian remained undeterred. "Your Grace," he began, "you are a formidable woman."

"I'm glad you recognize that!"

"I have no wish to make an enemy of you. However, I am compelled to inform you I am not a hapless young buck who will allow himself to be herded meekly back into the streets because you so desire. I wish to see Devon. Alone," he stressed.

She didn't back down. "And I must ask the nature of your visit."

Sebastian surged to his feet. "Your Grace, that is between Devon and me. She is a grown woman, and I do believe the choice to see me should be hers, not yours."

"You are right," she startled him by saying. "But first I've something to say to you. Devon told me last night how you endeavored to see to her education, how you taught her to read and write. But I pride myself on the sharpness of my mind, particularly in light of my advanced age. I am not a doddering old ninny."

And he was in no mood to be lectured. "Your Grace, I respect you far too much to even think such a thing." He forced a calm he was far from feeling.

"And I have always respected you as well, my boy. But I am not blind," she declared. "I saw the possessive way you gazed at Devon yesterday, the overly familiar way you spoke to her, and touched her. I saw the way she refused to meet your eyes and your reluctance to let her go. Now, I have never been one to pry—"

"Then don't," he said curtly.

"Listen to me, Sebastian, and listen well. I am grateful to you for rescuing her. But I heartily disapprove of the way you kept my granddaughter beneath your roof under circumstances that could certainly be construed as compromising. Judging from what I saw of the two of you, I have every right to be concerned. She tried to hide it, but there were tears in her eyes when she spoke of you last night. And anything that distresses my granddaughter also distresses me. Do we understand each other?"

He lost his temper then. "Perfectly," he said grimly. "Now may I see her or must I tear this house apart until I find her?"

Devon had joined her grandmother for breakfast, but by noon she had a horrible headache. Everything had happened so fast. Her mind was still whirling. She was vastly relieved when her grandmother suggested a nap. Indeed, she'd have liked to spend the rest of the day in relative seclusion, but her grandmother had asked that she join her for tea at half past three.

Her slippers made no sound as she crossed the massive domed entryway toward the drawing room. The spiral of angry voices reached her ears. One was the duchess's.

The other was Sebastian's.

She did not mean to eavesdrop, but one of the doors stood cocked ajar. The mightiest hand from above couldn't have kept her from stealing toward it.

They stood toe-to-toe, the marquess and the duchess. Under other circumstances, she might have laughed. Her grandmother, whose snowy white head scarcely reached the middle of Sebastian's chest, appeared as though she'd like to throttle him with her bare hands. Sebastian's expression was no less intense.

"Now may I see her," he was saying in that imperious tone she knew so well, "or must I tear this house apart until I find her?"

Devon stepped forward. "There's no need for that," she said calmly. "I'm right here."

Two pairs of eyes swung her direction.

The duchess immediately hobbled to her side. "My dear," the duchess clucked, "you needn't see him now if you don't wish to."

Devon summoned a tiny smile and squeezed her shoulder. "It's all right," she murmured.

The duchess gave a nod. She left the room, but not before she turned and glared daggers at Sebastian.

They were left alone. Slowly Devon transferred her gaze to Sebastian. He was impeccably dressed as always, in tight fawn breeches and black frock coat. The very sight of him made her heart lurch.

He tipped his head. "How are you?" he queried

softly. His lips crooked up in a tender little smile that made her ache inside.

Devon couldn't return it. Instead a painful, bitter wave of emotion battered her. "I'm fine," she returned coolly. "Why would you think otherwise?"

He blinked. "No reason," he muttered. He gestured toward the sofa.

"May we sit?"

"Certainly."

She took a seat at the end of the sofa. A mistake, for he sat on the chair next to it, so close their knees almost brushed. A treacherous warmth shot through her at his nearness. She fought against it with all that she possessed, suddenly trembling inside.

"This is awkward," he said.

"Is it? I hadn't noticed."

He said nothing, but she felt his gaze scouring her features, as if he were puzzled.

She sat very still while he took her hands.

"Devon," he said huskily, "I came here to ask you a question."

"What question?" It was odd, the way she felt, as if she weren't the one who sat here with Sebastian—as if she were a stranger.

A shattering pause, and then, softly, he said, "Will you marry me?"

Her heart gave a feeble thud, then began to thunder. Her blood rushed in her ears. She was surely losing her mind. No, she thought vaguely, it couldn't be. Sebastian . . . asking her to marry him?

Oh, God. *God*.

A rending, tearing pain sliced through her. Two days ago she'd have hurtled herself into his arms, crying out in unbelievable joy. But his proposal . . . *this* proposal . . . came too late.

A curious tightness settled over her.

"No," she said succinctly.

The flicker of uncertainty that flitted across his handsome features was gratifying. Little did he realize she was simmering inside.

"I beg your pardon?"

There was no need for pretense. There never had been, not with the two of them.

She withdrew her hands and linked them together in her lap. Baldly she spoke. "I said no. I will not marry you."

His every feature seemed to freeze. He was shocked. Stung.

But he was also angry. His lips compressed. He looked utterly ominous. He got to his feet, towering over her, his jaw clenched hard. His eyes narrowed dangerously. "You can't refuse me."

Her own glinted. "I believe I just did." Softly, almost whimsically, she met his regard. "You don't understand, do you? No, of course you wouldn't. No doubt you, my noble lord, expected me to fall on my knees and gush my gratitude that you would deign to marry me, a nobody. But I confess, I'm curious. Would you have lain with me if I were a proper lady? If Penelope Harding were to be your bride, would you have taken her to your bed without benefit of marriage?"

A dull flush crept beneath his skin. With his hand he made a curt, dismissive gesture. "It does not signify," he said shortly. "I had no such feelings toward Penelope."

"It does signify!" Devon hissed, and all at once she

was on her feet. "To me it signifies! Tell me, Sebastian. It's a simple question, is it not? Would you have made . . . Oh, how shall I put this? Would you have made advances toward your future bride? To any woman you would have considered making your wife? A kiss, perhaps, I think. But no more, surely. You see, I know you. The woman you would take to wife . . . You would have waited till your wedding night to make her yours."

He made a sound. "Do not belittle what we had"—his gaze drilled into hers—"what we *have*. Why, you make it sound as if I used you for my own pleasure!"

"Perhaps you did!" she shot back. "Perhaps I was just a woman to *tumble* to ease your need!"

"I did not *tumble* you!" Anger kindled in his voice. "By God, Devon, you make me want to shake you . . . And you forget, you wanted me as much as I wanted you!"

This time she was the one who flushed. "I did," she allowed. "I blame myself as well, for I allowed you liberties that should only belong to a husband."

"Goddamn it, that's what I want. To be your husband!"

Her laugh was brittle. "I recall differently. That day with Justin at Thurston Hall, you made your feelings abundantly clear . . . you would bed me, but you would certainly never *wed* me."

"I came here to rectify my mistake. I was wrong, Devon. Wrong. I was a fool. I knew it the other night. Oh, I know you may not believe me, but I swear, I intended to ask you yesterday morning. But then the duchess arrived, and . . . and I'm asking you now. Again. Marry me, Devon. *Marry me.*"

Tears slipped down her face. She dashed them

away. "You're right," she said flatly. "I don't believe you. And I will never marry you."

"Devon, listen to me! I came here to explain—"

"What, that you've reconsidered? Well, *I* need not consider at all, sir. You are a hypocrite, you who pretend to be so staid. So proper. But I have principles too. I have feelings. No doubt you regarded me as no more than a convenience to warm your bed when it suited you. Who would know? After all, what was I but a woman of no consequence."

"You know better than that, Devon." Sharply he censured her.

In some part of her, Devon *did* know it. Her conscience stabbed at her, but she was too full of angry hurt to listen, overcome with the starkness of betrayal.

"Only a fool wouldn't see through you, and I am not a fool. You wouldn't consider making me your wife when you believed me a street urchin. Ah, but what do you know! Bastard I may be, but now that you've discovered my grandmother is a duchess . . . apparently now you've deemed me worthy!"

She looked at him then, her mouth quivering. Her voice trembled with all that she felt. Buried in her fury was a world of anguish. With every word, conviction gathered full and ripe within her.

"You wouldn't have me, Sebastian. *You wouldn't have me.* Well, now I won't have *you*! You thought I wasn't good enough for you. But you—you're not good enough for me!"

Strong hands clamped down on her shoulders, dragging her close. The cast of his jaw was rigid. "You love me," he said tautly. "I know it."

"Oh!" she cried. "You presume too much, sir!"

His eyes impaled her, as stormy as the seas. "Yes,"

he said fiercely, "I do presume, for I know you too, my little love! The night I made you mine will burn in my soul forever. I will never forget the way you melted when I kissed you—the way you shuddered when I came inside you! And when it was over . . . Remember what you said? 'I belong to you,'" he quoted. "You said you belonged to me!"

Devon fumed. "And you have just reminded me of something as well. What was it? Ah, yes, now I recall. To hell with the future, you claimed. To hell with duty. Well, my lord marquess, to hell with *you*!"

Twenty-six

Looking neither right nor left, Devon climbed the curving staircase straight to her room. After closing the door, she strode to the seat set beneath the high, mullioned window on the wall opposite the bed. Picking up a frilly pink pillow, she stared into the shadows that had begun to fall over the city.

There was a knock on the door. "My dear?"

It was the duchess. The door opened a crack, and the elderly woman stepped inside. Feeling utterly empty inside, Devon watched her halting gait as she crossed the room.

"My dear, forgive the intrusion, but I had to see for myself that you are all right."

"I'm fine," Devon said dully.

The duchess peered at her. "Why, you're shivering!" she fretted. After rifling through the armoire, the duchess tugged a shawl over Devon's shoulders.

"It breaks my heart to see you so miserable, child. Is there anything I can do?"

Devon gave a shake of her head. Perhaps the old woman meant well, but she had no intention of discussing Sebastian with anyone, most certainly not her grandmother.

"My dear, I could not help but overhear."

No doubt, Devon thought numbly. Of course she'd overheard. No doubt everyone in the household had overheard.

"Of course you needn't marry Sebastian if you don't want to. Indeed, you needn't ever marry."

Devon's fingers curled around the ends of the shawl. "Truly?" she whispered.

"Unless it's what you want, of course. Call it selfish, but I'm quite content to have you all to myself." The duchess smiled slightly.

"Thank you for that . . . Grandmama." Odd, but the word suddenly didn't sound so foreign on her lips.

The duchess leaned on her cane. "When I was a girl, every marriage was arranged. Your grandfather and I got on well enough together, but the world is beginning to change, and I daresay, it's about time. More and more one hears of those those who choose to defy convention and marry for love. They are lucky, I think. Indeed, to marry for love . . . why, it's what I wish for every young woman." The duchess's tone had grown very softly whimsical. "Ah. But I can see you would rather be alone, my dear." The duchess turned.

But all at once to be alone was the very thing Devon *didn't* want. "Grandmama, wait," she cried. The duchess turned back inquiringly. "Please stay," she said haltingly. "Please." An unbearable ache then crowded her chest. Suddenly her shoulders were shaking soundlessly.

The next thing she knew, the duchess sank down beside her and gathered her close. Neither of them questioned what happened next. There existed between them a bond that transcended time, the years spent apart. "Cry, dear, if you must."

Devon turned her face into her shoulder. "Grandmama," she choked out. "He . . . I . . ."

She could manage no more. Nor, it seemed, was there any need.

Holding back her own tears, the duchess patted her shoulder. "I understand, my dear. Truly I do."

And indeed, the duchess did.

The effects of an entire bottle of brandy did little to quell Sebastian's guilt or his pain. Self-loathing poured through him like boiling oil. Hunched over his desk, he jabbed his fingers into his forehead, as if to gouge out his memories . . .

He started when a small, warm body sidled into his lap. A cold, wet nose nudged beneath his palm.

Blurry eyes focused on the furry little creature. In some distant part of his mind, he marveled that he'd remembered to bring Dumpling and the pups. "Dumpling," he said, "she's not here."

The mongrel tipped her head to the side and whined. And now they were all here—the General, the Colonel, the Major, and the Captain—pawing at his knees and whining pitifully.

He lunged to his feet. "She's not coming back," he shouted. "Don't you see, she's not coming back!"

The whining ebbed. One by one, the little creatures lined up in a half circle before him. He groaned. In the end it was those sad, soulful eyes that sent him stumbling headlong through the doors.

Before he knew it he was standing in the library. Devon's favorite room, he recalled with a pang.

If I lived here, came the echo in his mind, *I should make it a point to read every book in this room.*

But she didn't live here. She would *never* live here, and the knowledge was like a stake through the heart.

He went a little mad then. Flinging out an arm, he swung it wide. Vases crashed and volumes toppled from the shelves onto the floor.

The door opened. The butler Stokes appeared, and several of the housemaids behind him. "My lord—"

"Get out!" he roared. "All of you!"

One by one they began to retreat. Justin had appeared as well, having just come home.

"Sebastian!" came his sharp rebuke. "Good God, what the hell—"

Sebastian's head came up. He regarded his brother through burning eyes.

"If you've come to gloat," he said through his teeth, "don't bother."

Justin simply looked at him in shock.

Sebastian closed his eyes. "Christ," he muttered. "I'm sorry. I shouldn't have said that."

Justin closed the door and looked him up and down. "You're foxed!" he said incredulously.

"Am I? I hadn't noticed."

"Sebastian, what the *hell* is going on? You were in a devil of a mood this morning so I left you alone. Now I return home to find the servants looking like you've beaten them to a pulp, and you reducing the library to a shambles!"

"That's not all."

"What, there's more?"

"There is. I yelled at Dumpling and the pups."

"Admirable."

Sebastian weaved toward a side table for another bottle of brandy.

Justin snatched it up before he could reach it. He pushed Sebastian into a chair. "No more of that for you," he said impatiently. "Tell me what's going on."

Sebastian slumped forward. He hung his head in his hands. "She's never coming back," he said in an odd, strained voice.

Justin caught his breath. "She's with her grandmother—"

"You don't understand," Sebastian ground out. "She's never coming back here."

"What do you mean?"

"I mean that she hates me, dammit! She *hates* me!"

Justin shook his head. "That can't be—"

"Believe me, it's true," Sebastian said bitterly.

Justin went pale. "Oh, Christ, this is all my fault."

"No, it's mine, Justin. *Mine*. You were right, Justin. From the beginning, I wanted her. I burned for her. Oh, I fought it. I told myself I could control my yearning for her. But then we went to Thurston Hall—"

"And I came up with that bloody, harebrained scheme to marry her off!"

"Don't blame yourself. Please don't. I was convinced it was the right thing to do as well. I thought it was the only way I could keep my hands off her. But that night with Evans and Mason and Westfield . . . She heard us, Justin. She heard us and she knew what we planned . . ."

"Oh, God."

"She cried, Justin. She *cried*. And I couldn't stand it. I should have left her alone, but I didn't. I told myself I wanted to make her stop hurting." His tone rang black with self-disparagement. "But I was selfish. I wanted her and I-I took her. And then you came back and saw us . . . Remember how she looked at me? Dry-eyed. Immobile. My God, I've never seen anyone who looked the way she did, as if"—he floundered—"as if she were bruised inside. And I did it. *I* put that look on her face."

Justin glanced down at his hands. His expression was drawn and tight.

"No!" Sebastian said sharply. "This is not your fault! Because you were right, you see. You've been right all along. I thought only of duty and obligation—and it all seems so petty now! My hesitation cost me everything! I was so blinded by my determination to avoid any scandal that I couldn't see what lay before my eyes . . ."

Justin's gaze never wavered from his face. Softly he said, "You love her, don't you?"

Sebastian nodded. His mouth twisted. "I thought I could make things right. I went to her and I-I asked her to marry me." A brutal silence descended. "She denied me. With tears streaming down her face, she denied me. Not once, but thrice. *Thrice*."

"She was confused, Sebastian. This whole business with the duchess—my word, I can hardly believe it myself."

"I know that. I know it," Sebastian stressed. "But truth be told, I can hardly blame her. I couldn't justify my behavior to myself, let alone to Devon! But in my arrogance, I never even considered the possibility that she would say no."

Little by little, the strength drained from his limbs until he was trembling. If he hadn't already been sitting, he'd have surely collapsed.

"I robbed her of her innocence," he whispered bleakly. "I robbed her of hope. I stole her pride. I thought only of my own, of duty and responsibility . . . and sacrificed Devon's in the bargain. I took everything from her, Justin. I *stole* it from her, and I will never forgive myself. *Devon* will never forgive me. *Never*."

Justin regarded Sebastian. "And that's it? You're going to give up?"

Sebastian's mouth twisted. "What! Don't you think I've hurt her enough?"

"She loves you, Sebastian. I saw it that day at Thurston Hall."

"I thought she did too. But now I'm not so sure. You didn't see the blaze in her eyes, Justin. The way she looked at me . . . she despises me!"

"I cannot believe that, Sebastian." Justin was adamant. "I was the one who was blind. I thought I was protecting her, and so did you. But you and Devon, it's so very clear . . . you belong together, the two of you." His half smile held a familiar trace of mockery. "Why, it's almost enough to make a skeptic like me believe in love."

Sebastian said nothing, but stared unblinking into the shadows.

Justin clamped a hand on his shoulder. "You'll change her mind."

"I won't!" Sebastian cried the words that tore

them both to shreds. "My God, Justin, you didn't see her!"

Justin pressed his lips together consideringly. Leaning forward, he wasted no time rapping his brother sharply in the forehead with his knuckles.

Sebastian's jaw fell open in shock. He lurched to his feet, staring at his brother.

Justin rose as well, extending an arm again. Sebastian's hand shot out and grabbed his wrist before Justin could knock him in the head again.

"Bloody hell," he swore, "are you trying to pick a fight?"

"Not at all," Justin intoned politely. "Though I do believe in your present state you'd lose."

"Then what the blazes are you doing?"

Justin regarded him levelly. "You are still my brother, are you not?"

"What the hell kind of idiotic question is that?" Sebastian demanded.

Justin raised his brows. "I thought perhaps a confirmation was in order," he murmured.

"What?"

A hand at his brow, Justin feigned great concentration. "Forgive my lapse in memory, but when Father died, he had allowed our financial affairs to fall into a state that was rather dire, had he not?"

"For pity's sake, you suffer no lapse in recall, Justin."

"And you are the man whose pragmatic approach restored our fortune, who began the seemingly insurmountable task of seeing to it that you, Julianna, and I were received in society without snickers or glares or whispers, are you not?"

Sebastian nodded tersely. "Your point?"

"Merely this. *My* brother would tackle the task of bringing home his beloved with the very same resilience and fortitude. *My* brother would not lose heart. *My* brother would not lose hope."

Sebastian was speechless. Somehow Justin's lecture penetrated his brandy-induced fog as nothing else could have.

Or perhaps . . . as no one else could have.

Emotion swelled his chest. His throat grew tight. His eyes stung. He'd always loved his brother, even when he was madder than hell at his wild recklessness, but never more so than now.

"Justin," he said hoarsely. "Ah, Christ."

Justin groaned. "Dash it all, don't go all sentimental on me!"

"I fear I can't help it. For I do believe I'm lucky to have a brother like you." He gave a rusty laugh. "I can't imagine having anyone *but* you as my brother."

Justin reached out and squeezed Sebastian's arm. "Nor can I," he said simply.

Twenty-seven

Every afternoon for the next week Sebastian presented himself on the duchess's doorstep and handed his card to Reginald along with the polite request, "I wish to call upon Miss St. James."

Each and every time Reginald disappeared, then returned with the same answer. "Miss St. James will not see you, my lord." Indeed, the last time even the stony-faced butler appeared a bit harried. "Indeed, my lord, Miss St. James asks that you not return."

Sebastian considered this. "Reginald," he said politely, "what were her exact words?"

The stoic-faced butler was suddenly not so unflappable. "My lord, I am not in the habit of using such—"

"Ah. I assume her language may not have been particularly polite?" Sebastian wouldn't put the poor man into the position of repeating his sweet little love's presumably not-so-sweet discourse.

Reginald was clearly relieved. "You assume correctly, my lord."

"I see," Sebastian murmured thoughtfully. "Will you give Miss St. James a message then?"

"Certainly, my lord."

"When she summons the courage to tell me herself, perhaps I *may* consider her request."

And indeed, it wasn't Reginald who opened the door the next afternoon, but Devon. She proceeded to tell him in no uncertain terms precisely what she thought of him. "And don't come back," she finished fiercely. "Ever."

And she slammed the door in his face.

Clearly he was getting nowhere, so he tried another tack. Every day for the next week, he penned a letter to his ladylove.

All were returned unopened.

Something had to be done, he thought grimly. Short of kidnapping her, muzzling her, sitting her down before him, and making her listen, he wasn't sure what it was. Indeed, he was pondering that very situation when Stokes knocked on the door of his study.

"The dowager duchess of Carrington to see you, my lord. I took the liberty of seating her in the drawing room."

Wonderful, Sebastian thought irritably. Had the duchess decided to light into him as well?

He nodded. A moment later he strolled into the drawing room. He greeted the duchess, then took the seat across from her.

"Your Grace, let us cut to the chase. I presume you've come on Devon's behalf—"

"I'm here because of Devon, but not on her behalf."

He looked at her sharply.

The duchess folded her hands across her cane. "The truth is, she doesn't know I'm here."

He hiked a brow. "Subterfuge, Your Grace?"

"I prefer to call it strategy, my boy."

Sebastian stared. "Your Grace?"

"The last time we spoke, my boy, you made it clear you wouldn't welcome my interference. Indeed, I believe you told me not to pry. And you may tell me to go to the devil again now, but before I say more, I have one question for you. Do you love my granddaughter?"

Sebastian could be no less than honest. "More," he said quietly, "with every day that passes."

"That's just the answer I was hoping for."

"I have every intention of making her my wife," he stated bluntly. He would have no misunderstandings. "By God, she *will* be my bride."

The duchess laughed softly.

Sebastian quirked a brow. "I take it I have your approval then?"

"Would it matter if you did not?"

He countered her question with one of his own. "It has not, has it?" He went on. "Indeed, you may recall, it was you who prompted me to begin my quest for a bride in earnest. I daresay, neither of us ever guessed it would be your granddaughter I intend to take to the altar."

The duchess chuckled again. "Not quite the bride you envisioned, though, is she?"

He frowned. "What do you mean?"

"The gossips found it a juicy tidbit when I revealed the news of my son's by-blow."

"Yes, I've noticed." Sebastian indicated the newspaper. It lay open to the gossip column, which featured a sketch of Devon sitting beside her grandmother atop an open carriage. "An amazing likeness, don't you think?"

"Quite so," the duchess agreed. "A few of my friends were horrified to discover I embrace her freely." Her mouth turned down. "Needless to say, they are friends no more. But it certainly hasn't stemmed the flow of invitations arriving each morning." She watched Sebastian closely. "But what of you, Sebastian? I know you've worked hard to see yourself accepted in society again since your father's death. If you make Devon your bride, it may well cause a stir. You will no doubt find your name on everyone's lips again."

Sebastian's jaw clamped tight. "The *ton* can talk all they want. I really don't care. My God, it's ironic, for that's the least of my concerns." His expression turned pained. "I mean no disrespect, Your Grace, but I do believe Devon would have accepted my suit before she discovered she was your granddaughter. Now that she has . . ."

"Yes, I know," the duchess said gently. When Sebastian glanced up sharply, she smiled slightly. "I'm sorry, my boy. I didn't eavesdrop deliberately. I fear it simply couldn't be helped. If it's any consolation, I regret that my timing appears to have been abominable."

"It's hardly your fault. But I must ask"—his tone went very quiet—"has she . . . spoken of me?"

"She keeps her feelings to herself," the duchess admitted. "I do not envy you, Sebastian. It appears our Devon has a stubborn streak. It's hardly escaped my attention that she won't see you."

"Nor will she answer my letters," he said grimly. "But I'll wait a lifetime if I have to."

There was a small silence. "Perhaps," she murmured, "you won't have to."

"Your Grace?"

But she made no answer. Instead she pushed to her feet with the aid of her cane. "Do not fret," she pronounced. "Sometimes we must simply avail ourselves of whatever opportunity comes our way."

Sebastian took her elbow and assisted her to the door. *Do not fret!* she'd said. How easy for her to say!

At the door she turned. "The Clarkstons are good friends of yours, I believe. No doubt you've received an invitation to their dinner party the Friday after next."

Sebastian frowned. It ran through his mind that perhaps the old gal was getting on in age, for what the devil did that have to do with his predicament? And—she was practically beaming!

"I have," he acknowledged, "and Justin as well. However, I fear I've not been in the mood for socializing—"

"A pity," she said gaily. "I'm so looking forward to it. Why, I vow the occasion warrants a new gown for both Devon and myself!"

And then she winked at him. The duchess *winked.*

Sebastian was still standing numbly in the doorway when her carriage rolled away.

The day of the Clarkstons' dinner party arrived. Devon had met the couple, William and Emily, when Grandmama entertained them at dinner one evening. Devon liked them immensely, for both were gracious and warm. But if she could have cried off, she would have. Throughout the past month, her grandmother had treated her as if she were a priceless treasure. Already Devon had come to dearly love this brash, outspoken old woman. They walked occasionally in Green Park, her grandmother leaning upon her arm; almost daily, they took the carriage along Rotten Row. Last week the duchess had taken her to the King's Theatre, where she'd seen her first opera—and gained her first glimpse of Prinny.

Clearly the duchess had no intention of hiding her from the world. Nor, it appeared, was either of them to be ostracized. The number of invitations that poured in each day was staggering. She couldn't help but remember what Justin had once said about the duchess: *I daresay the devil himself could be received in society if he was received by the duchess.*

But the duchess chose only a select few invitations. Devon was aware that the duchess had curtailed her activities so the two of them could get to know each other, to give her time to adjust to her new life. Her grandmother, she decided, was a woman of wisdom. Where Sebastian was concerned, the duchess did not question or lecture or pass judgment.

But Devon could not talk about Sebastian to her grandmother. Her wounds were too fresh, the hurt too deep. She did not want to see him, and at first she was fiercely angry at his arrogance. Did he truly think he could step into her life as if nothing had happened? She wanted nothing to do with him! Indeed, she was glad when his daily appearances ceased and his letters stopped.

A thousand times she replayed that horrid scene in her grandmother's drawing room—the foolish, terrible accusations she'd flung at Sebastian. If only she could take it back, she would!

Yet from that wretched memory a shaky confidence began to grow, a fledgling courage that blossomed into a frail tendril of hope. It wasn't as if he'd *had* to ask her to marry him. It wasn't as if his hand had been forced. He'd known full well that if they wed, shame and scandal might follow.

He hadn't cared. *He hadn't cared.*

Only then was she able to search the depths of her heart and seek the answers that so eluded her. Only then did she discover one of life's deepest truths—that dreams sometimes had a way of changing. Or perhaps it was simply that *she* had changed.

No matter how hard she tried, no matter how much she might have wished to, she could never stop loving him. *Never.*

Nor did she want to . . . for it was then she realized she was carrying Sebastian's child.

She sat before the mirror the night of the party, dressed in a gown of shimmering silver. It was odd, really, how much her life had paralleled that of her mother. Odd how the present sometimes had a way of shouldering the past. For she, like her mother before her, had fallen in love with a blue blood. Sebastian too had been so determined that he would never repeat the shame and scandal that marred his childhood.

But there was a difference, a vast difference. And in that moment Devon made a vow. She wouldn't spend her life as her mother had, mired in regret.

And Sebastian would never abandon his child. He would never abandon *her*.

For all her penniless upbringing, Devon had known her mother's deepest devotion. Sebastian, on the other hand, for all his wealth and privileged upbringing, had never truly known his parents' love, not the way that she had.

And she would not deprive their child of the one thing neither of them had ever truly known . . . the security of knowing he or she was loved by both mother *and* father.

She must go to him. She must *tell* him.

She had only to find the courage.

The duchess commented on her state during the carriage ride to the Clarkstons. "You're so quiet, my dear. Are you feeling well?"

Devon bit her lip. "I'm just tired." It was true, after all. She disliked the idea of keeping secrets from her grandmother, but she could hardly tell her before she told Sebastian.

Her eyes widened at the line of carriages before the Clarkston mansion, waiting to deliver the occupants. "Grandmama, I thought you said this was a small, intimate affair."

"Oh, it is, my dear." A pause. "For the Clarkstons, that is."

Devon sucked in a breath. "Grandmama—"

"You'll do fine, my dear." The duchess squeezed her hand.

And somehow, Devon knew she would. Oh, but the tales that would surely be flying about the city tomorrow! Faith, but she did not relish the prospect. She'd been vastly irritated when the sketch of her likeness appeared in the gossips. Indeed, she could fully understand why Sebastian despised scandal so much!

Inside, they were greeted by William and Emily. More than a few heads turned at their entrance, but Devon kept her chin high, a smile on her lips as they chatted with the host and hostess. William strode off to greet another newcomer, while Grandmama stood talking with Emily. Devon listened idly, allowing her gaze to wander.

And then it happened . . . Her heart lurched. Sebastian was here. *Sebastian.* The sight of him was like a blow to the chest. Her breath left her lungs, and she could not breathe.

And on his arm was the most strikingly beautiful woman she'd ever seen in her life. Chestnut-haired and petite, clad in a gown of deepest blue, she was even more stunning than the fair Penelope. White-gloved fingertips were curled possessively into the curve of his elbow. Even as Devon watched, the fingers of her free hand reached up to stroke his cheek. In return Sebastian laughed, then bent to kiss her cheek.

She died a little inside in that moment. Turning, she wrenched her gaze away. But just as quickly, a white-hot rage boiled in her blood. No wonder he had not called on her in the last fortnight. Obviously he'd wasted no time resuming his search for a bride. Oh, but it hadn't taken him long to find a potential replacement! He was clearly enraptured with the enchantress at his side.

In some distant part of her, she noticed their hostess was gone. It was then she saw that Justin was there as well. She'd have said hello, if only . . . She glanced at her grandmother. She couldn't stay. She *couldn't*. She would plead if she must. Beg—

"Hello, Devon," said a familiar voice. "Your Grace."

Devon stiffened. A nod to the duchess, and then he was standing directly before her. Reaching out, he snared her hand and brought it to his lips.

Devon was incensed. How dare he kiss her hand after kissing that other woman! She tugged it free as soon as he straightened.

"Your Grace, do you mind if I steal your granddaughter away for a few moments?"

"No, of course not." For the life of her, Devon didn't understand why her grandmother sounded so bright. "Why, there is Lady Robinson." Her cane thumping, the duchess started across the room.

Eyes snapping, Devon forced her gaze upward. Oh! How dare he smile so benignly! She longed to smack his cheek.

"It's good to see you again," he murmured.

Devon bristled. A footman passed by, offering champagne. Devon accepted it, downing it quickly before settling her gaze on him.

"I fear I cannot return the sentiment," she stated coolly.

"You're still angry."

"I am not. Why, I've scarcely given you a thought."

"I know better," he said gently.

Her chin jutted out. "Obviously you cannot say the same. But tell me of your search for your bride. Has the fair Penelope been forsaken for the lovely lady on your arm tonight?"

His smile widened. Oh, but the man had no conscience!

"My search for my bride was over the night I met you, Devon."

"Rubbish," she said baldly. Her chin hitched to

the place where he'd left his lovely companion. "You appeared quite besotted."

Sebastian had glanced over at the vision in blue, then back to her. "I will not lie, Devon. I care for her. I care for her deeply."

Devon had thought she could hurt no more. But his words were like a knife twisting inside her. Yet somehow she managed to mask the pain tearing through her.

"Then perhaps you'd best tend to her," Devon snapped, "for now she's with Justin. And . . . oh, my, it appears you have competition, my lord. They're in the corner with no one else about. Oh, dear, but it would never do to lose your intended to your brother—"

Her glass was set aside, her hand settled into the crook of his elbow.

"Sebastian!" she hissed.

"Hush," he said almost sternly.

It was beyond bearing. Beyond belief. For he was leading her toward *that woman*.

She would have pulled away, but she couldn't, not without causing a scene.

They stopped before Justin and the woman. "Devon, no introductions are needed for my brother."

Devon gave a brief nod of greeting to Justin. And—oh, she didn't want to look, but the woman was even lovelier than she had imagined. Huge eyes of china-blue regarded her in turn. Lips the color of crushed pink roses tipped up at the corners.

"Devon, it is with the greatest pleasure that I present my sister Julianna, newly returned from the Continent only yesterday. Julianna, Miss Devon St. James."

Devon was too shocked to say a word.

Not so with Julianna.

"So this is Devon! Oh, Devon, but I've heard so much about you, I-I almost feel I know you! Oh, and please forgive my forwardness, but a handshake simply won't do!" Reaching out, Julianna gave her a quick, fierce hug.

Devon finally found her manners. "The pleasure is all mine, I assure you." The first genuine smile of the night finally appeared. "Sebastian once told me you had a voice like pure sunshine. I do believe it's true."

Nonetheless, she was still reeling when Sebastian guided her onto the terrace. She was *not*, however, smiling when they halted a short distance away from the doors.

Devon glanced around to make certain they were alone on the terrace. "You might have told me Julianna was back, instead of letting me believe—"

He laughed outright. "Oh, but it was an opportunity too precious to resist. Besides, I liked seeing you jealous."

"I wasn't!" she denied. But she had been. My God, she'd been almost eaten up with it.

"Let me get this straight. You don't want me, but you don't want anyone else to have me either."

"Yes . . . I mean no!"

A jet brow climbed high in wicked amusement. "What, Devon, don't you know your own mind?"

In all truth, she didn't. Her stomach was knotted, twisting inside her. She felt dizzy, almost sick.

"I knew I should have stayed home," she muttered. A sudden thought struck then. "You knew I'd be here, didn't you?" Her lips compressed. "You and my grandmother arranged this, didn't you?"

"My love," he said with a chuckle, "I highly doubt either your grandmother or I had any influence on the Clarkston guest list."

Must he be so rational? Her eyes flashed. "Stop laughing at me!"

He did. But now his regard was burning and direct. He had stepped near, so near she could feel the raw, sheer power of his presence, so close the familiar scent of him swirled all around her. But all at once her knees were shaking. She felt so strange, her head spinning so that she could scarcely hold her head up.

"We need to talk, Devon. We need to—"

"No," she moaned. Heaven help her, the sickness churning in her belly was rising, burning her throat.

"What do you mean, no?" His expression was black. His tone like thunder. "Goddamn it, Devon—"

"Not now." She clamped her hand over her mouth and rushed past him.

His expression underwent a lightning change. "You little fool! It's the champagne. You shouldn't have swilled an entire glass—"

She shook her head in fervent denial. The rest of his explosive speech seared the air above her head.

But Devon didn't hear. She was busy retching in the bushes next to the bench.

In all her life she didn't know when she'd been so embarrassed. Of course it could have been much worse. Somehow he'd managed to hail Justin and order his carriage brought around to the front. Justin hadn't even batted an eye when Sebastian carried her around the side of the house and into his carriage; of course, she'd been too miserable to care at that particular moment. But at least no one else inside had seen. She could only imagine the stir *that* would have caused.

It wasn't far from the Clarkstons to her grandmother's mansion. Sebastian spoke very little, but his countenance was thin-lipped and grim. His hand was solicitous as he helped her alight, but she sensed his mood was no longer tender or amicable. A half-hysterical giggle rose in her throat as he escorted her into the house. Perhaps he should have known by now to expect the most *un*ladylike behavior from her!

"Are you able to manage the stairs on your own?"

"I'm fine," she murmured. Now that the contents of her stomach had been purged, she felt much better.

"Then go change. I'll wait for you here."

Devon bit her lip. "Perhaps we should send word to my grandmother—"

"Already done," was all he said. "I expect she'll return momentarily."

Devon climbed the stairs, her heart hammering, her breast roiling with confused longing. In truth, she hoped her grandmother *didn't* return soon. There was so much she wanted to say. So much she *needed* to say. But, in all truth, she wasn't quite sure how to go about it—or even if she was elated or terrified.

Her room was dark, for she'd told Meggie, her maid, not to wait up for her. Aided by the moonlight streaming in through the window, she lit the bedside candle. But just before she closed the door, an eerie tingle raised the fine hairs on the back of her neck.

"Hello, dearie. I've been expecting ye."

Her blood seemed to curdle in her veins. She knew that oily voice. She knew, even before she turned, that it was he who stood behind her . . .

Harry.

Twenty-eight

A sick dread twisted inside her. In panic she eyed the door. She dove for it, but he was too quick for her. Iron-hard fingers dug into the soft flesh of her arm. He yanked her against him.

"Let me be!" she cried.

She tried to jerk free, but it was no use. He seized her in a bone-crushing grip and shoved her against the wall, then snatched a candle high. The flame wavered so wildly, she feared it would catch her hair and gown afire. Bold black eyes roved over her features. His sudden, grating laugh made her long to shrink away. "I think not, dearie. Eh, I think not!"

"What do you want with me?" she asked coldly.

Thin lips flattened into a nasty smile.

"Oh, come now, dearie! Ye killed Freddie! Did ye really think I'd let that pass?"

"How did you find me?"

He grinned. In answer he drew a rumpled piece of

paper from his jacket. Devon suppressed a groan. The sketch from the gossips!

"Oh, but it wasn't hard, not once I saw this!" He gave a cackling laugh. "Jes' when I'd begun to think I'd never find ye, 'ere ye be! And lucky fer me, I've friends who can read!"

His slimy gaze ran over her. He rubbed the material of her gown between his fingers. "Don't know how ye did it, dearie, but yer circumstances 'ave changed a bit since the night ye killed my brother."

Devon wet her lips. "What is it you want?" she asked again.

"Oh, I think ye know what I want." He gave her a wink—and a slashing movement across his throat.

Devon clung hard to her self-control. She wouldn't scream. She wouldn't weep. It would please him too much if she showed her fear.

She was lucky, she supposed, that he didn't kill her then and there. Devon was under no illusions as to his intent.

"Is it money you want? My grandmother will pay you." Her voice rang out loud and clear. The door was ajar. Her room wasn't far from the landing. Pray God, Sebastian hadn't wandered into the drawing room to wait . . .

"Damn right she'll pay, and then you'll pay for what ye did to Freddie. I'll be rich," he crowed, "and you'll be dead!" His black eyes gleaming, he seized her arm in a bruising grip. "Now, bitch, I do believe it's time we left."

"Do you expect to simply walk out the way you came in?" Inwardly she was quaking. She marveled that she dared to goad him so!

His eyes glinted. "Oh, we'll be leavin' a different way than I came in. Now, where's yer granny?"

"Asleep down the hall," she lied.

"Then we'll 'ave to be quiet, now won't we?" He grinned, opened the door, and pushed her into the hallway.

Deliberately she stumbled.

He jerked her upright. "Try that again," came his fetid breath in her ear, "and I'll gut you here and now!"

"But then you wouldn't have your precious money, would you?"

Harry retaliated by twisting her wrist behind her back. Pain shot through her arm; she feared it had been wrenched from its socket.

Harry halted, peering down toward the entrance hall. Devon strained to see as well; God above, Sebastian was nowhere in sight!

Behind her she felt Harry's fingers steal into his coat, feeling for his knife.

"Sebastian!" she screamed. Even as the sound left her throat, everything inside her wound taut. She steeled herself for the jabbing slice of Harry's blade—ah, but she remembered it well, the sensation of searing fire burning through her, a red-hot poker. She prayed it would be quick, mercifully swift this time . . .

But there was no pain.

Only the most blessed sound in the world . . . the sound of Sebastian's voice.

"There's no need to shout, love. I'm right here."

Harry whirled. Her eyes had barely adjusted to the gloom when she glimpsed a tall, spare figure detach itself from the shadows.

A clenched fist shot out and connected with the point of Harry's jaw. Harry's head snapped back. There was a grunt, then he slumped to the floor without a sound.

The next few hours passed in a blur. The police were summoned. Harry was led away by two burly, uniformed figures—he had obtained entrance through the attic, it appeared. Afterward both she and Sebastian spoke to the constable. Devon only half remembered what was said, but everything was out in the open—Freddie's death, how he'd tried to kill her. The constable quickly assured her no charges would be brought. "Indeed," he pointed out, "the world is well rid of him. Nor," he added forcefully, "will Harry be bothering you or anyone else again. I'll see to that."

It was Sebastian who saw him to the door. Grandmama announced her intention to retire, kissed Devon on the forehead, and looked at Sebastian. "I trust you're able to see yourself out," she said crisply.

Sebastian gave a silent salute. Devon, meanwhile, made her way into the drawing room and sat, still rather dazed. She looked up when he strode through the doors. He closed them both, then turned to face her.

The air was suddenly alive with the force of his presence. Devon's heart lurched. Never had he been so handsome, the firelight flickering over his form.

Four strides brought him before her. He sat, catching her hands within his, his grip warm and strong. For the longest time he said nothing, his long fingers idly toying with hers.

"Well," he said. "It's finally over."

Devon nodded.

"Are you all right?" he said gently.

"Yes," she murmured. But her heart was suddenly quivering.

Sebastian frowned. "What is it?"

"Sebastian," she said helplessly. Her breath tumbled out in a rush. "Oh, Sebastian," she cried, "there's so much to say, and I don't even know where to begin!"

"You don't have to say anything."

There was such melting tenderness in his tone that her heart and eyes spilled over. "Oh, but I do. I do!"

With a groan he caught her against him. "Don't cry, love. I can't bear it when you do . . . I love you, Devon. I love you . . ."

A rush of emotion poured through her, leaving her dizzy and weak. Her throat aching, she wrapped her arms around him and clung. "And I love you too," she said with a watery half sob, "but then you knew that, didn't you?"

His eyes darkened. His gaze roved her upturned features. "I did," he admitted with a little laugh, "but God! it's good to hear you say it!"

He kissed her then, a long, drawn-out kiss of infinite sweetness.

Reluctantly he released her mouth. Drawing back, he traced the smile on her lips. "What is this for?" he murmured.

The merest hint of a smile grazed his lips.

Devon snuggled against his heat. "I was just thinking of the last time we were alone together in this room." Some little imp inside compelled her to tease him unmercifully. "Do you recall?"

Sebastian slanted a brow. "That particular recollection is one I should like to forget," he put in dryly.

"Ah, but you asked me a question . . ."

"I remember that question."

Shyly she laid her fingertips alongside his jaw. "Were you to ask me again," she whispered, "my answer might be quite different."

"I see." His tone was grave, but his eyes had begun to twinkle as well. "And what would that answer be?"

"Why, yes, of course I shall marry you. You are quite persuasive, you know."

"I rather thought *persistent* was the better word."

"Well, that too," she allowed.

He would have kissed her again but she stopped him with a finger on his lips. "Wait," she said breathlessly.

" 'Wait,' she says," he grumbled. "Must I wait forever?"

"Ah, but you are a patient man, are you not?"

"Not," he warned silkily, "when it comes to you."

"I see. And what about when it comes to children?" She was almost afraid to look at him, just as afraid not to.

There was a shocked silence.

"Devon," he said carefully, "are you saying what I think you are . . . ?"

"Yes." She pressed his hand against her belly. "You're going to be a husband—and a father, Sebastian. You don't mind, do you?"

"Mind?" His fingers moved against her belly, a feather-light caress that moved her beyond measure. He laughed, the sound husky. "My word, no. I've always wanted a houseful of children."

Devon smiled.

Wicked amusement danced in his eyes. "*Now*, my soon-to-be-wife, may I kiss you?"

She reached up and twined her fingers in his hair, bringing his mouth to hers. "Yes," she breathed. "Oh, yes . . ."

Epilogue

They wed less than a fortnight later, in the chapel at Thurston Hall. It was a small, quiet ceremony, attended only by the closest of friends and family. Devon wore an exquisitely layered gown of silk and lace.

The ceremony concluded, there were no tears—well, except for Grandmama and Julianna, who had sniffled throughout. When the two were pronounced husband and wife, Devon lifted shining, love-misted eyes to her husband.

Sebastian, his eyes wickedly agleam, locked his bride into an all-encompassing embrace and proceeded to kiss her with thoroughly unabashed, breath-stealing ardor.

Oddly enough, it was Justin who, a brow quirked high in sardonic amusement, loudly cleared his throat, causing them to reluctantly break the seal of their lips.

Scandal was the last thing on Sebastian's mind in the days before the wedding. In light of Devon's daring rescue by Sebastian, the women of the *ton* clasped their hands together and sighed dreamily, declaring the match wonderfully romantic. From the moment the betrothal was announced, a host of good wishes poured in. Of course, the nuptials of the marquess of Thurston caused a bevy of young misses to sigh their disappointment that the most eligible bachelor in London had been lost to another. From the moment the pair were glimpsed together arm in arm, scarcely able to tear their eyes from each other, it was clear to any and all that these two were meant for each other.

They spent the last few months of Devon's confinement at Thurston Hall. And it was there in his chamber, in the immense four-poster where Sebastian had made love to no other woman but his wife—the bed where he'd vowed his children would be born—that Devon strained and heaved and struggled to bring forth their firstborn child.

Her pains had come a few weeks early, a blessing Sebastian told himself, for she'd shown the effects of her pregnancy almost immediately. By her seventh month, she was . . . well, there was no delicate way to put it, positively huge. Of course, he assured her daily that she was the most beautiful creature on this earth . . .

For she was.

From the outset, he'd taken his place at the head of the bed, much to the midwife's disapproval. He tried to make himself useful, whispering encouragement, wiping the sweat from her brow, when in truth he'd never felt so helpless in his life. His heart contracted. Ah, but she was so brave, turning her cheek into his palm and teasing him between pains, as if to reassure him!

Devon's pains were almost constant now. Her back arched, and she gave a tiny little moan, the first she'd made. Her entire body quivered, and then he could only stare in mingled fear and fascination as a small head, dark as his own, came into view. A pair of narrow shoulders came next, a round little belly. And then . . .

"A boy!" came the midwife's cry. "Oh, a handsome wee one, he is!"

Devon immediately held out her arms. "Oh, let me hold him!"

Sebastian watched numbly as the midwife cleaned the slippery little body, wrapped him warmly, and pressed him into his mother's arms.

Sebastian had risen to his feet. Devon pressed her lips against the babe's scalp and reached for Sebastian's hand, beaming. He squeezed her fingers.

"Devon—"

All at once she gasped. "Oh, my," she said weakly. "Mrs. Carver—"

Mrs. Carver had already assessed the situation.

Sebastian's face went ashen. "What?" he cried. "What is it? What's wrong?"

The midwife thrust his son into his arms. "Here, my lord," she advised cheerfully. "It seems there be another one a-coming."

Clutching the small, squirming bundle that was his son, Sebastian dutifully did as he was told. He was still marveling when the midwife departed a short time later.

Devon latched on to his free hand and tugged him down beside her, her smile brilliant.

She laughed at his dazed state. "Sebastian, you're looking rather befuddled! Now come and meet your daughter."

He swallowed and spoke the first thing that popped into his head. "My God," he said with a shake of his head, "when I said I wanted a houseful of children, I thought we'd be starting with one, not two . . ." He stared at the golden head nestled into the crook of Devon's elbow and swallowed. "May I hold her?"

Devon eased the other little bundle into his other arm. Holding both son and daughter, he lost his heart yet again . . . A tremor of emotion rushed through him, emotion that was unbearably sweet. He kissed four flailing, tiny fists—and then his wife's waiting lips.

Later, with the babes tucked snugly away in their cradles, he climbed into bed and carefully gathered his bride against his length.

Devon was on the verge of sleep when a sudden laugh rumbled beneath her ear.

She lifted her head from his chest. "What is it?" she murmured sleepily.

"I was just musing on what the last year has brought me. When I began my search for a bride, I never dreamed I'd find her that very night—and right under my nose!"

"What, sir, are you complaining?"

"Not at all." His arms engulfed her. He pressed his mouth against the curls at her temple. "I love you," he whispered. "I love you madly, in a way that makes me giddy with happiness, and rich in a way that has nothing to do with wealth."

Her throat grew achingly tight. "Oh, Sebastian," she whispered, "that's the way I love you too."

Their lips clung in a long, unbroken kiss. When it was over, he smiled crookedly.

"In truth, I have but one wish."

"And what is that?"

"That Justin and Julianna find what we have found together."

Devon snuggled closer. "I daresay we are proof that love can be found in the most unexpected places."

"Do you think so?"

"I do. Despite the fact that Julianna has vowed that no man will ever turn her head, something inside tells me that someday she will find a man who will sweep her from her feet and make her as happy as we are." She chuckled. "But your brother . . . why, I fear it's hopeless!"

"I know," Sebastian laughed. "I wonder if the woman exists who can tame such a rogue!"

"Well," Devon murmured, "we shall simply have to wait and see, shan't we . . ."

Samantha James knows
how to write romance.
And she knows that for every
PERFECT BRIDE,
there must be
A PERFECT GROOM.

Don't miss yours!

He's arriving in December 2004

A PERFECT GROOM
by Samantha James
from Avon Books

Coming May 2004

Party Crashers

by Stephanie Bond

Jolie Goodman's life's a mess. Her boyfriend vanished months ago—with her car! She's broke and working in the Neiman Marcus shoe department, selling tantalizing but financially (for her!) out-of-reach footwear to the women whose credit cards aren't maxed out. And now, the police have come looking for her . . . thinking that she has something to do with her boyfriend's disappearance! But sometimes selling sexy shoes is just as enticing to men as wearing them.

Jolie glanced at the doorway leading back to the showroom, then to the fire exit door leading to a loading dock, weighing her options. She had the most outrageous urge to walk out . . . and keep walking.

Is that what Gary had done? Reached some kind of personal crisis that he couldn't share with her, and simply walked away from everything—his job, his friends, and her? As bad as it sounded, she almost preferred to believe that he had suffered some kind of breakdown rather than consider other possible explanations: he'd met with foul play or she had indeed been scammed by the man who'd professed to care about her.

The exit sign beckoned, but she glanced at the shoe box in her hands and decided that since the man had been kind enough to intercept Sammy, he deserved to be waited on, even if he didn't spend a cent.

Even if people with vulgar money made her nervous.

She fingercombed her hair and tucked it behind her ears, then straightened her clothing as best she could. There was no helping the lack of makeup, so she pasted on her best smile—the one that she thought showed too much gum, but that Gary had assured her made her face light up—and returned to the showroom.

Her smile almost faltered, though, when Mr. Beck Underwood's bemused expression landed on her.

She walked toward him, trying to forget that the man could buy and sell her a thousand times over. "I'm sorry again about running into you. Did you really want to try on this shoe or were you just being nice?"

"Both," he said mildly. "My sister is going to be a while, and I need shoes, so this works for me."

At the twinkle in his eyes, her tongue lodged at the roof of her mouth. Like a mime, she gestured to a nearby chair and made her feet follow him. As he sat she scanned the area for signs of Sammy.

"She's behind the insoles rack," he whispered.

Jolie flushed and made herself not look. The man probably thought she was clumsy *and* paranoid. She busied herself unpacking the expensive shoes. "Will you be needing a dress sock, sir?"

He slipped off his tennis shoe and wiggled bare brown toes. "I suppose so. I'm afraid I've gotten into the habit of not wearing socks." He smiled. "And my dad is 'sir.' I'm just Beck."

She suddenly felt small. And poor. "I . . . know who you are."

"Ah. Well, promise you won't hold it against me."

She smiled and retrieved a pair of tan-colored socks to match the loafers. When she started to slip one of the socks over his foot, he took it from her. "I can do it."

"I don't mind," she said quickly. Customers expected it—to be dressed and undressed and redressed if necessary. It was an unwritten rule: *No one leaves the store without being touched.*

"I don't have to be catered to," he said, his tone brittle.

Jolie blinked. "I'm sorry."

He looked contrite and shook his head. "Don't be—it's me." Then he grinned unexpectedly. "Besides, under more private circumstances, I might take you up on your offer."

Heat climbed her neck and cheeks—he was teasing her . . . his good deed for the day. Upon closer scrutiny, his face was even more interesting—his eyes a deep brown, bracketed by untanned lines created from squinting in the sun. Late thirties, she guessed. His skin was ruddy, his strong nose peeling from a recent burn. Despite the pale streaks in his hair, he was about as far from a beach boy as a man could be. When he leaned over to slip on the shoes, she caught a glimpse of his powerful torso beneath the sport coat.

She averted her gaze and concentrated on the stitched design on the vamp of the shoe he was trying on, handing him a shoehorn to protect the heel counter. (This morning Michael had given her an "anatomy of a shoe" lesson, complete with metal pointer and pop quiz.)

The man stood and hefted his weight from foot to foot, then took a couple of steps in one direction and came back. "I'll take them."

A salesperson's favorite words. She smiled. "That was fast."

He laughed. "Men don't have a complicated relationship with shoes."

Coming June 2004

And the Bride Wore Plaid

by Karen Hawkins

What is to be done with Kat Macdonald? This Scottish miss is deplorably independent, and unweddably wild. But while it's impossible to miss her undeniable beauty, it's also impossible to get Kat to act like a civilized lady. Still, even she cannot resist Devon St. John. A man born to wealth and privilege, he has no intention of ever settling down with one woman . . . until he meets Kat and realizes that his future wife will, indeed, proudly wear plaid.

Devon lifted a finger and traced the curve of her cheek, the touch bemusingly gentle. "You are a lush, tempting woman, my dear. And well you know it."

Kat's defenses trembled just the slightest bit. Bloody hell, how was she to fight her own treacherous body while the bounder—Devon something or another—tossed compliments at her with just enough sincerity to leave her breathless to hear more?

Of course, it was all practiced nonsense, she told herself firmly. She was anything but tempting. She looked well enough when she put some effort into it, but she was large and ungainly, and it was way too early in the morning for her to look anything other than pale. Her eyes were still heavy with sleep and she'd washed her hair last night and it had dried in a most unruly, puffy way that she absolutely detested. One side was definitely fuller than the other and it disturbed her no end. Even worse, she was wearing one of her work gowns of plain gray wool, one that was far too tight about the shoulders and too loose about the waist. Thus, she was able to meet his gaze and say firmly, "I am not tempting."

"I'd call you tempting and more," Devon said with refreshing promptness. "Your eyes shimmer rich and green. Your hair is the color of the morning sky just as the sun touches it, red and gold at the same time. And the rest of you—" His gaze traveled over her until her cheeks burned. "The rest of you is—"

"That's enough of that," she said hastily. "You're full of moonlight and shadows, you are."

"I don't know anything about moonlight and shadows. I only know you are a gorgeous, lush armful."

"In this?" She looked down at her faded gown with incredulity. "You'd call this gorgeous or lush?"

His gaze touched on her gown, lingering on her breasts. "Oh yes. If you want to go unnoticed, you'll have to bind those breasts of yours."

She choked.

He grinned. "And add some padding of some sort in some other areas."

"I don't know what you're talking about, but please let me up—"

"I was talking about padding. Perhaps if you bundled yourself about the hips until you looked plumper, then you wouldn't have to deal with louts such as myself attempting to kiss you at every turn."

She caught the humor sparkling in his eyes and it disarmed her, even as the thought of adding padding to her hips made her chest tickle as a laugh began to form.

"Furthermore," he continued as if he'd never paused, "you will need to hide those eyes of yours and perhaps wear a turban, if you want men like me to stop noticing you."

"Humph. I'll remember that the next time I run into you or any other of Strathmore's lecherous cronies. Now, if you'll let me go, I have things to do."

His eyes twinkled even more. "And if I refuse?"

"Then I will have to deal with you, myself."

"Oh-oh! A woman of spirit. I like that."

"Oh-oh," she returned sharply, "a man who does not prize his appendages."

That comment was meant to wither him on the vine. Instead he chuckled, the sound rich and deep. "Sweet, I prize my appendage, although it should be *your* job to admire it."

"I have no wish for such a job, thank you very much."

"Oh, but if you did, it would then be my job to wield that appendage in such a way as to rouse that admiration to a vocal level." Devon leaned forward and murmured in her ear, "You have a delicious moan, my sweet. I heard it when we kissed."

Her cheeks burned. "The only vocal rousing you're going to get from me is a scream for help."

A bit of the humor left his gaze and he said with apparent seriousness, "I would give my life trying to earn that moan yet again. Would you deny me that?"

Coming July 2004

I'm No Angel

by Patti Berg

Palm Beach's sexiest investigator, Angel Devlin, knows that a tight skirt, a hint of cleavage, and some sky high heels will usually help her get every kind of information out of any type of man. But millionaire bad boy Tom Donovan has something up his custom-made shirt sleeve, and even though Angel is using every trick she knows, it's proving far more difficult than usual to get what she wants.

Tom grinned wickedly. "I caught you."

"But you didn't come after me."

"I hoped you'd come back."

"Why? So you could personally haul me off to jail?"

Tom shook his head. "Because I liked the feel of your hands on my chest and your lips on my cheek. If I hauled you off to jail we'd end up enemies. The fact that you came back means there's a chance for more."

"You know nothing about me but my name." *And the feel of my body,* Angel thought, just barely hanging on to her composure as Tom's hands glided down the curve of her spine, then flared over the sides of her waist and settled on her hips. "Why would you want more?"

"I paid Jorge for a lot more information than just your name," he said. "I know you're a private investigator and that you cater to the ultra-rich. I know that your office-slash-home is right here on Worth Avenue in a building you share with Ma Petite Bow-Wow, the local pamper-your-pooch shop. And if Jorge knows what he's talking about, you're thirty years old, five feet eight inches tall, weigh one thirty-two—"

"Thirty-one dripping wet."

Tom grinned, his laughing gaze locking onto hers. "Should we get naked and dripping wet and weigh each other?"

"Not tonight."

"It's close to midnight. It'll soon be tomorrow."

"Are you always in such a rush to get naked and dripping wet?"

He shrugged lightly. "Depends on the woman."

"Trust me, I'm the wrong woman."

"I disagree."

The music picked up tempo and so did Tom's moves. He spun around with Angel captured in his arms, the heat of his embrace, the closeness of their cheeks, and the scent of his spicy aftershave overwhelming her, making her dizzy.

And then he slowed again. His heart beat against her breasts. Warm breath whispered against her ear. "From what Jorge told me—that you wear Donna Karan's Cashmere Mist and Manolo Blahniks if you can get them on sale—you could easily be the right woman. Of course, there's also the fact that you're soft in all the right places. And going back to your original question, *that*, Angel, is why I want more of you."

Angel laughed lightly. "Jorge was a virtual font of information."

"I figured the soft-in-all-the-right-places part out for myself," Tom said, his hands drifting slowly from her waist to her bottom.

She leaned back slightly and gave him the evil eye. "Excuse me, but we don't know each other well enough for you to touch me where you're touching me."

A grin escaped his perfect lips. It sparkled in his eyes and made the dimple at the side of his mouth deepen as his fingers began to slide again, but not up to her waist. Oh, no, lascivious Tom Donovan's fingers slithered down to her thighs.

That was the first really big mistake he'd made since he'd chosen to follow her.

His fingers stilled, his eyes narrowed, and she knew he'd found the one thing she didn't want anyone to find.

Again his hand began to move, to explore, gliding up and down, over and around the not-so-little-lump on her right thigh. His eyes focused even more as his gaze held hers and locked. "That wouldn't be what I think it is, would it?"

Angel smiled slowly. Wickedly. At last, she again had the upper hand. "If you think it's a slim but extremely sharp stainless steel stiletto that could carve out a man's Adam's apple in the blink of an eye, you've guessed right."

One of Tom's dark, bedeviled eyebrows rose. "I never would have expected a sweet thing like you to carry a stiletto."

"That, Mr. Donovan, just goes to show that you really don't know as much about me as you think you do."

Coming August 2004

A Perfect Bride

by Samantha James

Sometimes expensive clothes and shoes aren't what does the trick . . . occasionally, men simply can't resist the power of a damsel in distress . . . an ugly duckling who unexpectedly turns into a gorgeous swan. When Sebastian Sterling rescues Devon, a wounded tavern maid, he thinks she's a thief—or worse. But underneath her tattered clothes is a woman of astonishing beauty and pride, who he quickly discovers could become his perfect bride.

Jimmy pointed a finger. "My lord, there be a body in the street!"

No doubt whoever it was had had too much to drink. Sebastian very nearly advised his man to simply move it and drive on.

But something stopped him. His gaze narrowed. Perhaps it was the way the "body," as Jimmy called it, lay sprawled against the uneven brick, beneath the folds of the cloak that all but enshrouded what looked to be a surprisingly small form. His booted heels rapped sharply on the brick as he leaped down and strode forward with purposeful steps. Jimmy remained where he was in the seat, looking around with wary eyes, as if he feared they would be set upon by thieves and minions at any moment.

Hardly an unlikely possibility, Sebastian conceded silently.

Sebastian crouched down beside her, his mind working. She was filthy and bedraggled. A whore who'd imbibed too heavily? Or perhaps it was a trick, a ruse to bring him in close, so she could snatch his pocketbook.

Guardedly he shook her, drawing his hand back, quickly. Damn. He'd left his gloves on the seat in the carriage. Ah, well, too late now.

"Mistress!" he said loudly. "Mistress, wake up!"

She remained motionless.

An odd sensation washed over him. His wariness vanished. His gaze slid sharply to his hand. The tips of his fingers were wet, but it was not the wetness of rain, he realized. This was dark and sticky and thick.

He inhaled sharply. "Christ!" he swore. He moved without conscious volition, swiftly easing her to her side so he could see her. "Mistress," he said urgently, "can you hear me?"

She moved a little, groaning as she raised her head. Sebastian's heart leaped. She was groggy but alive!

Between the darkness and the ridiculously oversized covering he supposed must pass for a bonnet, he couldn't see much of her face. Yet he knew the precise moment awareness set in. When her eyes opened and she spied him bending over her, she cringed and gave a great start. "Don't move," he said quickly. "Don't be frightened."

Her lips parted. Her eyes moved over his features in what seemed a never-ending moment. Then she gave a tiny shake of her head. "You're lost," she whispered, sounding almost mournful, "aren't you?"

Sebastian blinked. He didn't know quite what he'd expected her to say—certainly not *that*.

"Of course I'm not lost."

"Then I must be dreaming." To his utter shock, a small hand came out to touch the center of his lip. "Because no man in the world could possibly be as handsome as you."

An unlikely smile curled his mouth. "You haven't seen my brother," he started to say. He didn't finish, however. All at once the girl's eyes fluttered shut. Sebastian caught her head before it hit the uneven brick. In the next instant he surged to his feet and whirled, the girl in his arms.

"Jimmy!" he bellowed.

But Jimmy had already ascertained his needs. "Here, my lord." The steps were down, the carriage door wide open.

Sebastian clambered inside, laying the girl on the seat. Jimmy peered within. "Where to, my lord?"

Sebastian glanced down at the girl's still figure. Christ, she needed a physician. He thought of Dr. Winslow, the family physician, only to recall that Winslow had retired to the country late last week. And there was hardly time to scour the city in search of another . . .

"Home," he ordered grimly. "And hurry, Jimmy."